MW00791334

GORDON ADLER

Here. I. Am.

A NOVEL

BEAVER'S POND PRESS

This is a work of fiction. The people, corporations, organizations, institutions, circumstances, and events depicted are fictitious and a product of the author's imagination. Any resemblance of any character to any actual person, either living or dead, is purely coincidental.

Edited by Kerry Stapley
Book design by Dan Pitts

ISBN 13: 978-1-64343-657-9
Library of Congress Catalog Number: 2022915013
Printed in the United States of America
First Printing: 2023
27 26 25 24 23   5 4 3 2 1

Beaver's Pond Press
939 Seventh Street West
Saint Paul, MN 55102
(952) 829-8818

www.BeaversPondPress.com

Dedicated to Richard Adler: 1922 – 1990

Warning:
everything in this story is made up,
and everything in this story is true.

1

Of all the things you shouldn't trust, the most common are the weather and people. People are irrational, and the weather's unpredictable. It's the mystery that never fails to excite me. Take this morning, Wednesday, August 24: A wispy layer of cirrus clouds hovers over Long Island Sound, and higher still, cirrostratus clouds glint like fish scales in a display my mother calls a mackerel sky. The blue, gray, and green high clouds will probably be replaced by a thunderstorm this afternoon, an exciting reading to record in my notebook. Tangy smells ride the humid, summery air at Quogue: seaweed, brine, and rotting bait. I follow my usual path to the beach, the grass giving way to the vines zigzagging along my route, racing me to the shore. Their summer blooms are white and violet against the rolling beige mounds of sand. To me, after spending many vacations out here, nothing smells of summer so much as Long Island Sound.

Staying low to the ground so I won't be seen, I scale up the last dune to the berm and lie on my stomach like an army scout. I take in the mile of sandy shore to Shinnecock Bay. Beyond it, the Ponquogue drawbridge reflects the sun like an old amusement-park ride.

Yelling kids and their mothers emerge from a row of summer houses built perilously close to the high-water mark along Dune Road. They cut through the dunes, carrying picnic baskets, blankets, and towels; an entire day at the beach tucked beneath their arms, waiting to be unfolded. During the week, the men of the summer families stay in Manhattan or Paramus and, like my father, return for the weekend, though this year my father hasn't come at all.

He's decided that the cottage my mother inherited is below us, as are the local and their kids . . . though he wasn't against using her money to build his business, Heald Shoes. That's why he's stayed in Manhattan instead of commuting like the other fathers: he's too busy at the store selling his signature invention, elevator shoes, with the well-known slogan *Now you can be taller than she is.*

In previous summers, I spent July and August at my attic desk (my favorite place in our cottage), working out advanced algebra problems, taking readings from my weather station on the roof, studying *Leavitt's Farmer's Almanac 1937*, and eating buttered corn and soft-serve ice cream at Buttrick's Creamy Cones. But this summer, I've been collecting climatological data for the Cooperative Weather Observer Program; 1938 is one of the hottest and wettest summers on record. I've also been observing two local boys, Carl and Jack Girardin, and their girlfriends, Margaret and a girl I only know as the one who works at the Quogue public library. All four of them are rising juniors. I still can't understand their behavior.

Usually, I hide in the dunes where they can't see me and study their every move, memorizing their expressions and what they do with their hands, how close they stand, and what prompts their laughter. I document it all in a BestEver notebook, with the date and time, just like when I watch the weather—only the four of them are even less predictable. If I just watch them long enough, I'll learn to fit in—at least that was my goal when I started watching them weeks ago. Before they arrived, I spent all my beach time alone, swimming in the Sound. If I learned to fit in, though, maybe I could have my first kiss by the end of summer vacation. For that, I have my eyes on the one I call the library girl.

Now, the foursome is fifty yards from me, laying their towels down like a row of large playing cards, a few feet from the falling waves. When my mother first inherited our cottage in 1932, I spent summer afternoons with Carl. We were both ten, and we were happy to collect shells, build sandcastles, splash around, and snap each other with our wet towels. Back then, it didn't matter what school I went to on the Upper East Side, or that his mother cleaned our cottage once a week during summer vacation. Now, six years later, he goes to Quogue Regional High School, and I'm a weekly boarder at Loomsfield Prep, up in Connecticut.

Carl sits, his arms wrapped around his knees, and lights a cigarette while Margaret rubs sunburn cream on his back. Jack and the library girl wade into the water and splash each other, laughing like they've never had more fun in their lives. This is one thing I've learned: always exaggerate. Whether it's feigned annoyance or pleasure, people my age amplify everything. Problem is, large gestures and loud voices make me uncomfortable. I'm more the shy type, which makes me wonder if I'll ever get my first kiss. All summer I've been living this hope—that somewhere, somehow, some good thing is going to happen, so I'll get my first kiss and be happy.

The four Quogue kids don't dive into the sea the way I do, letting it swallow me whole. They hang back and seem not to want the water to go above their knees. The ocean makes me feel small, but in a good way, like I'm part of something bigger; other kids just make me feel small, like I'm on my own. The first summers we spent at Quogue, I stood on the beach every morning.

At that time of day, the water was usually calm and vast as the desert where I once went to summer camp just outside Gallup, New Mexico.

But Long Island Sound never felt lonely. I imagined amazing sea creatures, and I was happiest underwater, surrounded by the distant booms of the waves and feeling the turbulence, my eyes open to the glittering surface. Two years ago, my uncle got me a snorkel and flippers and it felt like I was always underwater: the first time I used it, I came across a starfish scuttling along the bottom, a school of bluefish, and a sand shark. None of them expected anything of me.

What I'd really like is to go swimming in the ocean with the girl from the library. I could show her how to body surf and what to do if you get caught in an undertow. I'm pretty sure this would be the best moment of my summer. But time is running out.

I get up from behind the dune, traverse the beach, and sit on my towel near the water line. Out of the corner of my eye, I follow their habits. I haven't talked to them all summer, and I've never said a word to the library girl. This is my last chance. But they're having such a good time, I don't want to interrupt and risk the library girl getting angry at me. Jack is piling sand on her feet, and she's giggling. Carl is strutting around the others, puffing his chest out, and saying things that make them laugh so loudly I can hear it from over here. My father does this with customers in his shoe store, and my uncle does this with women—especially the waitresses at the Big Hat luncheonette where we sometimes meet. Charm and humor seem to be everywhere, but impossible to conjure.

Carl sneaks a furtive kiss on Margaret's cheek. She turns away from him, then pushes back her hair to more fully expose her face. To me, this is an invitation. Now Jack leans over and tries to kiss the library girl, but she pushes him away. Thank god. Unlike Margaret, she really means it, gets up and steps away, warning him with a fierce glower not to step any nearer. Jack hops to his feet and stands over her in a huff, his thumbs pulling at the waistband of his Jantzens. He clearly feels slighted and entitled to a kiss. But why? I wonder.

Now Carl kisses Margaret on the mouth, and she pushes him away, pretending not to like it, but giggling like maybe she does. He's got this confidence, like he knows she won't stop him. I keep wondering how he knows this, like how my uncle stops the waitresses in Big Hat in their tracks, even in the middle of the lunchtime rush.

I imagine Carl and Margaret having intercourse. These days, I imagine everybody having intercourse: my teachers, classmates, girls from Quogue Hall, my aunt, customers in my father's store—even my parents. Last year, in human biology, we learned about sexual intercourse. I overheard classmates calling it mattress polo. Right now, I'm imagining Carl and Margaret playing mattress polo. To turn off the pictures, I recite every quadratic equation I can think of.

The four of them get up and stand around for a few moments in silence, like they can't decide what to do next. Carl runs his hands through his slicked-back hair, his head cocked to one side, then kisses Margaret on the neck. She wraps her hands around his neck and raises one foot off the sand, like in an advertisement for men's cologne. They head in my direction, toward the bridge, but this time, instead of going into the water to avoid them, I'm staying where I am.

Carl and Margaret ignore me, wandering down the beach, kicking sand at each other, giggling. Carl doesn't look at me or say hello, even when I wave. It's been two years since he acknowledged me, and I still don't understand what happened or why.

The library girl walks right up to me. "You're Ben, aren't you?"

I nod, stuck for words.

"I'm Peggy." She runs a finger over her lips. "I've seen you at the library."

"I've seen you too."

"Your father owns Heald Shoes." She sounds impressed, and I can hear my father's voice on my sixteenth birthday telling me about what women want: *a man in charge*. I'm not sure if that's what *he* is. And I'm not in charge of much of anything except my homework, my weather notebook, and my swim workouts. I wonder if Peggy would be impressed by my dream to be a math professor, and not the son of a "father-and-son" shoe company.

"Let's go, Peggy." Jack tugs on Peggy's sleeve.

"Wait, will ya?" she says, swatting his hand away.

He takes a few steps back, pouting. "Come on, Peg. Why do you want to talk to a giant weirdo?" She doesn't seem to mind Jack calling her Peg. She's staring at me in a way that's unlike any expression I've seen before; her mouth is twisted in a half smile, half frown. I wait for her to tell me what she's thinking, but she's not going to. By the time I figure this out, the moment has passed.

Jack, who's a full head shorter than me, sneers. "Jeez, Peg, we gotta go." Peggy has these really blue eyes. I wonder if she'd mind if I called her Peg.

"What are you guys doing?" I say.

"Going swimming up by the bridge," she says.

I'm hoping she'll ask me to come, but I don't know how to show it in my expression. I stare at her until her gaze wanders. Before she can leave, I blab the first thing that comes to mind.

"It's going to be over eighty-five this afternoon, and the humidity's at least ninety percent." I'm ashamed because it's the wrong thing to say, even if it's true. I want to sink into the sand next to the lone bleached shell between my feet. I imagine crawling inside it, and Peggy's hand swooping down and putting me in her pocket.

"OK, well, we've gotta get going," she says, but it sounds like she's saying she's sorry to leave.

I want to touch her tanned shoulder, but my arm won't obey. And now she lets Jack pull her away from me by the strap of her tank top.

Twenty feet away, they stop. Jack is eyeing his brother, the fingers of his right hand still looped under the strap of Peggy's tank top.

She turns back toward me, watching me for two seconds. I'm lost in her eyes; then she waves and tucks her hair around her left ear. I've seen this before, with Margaret. Is it an invitation? Carl would know, but I just stand in silence and let her leave.

Jack wraps an arm around Peggy's exposed waist. He catches me still watching them and gives me the finger.

"Loser," he shouts, and bends over with exaggerated laughter.

Peggy pulls away and jabs him twice in the arm.

He clutches his arm and falls to his knees dramatically. She's laughing like she really thinks it's funny, like Margaret laughs at Carl, and then she kneels down and they kiss.

All I can think of is *loser*. I don't want to be standing here, wasting my summer vacation, when I could be swimming and observing the weather. I quickly wade into the water, my legs numbing from the cold. Then I dive in, letting the ocean consume me. I glide along the sandy bottom, beneath the rough surface, weightless and free, safe from the world above.

2

Before lunch, I find my mother in the kitchen arranging Amazon lilies in a black hand-blown vase. I like watching her arranging flowers, although at times she seems lonely and I feel sorry for her, which I don't like. No kid should feel sorry for his mother. She hears me come in and stops, glancing at me. Her face is kind of puffy, like it's filling with water. Her cheeks are pale. Since she got back from East Africa in late June with her friend, Dr. Lenz, she's been having all sorts of odd symptoms: swollen lymph nodes, headaches, sore joints, swelling of her hands and feet.

Oddly, she has phases of relatively good health too, when her skin is rosy, and although her cheek bones are more pronounced, in these periods I see the mother I had before last June: the mother who takes care of her appearance, who styles her long, layered bob, keeps perfect nails, and is attentive to every detail. The mother who does research work with Judge Anna Kross for New York's orphans and volunteer tutors at New School, who welcomes creative types into a pied-à-terre she's rented on the ground floor. This mother is so sure of herself, so much taller than her five feet, six inches. Last May, when a fire erupted across the street from our Manhattan apartment, she opened our door to everyone from that building, made spaghetti, and called around the city until she'd found places for them all to stay. The things I've learned about her from others—lawyers, educators, psychiatrists, doctors, artists—make her seem important and heroic.

But Dr. Lenz, a renowned tropical disease specialist, doesn't know what's ailing my mother. Her theory is that it's a mosquito-borne disease—not malaria, but maybe dengue or chikungunya.

I catch my mother's glance. "I'm back," I say.

"Did you run into those kids from Quogue?"

"Yeah, but we didn't really talk. Besides, Dad says I shouldn't be hanging around too much with them."

She shakes her head gently from side to side. "Don't worry about what your father says, he doesn't know them." She gives me a long stare, more of an inspection, actually. "Your face is red. Did something happen?"

"Body surfing is all." I'm struck by something I've never thought consciously before . . . how easy it has become for me to lie to my parents, how effortless it is to hide myself from them.

"It's been my experience that boys your age often overestimate their abilities. When your father was a young man, he did all sorts of crazy things. He once rode a motorcycle all the way Michigan to enroll in flight school. I must admit, he cut a dashing figure in his leathers and goggles." She smiles, her face warming with the memory. "Ben," she says. "You know how dangerous the ocean can be."

"Nothing happened."

"Remember how you used to go crabbing under the bridge and body surfing with the Girardin boys? I was so worried about you." She comes back to the counter by the sink and slices off the ends of a clutch of pink roses. "I bet you don't remember what happened our first summer here. You were two. You waded into the ocean and just sank, right to the bottom. We thought you'd drowned. I was sure, and they were the worst minutes of my life. I thought my heart would explode. But thank God, your father found you lying on the bottom, staring up from two feet down, eyes wide open, with the most peaceful smile."

"I don't remember that." I kiss her on the cheek, which is cool and smells like roses. On the table next to the vase is her dog-eared copy of *Civilization and Its Discontents.* I wonder if my mother is one of the discontents.

"Ben, hand me that paring knife, would you?"

"*Eucharis grandiflora.*"

She smiles, pride in her eyes. "Did you already do your weather maps today?"

"Hot and humid for the next few days."

"I've got a headache from the humidity." She rubs her palms together. "And my joints hurt." She puts a vase of lilies on the windowsill where the midday sun hits. She shifts to the side, leaning toward the window. She stares out at the tidal pond with the raft my father built. She seems far away. She turns to me, but doesn't acknowledge me. "So much to do," she says, tugging at the loose skin on her neck, which is like crepe paper. "I need to pack for the trip back to the city tomorrow. More tests," she says in a low whisper. "And Dr. Hedjhal will be here in an hour."

Dr. Hedjhal is my Loomsfield Prep math teacher. "Did Hedjhal say what he wants?"

"Something important, is all he said." She lowers her chin, stares at her desiccated hands, and frowns. "Why don't you wheel out the drinks trolley, with four glasses, lemons, some ice, and those gold tongs your father bought me for my birthday." She runs her eyes over me. "And put on some decent clothes, like that new long-sleeve polo with the adorable golden-fleece logo we bought at Brooks Brothers." By decent clothes, my mother means "clothes that won't embarrass me."

"I'll put on the blue one," I say, and go off down the hall to leave my mother to her preparations.

3

In the attic where I've been living this summer, I put on my Brooks Brothers blue polo and check the barometer: it's dropped to 1015 millibar, and if rain comes it will drop to 1013.2 millibar level. In the elevator, I push the button for the ground floor, and the lift starts descending with creaks and groans. My father had it installed, he claimed, so my mother wouldn't have to walk up the stairs, but I think he did it for the luxury. He wants the kind of Newport, Rhode Island, estate that lets him stand on the patio and watch the America's Cup through French binoculars. And I guess to his thinking, an elevator goes hand-in-hand with an estate like that. From the utility closet on the ground floor, across from the elevator door, I get the drink tray and wheel it out the side door, the wheels creaking along the curved flagstone path, up a slight incline, onto the front patio next to my father's unused barbecue grill.

I sit on one of the rattan chairs and wait for my mother. On either side of the patio are two blue wisteria trees my mother got the summer before last from Dr. Lenz. It seems odd to me that my mother's doctor would give her two trees for no reason. My mother says they provide shade for our guests, but we never have any, at least not when I'm here. She's been grafting and staking the stalks, so now strong, twisted trunks have scaled the sides of the trellis that arches over the patio, and their thick, blue blooms make a flowery roof like a waterfall. From here on the patio, the two things I love the most in Quogue—the sky and the Sound—are perfectly framed. The wind has come up, gusting to thirty-five knots or so. Onshore. South-southwest. I sit up straight to see the water, which has gone gunmetal gray. The surface is all riled up, and the sand is covered in white foam where the waves hit and wash back down the sloping beach.

My mother comes out the back door from the kitchen. She's wearing the helmet she has on in all her African photographs—she's removed the mosquito net—and she's limping. She's trying to carry herself straight, but she's listing to the side with each limp, as though her inner ear is out of kilter. By the time she reaches the patio, the cirrostratus is thicker, spreading across the sky. Underneath it, a mile offshore, rain is angling down from a tower of cumulus clouds in gray-white slants that are sweeping toward us.

"Staring at the water again?" she says, taking a long, slow breath from her chair. "I should have thought you'd have had your fill of the ocean for one day."

"I was imaging what it would be like to get caught in an ocean storm. Ten-foot waves are too powerful for most lifeguards, even, and cottages along Dune Road would be damaged."

My mother harrumphs. "Good heavens, Ben, must you fill your head with such sordid thoughts?" She inspects the blue veins on the backs of her hands.

"Dr. Hedjhal really didn't mention why he's coming?" I say.

"No, dear, nothing I can remember," she says.

The truth is, I wouldn't put it past my mother to invite Dr. Hedjhal. My last year at PS18, in 1936, she had me seeing Dr. Otmar Groopman, a bald psychiatrist on Madison, who wore tweed jackets with leather elbow patches. He asked me questions

I didn't want to answer. *How did you feel when the Spanish kids in PS18 beat you up?* It was great being punched at knifepoint. *Do you like helping your father in the store?* Who doesn't love elevator shoes? *How do you feel about your mother sending you to me?* It's even better than eating ice cream. At the end of that summer my mother and Dr. Groopman banished me to Loomsfield Prep, where, free from the taunts and bullying at PS18, my lowest grade as a sophomore was an A and my lowest test score was 99 percent, which I got on Friday, November 13. I forgot the + sign in a quadratic equation on a Math 2 pop quiz, a bit of careless-ness that bothered me until Thanksgiving.

While I'm wondering what to say next to my mother, Dr. Hedjhal's Model A rolls across the crushed-shell driveway; the engine cuts off, a door slams, and a tall figure comes around the corner of the house.

My mother is already on her feet, smiling through her pain. She is a champion of small talk, and when guests come, she regales them like a concert pianist. I don't know how to make small talk; I never learned the rules. Sometimes I talk about the weather, but adults get bored with the names of clouds and pressure systems. Then I'll be at a loss for words, standing with my arms crossed not knowing what to say. That happened to me when she introduced me to one of her writer friends. "This is Winston Rogers—he wrote *Three Miles to Paradise.*" I'd never heard of Mr. Rogers, and I'd never read his book. Was I supposed to talk about his shoes—cordovan loafers with buckle straps? So I said hi, and silence fol-lowed until my mother started telling Mr. Rogers all about my grades at Loomsfield and my swimming exploits, as if I weren't standing beside her.

Dr. Hedjhal stops at the edge of the patio, displaying a mouth-down frown. My mother greets him with a handshake and asks if he found the place all right. He's confused, since he obviously found the place. She says, "Have a seat, professor."

"I'm no longer a professor, Mrs. Heald."

"Florence."

"Dennis," he says and comes over to the chair across from me, setting a thick book on the glass-top table between us.

I skirt around it, grinning like a moron, and hold out my hand, which he takes in a surprisingly hard grip, giving it a firm surprise-you squeeze. "Nice to see you, Ben."

"Dr. Hedjhal, hi."

"How's it going, Ben?"

"Fine. Great. Just went for a swim."

My mother's beaming. "Don't be rude, Ben—ask our guest if he'd like something to drink, or a sandwich."

The thick book is a textbook. It's at least three hundred pages and bound in blue cloth. I'm not clear why he's brought it, since he taught my Math 2A class last semester without opening the textbook or notes. Rumor has it he taught his graduate courses at NYU without the book, referring from memory to specific pages and problem sets. That was before he was forced out.

Two chairs are free—one next to my mother, who's got pride on her face, and one next to Dr. Hedjhal, who's standing there nervously, as if he's afraid to sit, like I am. I still don't know the rules about where to sit. Before I can decide which chair, my mother tugs at her throat again. "What can I get you to drink, Dennis?"

"No trouble, Mrs. . . . uh, Florence."

"Not even a ginger ale?" My mother's got this idea that ginger ale is the cure when nobody knows what to say. At school mixers, I'm always holding a ginger ale.

My mother pats the cushion on the chair next to her. "Ben, come sit down," she says, giving me an elated smile.

A cumulus tower blocks the sun, and the wind gusts colder than before.

I'm shivering now in my shorts and my double-knit polo. Dressed for the beach, not for drinks, I sit next to my mother, but I'm thinking we should go inside.

Dr. Hedjhal is still standing, his eyes bugged open, as if he's surprised to see me. He picks up the book, reads the title to himself, moving his lips, then holds it between his two hands like some sort of prayer stone.

"Dr. Hedjhal, do sit; no reason to stand on ceremony."

Hedjhal folds himself into the chair. He raises his tired eyes to my mother. He clears his throat. "As I was saying when we spoke on the phone, Ben's a brilliant math student. I have high aspirations for him."

My mother ruffles my hair.

Hedjhal pushes his glasses up onto his forehead and focuses intently on my mother. "What I'm suggesting is that Ben skip ahead to his senior year in the fall and apply to MIT. I believe he can win a scholarship." He studies his watch, a heavy stainless-steel job with a blue face. "Compared to the seniors, he's behind in math, so he'll have to do a couple years of math by the end of October." He drums the fingers of his right hand on his chest. "I'm prepared to tutor him, but it's not going to be easy, even with his talent."

My mother is touching her face with her fingers. "Give us a few days to think it over, Dennis. I'd like to talk with his father."

I don't need to think it over. I've got enough time for girls and calculus. "Yes," I say.

"Yes, what, dear?" My mother is alarmed at my un-thought-out answer.

"I'll do it."

"Dear," she says, "we should discuss this with your father." Her face is pinched with disapproval.

"OK, but I'm doing it." My own stubbornness surprises me: this is the first time I've ever stood up to my mother.

She opens her eyes in astonishment.

Hedjhal stands again, picks up the book, and holds it out to me. I take it, feeling the heft: *Calculus for the Practical Man*.

"Your first assignment is 'Chapter 1: Fundamental Ideas. Rates and Differentials.'"

I flip through the first thirty pages. With each topic, my excitement builds: *the derivate as concept, average rates of change, secant lines, derivate as slope of a curve.*

"Are you sure we can't offer you some sustenance for the road, Dennis?"

"I'm fine, Florence, I need to be getting on."

"Thanks for coming," my mother says. "We'll be in touch."

"My number's on my card," he says. He hands her a frayed business card, walks around the coffee table, takes his careful steps down the flagstone steps, and disappears, leaving without shaking hands.

"What a nice man," my mother says, putting the bottles and glasses in two perfect parallel lines on the drink cart.

I nod. "He's a genius. Everyone at school says so. He was the youngest tenured math professor ever at NYU. He teaches us math without notes or a textbook, but he knows every page by heart," I say, gazing out at the ocean, where dark clouds are gathering for the late-afternoon thunderstorm I've been expecting. Sporadic lightning flashes inside the cumulus clouds, like fireworks blinking in fog.

"Is Dr. Hedjhal a good teacher?" my mother asks, regarding me thoughtfully.

"He can explain the most complicated theorems in clear, simple ways."

She closes her eyes for a moment, as if she's searching inside for her words. "I need to pack my things for our drive back to the city," she says. And then she stands, makes a pained face, and turns away, taking three slow, deep breaths before pushing the drink cart toward the house. The wheels clank against the rectangular flagstones, limp, as if on rusted knees.

I have a feeling I've never had before, like I'm at a threshold of some sort. I'm about to begin a new and exciting time in my life: a crash course in first-year calculus, skipping my junior year, and applying to MIT. A time of bigger challenges, bigger stakes, and bigger rewards. It makes me smile, now that I know my mother isn't watching.

⧗

Two hours later, after cleaning the kitchen, stripping the beds, draping the furniture with sheets, and packing our suitcases, the house behind us is finally locked up tight, and we're sitting in the car in front of the garage, listening to the rain hit the roof. My mother grips the wheel and turns to me. "I'm feeling a little dizzy," she says, removing the keys from the ignition and holding them out to me. "Can you drive us into the city?"

"With my learner's permit, I'm not allowed to drive in New York City. And I shouldn't be driving here. What if the police pull us over?"

"I'll tell them who we are. Since your father made that deal with the policemen's union, they're probably wearing Heald shoes."

"Thousand Milers," I say, starting the car and easing it out of the driveway.

"Your father gives to the policemen's union—they'll let us off with a warning."

A few minutes later, we follow the black ribbon of Dune Road, which, like some of the summer cottages, is perilously close to the high-water line, vulnerable to big waves and storm surges. During full-moon high tides, seawater sometimes runs across the road. I steer us through Quogue center toward the highway, careful to avoid the streams of water flooding the gutters from the downpour.

In a quiet neighborhood, we pass a row of ranch houses with white fences and the same dripping mailboxes out front. We thump over a silent policeman, a bump in the road to slow traffic where children cross. My mother groans. She must see my worried expression. "Just a silly little pinch," she says, staring down at her hands, which are folded like she's praying.

A cat runs in front of the car. I swerve to miss it.

"Be careful, Ben," she says.

I ease off the gas and shift down a gear, and the car slows.

"Somehow the idea of you skipping a grade and going to MIT isn't . . . what I was expecting."

"MIT has an atmospheric sciences department and some of the best mathematicians."

I wait for her to say something, but she's far away for a few minutes. Then she swivels her head, reaches out, and touches my shoulder. "No matter what happens, I'm so proud of you, Ben."

"What do you mean?"

"We don't know how your father will react; he may have other ideas about your future."

"Like what?"

"I don't know, Ben. Nothing specific, I mean, just . . . we don't know."

A jolt of worry squeezes my stomach, but I wait it out and think of more quadratics.

In Westhampton, we pass another row of mailboxes. None are the same size or shape; they're blue, yellow, and green. One is a dolphin, and another is a miniature log cabin.

"I don't understand why people want their mailboxes to stand out in design. Mailboxes should be standard yellow boxes with hooks for newspapers." She shakes her head in disapproval.

"We had a mailbox when I was girl. I loved going out to get the mail. It was so exciting, opening the front door and slitting it open; you never knew what you might find. I miss that in the city." She puts her head back, eyes closed. "Your grandfather built the mailbox at the Quogue cottage. He even put those nets on it so it's like a real lobster pot that catches the mail. If he hadn't built it, I'd take it down, but it reminds me of him. Such a kind, soft man."

We stop at a red light. I have an urge to touch her cheek, or maybe her hand. But I don't.

She opens her eyes, leans over, and gives my wrist one of her I-love-you squeezes, and the warmth spreads through me.

4

The next morning after breakfast in our rooftop apartment, which was advertised as a "mansion in the sky," I write *Thursday* in my new calculus notebook and start reading about rates of change and first derivatives. Across from me, my mother is reading the July issue of *Vogue*, open to "Paris Temperature," an article about a visit from British royalty. She puts down the magazine and rubs her temples with her forefingers.

She touches my math book. "Calculus?"

"My first assignment for Dr. Hedjhal."

"How do you make sense of all those squiggles and Greek symbols?"

"I see each one as a different color or shape."

"Of course you do, dear," she says, giggling. "How naïve of me."

"I love calculus already. Accidents don't happen in calculus; everything leads logically from one thing to another. You start with the initial facts and apply the law of motion. Then, with calculus, you can predict the future, or recreate the past."

"I wouldn't mind predicting what I've got," she says.

"If we had a calculus of the weather, we could predict dangerous storms."

"You're an optimist, if nothing else, Ben Heald." My mother gets up slowly, putting both hands on her knees for support. She's swaying a little and grips the edge of the table with white knuckles, holding her breath for a long time. She smiles at me but makes no effort to speak.

"What's the matter?" I say.

She breathes out with a whooshing sound. "I've got this infernal headache."

"Maybe we should call Dr. Lenz."

"What can she do?" she says, lifting one shoulder.

"Give you something for the pain, maybe an aspirin."

"She always tells me the same thing: go easy and get enough rest." She rubs her temples with her index fingers in little circles. "Dr. Lenz says that whatever I have, it's going to get better with a drink of water and a nap." She lets go of the table, walks to the sink, and drinks a glass of water. Then she picks up a sponge, wipes the counter, and scrubs the inside of the sink. She dries both with an edelweiss-patterned dish towel she bought in Zurich. She rinses the glass, rubs the inside until the towel makes a squeaking sound, and sets it on the shelf above the stove with a groan.

Before my mother went to Africa with Dr. Lenz, she was a pert, sharp-eyed conversationalist. Her countless friends were happy to talk with her about almost anything—Freud, child psychology, the New School, modern theater, poetry, and art. Since she got back in June, the batteries that powered her conversation have died, and she's often silent or far away in her own pain.

She turns back toward me, one hand clutching her right side, the wrinkles at the corner of her eyes scrunched up. "Mind if I put on the radio?"

It's not really a question. It's my mother's kindly way of telling me.

I'm relieved by the change of subject.

She traverses the kitchen to the radio, bends down slowly, and turns it on.

"Philco fifteen-tube 37-116 console," I say.

She shakes her head, smiling again. She manages the rest of the way to the table like she's walking on glass and sits with an "ahhh."

From the large brown box in the corner comes the voice of Henry Morgan, the radio personality who's helped make Heald Shoes—and my father—into a national brand.

"Good morning, here's Morgan. Incidentally, I'm the only man alive who's truly acquainted with the life story of Old Man Heald, the shoe putz. Tonight, I tell all. Artie Heald, as a little putzer, was known to his chums as Shoeless Joe. He had no shoes. His father had no shoes. His mother had no shoes. The shoes had no shoes.

"This preyed on the young man's mind. Stinky, ah, Shoeless, used to lie awake at night thinking about pictures he'd seen in the papers of men—yes—men wearing shoes. When at last he'd fall asleep, he'd lie in his bed dreaming of white leather. Luckily, his dream came true when his father opened a footsie shop.

"Later, after the young munchkin Heald quits the third grade with a 'Doctor of Footsies,' his father is killed by a grand piano that falls off a hoist, so the munchkin family needs money, and munchkin Heald decides to open his very own footsie shop. He walks into a radio station and asks to buy time to advertise his shoes. This was years ago, and unfortunately, he was told that radio hadn't been invented yet. That was all right with Heald, since he had just discovered that money wasn't everything, but soon after, he managed to forget that fact—he quickly opened ten Heald footsie stores, made a few million, and complained about the cost of storing gold at the bank. At the age of forty-five, young man Heald, who was now being called Middle-Aged Heald—well, you all know the rest, this lonesome millionaire with nothing to keep him company but the employees of his twenty stores and union members—meets me at the radio station and buys airtime to advertise Heald Elevator Footsies. The first night, I called him Old Man Heald. He was furious and threatened to end the radio campaign. From then on, it was touch and go. You remember us: Touch Heald and Go Morgan. But then everybody in New York, including the pigeons, knew Old Man Heald. Today, Heald has twenty stores. That's as far as I got with this. For further detail—startling, revelatory—an exposé on Old Man H, come to me. Well, that's as far as we're going to get tonight. If you want to know more about Young Man Heald, the lurid details and juicy exposé, give me a call. And remember, folks, Heald Shoes: Now You Can Be Taller Than She Is."

"Why does he say that Father started the business?"

"Henry Morgan plays loose with the truth, dear."

"I thought he inherited it after Grandfather died in that piano accident."

"He did—they were moving a piano from the third floor, a strap holding it broke, and the piano fell thirty feet and crushed him, right in front of the store."

"But he's lying."

"It's marketing and public relations," she says jovially.

"So, it's some kind of a gag?"

"Your father says that what matters isn't really the shoes—shoes are pretty much all the same, except the elevators—so people remember the Heald stories and how much Morgan makes them laugh." She lifts her eyebrows as if we're in on something about my father, like maybe he's full of it. "A year ago, late August, Henry Morgan referred to your father as Old Man Heald on his daily WROR radio hour. Hundreds of people came into the store on the sixth asking for your father's autograph. Every morning, twenty-five people were waiting for your father to open. Every day in September, more than one hundred customers bought shoes from Old Man Heald."

The phone in the front hall rings. "That's for me. Probably Dr. Lenz." She patters across the kitchen tiles in her house shoes and takes the call. She doesn't say much, and I can't make out the words, though her voice is rising and falling with cheer. "OK, then," she says louder and more forcefully. "I'll tell him." She puts the earpiece back in its cradle and returns. "Your father wants you to come to the store."

"I'm doing my calculus."

"You can finish it later," she says, poking the back of my hand softly.

"What about what I want?"

She gives me a big I-understand smile.

"Calculus is important to me—you heard what Dr. Hedjhal said."

"Please, Ben, go to the store. If you won't do it for your father, do it for me."

I don't understand what going to the store does for *her*. Judging by her tone, I'm not getting out of this; I have no argument. "OK."

Half an hour later, I'm on my way under a dark-gray sky—it's 8:30 a.m. but could easily be dusk—to visit Heald Shoes at Forty-Second Street and Sixth Avenue, my father's branch. It's the headquarters of the twenty Heald Stores in New York, Boston, Philadelphia, and Washington. Heavy rain has been flooding Manhattan's streets since my mother and I returned from

Quogue late yesterday afternoon. According to my rain gauge on the roof, in the last eighteen hours, 2.82 inches of rain has fallen, an inch more than the September monthly average. Lightning blitzes over the suburbs to the west, and the air over the city has the sweet, pungent smell of ozone. It's a lousy morning to be out.

Coming to the Heald Shoes store makes me feel tense and pressured, like I'm not supposed to be who I am. To the left of the entrance is a fifty-foot wall with a fading mural: *Heald Shoes for Men—Build Your Ego, Amigo! Now you can be taller than she is.* Heald Shoes is synonymous with Heald Elevator Shoes—men's models with hidden two- to three-inch lifts in the heels. Shoes made for men who aren't confident enough to accept who they are. Seeing the gingerbread around the entrance and the metal lamp my father bought in Cairo during a Cook's Tour of Egypt in 1932, I realize the store also makes me feel hopeless. It's my father's dream, not mine. In the same building is a collection of failing shops: lighting fixtures, a chiropodist, Professor Shtisel's Beauty Parlors, and Leo Morse's Nursery Novelties.

When I was ten, I got all excited when my father talked about the business. He was so animated. I wanted to feel that way. I eagerly helped around the store. He nicknamed me Little Jeremy, after Jeremy Bentham, who, at age seven, wrote a history of Rome in Latin. "Someday we'll be partners," he'd say. "That's why I want you to shadow me when you're here; learn the business. Imagine the awning—in huge, ornate, black letters we'll have 'Heald and Son.'" I imagine a flag with Heald and Son written in medieval letters, flying over my father's castle, a dark somber place with cold, breezy rooms. The first time he said that, I reminded him I was only ten. He told me it's never too soon to learn the ins and outs. Heald and Son. A promise then, and a threat now. Lately, my father talks about Heald and Son more and more often, as if repeating it will make it true. I hate shoes, only he doesn't know that yet, since I've been keeping it a secret for six years.

When I get to the store, the sales guys—Miler, Goldstein, Hirschmann, and Sturm—are lining up the shoes in the racks using a T-square, my father's technique. My father has his own hiring principle: *Only hire men who'll do anything to keep the job.* It's not clear what *do anything* means, but it includes running errands for my father, like meeting women at Grand Central and taxiing them to the Pennsylvania Hotel, buying flowers and rings and necklaces that he never brings home. The sales guys will never get a higher-paying, more prestigious job. All four started as stock boys, then got into sales in smaller stores like the army-navy supply shops, then the big chain stores: Thom McAn, Bonwit Teller, Kaufmann's, and Macy's.

I stand by the rack of women's pumps and watch my father, a small, wiry man with a tall aura and the energy of a wasp on amphetamines. Perversely, although he's five feet, five inches tall, he won't wear Heald Elevators, which he refers to in private as "an admission of defeat" (or, more accurately, "da feet"). Customers call him "Flex" and "Big Artie."

Sweating profusely and dabbing the dome of his head with a paisley handkerchief, he checks the rows of cordovan Elevator brogues, the ones with perforated toe caps, size six to fourteen. He gives Bob Miler a genial smile until he checks the top row with his T-square. One shoe is an inch out of line. Suddenly he loses his temper, balls up his small fists in Miler's face, and yells, his eyes bulging, "For Christ's sake, Bobbie, it's the End-of-Summer Blowout! I told you, presentation is half the battle, so line 'em up." Miler gives my father a defeated smile and stares down at his own polished Heald Oxfords.

Seeing this, my stomach constricts nervously, since my father may, at any moment, turn his skittish frustration on me.

But he doesn't, and my shoulders relax with relief. Still shaking his head at Miler's carelessness, my father hurries to the front door, unlocks it, and swings it open. Women with hats as big as umbrellas and men in wide suits flood the showroom. Big Artie is running around like he's plugged into a 220-volt socket. He shakes hands and pats people on the shoulder, catches their eyes and makes energetic conversation: *that's right, absolutely, I get it, tough break, sure let's do that, round of golf, meet you at the Harvard Club, what can I do you for?* He may be in a buoyant mood, but his exaggerated zest makes him seem smaller, like the shoulders of his suit are too wide. He's trying so hard, which makes me feel bigger than he is, when what I want to feel is protected.

He spots me standing off to the side behind a rack of espadrilles. He joins me, beaming like he hasn't seen me in years. Out of breath, he lights a Lucky and takes a drag like he's sucking the life out of it. He retrieves a black wingtip off a shelf and returns, stroking it slowly. "Feel this," he says.

I run my fingers over the perforated toe, unimpressed.

"Those guys in the factory at Endicott do a bang-up job."

"Sure do."

He sweeps his hand 180 degrees. "This will all be yours someday, hopefully when you graduate from Loomsfield, but you never know *when*," he says. "After what happened to your grandfather . . . something might happen to me."

"Like what?" I say, clenching my jaw at the thought.

"Fuck knows. Hit by a bus, fall into the Hudson, hit by lightning. Something, anything." He says this in a cheerful tone, like he can't imagine anything cutting his life short.

I put the wingtip back on the shelf, out of reach of his ruler. My first thought is, too bad no one's invented paternal calculus so I'd know when I might have to come into the business or run away. This is a perfect chance to remind him that I want to be a math professor. He knows it, actually, since I've told him at least ten times, but each time, he just went on talking about Heald and Son. So, I created a personal rule: never talk about my dreams with my father, even if I want to cry. This time, I obey my rule. I nod my agreement and let his vision of our future stand. Why I still obey my rule, I don't know, since I'm a foot taller, stronger, and I just learned that I'm going to skip a grade and maybe go to MIT. And yet, I notice that I'm slumping again, and won't say a word when we meet our first customer of the day.

My father reaches up and puts his hand on my chest, his stubby fingers splayed. "You've got to keep an eye on quality. Our customers want shoes that feel new after a thousand miles."

This is one of his exaggerations. He sells heavy-duty work shoes, Heald Thousand Milers, to New York State's Irish beat cops, but after a thousand miles, their uppers are scuffed, and the heels are worn as thin as cardboard.

"I thought we're selling stories."

"Yeah, that's Morgan's department, but we gotta guarantee quality. Quality is like the table stakes in a poker game. You gotta have quality to get into the game. Most chain stores have quality shoes. We need a story people can identify with. We're not selling shoes, we're selling stories, like a short man buys the elevators, gets the tall honey, and schtups happily ever after."

"But what happens when he takes the elevators off at home?"

"That's not the point. We're selling hope and optimism, confidence, like the movies. Get it? We're leaving love marks."

"Mm-hmm." I have no idea what he's talking about. So far

as shoes go, I've been wearing the same Bass Weejun loafers for three years. In junior high, to keep my father happy, I helped in the store on Saturday mornings before swim practice. I was willing to get interested in shoes and the shoe *business*—sales, marketing, and branding—but I ended up spending most of my time helping my aunt do the accounts, thinking about kissing her, and tracing storm fronts on my weather maps.

"You're with me today, Bentham," he says for the umpteenth time in my life.

"I'd rather work on the books."

"We both know you're not a sales guy," he whispers, squeezing my wrist. "Too much the introvert, and that's ok, but you gotta understand how sales works, how to engage customers, so you can assess the sales guys."

This means I'll spend the morning hovering at his side like a pilot fish while he chats with customers. My father remembers the name of every customer, and often other quirky details, like the name of the family dog or the university where one of the children is studying, even the degree they're studying for. I don't know how he does it. I can remember long strings of numbers and complex formulas, but I need to hear a name five times before it's burned into my memory.

Larry Rosenblatt, a wide man with horn-rimmed glasses and a tailored pin stripe suit, is inching toward the rack of elevator shoes—which is emptying out quickly. My father has idolized him ever since he heard that Larry earned millions shorting the market in 1929.

My father practically lunges toward Rosenblatt, whose back is to us, with me trailing. They shake hands, my father asks about his two daughters. Rosenblatt ignores the question. "You must be Ben."

"Right," I say.

"Your father says you're a math genius."

"I don't know about that," I say. "I'm pretty good at math and science." My father, I see, is tapping the ends of his fingers together with short fast motions.

"Take it from me," says my father. "The kid remembers every word he ever read."

Rosenblatt nods approvingly.

My father smiles, working up his charm. He's like a vampire getting ready to leave one of his love marks. "You need a new pair of elevators, Larry?" he says with amplified good cheer, like a master of ceremonies.

Rosenblatt turns a black Oxford in his hands, like he's inspecting a work of art.

"What are you needing today?"

"Two-inch lifts, black, no perforations—"

My father flashes a huge I-know-what-you-need smile.

"A few inches for my birthday," Rosenblatt says, giggling.

"I can't help you with *that*, Larry—"

Rosenblatt blushes. "I meant my wife wants me to be taller than she is when we go to the Met. She says I should be at least as tall as a millionaire."

"I can sympathize. My wife says the same thing."

This is a lie; my mother never mentions money nor my father's height, but Rosenblatt seems to be enjoying it.

"I can help you *stand more erect*," my father says with an exaggerated wink. He's beaming like a boy in a candy shop, which makes me feel older and more confident than he is, which is not the way I want to feel about my father.

Rosenblatt takes a pair of black monk straps from my father. "These are perfect."

"Me, I've got two pairs," my father says, lying again. "Remind me of your size?"

"Size of what?" Rosenblatt winks at my father.

"Whatever needs *lift*ing, Larry"

"Nine and a half, ten, double EE."

My father turns to me. "Get Mr. Rosenblatt a pair of size tens."

I reach up, my chest even with their heads, and take down the last pair of tens, offering them to my father like wampum.

He brings one of them to his ear as if he's listening for something inside. "You can hear the ocean in front of your East Hampton deck."

Rosenblatt takes the shoe and holds it to his ear. "I'll be damned," he says.

"That's our last pair," I say. And that's the end of my small talk. Like yesterday at the beach in Quogue, I want to sink into the floor.

"Half price," says my father. "Gotta clear the inventory."

"Thanks, Old Man."

"Welcome, Larry," My father's big smile has returned. "You have yourself a great day, Larry." Something overplayed has crept into his voice, just like the Girardin boys on the beach. He punches Rosenblatt in the upper arm. "Knock it out of the park."

Rosenblatt laughs really loudly. I don't know why. My father's words aren't funny. They make me uncomfortable. Something in his voice when he emphasizes the word "welcome" sounds strained, and the baseball metaphor makes no sense since Rosenblatt, who has narrow shoulders and a paunch, could never have been anything but a high school batboy. My father's groveling and the false flattery make him seem desperate for attention, which lessens my admiration for him even further.

We watch Rosenblatt leave the store, good cheer on his face.

"That's how it's done," my father says, grinning at the awning over the front door, imagining my future of love marks and heel lifts, Heald and Son.

5

The day after shadowing my father in the Heald Store, a drizzly Friday, August 26, at eleven o'clock, I'm waiting for my uncle Jesse in the Big Hat diner. I check my watch, though I always know what time it is, as if a clock is ticking inside me. He's late, as he does everything slowly, like the pro Yankees pitcher he once was, lobbing the occasional off-speed pitch between fastballs, moving with easy, well-put-together confidence. I often dream of growing up to be like him: self-assured, so attractive that both men and women stare, never taking things too seriously, laughing at my father's demands, as if he knows that my father's bark is worse than his bite.

The bell attached to the door rings, and my uncle saunters in. Everybody standing in line at the counter stares. He ambles by the double counter and four tables, slightly bow-legged and limping from a hamstring injury years before; removes his Stetson Tom Mix hat; and bumps his head against the empty bulb socket dangling from an exposed electrical cord. For a minute, he is the town sheriff in Tombstone, Arizona: tough on rustlers, soft on the women in the saloon.

My uncle grins at two waitresses who are hovering in front of signs for the forty-cent chicken-dinner special and ads for laundry services, plumbing, air conditioning, bread, a dairy, and a supermarket. They giggle and whisper, smiling too much and turning red. He stops at my table, leans toward me, and speaks in a low, quiet voice. "I love this place. It hasn't changed since I started coming here in 1920: same Big Hat Bar-B-Que poster from Yosemite and the cowboy hat nailed to the wall."

He's much larger than the last time I saw him: wet sand seems to have filled his shoulders and chest. When I stand up to greet him, he skirts the table and wraps his arms around me, and all at once I feel like a kid, moored and safe—the opposite of my father, who makes me feel like I'd have to protect him in a fight. Whatever conversation my uncle proposes—horse racing, real estate, his Heald store on Madison, family stories, my swimming, or Loomsfield—I never feel overwhelmed. With my uncle, I can say what I think and feel. Around my father, I always rehearse what I'm going to say so he won't get angry and start nipping at my ankles like a small, aggressive dog.

"I thought you were going to meet me outside," my uncle says.

Is he accusing me of something? This could be a trick question: why didn't I wait outside if I wanted to see him? "I got soaked," I say.

Unperturbed, he picks up my math textbook. "Homework?"

"Calculus."

He puts the book down. "Can I help you?" he says, winking. "I'm an addition and subtraction demon."

"I was just finishing up." I close my calculus book lightly.

"Truth is," he says, "I'm already out of my depth with algebra—too many Greek letters." He pulls the book across the table toward him, opens to a page on second derivatives, and nods. "You know how to do this?"

"I'm not sure, I just learned it."

"Ben, don't be afraid to acknowledge how smart you are," he says, running his large hands across the worn blue cover of the textbook. "Modesty looks weak, and some people will take advantage of you."

"The boys at school make fun of me."

"They're jealous because they know you're smarter than they are." He gazes at me approvingly, reaches his muscled arms around the napkin dispenser, and presses warm palms against my cheeks. His Old Spice cologne, a Christmas present from my mother, hangs in the air. Old Spice seems like a present she should have given my father—he got French silk ties—not my uncle, and I wonder how this might be significant. Maybe she just knows what the two of them like. Or maybe she knows more.

My uncle squeezes my shoulders. "Still doing the four-hundred and eight-hundred freestyle?"

My father has never asked me this question. "Personal best times last May at the New England Prep School Championships. I do the one-hundred and two-hundred backstroke in Loomsfield relays too, but freestyle's my best."

"I once had a decent slider and sinker," he says in a warm whisper. His eyes sparkle with green flecks. "But my ninety-five-mile-an-hour four-seamer was my best." Something in the memory clouds his face—maybe it's the pitch that tore his rotator cuff and ended his career. He gives me a hard glance, muscles at the corner of his jaw knotting. He fishes a flask from his inside jacket pocket and takes a swig—his Adam's apple slides up and down—and the hardness leaves his face.

The low, steady chitchat of the lunch crowd gets louder as the smell of grilling burgers fills the diner. From the radio console behind us, Billie Holiday sings "They Can't Take That Away from Me."

"How's school?" he asks.

For a heartbeat, I can't decide how much to tell him. "My

math teacher recommends that I skip junior year, graduate a year early, and apply to MIT."

My uncle comes around the table and loops an arm over my shoulders. "I'm so proud of you."

He's so close, my breath knots at the back of my throat. I never let anybody this close, but it feels right. "I'm scared," I whisper. I pick up the calculus book. "I'm not sure I can learn this in two months."

"It's all right to be scared."

"Were you scared when you pitched your first Yankees game?"

"My first start, against Boston, I was so scared that my first pitch went high and wide into the backstop." He hugs me, which feels as good as solving a complex derivative: for a time, everything makes sense.

He loosens his arm and sits again, runs his hand in a smoothing gesture over his sun-bleached hair, like a Western movie poster that's come alive. "Reason I came," he says, "I need your help."

I can't imagine what my uncle wants from me. I'm afraid he'll ask me to do something illegal, like the time he asked me to deliver a bag full of cash to the head of the Irish Policemen's Union. *Just ring the bell, tell them who you are, and hand over the money.* Only it wasn't that easy: a beat cop showed up and almost nabbed me. I ran ten blocks full speed until he gave up chasing me. I imagine this time could be worse: I'll be caught, expelled from Loomsfield, and rejected by MIT. But I don't want to let him down, since he's like a friend and a father. So, I just smile like a doofus and wait for the bad news.

"For two years, I've been trying to go legit, divesting my side businesses and getting out of some bad arrangements with some bad people." The force of his words seems to compel my uncle to talk more than usual. "Last spring," he says, with a theatrical pause. "I bought a hotel in Florida." He throws his head back, tips a silver flask upside down, and swallows a terrific mouthful of whiskey. "Whispering Palms, in Islamorada, a couple of hours south of Miami," he says. "It's got three main buildings, a building with a reception, twelve bungalows, a pool, a restaurant, a tiki bar, and a jetty with a sixty-foot Trumpy yacht."

I suspect, by the indirect way he's getting to his point, that I'm not going to like what I'm about to hear. My father has been telling me for years, *Everything your uncle touches turns to ash.* My thoughts jump ahead, rehearsing my way of trying to get out of whatever he wants from me. I want to go back to the part of the conversation where we were talking about calculus and MIT, or maybe his fated game with the Yankees.

"I'm in trouble with a guy from the North Jersey Syndicate."

"Like Meyer Lansky, you mean?"

"Yeah, like that." He turns away from me, lights a Lucky, and fills his chest with a long, slow drag. "For the down payment on the hotel, I took cash from savings, but I needed another fifty k, which I borrowed from Abner Zwillman."

"Who?"

"Zwillman imports whisky from Canada—got his start during Prohibition and still owns the whisky trade in New York from his headquarters in New Jersey."

I repeat one of my father's favorite expressions: "A gentleman gangster is still a gangster, even in an Italian suit."

"Your father wears Italian suits," says my uncle, grinning.

It's a family secret that my uncle runs bars in the basements of the Heald store locations. During Prohibition, they were speakeasies and he made a killing, but when Prohibition ended in 1933, he converted them into bars and gambling dens and, in some places, what my mother refers to as "dens of iniquity," by which she means brothels. *To keep a positive cash flow*, my father says, though I don't see the connection between Jesse's bars and the shoe company.

My uncle stares at his folded hands, the scars from baseball injuries crisscrossing his white knuckles. "Zwillman gave me until the end of September to pay him back at twenty-five points." He glances at me for a moment, showing a hard jaw line and the tanned planes of his face. "I figured I'd make enough money from the hotel to pay Zwillman back on time. With the Florida East Coast Railway running from Jacksonville to Key West, Flagler's opened the Keys to tourism. The hotel's fully booked," he says, but then his voice breaks. "But I'm hemorrhaging cash." He extends his legs and crosses one over the other, taking his time.

"The favor?" I say.

"Review the business plan for Whispering Palms." Though he says this with a soft, melodic voice, he's leaning toward me with broad shoulders. This I clearly a demand, not a request.

"I don't know anything about business plans."

He waves a hand dismissively. "You don't need to. When you were fourteen, you got nervous around people, like you were allergic to them, but when it came to numbers and equations, you found a mistake in the deductibles in our tax filings that saved us thousands." He sets his Lucky in the ash tray, composes himself, and turns to face me. "I know you'll find the mistakes in my business plan. You know why?"

"Why?"

"Because . . ." He raises his eyebrows expectantly. ". . . I'm depending on you."

"I don't know."

An awkward silence joins our table.

My uncle looks at me with bright points of green light in his eyes, leans back, and puts his boots on the table, as though he's in a saloon. I don't know what it is about him, but I can't stop staring at him. My mother says he's beautiful *and* handsome, which may be true. I'm not sure. But I am sure that something happens in my brain when I look at my uncle. Maybe it's a chemical, like when I solve a complex math problem, see thunderheads piling up, or stand by an empty indoor pool. This is what women—and some men—feel when they look at him: you want to be near him, in his orbit, safe from problems and stresses. And maybe you want to have intercourse with him.

"I need your help," says my uncle.

"Why don't you hire a forensic accountant?"

"Gotta be someone I trust one hundred percent."

I'm flattered, but my stomach is fluttering. "What if I make a mistake?"

"I'll take the hit."

"My father says I shouldn't help you because you deal with shady, dangerous people like Zwillman."

My uncle pinches his eyes shut. Lowers his feet, stands, hunches forward, and rocks back and forth in front of the table, stroking the hair above his ear. "Listen, Ben, your father and I have a history. He claims I threw him down the stairs when he was eight. Never happened. I could tell you more, but I can't go into it now; one day you'll understand why." He settles back into his seat, picks up my calculus book again. "The point is," he says, tapping the book against the edge of the table, "my shoe partnership with your father is built on layers and layers of lies. We lie to cover our previous lies, and neither one of us ever says, 'Hey, we gotta stop lying to each other.' So now, we have a pile of lies like a huge mountain of burning tires. It stinks, the smoke burns your eyes, and you can't put it out, and neither one of us mentions that it's burning."

Now I stand up, leaning toward my uncle. "What do I get?"

He frowns and thinks for a moment. "Name your price."

As I'm about to tell him, the waitress, a mid-twenties woman in a tight-fitting Big Hat uniform with a bronco rider logo on her chest, comes over balancing our lunch on a tray. In a couple of swift motions, she sets our roast beef specials and root beers on the checkered place mat.

"Took long enough," my uncle says.

"Lunch rush," she responds, annoyed.

When I look up to see if she's angry, she winks at me.

"Anything else for you, honey?" she says to me.

I get the sense she hopes I'll want something else, so she can talk to me some more. For a moment, I'm confused, then I say the safest thing I know. "I'm fine."

She sashays away; stops at the counter, where she bends forward to take a red bottle off a lower shelf; then comes back. "Ketchup, handsome?" she says to my uncle, her hand lingering on the bottle.

"Honey, I want more than you can give," he says, patting her buttocks gently.

She giggles, and her face reddens. "You two cowboys want anything else, just holler." It comes out *hollah*. She walks away, her starched uniform making a sound like the rustling of hotel sheets.

"She likes you," my uncle says.

"You mean she wants to have intercourse?"

"Whoa, sailor, not so fast."

"You mean she's interested in getting to know me?"

"Maybe. If you have a good conversation."

I gaze at my uncle, trying to gauge from his expression if he means what he says about the waitress liking me, or if he's just trying to make me feel good so I'll agree to check out his business plan. It's not clear to me, and I can feel myself getting confused again because the subject embarrasses me. I manage to stay calm enough to say, "Can a good conversation lead to a kiss?"

"Sure. Most women want to get to know you before they'll kiss you."

"Can I ask you something?"

"Shoot."

"I want to know how to get my first kiss."

He nods approvingly, a smile loosening the tight wires of his face.

"OK," he says. "Do you have your eyes on a special girl?"

"Peggy."

"How do you know her?"

"From the Quogue beach," I explain, my uncle staring at me intently. "But she's not interested."

"How do you know?"

"She's always with Jack Girardin."

"Do you talk to her?"

"I tried last Wednesday, but I didn't know what to say. I told her the name of a shell and the weather forecast. Before she left with Jack, she told me maybe we'd see each other at the public library."

"Do you think you have a chance of going out with her?"

"I don't know. I heard what she said, but it was like a code I couldn't break."

"Like what?"

"When she said, 'You're Ben Heald,' she could be stating a

fact, or expressing surprise. Maybe she likes me, or maybe it means she noticed me and remembered my name but that's all."

"Most girls are thinking, *How would it be to kiss Ben?*"

"Me?"

"So maybe Peggy is thinking, *I like the look of Ben, but I don't think he's boyfriend material.*"

"Boyfriend material?

"You know . . ."

"Intercourse?"

"Or maybe kissing." He pulls at his chin with his thumb and forefinger. "Rather than saying, 'Hey Ben, I like you but I'm not going to kiss you,' she says, 'Maybe we'll see each other at the library.' She's leaving her options open."

This had never occurred to me before, that Peggy might be intentionally vague in order not to commit herself. So now I ask my uncle the next obvious question: "How do you know which option?"

"Experience. Talking with women." He thinks for a moment. "Before Peggy will kiss you, you need to have a conversation with her."

For several moments we sit in silence. It feels good to have my uncle pay attention to me, like I'm the only person who matters to him, unlike my father, who always has his eyes peeled for another customer or a woman in a tight dress.

"My experience, you can't learn to hit by talking about hitting; you need to get into the batting cage." He stands, gets into a batter's stance, and takes an imaginary swing. "Boom," he says. "Deep left field, over the fence." He grins. "Home run." Then he drags a third chair over next to our table, so it's facing him. "Sit," he says. I sit, and he refolds himself into the chair opposite.

"What is this?" I ask.

"Bear with me . . ." he says patiently.

"I'm not much at baseball."

He grabs my knees. "Tell me your strategy for talking with a girl."

"I just did."

"That was the old Ben," he warned. "You know what doesn't work—"

"Talking about shells and the weather."

"So, what questions keep a conversation going?"

I stare at him. "The actual questions?"

"Yeah, what you'd ask, say, if we met Peggy outside on the sidewalk."

"I have no idea, I haven't read a book about it. My conversations die after two sentences, which are usually about the weather or math."

"Every time she answers a question, you need to keep her talking about that. If you only have four unrelated questions, you'll be asking for the check after three minutes. So, let's practice. Imagine I'm Peggy. You start," he said, sticking out his jaw.

"How old are you?"

"Sixteen."

"Did you have a party?"

"Yeah, we had a big party. Then three of us went to the movies."

"What movie?"

"*The Hurricane.*"

"I liked it, too. The special effects of the hurricane were amazing. What did you like about it?"

My uncle smiles. "Good, so now we've got a common interest."

"So, I need to prepare questions to ask girls, like a script?"

"Like a deck of cards, each card with a question." He keeps

his patience through a long sigh. "You meet a girl; you pick a card."

"So, I should write my questions on cards and carry them in my pocket?"

"Not exactly," he says, impatience in his voice. "You memorize the questions."

"Like I memorize certain functions and math rules."

"Exactly." He grabs the saltshaker and dusts salt into his palm, licking it off. "Just need some tequila."

I take this to mean our conversation is over, though I'm not sure, since I'm lousy at reading other people's signals. "I'll memorize some questions and try them out the next time I see Peggy or talk to another girl."

"I'll bring you the business plan tonight."

"I'll have it done in a week."

"Sooner."

"You didn't tell me that you're afraid you're going to go bankrupt."

"Half right. I'm afraid I'm going to go bankrupt and they're going to kill me." He smiles and gets up from his chair, drops a ten-dollar bill on the table, turns with a wince from the torn knee ligaments he sustained in high-school football, and walks gingerly down the row of tables, like a lawman who's been grazed by a bullet. The waitress from before says to no one in particular, maybe to herself, "That's Gary Cooper," and every head in the diner turns to watch him go.

6

After lunch, my uncle and I head back toward the Fifth Avenue store through a light drizzle. Clouds shroud the tallest buildings. My uncle saunters beside me, his arm lassoed over my rounded shoulders like a heavy rope. "Did you know," he says, "the old reservoir had one of the largest Hoovervilles in the US? Forgotten Men's Gulch. Tourists lined up to watch Ralph Redfield, an out-of-work tightrope walker." He animates his face like an actor playing a man animating his face. "Sometimes I can't believe our luck, surviving the Depression."

"Lease holds, right?"

"Something like that," he says, and I believe he's lying.

My uncle is moving surprisingly fast, so I straighten up and walk double time. We pass three middle-aged saleswomen smoking in front of a Bonwit's. They appraise my uncle with the same hungry stare Margaret gave Carl on the beach. They're tittering, embarrassed by his presence—his handsomeness—and one of them, short and curvy, in a proper cardigan, exclaims, "Mr. Cooper, can I get your autograph?"

My uncle stops, and she offers an open match book and a pen. My uncle smiles; her face goes crimson. He signs *"Gary Cooper,"* and says, "Happy to oblige, ma'am." After she walks away, there's a short silence. Then his serious face is unraveled by the familiar high-wattage smile—not the weak smile I used on Peggy.

"I can't believe you did that," I say.

"A time will come," he says, "when you'll choose to be whoever people need you to be without losing yourself. You'll be signing matchbooks 'J. Weissmuller.' Hearing this, something shifts inside me. I picture myself as Johnny Weissmuller, signing autographs after winning another hundred-meter freestyle race. And unlike conversations with my father, this one is making me feel bigger, not smaller.

Five blocks later, at 1:00p.m., we stop outside the store. The windows are fogged from the inside, obscuring the features of the customers who linger alone or chat in pairs. My father is still rushing around in a blur, chatting up strangers, grabbing men by the arm, kissing women's hands like he's got an audience with the queen.

"Your father never stops." For once, my uncle sounds impressed. "Wind him up first thing in the morning, and he runs all day." He squeezes the back of my neck. "I'm not built like that, and neither are you. We've got nothing to prove—we know we're good." I'm not sure this is true for him, but I'm sure it's not true for me. I bet he's kissed a thousand girls; I've kissed exactly zero.

"My father is proof of Newton's first law of motion," I say. "An object in motion stays in motion."

My uncle wags his head, then gives me a friendly punch in the shoulder, one teammate to another. "You ready, boyo?"

"What?" I feel myself flushing, because I'm so happy to be with him, calling me boyo, like a Yankee teammate. But the feeling fades, replaced by worry, as I imagine another talk with my father ending in disappointment.

"I'm going to tell him about Whispering Palms."

"He's not going to like it."

"He never approves of what I do, which is why I gotta try to patch things up."

"Just Whispering Palms, right? Not the business plan."

"Don't you worry, kiddo." He wheels around to wave at a woman walking by on the wet sidewalk. The air ripples with the motion of his large pitching hand. She keeps walking, her heels clicking on the pavement. Then she stops, turns, smiles, and waves back, waits three seconds, and walks on. "That, Ben, is the start of a conversation."

My uncle follows me into the showroom. Immediately, I'm in my father's world: tanned leather; Eagle brand shoe polish; and Hero, his French cologne. The morning crowd has thinned, but by midafternoon at least twenty customers are milling about the half-empty sales racks. At first, my father doesn't see us, as he's deep in conversation with a middle-aged woman in a sheath dress and black turban hat with a butterfly pin.

"Handsome woman," my uncle says. "One thing you can learn from your father is how to talk to women."

"He's always selling something; I'm not selling anything."

"That's where you're wrong, Ben—you're selling yourself, or rather a conversation with you. Your father," he says in a baritone whisper, "figured out when we first inherited the store in 1919 that everyone, men and women, thrill at personal attention. In a few minutes, he creates a relationship with every customer. For them, that's better than no attention at all."

My throat constricts. "I c-c-c . . . an't d-d-do that." Embarrassed by my lapse, remembering my years as a stutterer, I take deep breaths and try again. "I'm not like my father."

"Mm-hmm," he hums. "Give it time, you'll find your own style."

My father spots us, extricates himself from his conversation, and marches straight over, winded and with red blotches on his cheeks. "Get out, Jesse," he says, kneading his fingers together and sucking air in through his nose.

My uncle puts up his hand, like the chief of the Lakota. "Hau."

"Go, now."

"I can't leave Ben with you; you might try to sell him a pair of shoes." My uncle bows slightly, which angers my father, then lowers his other hand toward the floor in an exaggerated gesture of surrender, which is ironic considering he could take my father down in three moves. "I'm not leaving," he says, apologetic but determined.

"But you will," my father says. "I warned you to stay away from my son."

"Your son?"

I wonder if my uncle's hard of hearing or whether he's implying something else. Whatever my uncle means, my father knows. He gulps air to lower his anger, but it's not working. His face flushes. He cocks his arm and stands with one leg behind the other, like a boxer posing for a fight poster.

My first response is to laugh at the Joe Louis imitation, but then I want to tell my father to stop. "You're ridiculous," I want to say, but I don't. "Everybody's staring at you," I say instead.

He gives me a combative glance, which I don't understand, since I'm just trying to spare him embarrassment.

Suddenly, my uncle, with a blur of motion, reaches out and clutches my father's wrist. I've never seen anyone move so fast. He goes from standing still to gripping my father faster than it takes his Stetson to hit the floor. My father gasps in surprise. He tries to break my uncle's grip, but his hand shakes and he's too weak to free himself. He stops resisting, the tension in his body leaking away like air from a balloon. Then he kicks away my uncle's Stetson. It hurts me to see my father like this, utterly defeated by his taller, more magnetic brother.

"You win, Jesse. Again. So what do you want?"

My uncle releases my father. "Truce."

My father cradles his arm like a broken wing. "Just go, I have nothing more to say to you."

My uncle takes a step toward my father. "Artie," he says. "I'll leave, but not without Ben, since you're forcing him to spend another afternoon in the store."

"Leave Ben here." My father is still trembling from the effort to free himself from my uncle's grip. It occurs to me that he's exhausted from talking with a hundred customers, or maybe he's sick, with shadows under his eyes like my mother's.

My uncle turns to me. His voice rises above the din of showroom chat. "He'll try to poison you against me and turn your own doubts about what's best for your future to his advantage." His voice has softened, more like Coach Winters, my supportive Loomsfield swim coach. "Go on, tell him your news."

"Tell me what?" There's acid in my father's voice.

My uncle and my father stare at me, waiting. I close my eyes and take a deep breath. "I'm skipping a grade and applying to MIT this year."

At first, my father stands in utter silence, his lips quivering. He grins—he knows something I don't. "Your mother told me."

I wait for him to say something, maybe congratulate me or tell me he's proud, but no. He considers my uncle, who now stands relaxed next to me, hands on his hips like a gunslinger.

"You may not think much of it," says my uncle. "But I think it's fantastic what Ben's doing."

"That doesn't matter."

"But I'm his—"

"It doesn't matter *what* you are; what Ben does with his future is none of your business."

"Imagine, the first person in our family to go to MIT," my uncle presses.

"He's my boy, and we've worked sixteen years for him to come into the business, and I'm not going to stand by and watch him throw away everything we worked for."

"Getting a degree from MIT is the big leagues, it's like playing for the Yankees."

"You wouldn't know, Jesse," my father says. "So stop trying to turn him against me."

"Jesse bought a hotel in Florida," I say. "And I'm helping him with his business plan." I'm shocked by own words, but I feel bigger than my father.

Now my father moves backward a step. "I asked you not to drag *my* son into *your* schemes."

"And I never agreed." My uncle's tone is nonchalant. "Ben's old enough—"

"—Ben doesn't know what's good for him, he's too young and he has no idea how the world works. MIT professor? A life of meetings, grading papers, fighting political battles for tenure, and all that for a pittance." My father whips around toward me. "You'll never be happy; you're accustomed to a certain lifestyle."

"The shoe business is *your* plan," I say, stuffing my hands in my pockets.

"My *good* plan."

"He's MIT material," my uncle says, "Heald shoes is a waste of his talent, like making Aristotle sell vacuum cleaners."

"I don't care about elevator shoes," I add, my eyes and mouth working on a smile that just won't materialize. And then, with reluctance, for fear of my father's reaction, "I don't need elevator shoes. I'm tall, like Uncle Jesse." I steel myself for his reaction to my comment about elevators, since it's the first time I 've said it so directly, surprising me and, judging by his smile, my uncle too.

"I don't know why you're so goddamned tall," says my father. His protruding, slightly yellow eyes narrow to slits. "Maybe you got it from your mother's side." He sounds like he's trying to convince himself. But it's not working. Sadness and confusion spread over his face.

I make an awkward step toward him, my gaze fixed on his mouth, but I say nothing and just stare at him.

His lips are quivering, and he's counting the floor tiles. He eyes me strangely, as if my words have taken him by surprise. He runs a hand over his ring of hair, then taps his bald spot with the ends of his fingers. Like most men who lose their hair, he's still surprised that it's gone.

I want to say something to help my father, who suddenly seems small and sickly, but I'm doing badly, standing in silence, lacking the skills to cheer him up. No witty quip comes to mind, so I say, "The forecast was right, the rain's letting up."

"That's my cue," says my uncle, cheer—or maybe contempt— raising his voice an octave. He rests his hand on the small of my back. "You did good, kiddo," he says. He backs up a few steps, turns, puts on his Stetson, and tips his hat to the handsome lady my father was love-marking. He exits the store and disappears into the crowd flowing down the sidewalk.

My father wipes his eyes with his sleeves. "Long day," he says.

"Sure is," I say.

"I don't want you checking Jesse's business plan."

"It'll be fun, and I'll learn something useful."

"That hotel he bought, it's a front."

This is news to me, and I'm not sure I believe it. Today, I trust Jesse more than I trust my father. "For what?"

"He's using it to wash the cash from his basement bars," he

says. He looks up at me and blinks. "You don't know, Ben; take it from me, you could get into trouble with some unscrupulous people, or maybe the police."

"I'm only going over his business plan to see if the numbers add up."

"And if they don't, he'll have you making a new one for god knows who," he hisses. "Your uncle's been in trouble with the Syndicate since his speakeasy days. And now they're demanding protection money. Those mob guys don't mess around. They'll push you off the transom of a boat with your feet in a tub of cement." For a moment, he considers what to say. "I can't stop Jesse, but I can stop you."

"I already agreed."

"Well then, un-agree," he whispers. "Believe you me, Jesse isn't a man of his word."

"OK, I'll think about that," I say, immediately feeling like a coward and not understanding my father's sway over me. I'm not going to think about it, I'm going to do it.

My father's cheeks puff out as he approaches me. And then he does something extraordinary. He nears me and rests a clammy hand on each of my cheeks. "If you get into trouble, he'll walk away." He kisses my forehead. "I'm the one who loves you, Ben. Never forget that. Your uncle always walks away, he just walks away, it's what he does best." And then my father turns and walks away too.

7

Later that afternoon, as I stand outside the Heald Shoes accounting office holding a pair of Heald brown-leather cordovan brogues my father just gave me—*a present for when you become my partner*—I can hear my Aunt Myrtle, Jesse's wife, if I can call her that, talking to herself inside. She's reading the numbers in a thick ledger. She does this out loud, her voice a substitute for paper and pencil; it's the way she's been doing the books and taxes since 1920, in her head, from memory.

From where I'm standing, checking her out through the window into her office, her face has no age. She could be thirty or forty-five, though she does have fine lines like tattoos, from her three-month ordeal at the Pilgrim Psychiatric Hospital out in Brentwood. My mother called it the Pilgrim, to make it sound like an upscale hotel. In June 1922, a year before I was born, my uncle had found her wearing only mismatched socks, sitting cross-legged on the living room rug, mumbling incoherently about the Bells, their neighbors, coming to kidnap her to make dirty movies. The neurologists and psychiatrists talked of a lobotomy, which would supposedly have separated my aunt's emotions and thoughts, thereby reducing her anxiety while retaining her keen numerical ability. The surgery entailed entering both eye sockets with an orbitoclast, a long needle with a metal handle on the end, like a miniature brass walking stick. The doctor would hammer the instrument upward into my aunt's brain and then mush it around. But my aunt and my uncle refused permission, so instead, she had insulin therapy—sixty convulsions from insulin shock, an ordeal she equated with dying every day for two months.

Then I hear what I believe is Aunt Myrtle's voice telling me to come in.

I press my face against the glass and tap three times, our signal, and she gazes up at me from under the geometrical bangs of her licorice pageboy. I go in, just as I've been going in since I was ten, ready to memorize receipts with her, a game we still play. Waiting for her to finish recording the day's receipts, I wander around, inspecting receipts, pay stubs, order forms for the factory in Schenectady, scribbled notes from my father, Heald catalogues, canceled checks, bills, sandwich wrappers, and the bowl of chocolate bars she still eats, a habit formed from her insulin shock treatments. I love filing because it brings order, putting everything in its place. Unlike my aunt, in my room at school, each book, notebook, notepad, compass set, ruler, abacus, and pencil has an appointed place. I can't work if my number 2 Ticonderoga pencils are lined up askew. I file my Loomsfield homework, tests, and quizzes in color-coded folders.

My aunt caps her pen—a Mozart-edition Montblanc from my parents' trip to Salzburg in 1935—and gently closes the ledger, so carefully it seems ceremonial. She comes over and hugs me like she hasn't seen me in years, so tight I can feel her breasts, stomach, and the soft skin of her cheek, and I immediately want to try a kiss. But, of course, I don't. When she finally lets me go, I grab a Snickers from the silver canoe-shaped bowl on the shelf beside me.

"You need to sign for the Snickers," she says, handing me the Snickers account ledger she's been keeping all these years in her top drawer. I sign with a flair. We both pretend to spit into our hands. I clasp her hand and feel the clunky Navajo turquoise thumb ring she bought when she visited me at summer camp in Gallup in 1935. She was the only one in my family who came to see me. She lets go and holds up her open palm. "You are hereby inducted into Snickers Knighthood." When I was kid, she read *The Sword in the Stone* to me. Those were some of the best hours of my life. I felt safe and warm, and since then, I've only felt like that with my uncle: peace, calm, comfort, and—yes—joy. I tell her everything, and two years ago, she helped me deal with being bullied by Spanish gangs in PS18. She suggested that I do their math homework, and I was never bullied again.

I bite into my Snickers and chew it slowly while I rewrap and pocket the other half.

My aunt suddenly gets up, swoops around the desk, and leans backward against it, facing me. "Come sit next to me," she says, tapping with her open right hand.

I do, and she sidles over to me, so close our thighs are touching. Again, her skin is like electricity buzzing through my thigh.

"So, Ben, are you happy with things?"

I have no clue what to say, since I don't know what being "happy" means. Happiness has many flavors: contentment, excitement, joy, awe . . . this time, I figure being happy with my life is about more than how I'm feeling. "My best possible day would be taking my weather readings, learning calculus, eating at the Big Hat with Uncle Jesse, then swimming, doing more calculus, and maybe reading *Buck Rogers and the Planetoid Plot*."

Her eyes narrow. "Something's bothering you." She slides her arm around my waist and grins, her teeth as white as chiclets. She presses her lips against my ear. "I think I know what."

"What?"

"Your father's pressuring you to come into the business."

I smile, since I thought I'd kept my frustration a secret.

"He's been planning this for years," she says softly, her face kind and warm. She wraps her arm around my neck. *She's too close.* She often touches my arms and legs, and I should be used to it, but I'm not. My forehead breaks out in a cold sweat.

"He never listens to me."

"He can't."

"So I'm not listening to him," I say.

"I'm not sure that's a smart strategy."

"It's my life, not his."

"You might consider your future from his point of view." She stares at me in silence. "He really believes you'll be happier in the business."

"Did he put you up to this?"

"Of course not. But you need to understand him better to convince him to let you follow your dream."

"I don't see why I should; he doesn't do that for me."

"You've got to put yourself in his shoes," she says, drumming her fingers on my thigh. "Here's something you don't know. He wanted to marry Laurel Lindblatt, but her parents wouldn't allow it because your father didn't have enough money."

I pretend to let this news sink in, but I really don't care.

"When your grandfather died, your father set out to get more money than the Lindblatts."

"I'm not like him, I don't need to prove anything."

"Maybe not." She shrugs. "Second, he's Old Man Heald, and he's been calling you his future partner since the day you were born. In his mind, it's not *his* business, it's the *family* business; it's your business, and he built it for you."

"I don't want to stand in Heald Shoes in a Heald store and sell elevator shoes."

She laughs as she slides away from me. "Ben, he's never going to stop." In her eyes, determination burns like a small, fierce flame. "You've got to stand up for yourself."

I level my gaze at her. "I can't."

"If Lincoln can free the slaves, you can say no."

This strikes me as a ridiculous comparison. "Lincoln was six feet, four inches. I'm only six feet." I meet her determined gaze and return one of my own. "When I'm swimming laps, my brain says, *Tell your father you want to be a professor; you're not cut out for the shoe business. Dr. Hedjhal says you have a one-in-a-million talent. You're shy and introverted, and when you think about sales, every inch of your skin breaks out in a cold sweat.* I never told my father outright that I'm not going into the business. Yesterday, during the Summer Blowout, I went to the store to tell him, but I couldn't. I thought of writing him a letter, but I couldn't figure out what to say. Afterwards, I went up to my room and cried. I couldn't do my calculus homework, because I couldn't stop feeling sorry for myself for going into the business."

"You can't persuade him with arguments."

"So, what am I supposed to do?"

"Don't debate," she says, sighing as though she really is dealing with a slow grade schooler. "Tell him you're not coming in, and that's that."

My aunt is expecting more from me than I can ever deliver. I say nothing.

"What are you afraid of?" she says

"My father will disown me. I'll have to leave Loomsfield. I'll never go to MIT. I'll end up alone working in a restaurant, and my parents will never speak to me again." I feel the chilly truth of it. "I'm afraid in some deep way. It's stronger than I am." I feel my face draw down. "It's like a negative charge."

"Your mother will never cut you off. I know her; Florence is prouder of you than anything. She talks about you nonstop, *Ben this, Ben that.*"

"I'm afraid she'll take his side."

"I don't think so. She wanted you to go to Loomsfield, your father wanted you to stay at PS18. Who won that argument?"

My aunt has got me wondering if I've misunderstood my parents' marriage. Maybe she's holding something over him. I have no idea. Can it be that my mother really has the final word? I wonder if that's true in business too.

In the ensuing silence, my aunt wraps her arms around me and holds me for the longest time. Her clothes smell like fresh laundry that has dried in the sun. She kisses my cheek. Then she lets me go and musses my hair. "We're all afraid"—she says in a voice that wouldn't wake a mouse—"of one thing or another."

After going to meet with my father in the showroom, my aunt comes back twenty minutes later. She's got a high-wattage smile now, like her face is lit from within by a candle. She sits behind her desk, and I sit across from her. She forms a steeple with her hands and peers at me through the triangle formed by her arms, like she's trying to focus solely on me. "So how was Quogue?" she says. "Tell me everything."

"Not much to tell."

"Ben Heald, not even I believe that."

"I went to the beach every day. Observed the weather."

"Well, did you meet anybody?"

"Mostly local kids."

"Girls?"

"I talked with one on the beach, Peggy, but she is with someone else."

"You like her?"

"What do you mean by *like*?"

"Did you kiss her yet?"

"No."

"Ben Heald," she says soberly, "Two months, you like her, and no kiss?"

I feel like melting into the floor. "Jesse's helping me get my first kiss."

"You want a tip? Show Peggy kindness, patience, understanding, empathy, and compassion."

"All at the same time? I don't know how to be all that."

"Start with patient." She stretches out the word *patient*. "Most men can't even manage that," she says softy. She moves back to her chair, sits with straight crossed legs, and reaches into the back of the bottom drawer. She pulls out a small yellow-white barrel, her Benzedrine inhaler. She unscrews the cap, fills her lungs, and sits back. With her eyes closed, she breathes out a long sigh. She opens her eyes again and says, "Doctor's prescription, for my fatigue."

"Benzedrine is amphetamine. It works in the brain to increase levels of dopamine and norepinephrine."

"That would be no way to talk to your Peggy."

"She's not *my* Peggy." I regret saying it already. *Loser.* So, I make another mental note to myself: talk like a normal person.

My aunt folds her hands in her lap, white skin with blue veins like fine nets. "How's your mother?" she says, giving me a curious stare. "Do they know what she has?"

"She was in Ethiopia, British Somaliland, Uganda, and Kenya," I say. "Probably a sub-Saharan tropical disease, most likely airborne or transmitted by insect bite, maybe a mosquito or a tsetse fly. She had an enlarged spleen, one of the symptoms of malaria, but Dr. Lenz thinks it's something else, like meningitis." I go on with what I'm comfortable with: simple, graspable facts. "The coverings of the brain and spinal cord get infected and swell up, with hearing loss and brain damage. Patients regularly die from meningitis."

Worry clouds my aunt's face. "Is she going to die?"

"Statistically? Good chance."

She wags her head back and forth. "I can't believe she really went with that woman doctor from Vienna," she says, her eyes sharp, taking everything in while giving nothing away.

"Dr. Lenz," I say. "She was doing research on diseases of sub-Saharan Africa. She's looking for a cure for African trypanosomiasis."

"Your mother just up and left your father alone," she says, more impressed than judgmental. "I hear Dr. Lenz is a member of the nucleus club." Seeing the confusion on my face, she adds, "She's in the life."

I take this to mean that Dr. Lenz is a lesbian. The word scares me since no one in my family has ever said it out loud. I'm confused.

Seeing my confusion, my aunt goes on. "Women who express attraction to other women."

I try to picture this, but I can't. "You mean they hold hands?"

"Of course, and more."

"Like kissing?"

"And other things too."

"Like what?"

"I leave that to your imagination, Ben Heald, or your human biology teacher." My aunt runs her forefinger over her lips. "I'm wondering," she says, in a voice normally reserved for a conspiracy, "if Dr. Lenz and your mother are more than doctor and patient."

"But my mother is married to my father," I say, my face burning hot. I've been wondering the same thing, though I haven't let myself say the words. And I have no idea what it actually means, that my mother and her doctor are *more than friends.* After all, why else would my mother, a hobby psychologist, go on a six-week trip to Africa with a tropical disease specialist? I'm not comfortable imagining my mother having intercourse, or whatever they do, with Dr. Lenz. We didn't cover that in human biology, though we did learn that scientists believe dolphins have same-sex relationships.

"Have I upset you?"

I shake my head back and forth.

"It's time to see the world as it actually is," she says, running her hands over the surface of the desk. "Dr. Lenz has no boyfriend, no fiancé, no husband, and no children," she says. "Can't say I blame her," she adds, grinning wryly.

I have never noticed this before, but now that my aunt says it, I realize I haven't been seeing Dr. Lenz as a person with feelings, just a doctor. I stand in silence, trying to order my thoughts and push away the pictures of my mother and Dr. Lenz doing things I want to do with Peggy. My stomach churns nervously, waiting for my aunt to say something. I envy how direct she is, since I avoid saying what I really think.

"We mustn't blame your mother," she says, leaning back so her chest stretches the cloth of her purple sheath dress, a fierce gaze on her face. "When she married your father, she couldn't have known that your father would never be home."

"He told me shoe sales plummeted after the 1929 stock market crash. With millions of people out of work, not buying shoes, Heald Shoes almost went bankrupt, so he stayed late at the office looking for renters for the most valuable leaseholds."

"If you consider the Rainbow Room and the Wyndham New Yorker to be offices." She wags her head, chin pointing down. "How many nights did your mother sit by the phone, waiting for your father to come home?"

"If we imagine four nights a week, times four weeks, that's sixteen times a month. Makes 192 times a year for, let's say, eighteen years, gives us 3,496 nights."

My aunt laughs; then a serious expression tightens her face. "Once she went to the Wyndham after midnight and saw your father's Stutz parked in a side lot," she says soberly. "She was inconsolable. So I'm thinking she decided to get into the life."

I feel my cheeks turn pink. My curiosity is piqued. I wait for my aunt to explain what my mother is doing with Dr. Lenz if they're together in more than a friendly way.

"Close your eyes," she says.

"Now?"

"Close 'em."

I hesitate, thinking maybe she's going to hug me again, but instead she says, "Do you have a crush on a girl?"

"What do you mean?"

"A desire to be with a girl you find really attractive and very special."

Now that's she's put it clearly, yes. "I guess so. Peggy."

"How do you feel when you think of her?"

"I want to kiss her."

"Well then, you have a romantic crush. You really, really like her. You fantasize about kissing, holding hands, or cuddling with her. You want to be more than a friend." She runs her finger down rows of numbers in the account ledger on her desk. "You feel that way about a girl, and men feel that way about women. But women can also feel that way about other women."

"So my mother has a romantic crush on Dr. Lenz."

"It's certainly possible," admits my aunt. "I once had a crush on my mother's best friend, Frieda Kline. During her visits, I found reasons to come into the living room so I could talk to her."

My aunt is right about one thing: I have a crush on Peggy, and I want her to have a crush on me. But she's wrong about my mother. She and Dr. Lenz were on a research trip; that's all. I wonder if my aunt has some hidden motive for telling me this. But I don't see it. What I do see are my aunt's eyes, which are as blue as a clear New Mexico sky, before she gives my hand another I-love-you squeeze, reminding me that I exist.

8

Out on the roof of our Fifth Avenue building after escaping from Heald Shoes through the back door, it's dusk, and my mother is ministering to her yellow hybrids in the small greenhouse she erected after her return from Africa. On a wooden shelf around the glass walls are her miniature trees: weeping fig, jade, lemon, and rubber. From a distance, she's a short, thin woman in a flowered housedress and Heald espadrilles, her favorite summer shoes. She's smiling, enjoying a few hours of energy, as she extends the shears in her right hand and deadheads one of the bright yellow roses. As I approach, she pricks herself on a stem cutting, then sucks on her finger for a moment. "Damn it," she hisses, then drops the shears on the floor and kicks them across the cement.

Seeing this, I'm taken aback. The reality of her newly unbalanced health has been gradually dawning on me—and probably on her too—since she's come back from her research tour with her Austrian-internist friend. She's been complaining of joint pain (neuralgia), and enervation that she's been chalking up to the wear and tear of her six weeks in East Africa. Two hours from now, she's planned her first pied-a-terre since last May, and she's been buzzing with excitement about seeing her artist friends again. The thorn prick is another reminder that her life isn't under her control, which, for my mother, is a serious challenge. Now, walking down the ficus lined path toward the entrance to the greenhouse, I see that she's talking to herself, her mouth half open in a toothy smile, her brow furrowed under her high forehead, a recurring feature of the Bowie women. My first thought is she's tired but fighting the constellation of symptoms. She's become a smaller, paler version of my mother. I wonder if she has anemia.

"I wasn't expecting you up here, Ben," she says, her voice edged with annoyance.

"I wanted to take my weather readings," I say, walking into the glass house, immediately surrounded by a sweet floral aroma that's at once earthy and humid. This is my mother's world, and I immediately feel like an intruder. Standing in a weak beam of between-cloud sun, my mother is clearly in need of a hug, but she never touches me, so I check my urge to embrace her. Last year, when we were doing the family Christmas card, the photographer asked me to sit close to my mother and put my hand on her thigh. I followed his instructions, and my mother batted my hand away. "Don't do that again," she said, her eyes narrow slits. Then, "Sorry, Ben, I don't know what came over me." She wriggled a few inches away from me.

She steps back and crosses her right arm over her chest, massaging her shoulder. "What's the forecast?"

"Rain." From the glass roof of the greenhouse, the light rain makes a quiet murmur.

For a moment her eyes wander, lost in thought. "Hmm, is this going to scare my guests off?"

"It'll let up soon."

"I've ordered finger food for thirty." Her assiduously manicured fingers flutter from her shoulder to her earlobe, which she tugs on lightly.

I can't tell if she would prefer some quiet before she starts putting on her hostess face—light brown makeup, darker eyebrows, mascara, and decent red lipstick. She deadheads another rose, drops the cutting in a plastic pale, puts down the shears, and steadies herself with both hands on the shelf. "Feeling a little light-headed." She realigns her shoulders and takes a firmer grip on the shelf. Rain is puddling on the glass roof.

"I'll get you a glass of water," I say, stepping nearer, where I can smell her lilac hand cream.

"That's very nice, Ben, thank you, but I'm OK." She doesn't let go of the shelf.

I put half a Fifth Avenue chocolate bar on the shelf next to her hand; she takes a nibble, then hands me the rest. The lilac fragrance around her is almost overpowering, mingled with the rubbing alcohol she's been dabbing onto her temples ever since Dr. Lenz told her it might reinvigorate her.

"Just look around; isn't this the most wonderful spot?" she says.

"It sure is."

"Well," she gives me a frail smile. "How are you, Ben?"

"Fine. Sure."

"You can be honest with your old mother."

"Dr. Hedjhal says I'll be ready for the MIT admissions test soon."

"Good," she whispers. She straightens up a little. "Listen," she says in a small voice. "If something happens to me . . ."

"What do you mean?"

"If it turns out I've got some serious disorder—"

"—But Dr. Lenz says you're getting better."

"She's just trying to cheer me up; she'd say that if I were dying." She lowers her head, closes her eyes for a few seconds, and opens them. "If whatever I have is worse than we know . . ."

"Like what?"

"Malaria, river blindness," she says, speaking quickly. "If I don't make it . . ." She gives me a thin smile. "I don't want it to affect your swimming or your schoolwork."

"The chances of you having either one, or something else, are one in *thousands*," I say with my most energetic voice.

"That's what I'm worried about," she says, clearing her throat, and for a moment it's quiet.

"All right."

"Well," she says, releasing the shelf to let her hands fall to her sides. "We'll have to see."

I nod. Again, I squelch the urge to hug her. I feel like the threat of her getting really sick is changing me, though I can't find words for how I'm feeling. If she ever gets malaria, my world and my father's world will go out of kilter—she takes care of everything that doesn't have to do with Heald Shoes. She's at the center of our lives, holding us in our orbits. "See you later," I say, and go off down the flagstone path, leaving her to her lonely offices. Gone is the urge to embrace, or touch, or peck her cheek.

Two hours later, my mother glides into the living room. How she moves so smoothly in high heels is a mystery to me, since the one time I tried walking in four-inch elevator shoes, I lost my balance and careened into my father, who steadied me by holding my wrist, the nearest he's come to comforting me physically since July 4, 1928, when he hoisted me onto his shoulders to get a better view of the Central Park fireworks. My mother might not be the first person you notice at a party, but by the end of the night, she is probably the only one you remember.

"Ben," she says, speaking in a whispery rush as she moves into the crowd, stopping a group of three men with four o'clock shadows and unkempt hair. "You've met Clifford Odets," she says to me while she rests an unquiet hand on his shoulder, beaming at him. "He wrote *Waiting for Lefty*."

"You already told me that," I say to her. "First performance on Sunday, January 6, 1935, at the Civic Repertory Theatre on Fourteenth Street. Seven vignettes on the themes of the power of unions, the corruption of big business, communism, and xenophobia, and the actors speak in working-class vernacular. The play breaks down theatrical boundaries with some of the players sitting with the audience."

"Your son's a theater buff," Odets says to my mother, not looking at me.

"Not really," she says, placing a hand on his hip. "It's just that he has a mind like a steel trap." She takes his hand and kisses him on the knuckles. They laugh, and he turns away, going back to his conversation with a tall, thin man wearing a baggy, brown cashmere jacket with a pipe in the breast pocket.

My mother swings her focus back to me. "He likes you," she says.

"He ignored me."

"You're just like your father, attributing the worst motives to people."

For a moment, things are strained. The space around us is buzzing with small talk and Count Basie's "One O'Clock Jump" coming from the Philco.

My mother's cheeks have reddened. "I love theater people. Sometimes I wish I'd married one," she says. "Oh, well. What difference would it have made, do you suppose?"

"I don't know," I say.

"Of course not, why would you?" It's then that she goes back to her plan for me. "We've got other people for you to meet," she says, like my social secretary.

This is the last thing I want to do right now. "Whatever," I say.

"Don't do that," she says, glancing away from me as if she's talking to someone else. But then I realize she's talking to me.

So, I try to show some enthusiasm for her this-is-our-genius project. "How many?"

"Just a few—we'll start with Judge Kross, whom I consider to be one of the finest legal minds in the city."

My mother raises her fingers to the shining hair that's curled behind her ear, as if her presence needs certifying. Then she walks over to a woman standing alone in a corner and gives her two French-style kisses, trying not to dislodge the round, tinted glasses from the woman's long, pointed nose.

I follow, a few feet behind.

My mother turns to me. "This is Judge Anna Kross. I've told you about her work on prostitution, domestic violence, and orphans." Smiling warmly at Judge Kross, she says, "This is my son, Ben, the family genius."

"Delighted to meet you, Ben. My goodness, you're tall for your age." She doesn't look delighted to meet me; her face is stern and serious, and so is mine, since I'm not delighted to meet Judge Kross or Clifford Odets, for that matter. "Your mother's been very helpful in our work on domestic violence," says Judge Kross, giving my mother a hug, which my mother returns with an awkward embrace and three stiff pats on Judge Kross's shoulder blades.

"Thank you, Anna," she says, admiration in her voice.

Judge Kross excuses herself with a smile, and my mother's gaze follows her across the room to the bar, her lips a tiny bit apart. "What do you think of Judge Kross, Ben?" she says.

"She's pretty serious," I say.

"Determined," says my mother. "It's not the same thing."

"Did she like me too, like Mr. Odets?"

"Ben, I told you not to do that."

"What did I do?"

"Get all snarky," she says. "Show some respect. Judge Kross is a force of nature." She smiles, then steps off past me into the milling crowd. For the first time since her return from Africa in June, her skin has a smooth texture and, except for the touch of gray around her ears, her hair has the almost-original luster, no doubt the work of an excellent hairdresser with whom she spent two hours this morning. Her eyes are sharp, and she seems to sparkle as she regales her guests with stories of her trip to Africa and, like my father, remembers important facts of everyone's lives: children's names, colleges of study, latest plays or novels, personal setbacks and triumphs. And all the while she's touching everybody on their shoulders and arms, or kissing them in greeting, even embracing a few, which, judging by my father's expression, delights him to no end. He spots me through a gap in the crowd and comes over.

"Want a gin and tonic, Ben?"

"I'm sixteen."

"Going on forty," he says with a boozy chortle.

I don't want to stay long enough to drink a gin and tonic. I'm tired of my mother's performance. I can't think of a polite way to leave. "I'll have Quinac, with lots of ice."

My father comes back with a tumbler and puts it into my hand. The cold from the crushed ice makes me shudder. He watches my mother with an expression of awe and admiration. "Your mother's in fine form," he says.

"I think something's wrong with her."

"Nothing's wrong with her that getting back into her old routine won't fix."

"She says she's fine, but she keeps holding her forehead, and she's walking like she has shards of glass in her shoe."

"She's just tired from the long travel," he says, with a quick snort.

"That was two months ago," I say, noticing for the first time a dense leather-spice fragrance around him. "I think she should get some tests."

"Is she at death's door?"

"No, but—"

"—No tests, no treatment. I'm not paying some clown with a stethoscope to tell us nothing's wrong with her." He sneaks a glance at me. "Besides, most specialists are connected to a hospital, and they'll want to send your mother to be jabbed by needles and god knows what other medical mistreatment." Now a faint smell of sweat mingles with his spicy leather aftershave. Weathering an evening with a room full of artists tests my father's small talk to its limits, since he never goes to theater, concerts, opera, museums, or bookstores. "The only way people come out of hospitals is feet first."

"Some people come out better."

"I'm telling you, by the end of August, she'll be our old Florence again."

"Great," I say, though he's deluded.

"Your mother's fine, got it?"

"If you say so."

"I do," he says, and parks his drink on a white doily from Bloomingdale's. "End of discussion," he says, shaking his head in exaggerated disgust, then pulling his cheeks downward with open palms, which gives him a psychotic look. He lifts his glass again, drains it one long gulp, chews on an ice cube, and slinks off for another gin and tonic.

My mother returns, excited but with gray ledges under her eyes. She sweeps her hand across the crowd milling around the living room in groups of threes and fours. "Isn't all this wonderful, dear?"

An awkward silence. "Great," I say for the second time, and for a moment feel stupid.

"I need a favor, Ben," she says.

I take a breath, hold it, and let it out slowly. "I've had enough introductions; I can never remember their names."

"I need you to keep an eye on your father. If he has more than one more drink, come get me."

"Where are you going?"

For a second, doubt tugs at the corners of my mother's mouth. "I need to lie down for a bit. I'm feeling headachy, kind of blah, and my knees hurt."

"Should I call Dr. Lenz?"

"No, dear," she says, with a momentary emptiness in her eyes.

"Your father thinks I just need rest," she says, scanning the crowd again, then smiling. "I don't know what's wrong. Maybe your father's right, it's nothing."

"Should I get you later?"

"In half an hour I'll be good as a new penny." She sounds like she's trying to convince herself, and she's certainly not convincing me. She touches her forehead again. "Is it hot in here, dear?"

"It's pretty warm, and humid." This time I lie, not to protect myself, but so she won't worry more than she already is.

Once I would have been happy to help my mother with her plan to stop my father from drinking too much. But this time I'm not. I told her yes, but I don't want to come get her if she's resting, because as I watch her walking away, greeting more guests one after another with a forced smile and an enthusiastic hello, I believe I know how she'll look in the future if she doesn't get more rest: a face pinched by headache pain and her mouth in a tight smile with every step she takes on achy joints. As she disappears into the sitting room, where she'll lie down on the couch with her eye shades, I watch my father nipping at another gin and tonic, and I accept my fate: I'm free not to go anywhere.

$$\frac{\sin\varphi}{n}=1 \quad \frac{1}{8\sqrt{2}} \quad \ln\frac{x+x\sqrt{2}+1}{x^2-x\sqrt{2}+1} \; ; \; \sin\beta = c_\nu \quad g'=-2\pi\nu g \quad \frac{1}{2}($$

$$g\left(x\sqrt{2}-1\right)\Big|_0^\infty = x \qquad \frac{\pi}{2\Gamma^\circ} \qquad \frac{5\nu_i \cdot 5\nu}{\sin\beta} = n = \eta\left(\mu, \qquad m=\lim\sum_{i=1}\right.$$

$$s, n_1, i_1) \qquad\qquad a^3 z \; ; \; n=$$

$$x^2\pi.$$

9

On Sunday morning, I study calculus for four hours and thirteen minutes, memorize a twenty-three-page chapter on integrals with upper and lower limits, and go to sleep completely exhausted, but still desiring more. What I find strange is how much more I want to know; it's like a new world is open to me, and I don't want anybody stopping me.

In the breezy, overcast afternoon, I go up to the roof again—my mother's in bed with a migraine and my father's at the store. I review my weather observations and try to predict the weather for September: unseasonably wet with periods of intense rain, unseasonably humid, with low-pressure systems flowing out of the coasts of Georgia and the Carolinas and a busy hurricane season. Of course, this is more a wish than a prediction, since I can't possibly know what's going to happen out over the Azores and what will make landfall in the United States.

On Monday, I wait out the morning in the store helping Goldstein, the oldest sales guy, with the August inventory, conceivably the most boring hours of my life. Then I go to the New York Athletic Club for an easy four-thousand-yard swim workout, which I've keenly missed, being alone in the water with my thoughts.

On Tuesday morning, the doorbell rings. I open the door to find the mailman, soaked from a downpour, with a book wrapped in rain-spattered brown paper. Wrapped sloppily and held together with some old red yarn, the package is another calculus textbook: *An Introductory Course of Mathematical Analysis.* Inside the front cover is a letter from Dr. Hedjhal. The handwriting could be a hybrid of Icelandic and Chinese. His indecipherable hieroglyphs add to the mysterious attraction I feel for his genius:

Here's the textbook for MIT Advanced Freshman Calculus. The chapters cover all the cornerstones of complex mathematical analyses . . . bounds and limits of sequences, integral calculus, and functions of more than one variable. Do as much as you can, work the examples at the end of the chapters. I'm expecting you to help me teach senior calculus this semester. See you in two weeks. DH

Now that my life has been upended by skipping a grade, I'm feeling smarter than ever for this chance, but I'm afraid to fail, afraid the Loomsfield kids will bully me back into my old roll: *Heald, the loser.* I'm afraid I won't finish the early chapters of the MIT introductory course, or the Loomsfield kids will mock me when I teach Hedjhal's class. I've already dreamed that I'm standing in Hedjhal's freshman geometry class naked, but when I try to run, my feet are stuck to the floor and the students are laughing. One of them yells, "Pencil dick!" and I wake up with my face afire with shame.

While I'm reading Hedjhal's note, my stomach does a pinch-and-twist, and I take a deep breath and hold it, like I learned to do to stay underwater for two minutes. The deep end of the pool is the safest place I know. But it's not only fear I feel. I'm also relieved to be going back to school to get away from the undertow of my mother's chronic sickness and my father's succession demands. It seems to me that I'm not known to my parents, so imagining my dorm room at school, my stomach calms. Then

I go back to my room to explore the new calculus book, more excited than I've been since climbing onto the train to summer camp in Gallup, where I saw my first fence lightning.

After lunch, I walk to the Big Hat to tell Jesse what's wrong with his business plan. He's late, so I wait outside, rain spattering my glasses. This time, I feel ready for our conversation. I've practiced what I'm going to tell him, because it's not good news. I realize with almost supernatural certainty, standing in front of the diner, that my uncle respects my word because of what I can do, not because I'm his nephew. And for just this moment, the shadow of my timidity that causes me to clam up in front of people—at my parents' parties, in my father's store, in front of my swim teammates, in my Loomsfield classes—has finally been banished.

My uncle shows up twenty minutes late. He's wearing the same white shirt and jeans as the last time, but now he has on a belt with a handworked silver-and-turquoise buckle that depicts a parrot under a banner which says *"Conch Republic."* "You eat?" he says, with no apology.

"At home."

"I could eat a buffalo," he says and flashes his big, relieved smile.

I need to say something, and I want it to be positive and hopeful, even though my news is anything but. "Well," I say.

My uncle's eyes fix on the legal envelope in my hand, and then switch up to me, as if he's trying to figure out what news I'm bringing.

"Well," I say again. "Shall we?" A phrase I learned from my

father, but have never said before in my life.

"Don't mind if I do," he says.

Inside, the air is heavy with the smell of western-cut french fries and Big Hat burgers with sweet ketchup-and-mayonnaise sauce and fried onions. We sit in the back, at our table, and I put the envelope in front of him.

Instead of opening it, Jesse leans back, and for the first time, doubt has turned the corners of his mouth downwards like two equation brackets. He pours cream into his coffee, adds two spoons of sugar, and stirs, his hand shaking slightly. His eyes come up to meet mine. "Well, Mr. Algonquin?"

"The good news is," I say over the two place mats and condiment stand on the table, "If you can make a deal with Zwillman, maybe work out an installment plan, or extend the credit for another twelve months, you'll probably survive, unless something unforeseen happens."

"Like what?"

"Snow, hurricane, flood, fire, red tide," I mumble. Words are failing me again; better to use fewer of them.

He casts an impatient smile toward me. He seems about to say something, then doesn't. He slurps some coffee loudly. And by refraining, he immediately takes over the conversation and my bad-news moment. I'm relieved. "What the hell's red tide?"

"A feared natural phenomenon that occurs along coastlines. The presence and growth of one can spell disaster for those who make their living using coastal resources, like hotel owners. A red tide happens when a few certain species of algae bloom, causing sea organisms to emit a toxin at an accelerated rate, resulting in a red or brown color." I sound like an encyclopedia and regret it immediately because I feel like I'm lecturing him, which I often do when I reel off something I read verbatim from memory.

"Jesus H.," says my uncle, gazing into his coffee at an image of himself. "That's bad," he says, looking out of place in his boots and jeans. But he doesn't seem worried or even bothered. It's as if he meant "that's bad" ironically.

"It's not good, that's for sure. But that's not all."

Feeling sure of myself now, I start with the easy stuff, telling him that the success of Whispering Palms is the longest of long shots. The business plan isn't detailed enough. It's got no nuts-and-bolts statement of how he's going to make money, including a pricing strategy and an outlay of the costs of keeping the whole thing running. He assumes that the guests will come because of the warm, sunny winter weather and world-class bonefishing, but this assumption can be questioned, since three hotels nearby are competing with him, and hurricane damage can close the hotel for an entire season. A normal hurricane season has more than twenty storms, and the likelihood of a dead-on strike to the upper Keys is pretty high. On top of all this, the list of planned ancillary services and organization chart is incomplete. He's got no marketing officer, no front desk officer, and no security detail. Nowhere in the business plan could I find an analysis of the weaknesses, like the fact that the hotel's under new management, and my uncle may not have the financial muscle to sustain the kind of publicity the hotel will require to get off the ground. And the list of the sources of income is incomplete.

"It's a fucking hotel," my uncle says, looking around the diner. His eyes stop on the waitress in the tight Big Hat uniform. "Nice chassis," he says, wetting his lips.

"She's really pretty," I say, trying to show him I'm a normal sixteen-year-old. I sip at my root beer float, stir it with the straw, and set it down next to the saltshaker.

"Excuse my French, but people pay to stay overnight, maybe fuck each other . . . not to get a manicure."

"It's not that clear cut."

"Fuck it is."

"No," I say, "You gotta figure out some things—not just over-nights—like are you gonna charge for the pool, meals, drinks, and laundry service? Will you have a banquet venue, or a shuttle service to the Miami airport?"

"I don't know, I didn't give it much thought," he says, pulling a pair of horn-rims from his shirt pocket and resting them on top of his head. "I figure my new CEO and manager would do that."

"But you need to know what you need to know, or your manager will take advantage of you."

My uncle's shoulders sink, and dark half circles appear under his eyes. He nips at his coffee. He gives me a sad smile. "OK, so I'm a victim of ignorance," he says, arranging his huge hands on the table. He says ignorance to come out ig-nor-*ance*.

"I've made you a checklist for improving the business plan."

He stares again at the waitress, inhales a few quarts of air, and lets them out slowly. "Any *bad* news?" he says, one corner of his mouth edging up in a smile that just won't happen.

"A few questions."

"Shoot."

"How much did you pay?"

"Two hundred thousand. Fifty thousand of which I borrowed from Zwillman."

"Points?"

"The usual, twenty-five."

"And how are you planning to recoup your investment and also pay Zwillman back?"

"The place is paradise. People love paradise. Bonefish, co-conuts, white sand, margaritas. The occupancy rate's ninety percent all year round."

"Uncle Jesse," I say. "You're missing the point."

A silence invokes itself. Outside, the rain has ceased pelting the sidewalk, leaving the air washed clean. A pair of self-conscious young women come in and take seats at a window table.

"Something for you?" Jesse winks at me, changing the subject, as if he knows more bad news is on the way, although I think he has no idea.

"Maybe," I say, embarrassed. "Listen, Jesse, maximizing occupancy isn't the goal."

"Of course, it is. The more guests, the better."

"No, it's not." I unfold a napkin, borrow his pen, and write *Profitability*.

"That much I know."

"You gotta *maximize* profit-a-*bil*-ity."

"That's great," he says, his eyes flashing. He grabs the pen from my hand, caps it, and slides it back into his shirt pocket. "Just fucking great."

"You've got to find a balance between occupancy and rate," I say. "You go above a certain occupancy, you've got more work, more wear and tear, which leads to more capital investment, and you get diminishing profits."

"Your father put you up to this?"

"He didn't need to. My conclusions are intuitively obvious, at least to anyone in the hotel business," I say. "You have to manage revenue. You might imagine 98 percent occupancy is good, but a slightly lower rate, say 95 percent, at a slightly higher per-diem price actually puts more money in your pocket."

I can see how hard he's trying to stay calm, watching the

other waitresses, the one with a bob and a uniform two sizes too small. I wonder how it would be to kiss *her*. I can't stop wondering about kissing the two young women who are drinking Cokes by the window.

My uncle sighs, but I have no idea whether he's sighing about my news or because he's interested in the waitress and she's not checking him out.

I could tell him it's going to work out fine, that I'm pretty sure he'll hit the sweet spot of occupancy, but I choose to let silence do its patient work and see if another reaction comes from him. But it doesn't. "Before you calculate your target occupancy rate, you need to figure out how many years it will take to make your two hundred k back and to pay back Zwillman."

"You do that for me?" he says.

"I'd rather not." The problem is, I'd rather do calculus than figure out the ideal occupancy rate of Whispering Palms. "I've got a lot of homework," I say, smiling what must be a weak smile, signaling that I'm going to cave, even if my father is dead set against my saying yes.

"Come on, Ben, help out your favorite uncle."

"You're my only uncle."

"So, help your only uncle," he says, giving me an I'm-with-you-on-this smile. "What's the problem?"

The waitress comes over and mills around behind my uncle, one hip thrust out, a hand primping the hair around her ear. I smile an; she throws me a glance, winks, and suddenly, I'm so embarrassed I close my eyes

"That your final answer? No?" he says, rolling the envelope into a tube and banging his thigh.

For the first time, I feel a twinge of pity for my uncle. I have the urge to pat his hand. I want to say something. I want to tell him how much I like our conversations in the Big Hat, how much I like spending time with him, how proud I am of my analysis of the hotel. I want to tell him how hard I worked on my analysis. And how haunted I was, worrying about how to give him the bad news. I want to tell him how much I liked that he trusted me to review the business plan, even if it means going against my father.

But the words just won't come out of my mouth, and the moment passes; we're in the Big Hat diner, my uncle scribbling notes on the napkin next to the word *profitability*. He stops writing, his pen poised over the white cloth, lifts his head, and smiles.

"OK," I say. "I'll do it."

"That was like pulling teeth," he says, cocking his head to one side to watch the waitress sashaying toward the counter, where she pours a cup of coffee for a gray man in a gray suit. "What d'ya say, Ben, another coffee and a piece of apple pie with two scoops of vanilla ice cream? To celebrate."

"Celebrate what?"

"Our little hotel project."

"My father's going to kill me if he finds out." For the first time, I hear the fear in my voice and have to admit that I've been kidding myself. I'm still worried about my father's reaction.

"Apple pie?" my uncle asks again. A forced cheerfulness has crept into his voice.

"No thanks," I say. I've caved again, but at least I'm free to go home and crack open *An Introductory Course of Mathematical Analysis,* which is almost as good as holding my breath under-water. Or imagining how it feels to kiss Peggy, the library girl.

10

After a long Tuesday night and Wednesday morning of studying sequences and series—the most interesting topic so far—I fall asleep with my head on the book like a hard pillow. I wake up at lunchtime on Wednesday, eat a ham and cheese sandwich, and decide to call Dr. Hedjhal.

Standing in the kitchen at one o'clock, I call his number. A humid, warm spring-like morning has dried the sidewalks and sides of buildings along Fifth Avenue. It's been a week since I talked with Hedjhal on the patio in Quogue, where I felt for the first time that my gift for math could get me out of the shoe business. Today I need his advice.

"Hedjhal residence," a soft, warm voice says. It's a man's, but not Hedjhal's.

"Hi," I say. "It's Ben Heald calling. I'd like to talk to Dr. Hedjhal. He sent me a book, with a note, and I'd like to ask him a few questions." My heart starts thumping against my chest. I have a bad feeling. Potentially I'm bothering him. He didn't mean it when he said I could call, it's just something he said to be polite. I begin putting the receiver back into its cradle, but I hesitate, unsure.

"Heald?" Hedjhal's low voice buzzes through the receiver, stopping me with my name. I didn't think he'd come to the phone, and now I'm trapped. I have to talk with him. "Ben?" Hedjhal's voice sounds a little put off, more annoyed than in class, when he's frustrated by my slower classmates. It's not a voice I want to talk to. There's a low cough, and then a scratchy clearing of his throat, and I suddenly feel this is a mistake. I should hang up and go to the store. "Heald, are you still there?" He sounds impatient now. Another cough. "What the . . . ?" he says, I assume to the man who answered. "He hung up."

"Dr. Hedjhal, I'm here," I say.

"He's still on the line. OK." Whoever owns the warmer, smaller voice—a friend, a brother, an uncle—also says, "OK" in the background.

"Did you get the book I sent?"

"Yes, sir."

"Good. Good. Well then, what can I do for you, Heald?"

"Well . . . it's just that . . ." I try to say.

"How's the calculus going?"

"Fine," I say, disappointed with myself for not getting to the point. "I'm calling about my . . . father."

"Ah, fathers," he says. "They're always busy putting their expectations on us. I see it every year at Loomsfield, fathers forcing their sons into careers they choose. Most of them get their way too."

"I . . ."

"Your father's pressuring you to go into the shoe business, isn't he?"

"I've been wondering how to argue with him that he should let me go to MIT."

"Impossible, Heald," he says with a tsk-tsk. "Arguments never change a father's mind."

"I don't understand."

"Is your father stubborn?"

"Yes."

"Have you ever seen him change his mind?"

"No."

"When they made men like your father, they perfected stubbornness."

"So, I should give up on MIT?" I ask quickly, feeling cornered and miserable. "Just let him get his way?"

"No, I'm saying an argument won't work; the only thing that will work is for you to tell him you're not coming into the business because you're going to go to MIT."

"He'll never go for that. He'll threaten not to pay, or to disown me, or never talk to me again."

"You're going to win a scholarship to MIT, provided you do your calculus this semester. You'll make so many new friends you won't miss your father, and you won't need his money because you're going to be a tenured professor one day."

The soft warm voice again, but not speaking to me: "We're going to be late." Then Hedjhal whispers, "OK, I'm coming; but first, the kid needs my help." More whispering. "Five minutes," says Hedjhal, "Ben, still there?"

"Yes, sir." My heart is gunning, my hand clutching the receiver through which I'm taking part in someone else's conversation. "I'm sorry, Dr. Hedjhal, I . . ."

"Don't be silly, Heald. I understand, you're in a jam; we can talk when you come back to school after Labor Day. Remember, you can't convince your father, you just need to present him with a *fait accompi*."

"A what?"

"A thing accomplished and presumably irreversible."

"I don't think I can do that."

"If you want to go to MIT, I don't think you have a choice." A pause. "Listen Heald, you don't have to do this before school resumes, so sit tight, and we'll meet in my office the first day back."

"Thank you, Dr. Hedjhal."

"We'll start reviewing your calculus then."

The soft voice again. "Dennis, we really have to get going." Then Hedjhal, "OK."

Then the line between us is empty. No goodbye. No closure. Just bad news, and then I'm alone and breathless in the kitchen by the open window. A girder of sunlight brightens the kitchen table in front of me, a reminder that maybe the wet summer spell is ending at last. But I still need a plan for getting out of the business. My latest idea is to ignore the problem until it goes away, like many problems that just solve themselves. But my father's not just going to go away unless he has a car accident or a grand piano falls on him outside the store, like it did to my grandfather. Mostly what I want to do now is swim, go to MIT, and have my first kiss.

In thirty minutes, I'm out the door, down the thirty floors to the lobby, and out into the street in the humid-but-bright sunny morning. I catch a cab to the store and spend a few hours checking receivables in my aunt's office, since she's gone to the doctor.

At four o'clock, the phone on the checkout counter rings. My father goes to the cash register, whistling like he's expecting a call from a supplier or a customer calling in an order. He holds the phone to his ear, his face growing whiter and whiter. He stops talking, but he moves his lips. He's absolutely still, like he's died standing up and *rigor mortis* has set in. Then he drops the phone, letting it swing on its cord like a pendulum. He pulls at his chin with wide-open, blank eyes, registering nothing. Then he lets his head sink almost to his chest and runs his hand repeatedly over his bald patch.

I leave the office and walk up to him.

"It's your mother . . ." He sighs. "It's . . . bad."

"What is it?"

"We need to get home," he says. "Now."

Five minutes later, in a blind panic, my father opens the door to the taxi, climbs in, sits back, and mops the wide slope of his forehead with a brown handkerchief. He blinks. His breath comes in short bursts punctuated by long delays. I've never seen him like this, and it terrifies me. He rests his chin against his open palm. "Not now," he says.

"What?"

"Not today."

I put my hand on his knee to calm his shaking. "It's going to be all right." Not even I believe this, since his dread has spread to me like a fast-acting poison.

"Your mother's . . ." His voice is pinched, with a high, whiny quality. I've seen him worried, anxious, even angry, but never so frightened. "Your mother's going to die." He says it, but he sounds as if he's putting the fact of it at a distance, and suddenly I want nothing more than for my mother to be well.

I've imagined this moment over and over since last June. But this sounds like a supernova of prodromes. I feel like I'm not in my own skin. I can't feel my feet. Adrenaline floods my body. My breath comes in short rapid gasps.

We rush out of the taxi in front of our building at Ninety-Eighth and Fifth. We look up at the massive rain-streaked façade, craning our heads back to see to the top, where we live.

Waiting for the elevator, my father is breathing quick, shallow breaths. "Can a person explode?"

"Why?"

"Maria, the housekeeper said 'Mrs. Heald *va a explotar.*'

"Theoretically, our organs could perforate or rupture. For instance, if you can't get rid of the gas in your system, your stomach and intestines would continue to expand beyond capacity."

The way my father stares at me, I realize he wishes I hadn't answered.

We ride the elevator to the penthouse and approach the door to our apartment. My father steps back. "My heart's gonna give out," he whispers behind me. "My teeth hurt."

Hurting teeth? That's your excuse? For a few seconds, I'm staggered by his cowardice. He's lost all authority over me. "When we get inside, you call the ambulance," I say.

Overpowering my reluctance, I make an awkward step into the front hall, my gaze fixed on the living room couch. My mouth and cheeks are working a smile that won't quite materialize. I stuff my hands in both pants pockets as if they're cold. I'm already doing this badly. I have no idea what to say or do. I take three tentative steps. "Mother?"

Silence. A smell of urine and roses. She's dead, I think, as my eyes adjust to the gloom.

"Mother?"

I walk into the living room, which is shrouded in the invisible fog of the soon-to-be-gone. Vomit splotches the couch, pillows, and blanket. A tang of urine and rose hand cream wafts off the curtains. My mother comes into view: Florence Bowie Heald. Lit by a thin slice of yellow daylight seeping in through a gap in the heavy curtains. Her cheeks and forehead have a lacquered shine, like sausage skin about to burst. In the ten hours since I last saw her, she's become the matron for death warmed over. It's shocking that on Saturday, at her party, though emaciated, she seemed pretty fine.

She takes a breath—flaking rasps and sawing snores—and opens her eyes. "Ben?"

I set a glass of water in her puffy fingers. She takes a sip, swallows, clears her throat with a retching sound, touches her left index finger to her lips, and hands the glass back, with the imprint of her lipstick. "Ambulance," she says, as pieces of her lungs break off and rattle around inside. She raises her head, the chords in her neck showing. "Ben," she says; her head flops onto the pillow, her eyes fall shut, and her breathing slows to a low gurgle.

My father joins me after all. "Is she going to be OK?" he croaks like an old frog.

"How should I know?"

I squeeze my mother's wrist. "She's got a pulse."

She exhales an audible breath, and then her fingers flutter to her frizzy hair. "Hospital."

My father blanches. "No hospitals," he says in a seething whisper.

I badly want to tell him he's being ridiculous—my mother's favorite line—because he's endangering my mother's life. But I make my usual choice to avoid a confrontation, so all I say is, "We can't help her here."

"We'd be putting her in the hands of mass murderers." He's against hospitals ever since his mother went into Mount Sinai in March 1917 for gallbladder surgery and was wheeled out nine days later a paraplegic—caused by a near-lethal overdose of barbiturates and benzodiazepines, he believes. He takes three quick steps backwards, catches his toe on the edge of the carpet, and falls. He lands with a hard thump and doesn't even try to get up, like a football player waiting on the field to find out how badly he's hurt.

Instead of feeling sorry for him, my first thought is that he's no use to me now. It's not a good thing for a boy to feel bigger, stronger, and more decisive than his father. I lean toward him. "You OK?"

"Fuck do I know," he says. I'm unsure whether he's impatient or despondent, so I offer my hand. He takes it gently, then scrambles to his feet, shaking his arms like a wrestler before a match. He grabs my collar, panting. "What if she dies?" His face is drawn; the lines around his mouth and eyes are black scratches.

"She's not going to die," I say, because that's what people say when they're trying to comfort a family member. But I'm not sure, because it's an ambiguous situation, and I don't do well with ambiguity.

My father stares at the rug, a replica of the Bayeux Tapestry. "Jesus, what a hideous rug. Your mother made me buy it in Paris." He turns away, seemingly more angry at her than anything else. "I'll call an ambulance," he says, heading for the kitchen, where he may or may not call, but he'll for sure take out the Canadian whiskey he keeps under the sink.

I take my mother's hand, light as a bird, and feel the faint rhythmic throbbing in her wrist. I bend down toward my mother's face, twisted with pain. "How are you feeling, mother?"

She opens her eyes. A burst of energy. Not a good sign: patients have been known to experience a sudden recovery minutes before they die. She speaks, but a gurgling in her lungs breaks up her words. "We never really know when it's time, do we?" She coughs and wheezes, gulps for air. "I don't think we get to know . . . every breath . . . a moment of luck." Her voice trails off.

On the coffee table are her "accoutrements" (her word): bloody tissues yellowed by pus, a metal tray with assorted pills, eyeshades, two syringes, three needles, a length of rubber tubing, a silver beaker with a long spoon, and a copy of *Know How To Live: A Course on Death and Dying.*

I put my mouth to her ear. "The ambulance is on its way," I whisper, that phony cheeriness again.

"Ben, promise me . . ." she says. Her trembling fingers tug at the loose skin under her jaw.

"What?"

"Seconal . . . in the bathroom." Tears come to her eyes. "You're a good son." Each breath, now louder, starts as a squeezing in, and rises in pitch like a bottle filling with water. There's a pause, followed by a moaning exhalation that spreads into an open, tissue-y clatter.

My father comes back with a glass of whiskey in his hand and stands next to me near the couch where my mother is breathing like a pneumonia patient. "Ambulance on the way."

I squeeze the water from a washcloth in a bowl and tamp her forehead.

My father puts down his glass. "Here," he says, holding out his hand. "Let me."

He dabs my mother's cheeks, until she asks him to stop. Miffed, he goes to the Philco in the corner—he's exclusively a Philco man—and turns on the radio, WJZ New York. Jazz, swing, and pop tunes are his antidote to every ill. The horns are oddly formal, a minuet, with a tight, repeating structure and harmonious violins way out of place. Fred Astaire comes on: *A voice inside keeps repeating You, You, You.* My father says, "Fred Astaire. Your favorite."

"Whatever gave you that idea?" she says, with surprising energy.

"You told me once," he says calmly.

My mother lowers her soft chin and stares down at her swollen body, then arranges her hands like a sick elderly lady, though she's only forty-two.

My father stares at her, uncomprehending. He nervously smooths the front of his shirt where his tears have spotted it.

She obliges him with a smile, putting his needs first, which is part of their arrangement. She coughs three shallow, staccato rasps, gropes for a tissue from the box on the table, rasps again, and deposits a green, gelatinous blob into a folded tissue. She folds the tissue into a tight ball. With her eyes closed, she says, "Is death a . . . a feeling? A sensation?"

I shrug. For a moment, I scan my memory for the answer from all the books I've ever read, but something about this moment, the gravity of it, enables me to refrain from answering what I know can't be answered.

She says, "Nothing I've done had an end. I saw myself obliquely, not the Florence who would die. Now I take a breath . . . do I get another one?" She closes her eyes and falls back into a deep snore.

I turn to my father. Tears glisten on his cheeks. He says, "Remember this moment, Ben. It may be the last time you see her alive."

I'm shocked that he would say this as though my mother isn't lying in front of us. It seems like admitting defeat, quitting a thousand-yard swim after six hundred yards. I want to say to him, *Pick a side, and that side is life, not death*, but he's sitting on the sidelines of the wrong team.

The sound of stretcher wheels creaking down the hall outside our apartment interrupts my frustration with my father. It's the sound of all the uncertainty of the world pouring in—my mother's labored breathing and my father's sobs—and I understand, for the first time, how easily life is one thing rather than another.

$p_i^3; \frac{\sin\varphi}{n}_{=1}$ $\frac{1}{8\sqrt{2}}$ $\ln\frac{x^2+x\sqrt{2}+1}{x^2-x\sqrt{2}+1}$ $; \sin\beta = c_\nu$ $g' = -2\pi Dg$ $\frac{1}{2}($

$g\left(x\sqrt{2}-1\right)\Big|_0^\infty = x$ $\frac{\pi}{2\Gamma^9}$ $\frac{\partial v_i \cdot 5v}{\sin\beta} = n = \eta\left(\mu,\right.$ $m = \lim\sum_{i=1}^m$

$s, n_i, i_i)$ $a_z^3; \ n=$

$x^2\pi\cdot$,

11

On Fifth Avenue, a sprawling hospital complex has the best doctors from Columbia University working in a vast emergency room and intensive care unit: the Flower Hospital. That's where we're headed in my father's yellow Stutz Bearcat, chasing the white Henney-Packard ambulance that's transporting my mother. My father is panicking as though the ambulance is a hearse.

The pounding rain hits the hood in thousands of little explosions, making it hard to see the cars in front of us. My father's driving is jerky: he hits the gas, pumps the brakes, and steers into turns too fast, the tires squealing. He runs a red light and nearly gets blindsided by a bread delivery truck, its horn echoing in my ears. I offer to drive, but he declines. At the hospital, he parks at an angle, taking up almost three spaces. He sees me critically eyeing his parking job. "Fuck it, let's go," he says.

Hovering around the door to my mother's room, not yet allowed in, my father starts saying he's sure, *sure as sin, three million percent sure,* my mother's going to die; that someone *up there* has it out for him, or maybe it's a conspiracy of her doctors, starting with that bitch Dr. Lenz, who's poisoning my mother with her damn Austrian homeopathic droplets. Since my mother went to East Africa with Dr. Lenz—it's still a mystery to me why she went—my father refers to Dr. Lenz as "that bitch," or "that woman . . . whose father was a mem-

ber of the Austrian Nazi party and is conspiring against the
fremdvölkische . . . people like you and me," so, "fuck her."

Every time he says it, I'm stunned because his hostility makes
me uncomfortable. At any moment, he could turn it on me or
my mother. I'm always trying to think of something I can say
to calm him, since his conspiracy theory is about as probable as
snow in September, but once he gets started, he tries to convince
me that powerful actors—doctors, nurses, ambulance drivers,
Egyptian spies—are the only possible explanations for the disease that no doctor in Manhattan can explain.

He caresses the closed green door and tries the smudged
knob, which strikes me as almost as sad as my father's expression.
I'm sure that instead of blowing his top, this time he's going to
start crying.

A piercing scream reaches us from inside an emergency room
at the end of the hall. It starts as a high-pitched wail, long and
drawn out, and trails off into a series of short whimpers and
pleads, "No, please, make it stop." The voice is unmistakably my
mother's.

The hallway is small now. My father doesn't cry. His face goes
pale. He gasps, rips a dollar bill into tiny pieces, and releases them
into the air in a miniature flurry. He says, "Fuck. Fuck. Fuck this,
and fuck everything up and down and twice on Sundays."

All I can do is smile at him and give him a reassuring nod.
But he won't be reassured. My mother's symptoms are too visible
and too immediate. Until now, they had been distant, belonging
to another world, another family, another time, and every sign
of improvement, a cheery note in her voice, a smile, resumption
of her daily activities like arranging flowers, he took as proof that
this episode in our lives would soon be a memory. But this is real,
now, and way too near.

Dr. Lenz sprints past, down the emergency-ward corridor, the crepe soles of her shoes squeaking on the tiles, and pushes through the doors into the operating area. A tall nurse with blond hair, no more than twenty, calls out, "Moved her to OP Two."

From behind the saloon-like doors, we hear Lenz: "Prep her for a spinal."

My father blanches and checks his watch, a gold clunker with a sapphire in the stem winder, a present from my mother on his fortieth birthday. He goes to the nurse's station, chats with the tall blond, and comes back shaking his head. "Your mother's having some sort of emergency, but they won't give me any more." He's got onions on his breath, mixed with the stench of fear-sweat. "You OK?"

"Yeah." Another lie. In truth, my mother's screams have set off a pain in my neck and disturbed my inner ear, so I feel like I'm standing on the deck of a boat in a rough sea.

He takes a cigarette out of a gold case and lights it. "I'm sorry about before, my little outbreak."

I nod, not knowing what to do with his apology. Of all the things he could apologize for, he chooses one of his tantrums, not his cowardice of the last hour, not trying to keep me away from Jesse, nor nixing my dream of MIT and trying to push me into the business. Five years ago, that would have been fine, because I viewed the business with a combination of awe and zeal, dazzled by the movie stars who bought Heald Elevators: Fred Astaire, Spencer Tracy, Mickey Rooney, James Cagney, Marlene Dietrich (my father fawned all over her when my mother wasn't visiting the store on Fifth Avenue), and Buster Crabbe, who won Olympic gold in the four-hundred-yard freestyle and played in *Tarzan the Fearless* and *Flash Gordon*. I wanted to be Buster Crabbe. But when I turned sixteen, last February, I felt a desire for more. I wanted to be me, only better: a freaky tall nerd who stutters, solves complex math problems in his head, and remembers every word he's ever read.

My father knows none of this, since he never asks me what I want, and I never tell him. Preoccupied, he moves one hand to his midriff and makes little circles, like he's rubbing out a pain. "When your grandmother died, I was standing beside her bed, right here in Flower. She kept crying out, 'I want to go home, I want to go home.' Her breathing became more labored, deeper, and slower with long pauses, then sudden gasps. I held her hand, but I don't think she knew it. Her cries got weaker, and her breathing stopped. It just ceased. I can't forget it; her body made this sound like a sigh as the last air escaped her lungs. I thought she was dead, but she kept moving . . . well, twitching. I called for a doctor, who came in, checked for a pulse, and said, 'She's gone.' 'But she's still moving,' I said. 'No,' he said. 'Your brain tricked you into seeing movements that never happened.' I excused myself, went into the men's room, and bawled my face off."

"Mother told me that your mother died of pancreatic cancer."

"Remember the combines we saw the first time I drove you out to summer camp in Gallup?"

"Outside Council Bluffs, Iowa, Saturday, July 14 at four o'clock. A big thunder- and hailstorm dented the hood, and we saw a green harvester as big as an airplane."

"You remember that?" he says with a smirk, returning his hand to his side.

"It was a metal monster."

"Your grandmother's cancer went through our lives like a silent threshing machine." He takes a few steps toward the door to my mother's room, listens for a moment, then comes back to me, still smoking. His movements are tentative, like a man released from a long hospital stay. He seems shaky, a little disoriented. "I'm going to need your help in the business now."

"I don't get it."

"Without you, we'll have to file for Chapter 11."

I let that sink in. It's patently false. "I don't believe you," I say.

"Believe what you want. I'm still going to need your help."

"I'm already helping."

"I mean more, and regularly, not just when it suits you."

"You want me to quit school?"

"Of course not, no, you need your diploma."

"So, what do you mean?"

"I was thinking you can work weekends—take the Friday midday bus from Loomsfield after lunch and go back on the Sunday-night Greyhound."

"Fridays, I have extra calculus and swim practice, and swim meets are on Saturdays."

"If you missed every class for a year, with your IQ, you'd still graduate, and swimming just isn't a priority." He makes a snorting sound. "If you were Buster Crabbe . . . but let's be realistic, you're never going to play Tarzan."

"I can win the New England Championships."

He gives me the side eye, listening to me at the edge of my words, and nothing's sinking in. "I gave up wrestling, college, and flying, from one day to the next," he says, his eyes as cold as frozen grapes. "So can you." Now he's staring up at the ceiling. He coughs, the equivalent of an exclamation point in his argument.

I pause. I need a new tack. "You told me you were too slow for wrestling, you didn't have the grades for college, and you were color blind for reds, greens, and browns, so the Air Force rejected you," I say. "Grandfather was running the business when he died. Jesse was playing baseball, so you had to take over."

"True." He lifts his eyebrows, not following my reasoning, it seems.

"But Mother isn't involved, so her being in the hospital doesn't change anything. And besides, I don't have much experience, and I'm not good at sales, you said it yourself."

"This way you'll get experience *before* we become partners. You can take over some of the administrative stuff, and cover for me when I'm preoccupied with your mother."

"This makes no sense." I may be yelling now.

"Who told you that life makes sense?" He hits his thigh with his balled fist. "Get over it."

"You're not giving me a choice." I'm definitely yelling now, and tears are blurring my eyes.

He closes his eyes, a tiny quiver of rage on his lips. "Two hours ago, you were sixteen. Now you're forty—sadly, childhood comes to an end."

"So now you get to decide when my childhood ends," I say, stunned. I feel like I'm going to hit him, or maybe put my hands around his neck.

"You think I wanted to take over the business? I didn't have dreams? We don't always get what we want just because we want it." He's openly hostile, and it suddenly occurs to me that he's enjoying this—since he can't control my mother's illness, he can control me. Seemingly to calm the moment, he pulls at the loose skin under his chin. "A needle as big as a pencil is puncturing your mother's spine, and you're whining about a bright future in the best shoe retailer in the whole fucking Northeast." Sweat drips down his temples, and his thin hair is matted. His bloodshot eyes move slowly my way, and for the first time I see that he's exhausted, shoulders hunched, face pinched, and a faint tremor in his hands. I wonder if he's sick. He interrupts my thoughts with his final argument. "This is how things work in our family."

This, of course, is no argument at all. It's a decree. Dr. Hedjhal was right—I will never convince my father with reason. But I'm not ready to say, "No." I just can't. I think, "No," but the word clogs my tongue and won't come over my lips, a relic of my childhood stuttering. I'm feeling frustrated and angry, and still have the urge to hit him.

"Do yourself a favor, Ben," he says, his voice cold.

"What's that?"

"Get over it."

"It's not fair."

"I already said, get over it." He gazes at his watch, then hitches up his pants and smooths his shirt, like he's getting ready to go out with one of his schtups. Then he turns away from me and walks briskly toward the waiting room. Not knowing what to do with my disappointment, I stand by the door of the room my mother was in, and think of swimming, the way water feels on my skin, smooth and cool; and the easy rhythms of my slow freestyle; my heart doing its patient work; no thoughts of my mother's swollen body or working in the store with my father.

My father returns with a Coke bottle in each hand. "Truce?" he says.

I say nothing because nothing seems about right.

He offers me a Coke. "Want one?"

"OK."

"Ben, think of it as an arranged marriage."

"Sure, that's a good idea," I say, giving him an accommodating stare, though I'm sure he hears my sarcasm. He's been using this arranged marriage line for years, claiming that the love built in such an arrangement is stronger than any romantic attachment, which fades with time. I can't imagine anything more horrible than an arranged marriage, just like I can't imagine spending more time in the business than short visits to my father.

"I'm offering you a place in the world."

"A place in *your* world."

"Stop feeling sorry for yourself; the color doesn't suit you."

But feeling sorry for myself seems about right. Waiting for Dr. Lenz to let us into my mother's room, I'm determined to find a way to avoid the family business. My time is running out.

12

An hour later, at seven in the evening, I'm still sitting in the crowded waiting room, waiting to see my mother. Three couples hold hands against their worry and grief. A gray-haired man reads the *Times*. A boy sleeps with his head on his mother's lap. An old Ukrainian woman with a headscarf is eating an egg and sipping tea from a thermos. She offers me an egg. I decline, stand up, and go to the window.

Outside, four stories below, the rainy first day of September gives the sidewalk a sad aspect. I've been here before, when my aunt had her appendix removed five years ago. Five years ago, my father stood in the same exact spot, under the dogwood tree, talking to himself and gesticulating like an irate cab driver. He radiated high energy, crackling like a Van de Graaff generator. The area around the hospital has remained the same: a line of four boxy ambulances; a fifth horse-drawn one, the white horse mottled with rain; my father's ostentatious yellow Stutz halfway up the sidewalk; the dark-brick walls of the surrounding buildings ; the busyness of Fifth Avenue.

But my father has changed. His straight back is slumped. His hair has thinned to a black shadow around his head. How surprised I am by how much he has changed in the last few hours. He stands in the sulfurous glow from a streetlight, smoking under his umbrella. He drops his cigarette, crushes it with his shoe, and walks back and forth as if he's following two parallel lines, fat drops of rain falling from the edge of the umbrella. He's wearing a crumpled white shirt with black suspenders that make him look like an exhausted commodities trader, not Flex Heald. He trudges with a bend in his spine that's only visible if you knew him before, when he was straight backed, the master of the salesroom.

For a second my heart seizes up. But not out of pity or sadness for my father, or my mother, which I oddly don't feel. It's for me. I'm feeling guilty because I should be more worried about my mother, when I'm actually frustrated that I have to put my life on hold for her; or rather, that I'll probably have to curtail my Friday afternoon calculus tutoring sessions, miss Friday swim practice and weekend meets, and stop helping Jesse with his Whispering Palms business plan, which I'm secretly enjoying.

Four stories below, my father tries to close his umbrella, but the runner jams and the black canopy catches a gust of wind, tumbling into the street, where a taxi runs it over like a broken bird. He puts his arms into the air, raises his face to the rain, and lets the water stream down his head and shoulders.

A tap on my shoulder. I turn. Not more than three feet away is the blond nurse my father was flirting with at the nurse's station. She's a little awkward, standing pigeon toed and staring up at me like a bashful girl. Her left eye, which is cobalt blue, has a slightly larger radius than the other, which makes her seem vulnerable. She could be Jean Arthur, or that type anyway, only younger. She's sympathetic, in a white uniform with a little blue tag on it: "Gloria. RN." She's not like the other nurses who wear their uniforms tight, daring you not to stare. Gloria wears hers loose, natural in the way it hangs and strains against her when she leans over. I stand up, aware that I'm ogling her, when a sudden, almost crippling urge—a sort of desperate longing—grips me.

"Ben?" she says.

"Yes," I say. "Gloria, right?"

She points at the tag on her chest, which I read over and over.

"Why was my mother screaming?"

She smiles at my bluntness, a "talent" my family laughs about. "LP."

"LP?"

"Lumbar puncture."

"They use a long needle for that, don't they?"

"Who made you a doctor?"

"That must hurt like a payara's eating her from the inside."

"Payara?"

"A kind of fish found only in the Amazon; it's got huge eyes and four-inch fangs."

"Oh, lord."

There's something dark and complex about Gloria that I can't read. She reminds me of my aunt: serious, focused, and level-headed, but caring and decent . . . and so attractive I feel sick to my stomach. I like her immediately. I stare at her lips and impossibly white teeth.

She notices that I'm staring and smiles, kind of shy. "I know what you must be going through; my father's been sick for two years."

"What does he have?"

"Lung cancer."

"I'm sorry," I say. "Since my mother got sick in June, I keep thinking, soon she'll be better."

We stand awkwardly like two strangers waiting for a bus.

My father comes back, soaked and puffy faced with dark

rings like smears of iron dust under his eyes. "Gloria," he says, leaning near to her chest. "Can't we visit my wife?" He covers his face with his hands, then he rubs his eyes. "Just want to say hello, won't stay long."

"It's against hospital policy." Gloria's eyes are flashing. "Dr. Lenz will be with you in a few minutes." Gloria adjusts her collar, her fingers awkwardly messing with a button. She looks behind her at the nurse's station, where three nurses are pointing at her and laughing. "Break's over," she says, her cheeks red. She turns to leave.

"Wait," I say.

She waits, with one brow raised.

I offer her my hand, we shake, and I do a little wave-like motion. Her back is already to me. I feel really stupid.

She's forgotten I exist. I'm here. She's not. Which is good, since she can't see my discomfort at feeling attracted to her while my mother is in agony three doors down.

Dr. Lenz arrives, a little breathless and wringing her hands. "Emergency appendectomy." This diminutive ball of energy and determination, MD and PhD, who my mother puts right up on a pedestal of scientific geniuses like Marie Curie, has been my mother's go-to doctor since her symptoms first manifested themselves in June. Back then, it was just swollen glands, headaches, and blurred vision. Lenz shakes my father's hand.

He promptly wipes it with his handkerchief. "Germs."

Lenz studies her clipboard through horn-rimmed glasses that are framed by her girlish black bangs. Her dark hair and glasses accentuate her blue-green eyes. "I am sorry about Frau Heald," she says.

"What's wrong with my wife?" My father's urgency makes everything he says sound like a threat.

"Difficult to say." Lenz pushes her glasses up on her nose and studies my mother's chart again—I should carry a chart, then I could avoid people's eyes—one hand clenched around a pencil, which she taps on her leg. "If things keep so progressing, she can from-the-inside, drown."

My mouth goes dry. "Lung congestion?"

"We've intubated, but the possibility of draining the lungs is limited."

My father moves toward Lenz, standing so close he could kiss her. "What does she have?"

Lenz steps back, raises a perfectly curved eyebrow, and keeps her cool. "Swelling of the lungs, abdomen, liver, and lower body. Perhaps hypothyroidism. It can also be encephalitis lethargica." She shakes her head but doesn't meet my father's eye. "We're doing tests for dengue fever, malaria, pancreatitis, maybe a tumor, liver failure, peripheral edema." Absentmindedly, using her sleeve, she polishes the stethoscope dangling around her neck. "Ach, we humans die of many causes, so many mysteries."

My father grabs Lenz's wrist, then immediately lets it go.

Lenz pulls away and gives my father cold eyes hardened by years of practice. "The experts at the College of Physicians and Surgeons don't recognize Mrs. Heald's constellation of symptoms."

"What's your best guess?" says my father.

"Hemorrhagic fever, malaria, Nile virus, sleeping sickness, phlebitis, a *komische* thyroid *Zustand*, um . . . *condition*."

"Your best guess is five hypotheticals?" says my father, staring at her bleakly, his mouth a ragged tear in his face.

"Excuse me?" says Lenz.

"Could it be anything else?" I ask.

"Maybe a parasite."

"With all due respect," says my father, "we'd really like to know what's wrong with my wife."

"A prognosis is a series of iterations of approximate guesses. We're surprisingly bad at it."

"When will you have something for me?" His voice is laced with hostility.

"I don't know," she says, translating direct from Austrian. "Medicine isn't bookkeeping."

"You're proof of that, Doctor," says my father.

Dr. Lenz's face goes bright red. After what my aunt told me—she's in the life—she's a mystery to me. It must not be easy dealing with patients, one minute friendly, one minute aggressive, and all the time in between wanting to be in the nucleus club doing who knows what women do with each other.

Tension fills the space between her and my father. I'm trying to ignore that fact that my father is probably going to say something he's going to regret, and that might jeopardize my mother's recovery. Words, I learned from watching him lose his patience with my mother, can scar. I squeeze the keys in my pocket until one of them digs into my palm.

My father shrugs. "I'm just saying."

Dr. Lenz lifts one shoulder and reads my mother's chart again. She's using it like a shield. "The reason that I came, Florence is back in her room now, you can visit her, but please, only short."

"Thank you, Dr. Lenz," says my father, retreating from his verbal attack.

"It's nothing," she says. "Follow me."

$p^3; \dfrac{\sin\varphi}{n}=1 \quad \dfrac{1}{8\sqrt{2}} \quad \ln\dfrac{x^2+x\sqrt{2}+1}{x^2-x\sqrt{2}+1} \quad ;\sin\beta=c_v \quad g'=-2\pi\vartheta g \quad \dfrac{1}{2}(1$

$g\left(x\sqrt{2}-1\right)\Big|_0^\infty=x \qquad \dfrac{\pi}{2\sqrt{9}} \qquad \dfrac{\partial v_i \cdot 5v}{\sin\beta}=n=\eta(\mu, \qquad m=\lim\sum_{i=1}^m$

$s,n_i,i_i)$ \hfill $a^3z; \quad n=$

$x^2\pi.$

13

Back at our apartment that evening, I come out of my room, where I've just completed a calculus chapter on implicit differentiation, and stand in the living room next to the couch where we found my mother. I expect to be sad, or at least upset at the memory, but being in the familiar room where my father played Benny Goodman and my mother read plays, the sight of the coffee table emptied of my mother's syringes and pill jars isn't a painful thing for me to hold in my chest, which surprises me. A day after my mother exploded—the maid's word—the living room has neither a positive nor a negative charge. I'd give it a PH of about seven. For years, no matter where I was—PS18, swim practice at the New York Athletic Club, or the Heald store— when I imagined the living room, I immediately felt safe and secure. But now, with fat, white droplets pelleting the floor-to-ceiling windows, I feel a sense of detachment. If anything, I'm bothered by the inconvenience of my mother's episode, since it could mean stopping my work with Hedjhal, or my swimming practice for the upcoming New England Championships.

I walk around the glass table, and skirt the two H-269 Halabala armchairs from Prague and; as I put my hand on the kitchen door, my father's whispered voice reaches from inside, probably standing in his favorite spot, right next to the sink. A louder voice from the kitchen, my uncle's low baritone, comes right after it. Through the peephole, a feature my father insisted on when he bought the place, his Mansion in the Sky, I see my father and my uncle framed like two characters in the round scope of binoculars. My uncle's shoulders are set, and my father is wincing, his hand over his solar plexus as if my uncle just hit him with a body shot.

I'm curious. I go into the kitchen as quietly as I can, and at first, neither my father nor my uncle acknowledges me. I'm invisible, and for once, I like it.

"Come on in, Ben," my father says. "You need to hear this."

"Thanks."

My father turns his attention back to Jesse. "I hope you're happy, Jesse," says my father, trying now to sound pleasant, no doubt for my benefit.

"I'll be fine," my uncle says.

"For once," my father responds.

"What's that supposed to mean?" All warmth is gone from my uncle's voice.

"Ah, forget it." My father splays his hand on his lower chest. He's been suffering from stomach acid since my mother's symptoms first manifested themselves in June, but then, he's been eating little and starting his day with a bagel and lox, and a whiskey soda. Then, to my surprise, he stands next to my uncle, goes up on his toes, and kisses him on the cheek, like a mobster greeting a made man.

My uncle draws back, a look of suspicion on his tanned face. "What did I do this time?"

"You recruited Ben to work on your business plan."

"Last I knew, that isn't a crime."

"You should have asked me first," says my father, cracking the knuckles of his left hand.

My uncle watches with amusement. He raises his chin, peering down at my father like a tall pitcher staring down at a batboy; then he raises his head, chin higher, the chords in his neck protruding. "You would have said no."

"True. That's because you don't get to make decisions about Ben." My father takes a long, pained breath.

"He's old enough to make up his own mind." My uncle opens his mouth to say more, but then lays his index finger against his lips, stopping himself. He turns his gaze to the ceiling, remembering something he's not going to share.

"He's my son," says my father, too loudly. "You gave up all rights years ago."

"You mean when you invested Florence's inheritance without asking her and lost it all in that scheme to sell women's clothes? You gonna tell me that didn't hurt your marriage?" Little points of irritation flicker in my uncle's eyes. "You violated her trust and lost her money. What happened between me and her was a natural outcome of your actions." He swallows hard. "No wonder she wants Ben to get away—"

"That's not true."

"She only supports you out of a sense of duty, pretending that it's a great idea for Ben to come into the business," my uncle says. "She wants Ben to get away so you can't bleed him dry, financially or emotionally, the way you bled her dry."

"You know nothing about my marriage, or what it's like to be married."

"No wonder you two were having troubles in '22."

"That didn't give you the right to . . ." hisses my father, swiveling around toward the sink where he left a bottle of Glenfiddich.

"Enough already," says my uncle, forming two fists.

"It's never going to be enough," my father yells, bending

over the sink and steadying himself with his flat hands on the counter, breathless.

I hear every word, but they might as well be talking in Diné Bizaad, the Navajo Nation language, because they're talking about things that happened before I was born, or when I was too young to be aware of them. For a heartbeat, I feel doubt, but looking at the hard line of my uncle's jaw and the hardness of his eyes, his substance gives me the courage to speak up. "What's never going to be enough?" I ask. Outside the kitchen window, a thunderstorm murmurs in the distance.

In the awkward silence that joins us, my father and Jesse stare at me, as if they've just remembered I'm in the room. That happens to me a lot, first at PS18, and then at Loomsfield. Other students see me, and maybe talk to me, but they don't really notice me, like I don't radiate enough energy.

Jesse raises his eyes, nods at my father, and then at me. "Your father blames me."

"For what?" I say.

"For pushing him down the stairs when he was six, hell if I know."

"Your uncle," says my father, his eyes settling on me. "Almost killed me."

I check my father, the scary, dark half circles under his eyes. He's grinning like he's won an argument, but it doesn't feel like he won anything. Something is hanging in the air between them, but they're not going to tell me.

"What's going on here?" I ask. But they're silent. Obviously, I'm getting no further, so I leave it be, but I can't stop thinking about it. What did my father mean by "You gave up all rights long ago?" Am I adopted, or did Mother have intercourse with a man who wasn't my father?

"We're not going to litigate this again," my uncle says, leaning toward me, then laying his hands flat on the kitchen table, palms down. "And it's not because I said so, but because we've got a case here that's been going on long enough, too long, and your father's sensible enough to know he's got to let it go. Everybody else has. But he's still blaming me for what I did after I ripped up my rotator cuff. I couldn't see my future then, but now I can; we can."

"So, now you can suddenly see your future. You call Whispering Pines—"

"—Palms, Whispering *Palms*."

"Whispering bonefish. There are certain things sensible people won't put up with, and what my brother, your uncle, did— it crossed the line." Tears are glistening in my father's eyes. This shocks me. I have only seen tears in my father's eyes once, on July 4, 1935, a hot, humid Thursday at two in the afternoon, when we took Myrtle out to Pilgrim Psychiatric Hospital on Long Island after she had her psychotic break. Jesse was too upset to drive, so we sat in the back seat with Myrtle between us, my father holding her hand and mumbling: *Myrtle, Myrtle, Myrtle.* "We agree on this point?" says my father.

My uncle picks up a pepper shaker, grinds the black powder into his palm, and licks it off. "I don't agree with anything," he says. "I was afraid to end up like Mother and Father, scrambling to sell a few more hats and gloves to pay the rent, sacrificing everything for their dream of a bigger shop. I remember when the shop wasn't doing well, and I wore a used baseball uniform with patches on the knees and elbows. I promised myself I'd never do that to a child." He steps back from the table and sticks his hands in his pockets, like a kid caught stealing from the cookie jar. "I was trying to be responsible."

"To yourself," says my father, with an expression of disgust.

"You're forgetting about Florence," my uncle says. "You're always forgetting about Florence."

"Forget? Never." My father's mouth twists. "I will never forget—or forgive."

"I was scared," my uncle says in a whisper that hints at pain. "And Florence was—"

"Stop! No more about my wife."

"You won't tell the truth, Artie, so I will. Your so-called wife was also involved."

"That's a prevarication, Jesse."

"Wrong." My uncle is looking straight at my father now. "I was afraid of failing at being you—hard working, good at the shoe business, dependable, a good provider."

My father stares at me for a few seconds. "What did I tell you, Ben?"

"When?"

He waves a hand at me. "Doesn't matter now. Point is, your uncle lies when he opens his mouth." He says this quietly. "So stay away from him, or you're going to be sorry."

"Then I'll be sorry," I say under my breath.

"Speak up."

"Then. I'll. Be. Sorry," I say, crossing the kitchen and heading out the door, leaving the two of them to it.

For a time, I wait outside the kitchen door again. But inside, talk has stopped. A decanter clicks against a heavy glass, and then there's scraping of a chair, maybe two, at the table. I'm anything but comfortable, yet curious about the conversation. I'm not trusting what I believed I'd heard: that Jesse is my father. How this involves my mother is a mystery to me: was I adopted? Did they have intercourse? I don't tolerate ambiguity very well.

Suddenly, the door flies open and my uncle comes out, leans down, and puts his face near my ear so he can whisper. "If your father finds out you're still helping me with Whispering Palms, he's going to be a tough customer."

"I want to help you, but I can't right now."

"I understand." His face is drawn with shadows like the area under a curve.

". . . because of my mother."

"She's pretty sick, isn't she?" he says, pursing his lips and letting out an audible sigh.

"They're doing a lumbar puncture to see what's in her spinal fluid."

"Your mother is a tough woman; I've always admired her." He stands straight again. "How much did you hear just now?"

"Everything."

"Your mother has put up with your father's antics for years."

This news that my father lost my mother's money and that something may have happened between my mother and Jesse has me really confused. And when I'm confused, I can't think clearly. So, I go back to Jesse's business. "Maybe I can help you after we know more."

"I'm proud of you, Ben," he says, patting the small of my back.

I smile and shake his hand, no clue why.

He smiles and lets himself out the front door; takes his slow, loping steps down the echoing hall; and is gone.

In the hours that follow, I try my best to tune out everything I heard. I'm tired of family dynamics that pit my father against my uncle over my uncle's irresponsibility, my father against my mother over my mother's money and my father's schtups, and my mother and Jesse against my father over what I suspect to be an affair. I already knew my father's position. He holds that my uncle has been shirking his Heald responsibilities since high school when he played baseball instead of helping in the men's accessory business, and then left for the Yankees farm system, leaving my father to run the shop. In his view, good sons do everything their parents expect, because their parents brought them into the world and sacrificed to give them a life, often giving up their own dreams. Though not yet out of high school, I've tried to meet my father's expectations about as long as I can. But when he ties the woes of the family and the business to my uncle, I want to punch him in the face, and my mother too, for giving my father justification for his beliefs. She's always demurring to him, even when I can see in her face that she doesn't agree with one of his fiats. And I didn't need to hear, as I just heard, that doing the right thing beats happiness because of the satisfaction you get from knowing you followed the rules of the family. I've watched my mother and father do the right thing, and look where's it got them: neither is happy. My mother's in the hospital with an unknown African disease, and my father's fighting with my uncle.

At nine o'clock, my father comes into my room, a scotch in his hand. When he sees me, he stops and swirls the ice cubes in his glass. "Your uncle and I love each other, and like all brothers, we fight like cats and dogs."

"What did you mean when you told him that I'm your son and he gave that right away years ago?"

"It's nothing."

"Then I don't understand why you were arguing about it."

"Ben, just let it go."

"It doesn't make any sense. I don't argue about things that don't make sense."

"The thing is, Ben, I love you; your mother loves you; that's all you need to know."

"But then why am I tall like Jesse?"

"Jesus, Ben, I don't have time for this," he says, reading his watch. "I'm meeting a big customer at the Rainbow Room in a few minutes."

This is clearly a lie: he has no business appointment. His "customer" is the Chemical Bank teller who's come by the store twice on Saturdays to buy espadrilles.

"But why did you say it?"

He releases a ragged, wounded sigh. He reminds me of the terrified pheasant we once hit with the car south of Norwalk— glaring eyes, ready to attack.

Without thinking, I drop my calculus number 2 pencil and put up my hands, like a cattle rustler caught by the sheriff.

"All right. This is the truth, and I swear it, Ben. I won't beg you to believe me, no matter how much I want to. Your uncle is self-destructive and deluded. When the Yankees cut him, he came back in sorry shape. He had married Myrtle who, as you know, is unstable. I've always tried to help him. But he won't accept my help."

"He told me his bar business and his scheme to sublet the lease holds kept Heald Shoes from going bankrupt."

"It was the opposite. I gave him money to keep his bars open, to start that goddamned speakeasy in the basement underneath his store, and the lease holds were my idea."

"You never told me this before."

"Of course not, you were a child! What should I have told you? That your uncle wants so badly to have a family that he's convinced you're his son? He wants so badly to relive his glory days pitching that he lies about his business success?"

"I don't understand. That would mean he and my mother had intercourse."

"Patently absurd, but that's how deluded and unhappy he is. He just makes things up, he lies to serve his own self-interest. You can't believe a thing he says." He puts his tumbler on my desk so hard I check for cracks in the glass. "I'm sorry, Ben. I wanted to spare you this, but maybe Jesse's right about one thing: you're old enough to make up your own mind."

"So, I'm old enough to choose to go to MIT?"

"Not quite. You're old enough to come into the business."

"But what if I want to be an earth sciences professor?"

"You're a Heald, and a Heald will always run our shoe business."

"And I shouldn't have helped him with his business plan?"

He walks over to me and slaps my cheek lightly three times. "*La famiglia viene prima di tutto, con te, la nostra eredità soprav-vive.*"

I know enough Italian to understand what my Old Man Heald, the faux gangster, said: "Family comes first. With you, our legacy lives on."

14

The next morning, for five minutes, I visit my mother. She's awake but barely coherent—no longer Florence Heald, the Manhattan socialite—a shriveled creature who's terrified and can't, or won't speak. Almost nothing Florence-like is recognizable. She's just beleaguered eyes behind glasses. I take the stairs to Dr. Lenz's lab two floors up. As I'm exiting the stairwell, a crack of thunder rattles the building. I go left down a sterile hallway with a linoleum floor and knock on the third door on the right. The door's label says, "Dr. Utte Lenz, Internal Medicine." I wait, but no reply comes, so I open it slowly. Sitting at a desk next to a fogged-up window that's bleeding white light, Dr. Lenz is hunched over a high-power microscope.

For a moment, I stand in silence under the anemic ceiling fan. What amazes me is how much I want to be here in the lab. I'm comfortable with the smell of formaldehyde and warm electricals. I'm happier among whirring machines and tubes than in a room where people are making chitchat and trying to get information from each other. Maybe I was born with only two genetic obsessions—science and swimming. Or maybe it's shyness or introversion. At any rate, Lenz's lab is a dream come true. I feel like I've been transported into the 1931 version of *Frankenstein*. Thunder shuttles the machines; lightning flashes in the window; red and green lights are blinking on two panels. I couldn't be more ecstatic.

"Dr. Lenz?"

"I'm busy."

"It's about my mother."

"Ach, Ben," she says, recognizing my voice. She stops scribbling on a yellow pad and lifts her eyes to me. "Your mother tells me you're planning on going to MIT?"

"If I can get in."

She goes into an adjoining storage closet and brings back a chair for me. Then she sits at her microscope, facing me.

"You know what my mother has, don't you?"

"Probably."

"Why didn't you tell us?"

"I am, in the moment, one hundred percent not sure."

"But . . ."

"But I believe it's African trypanosomiasis."

"Sleeping sickness," I say. "I've read about it."

"Yes."

"My mother's not responding well to treatment, is she?" I ask, though I know this already. I know more than I'm comfortable with about the likely course of my mother's disease.

"No. She's showing symptoms of late stage two, maybe early stage three. Your mother is showing signs of madness common in the last stages of rabies, and her personality is changed. Last night she had hallucinations and threw her dinner on the floor. These are symptoms of stage three sleeping sickness."

"My mother had a tantrum?"

"She flew into a rage."

"My mother doesn't know how to throw her dinner on the floor."

"Not the Florence you know, but she's not your mother." She gives me a frosty frown. "I have known Ugandan victims who

beat their children and attack family members with machetes."
She brings her feet forward and places them flat on the floor.
"Yesterday when her nurse—"

"—Gloria?"

She smiles. "When Gloria tried to wash her face, she screamed
with pain."

"If this goes on, what happens?"

"She will lapse into a coma and die," she says. "Everyone with
the parasites found in a blood test also has to undergo a spinal
tap to see if the parasites have reached their brains. If they have,
patients suffer through a complex, and sometimes dangerous,
intravenous regimen requiring hospitalization. That's why we
needed the spinal tap, to detect if the parasites have reached her
brain."

"And if they have?"

"She'll undergo an intravenous regimen with an arsenic-based
drug. It can be life threatening." It's quiet. Then she gets a metal
cup from a drawer, unscrews her thermos, and pours me a coffee.
"Coffee mélange," she says, "Austrian specialty, from Innsbruck,
my home." As I take it, she says, "I was with your mother the day
I think she contracted the parasites."

Much to my horror, I find myself staring at her lips, wanting
to kiss them.

"That must be why you're here, to find out how I let this
happen," she says. "Your father blames me."

"No."

"I ask myself that question again and again," she says. "Your
mother did nothing wrong. We did everything carefully. I won't
forgive myself if your mother doesn't make it." She folds her feet
back under her chair. The straps on her sandals are loose, their
surface colored from years of rounds.

"So, my mother's not contagious?"

"No."

I watch her. She turns sideways on her stool, revealing two racks of test tubes on the table behind her, one with what I take to be blood and the other with pink liquid. She hoists her glasses up the bridge of her nose and smiles. An electric desire buzzes in my stomach, which reminds me that I want more than a kiss. She tips her head slightly, so the light from the window shines on a loop of shiny black hair behind her ear. "Something's bothering you, Ben."

"My father wants a different physician in a different hospital."

"Why?"

"He thinks you and my mother are—"

"—Ach, so." A laugh comes up out of her chest. She pats me on the arm. Then, all nonchalant, as if it's of no consequence, she says, "I believe you must ask your mother about these matters." She's deflecting, which I take to mean *yes*.

I nod. This inadvertent news hurts me unexpectedly, the thought of my mother and Dr. Lenz . . . For a moment, I'm numb. The only thing I feel is my heart, the bumpety-bumpety of tachycardia.

"Listen, Ben. Your mother and I are good friends, we've known each other ten years. She talks about you often," she says. "Don't judge your mother too harshly, Ben." She sips her coffee, which leaves a dot of foam on her lip that she wipes away with two fingers. "Your mother says the day you were born was the happiest day of her life." She takes another sip and lets out a long breath. "I'll tell you a story." Her eyes take on a sad hue. "The day on which I tell my father I'm lesbisch—"

She must see the confusion in my eyes. "—I like women," she says. "So, my father returns home from his candle factory in

Innsbruck, I was practicing my words for weeks. I was seventeen and in gymnasium—high school. I believe I'll be happier than if I try to hide it. He sits in the living room reading his *Kronen Zeitung*. I say, 'I like girls.' He reads on. 'I've had feelings for girls since I was seven years old.' He turns a page. 'I'm telling you because I want to share my feelings with you.' He drops his newspaper on the rug, stands up, and says, 'You are a faithless demon,' and slaps me so hard my ears are ringing. 'We will never speak of this again,' he says and departs. He died in 1935, without ever speaking with me again." She goes back to the microscope, coaxes a slide out from under the lens, and inserts it into a wooden holder. She glances at the overhead fan, which is pushing formaldehyde smells into our faces. She squints at me over the top rim of her glasses, like a stern schoolteacher.

I go back to my comfort zone, questions about my mother's illness. "What did you find in my mother's spinal fluid?"

"Traces of blood."

"Does that mean she had an aneurysm?"

"Her brain is bleeding." She swallows hard. "It could be that vectors are causing trypanosomal lesions of her cerebral membranes."

This thought makes my gorge rise. "Now what?"

"I'll try a new method for examining her cerebrospinal fluid. I'll use centrifugation of ten milliliters so I can examine the deposit. If I find trypanosomes in her CSF, we have confirmation—"

"—that they crossed the blood-brain barrier."

She nods.

"What's the treatment?"

"I run an experimental regimen with tryparsamide."

"A derivate of atoxyl?"

"How do you know that?"

"I remember almost everything I read. My mother says my brain is a sponge."

"Well, yes, it's basically arsenic. It has worked on cattle."

"That doesn't mean it will work on my mother." I feel a tear in my left eye. Dr. Lenz raises an eyebrow.

"From this course, she can die. Arsenic disrupts the cellular process that produces molecules to transport energy throughout the body's cells so they can perform the tasks that keep a person alive. Arsenic leaves a body well short of what it takes to keep up even the most basic cellular processes, such as neurological and cardiovascular systems, and can make it difficult for muscles to work. This treatment can eventually cause multisystem organ failure, most likely driven by cell death and hemorrhaging." She taps a pencil on her open palm. "It's possible, if she recovers, her optic nerve will be compromised."

"She'll go blind."

"Or walk in circles." She cuts off a laugh, slides her glasses off, and lets them hang on their chain. "If your father upsets her, she can die."

"How much time do we have?" I ask.

She studies her watch, a new gold duo-dialed doctor's model. "Forty-eight hours will determine her fate." Her pretty head and face and eyes are next to me, and I'm staring at her lips. She scans a paper with columns of data, making an *mmm* sound. "If she's not out of the woods in two days, she will not recover."

"How can you be so sure? I mean, statistically, she could recover."

"That chance," says Lenz, peering over her glasses like a stern librarian, "is disappearingly small. I've seen more than a thousand patients die of sleeping sickness."

"I don't know what . . ."

She reaches out and cups her hand over my cheek, so close I can smell coffee on her breath. "Ben, accepting our own death and the death of others allows us, finally, to accept life."

Something in her voice, hoarse and flat, tells me my mother's death by arsenic poisoning, upset, or one leading to the other is her expected outcome. Even when he's exhausted and trying to stay calm, like before with Dr. Lenz, my father radiates stress and often manages to get into verbal jousting matches. Something about imagining my father upsetting my mother so that she has a stroke and dies in front of us terrifies me. Nobody wants to see someone die. Until now, her dying was a concept that I could live with, because it seemed like a geometric theorem, abstract and governing a world that I could observe but that didn't touch me or bring me to tears. For the first time since we found her lying on the couch, swollen beyond recognition, I'm afraid. I recognize the signs: my hands and feet feel like they're dangling in ice water, and I have searing pain in my chest. If she goes now, it's not enough. It's never enough time when you know the person who's dying. I have things I want to say to her, like "I love you," but I don't know how. We don't use those words. The Healds, it's now clear to me, are governed by emotional reluctance.

15

The next morning at eleven, a busy Saturday in the store—my father's left Goldstein in charge—my father and I are sitting in his car, headed for the Flower Hospital. Rainwater swooshing under the tires makes a rushing noise. The wind strips leaves off the oaks along the park. They stick to the windshield where they get smeared by the wipers. My father throws his scarf onto the back seat, then smiles at his brilliant aim. I give him a thumbs-up, but his focus is on the road. I wonder if he's forgotten that I exist. I'm here. He's here. But in another sense, we're in separate worlds.

He taps on the wheel with his thumbs and stares straight ahead. "You worried about your mother?"

"Sometimes."

"It's scary, isn't it?"

"Sure."

"Now that our lives have been blown up and turned topsy-turvy, we need to be asking ourselves what's next. How do we deal with this? Jump into the Hudson? Launch a boat from Quogue, head for the Bahamas, and never come back?" He swivels his head to see me, looks back at the road, and brakes for a Yellow Star Taxi, with its soft, rounded edges. His eyes blink, and for two city blocks, until we stop at a light, he seems far away.

"I was reading a book on tropical diseases," I say. "Mother may have cassava mosaic disease."

"Cassava what?"

"CMD. It's a virus, first reported in East Africa in the late 1800s. From 1900 to 1920, an epidemic in Uganda killed two hundred thousand people." I look hard at him, trying to gauge his reaction, to see if he's worried. But cassava mosaic doesn't seem to trouble him the way it troubles me. I don't want to talk about my feelings. I'm tired of the adults around me telling me that I'm worried. It's none of their business, except maybe Dr. Lenz. So, I give him the silent treatment until we get to Dr. Lenz's office a half hour of heavy traffic later.

Lenz's office is across from my mother's room on the Intensive Care ward. My father and I go in and sit across from her at her gray metal desk like two delinquents.

Lenz sighs loudly and shuffles some papers while she says, "During the tests, I did screens for malaria, meningitis, hepatitis, trypanosomiasis, and cassava mosaic."

My father leans toward me. "You were right," he whispers with pride.

"The tests," says Dr. Lenz, holding a single sheet of paper in front of her, "show no signs of cassava, malaria, or hepatitis, but that leaves meningitis and trypanosomiasis. I'm betting on trypanosomiasis. The parasites have crossed the blood-brain barrier. This is why I have now found trypanosomes in large numbers in the circulating blood of your wife. Her lymph nodes and spleen have been invaded—they're swollen, soft, and tender. So, it's not meningitis. She has a spiking fever and delayed sensation to pain, symptoms characteristic of this stage. In the more severe East African form of sleeping sickness, *T. brucei rhodesiense* infection, toxemia becomes so profound that the patient dies within months. The West African type, *T. brucei gambiense* infection, shows a delay of one or more years before the trypanosomes invade the brain and spinal cord."

"Which type does she have?"

"We were in East Africa, so probably *T. brucei rhodesiense*."

"Probably?" My father leans forward with his forearms on his knees, as if getting nearer to Dr. Lenz will help him process the words. "What's the prognosis?"

"Well, if the arsenic treatment fails, she'll have more and more neurological symptoms like severe headache; mental dullness; apathy; a weary, shuffling gait; tremors; spastic or flaccid paralysis; chorea; and a profound sleepiness that develops during meals or when Florence is standing or walking. Then comes increasing emaciation, coma, and death. I'm hoping if we can't rid Florence's body of the parasites, we can at least make her a carrier so she will live for years." Dr. Lenz takes another peek at my mother's chart. "I'm meeting with experts at Columbia to get some colleagues' medical opinions." She lets out a long breath. "I'm going to start the treatment with arsenic this afternoon, so we can determine her response."

Dr. Lenz turns away from my father, focusing hard on my mother's chart.

"Don't turn your back on me, Doctor—I'm not done talking to you."

Dr. Lenz stops, clutching my mother's chart to her chest like a stop sign. "With all due respect for your stress, Mr. Heald, show some respect or you'll have to leave."

My father looks at her uncertainly, maybe stifling the urge to say more. Then he blinks and goes on. "You don't know what kind of sleeping sickness, you don't know how she got it, who's at fault, whether she wasn't careful, you don't know if your treatment will work, or, worse, if it's going to kill her," he yells. "You don't know shit, is basically what you're saying."

"If you don't approve of my treatment, you can take Mrs. Heald to Columbia or somewhere else."

"This is an admission of defeat, Doctor." My father crosses his arms, rocks forward, then bangs his hands on his thighs. "Fuck, fuck." He's grinding his teeth and twisting up his face. He wags his head quickly back and forth. He mumbles "fuck" under his breath, unfolds his arms, and wipes his nose with the back of his hand. He stands up quickly, heads for the door, and stops to whack his hand on the filing cabinet. "Sorry," he says, grabs his coat, and leaves.

"Your father is taking this very badly," says Dr. Lenz.

"Three people in his family were pronounced dead here."

"That's unfortunate," she says, though it sounds like she's said it a thousand times and doesn't care, which is how I probably sound when I make small talk.

"How's my mother doing now?" I ask.

"She's conscious and coherent, doing well considering the constellation of potential symptoms. Your mother is a strong woman."

"Is she dying?"

"That's a possibility," she says, scanning the rows and columns of numbers on the paper in front of her. "But it's not the only possibility."

16

Later that afternoon, while my father is at the bar of the Pennsylvania Hotel, I head to the New York Athletic Club for a workout. An unusual sight greets me as I walk into the narrow, low-ceilinged swimming pool: in the humid smell of chlorine, under the blue-haloed lights, Otto Wahle, the Austrian-American thousand-meter freestyle medal winner at the 1900 Paris Olympics, is doing his laps. He's in the first lane, by the wall, where the tiles are stained brown. He's now in his fifties, but he still swings his arms in wide, slow arcs, kicks easily, almost as an afterthought, and makes slow flip turns. On the deck by lanes two and three, four swimmers, members of a relay, it seems, listen to Doc Woodworth. He's dressed in his usual UCLA shorts and sweatshirt, with a whistle and stopwatch around his neck. Doc Woodworth grew up in Sarasota, Florida, and was the Junior National record setter in the hundred- and two-hundred-yard individual medley, and an NCAA All-American in six events at UCLA, where he swam for the Bruins before earning a PhD in applied mathematics. Except for Hedjhal, he's the closest thing I have to a mentor or a friend. Around both, I feel cared for and respected, and I couldn't be happier.

I go over to the group and wait for Doc Woodworth, who, when he sees me, tells me to do five hundred yards of easy freestyle to warm up. "Like Wahle, go easy for now," he says.

"He's over fifty," I say. "He can't go hard."

"But he still knows how to warm up," says Woodworth. "And besides, in the one-thousand-meter free, he'd still give you a run for your money."

"That's not likely, Coach."

"Do you have to take everything literally, Heald?" he says, shifting his big, meaty face to the side, leaning toward me like a big kid. "My point was, don't overdo it today."

"Yeah, well, I'll try not to sprint." What Doc Woodworth doesn't seem to understand, just like Coach Frank at Loomsfield Prep, doesn't get, is how good it feels to swim hard, "into the purple," which is well named given the color of my face after most workouts—the burning lungs, pulsing blood, and my arms straining with every recovery.

I dive in and swim the first twenty-five yards underwater, flutter-kicking with my arms out front like an arrow. At the end of the pool, I do an easy open turn, push off, and then I'm gliding, pulling, kicking, rotating, catching the water with open palms, fingers spread slightly. I love the rush from the other swimmers in the lanes next to mine, like the sound of a fountain. I taste the blue-green water, glide through the emanating bluish cones from the underwater lights. My heart beats hard, but smooth. After my five-hundred-yard warm-up, I rest at the end of the pool. Doc Woodworth comes over and gets down on his haunches, so close I can see the individual pores in his skin. "Fifty repeats of one-hundred-yard freestyle at one minute, five, with thirty seconds of rest." He plays with his stopwatch. "You do that?"

"Sure," I say.

"I don't want to see you vomiting, but I also don't want to see you dawdling, Heald. Keep it in the red zone." Woodworth's crude color-coded zone system is based on the desired intensity of physical work, and is defined by five colors, from white, the easiest; to purple, the most intense; with red in the middle. "Remember," he says, "Red is where you're building endurance and getting in continuous yardage."

In all, it's the perfect workout for my goals: the September New England Prep School Championships at Andover Academy, where I'm going to do the thousand-, five-hundred-, two-hundred-, and one-hundred-yard freestyle. My best chance is in the thousand and the five hundred. I'm not a natural sprinter.

During the set, I force myself to slow down, but I sprint the last five yards of each lap. The rest is slower than my father swims. I finish the fiftieth hundred-yard repeat and hold on to the gutter of the pool.

Doc Woodworth is shaking his head with dents of annoyance at the corners of his mouth. "Your splits on those hundreds are four seconds slower than your recovery pace."

"It seemed about right to me."

"You keep this up, you'll be as slow as my grandmother at the New England Championships . . . and she's dead."

"OK, Coach."

"No, not OK. I see someone who's swimming more slowly than a manatee." He's all swim-coach business-y now, as if some of my previous workouts he's watched have flashed up into his brilliant mind's eye.

"What am I supposed to do?"

"Listen. Just listen. Is that so hard, Heald?"

"I don't know what you mean. When I swim freestyle, my ears are underwater."

He takes two steps back, as if he needs space for his vexation. "Listen to your body. Maybe a better word is *feel*, — you need to *feel* your heart rate, your lungs, your arm, back, neck, and leg muscles."

"I'll try, Coach." What he doesn't know: I don't listen when I swim; I do calculus problems or try to predict the next week's weather based on the observations in my notebook. But I'll try it his way, since he has twenty years of swim coaching and was, himself, a four-year Letter Man with the UCLA Bruins, and twice swam on Olympic relays, doing the backstroke leg. Woodworth knows swimming. He knows speed. And he knows stroke mechanics; he applies his graduate work in physics to his coaching. The man misses nothing. He's the Dr. Hedjhal of swimming. Why a man with a master's in applied physics from UCLA, where he captained the swim squad, is coaching remains a mystery to me.

After ten fifties, Woodworth flags me down with a wide wave of his arms.

"Not good?" I say.

"I told you to stay in the red zone, but you're in the white zone, like the color of my grandmother's doilies."

"I'm trying to relax, focus on form, keep up a consistent pace, with no dropping off. A little above active recovery."

"That was inactive recovery. Last week you're puking on the deck when I told you to go blue," he says, shaking his head, as if to rid his face of the scrunched-up forehead and the one raised eyebrow. "Today you're swimming like a slow loris in a Speedo." Our camaraderie is paling. "You've got the New England Prep School Championships in two weeks, and you're napping in the water."

"We could start taper today."

"We'll start taper when I say. It's too soon." His eyes get all crinkly at the corners. "Swimming fast is all about head and heart, one square inch of real estate up here and down here," he says, pointing at his temple and his heart. "And now you're making that grim face, like you don't follow what I'm saying."

I follow what he's saying, but I don't agree. "I understand," I say.

He goes on. "Are you in some sort of trouble?"

"No, sir. Just family stuff."

"Is something wrong?"

"No, sir."

"Your heart and brain aren't in the water with you."

"I'm thinking about stuff."

"About what?"

"My mother's really sick, and my father wants me to come into the shoe business."

"My view? Sons should disappoint their parents," he says, with a solemn face. Doc Woodworth has a dry sense of humor and never gives away whether he's joking. "That's how you figure out who you are," he says. "Make sense, Heald?"

"Sure, I think so." This is a lie.

I rely on my math and swimming skills to put myself at ease and feel right about things. With them, my mother's trypanosomiasis, my father's expectations, and the question of who is my father are just plain easier. The risk of this is, of course, that if I have bad day in the pool or can't do a Fourier transformation, I'll start doubting myself, which usually makes me uncoordinated and scatterbrained. But the worst part of my swimming too slowly is that I've disappointed Doc Woodworth. I feel like an imposter. I wish I could tell Doc Woodworth more about my mother and father, but I can't. He's my coach, and he intimidates me. This, of course, isn't news.

"As for today's sets," says Woodworth, "It's OK to have an off day." He points to the crew-cut, lanky figure hoisting himself out of lane one. "Otto Wahle's still spooling his yardage, sticking to his pace." We watch him, still fit in his fifties, walk to the shower and rinse himself off, slowly and meticulously, just like his swimming. "You think old Wahle never had an off day?"

"I guess not."

"It's OK to get it wrong and miss your times, Heald. You're accustomed to winning in the water. But it's OK to lose, to lose often, and to lose time and again. A bad day in practice builds character, shows us how to keep on when the going gets tough, and teaches you that you are always stronger than you think you can ever be," he says, resetting his stopwatch. "You need to learn to lose now so you can win the five hundred and the thousand at the New England Regionals." His face is intelligent and friendly at the same time. "You have a real shot, but so do the other guys. You've got to be all in; bring your brain and your heart into the water with you."

"I'll tell them," I say. "I think they're both free."

Woodworth's face breaks into a smile. "So now," he says, "Give me ten one-hundred-yard repeats at two hundred pace, breathing on every third, fifth, seventh, and ninth stroke, with a strong push off."

"Twenty-second rest?"

"That'll do." His eyes focus on me. "And Heald."

"Yes, Coach."

He puts a foot up on the starting block with his stopwatch on his open palm. "Don't be so hard on yourself. Lose a little, but only in practice. You'll thank yourself in the end."

17

On Monday morning, my father and I find the door to my mother's new room cracked open. I hear her cough and turn over. Then Dr. Lenz says, "You may feel a little pinch, but it's nothing like an LP."

To which my mother says, "I feel like a human pincushion," and laughs. Another cough from inside. Again, Dr. Lenz's soft voice, "Florence, sit back." Cough. "OK, I'll sit back. That I can do."

My mother is a tryer. She's always been a tryer, which I never liked about her, because it makes her seem terribly needy.

"Why the fuck did they move her again?" my father asks.

"Well, I don't know," I say irritably.

"Every time they move her, she's one step nearer to the morgue," he says. "Jesus, can't they just let us go in." We never go in before Dr. Lenz invites us, which is something else I don't understand. It has nothing to do with hospital policy. I suspect it has to do with my father's feelings about Dr. Lenz, which are complicated. First, he stands close to her. Once, he put his hand on her hip. Then he gets angry and accuses her of not being a real doctor.

"I've gotta take a leak." My father is already hitching up his pants. "Christ, thirty times a day." Yesterday he said he thinks he has a urinary tract infection, which hurts, he said, "like a red-hot catheter."

While he's gone—his trips to the urinal last longer and longer these last weeks—Dr. Lenz pokes her head out the door. "You can come in now, Ben."

"Why did you move my mother again?"

"Five-alarm fire last night. We needed the ICU beds," she says. "In case you have any questions, I'll be back in fifteen minutes."

My mother's new room is drab green, with a cut-glass ceiling light, a pressed steel cabinet, and, behind it, a black stain spreading upward from the radiator. A filament of light shines through the window and brightens the bedspread over my mother. Death warmed over in the spotlight.

I imagined I'd find her like before—gaunt, maybe, but still the old Florence Heald. But the arsenic treatment has hollowed her out and given her skin that matches the white-green walls. Shadows line her face. She's withered to a dried-out version of her zaftig self, the Christmas lights inside her almost out.

My heart is rocketing. I squeeze my hands into fists, thinking she might stop breathing any moment. I need a strategy for small talk. In my softest voice this time: "Mother? Are you awake?"

"I think so," she whispers, her forehead damp with sweat. "Is that . . . is that you, Ben?"

"Yes," I say, putting a smile on my face. "How are you feeling?"

She moans, her face contorted. "I've been... I've been... better."

"Before Father comes back, I've been . . . I've been . . . better."

She leans forward. "Come here, take my hand." She reaches out her hand, which feels in my palm as light and weak as feathers.

"What, Ben . . . did you want . . ."

"I heard Father and Uncle Jesse arguing about something

that happened in 1922, and Father said that Jesse gave up all his rights back then."

"I can't imagine . . ."

"Jesse said you and Father were having troubles. That was the year I was born."

"What . . . ?"

"It made me think that Uncle Jesse is my biological father."

"Maybe the two of them were arguing . . . about business."

"That doesn't make any sense. What kind of trouble was he talking about?"

"I'm tired, Ben," she blurts out with surprising force, before she lets her head plop onto the pillow, her eyes closed and one hand at her throat.

"If you and Uncle Jesse—"

"Enough, Ben," she says, wiping her nose and eyes with a blue handkerchief, inspecting it for evidence of her disease. "I need to have this laundered."

"Just tell me, please." I'm feeling trapped and miserable.

"Let this go, Ben. It's irrelevant." She laughs, more brightly this time, and now she's ready for one of her lectures. "Dr. Long warned me that you were going to be a handful—highest IQ score, wanting to know everything and for everything to make logical sense. But your father and your uncle are regular people. They say things that make no sense."

"But—"

"Life is messy, people are complicated." Her eyes open wide with exasperation. "I'm your mother and Arthur's your father." She coughs, although she also seems to be laughing. She's shaking her head, trying to talk through another cough. She opens her mouth, but her words encounter obstacles on the way down to her lips. "Sometimes in life . . ." Another cough, but with a smile. ". . .

no amount of information helps . . ." Rasping cough, eyes closed. And then she manages ". . . and we never achieve clarity."

⧗

Ten minutes later, my father comes into the room. "So," he says. "What's news?"

"Your fly's open," I say.

"Guess I'm distracted," he whispers, fiddling with his zipper. "Man, it burns." He subsides back into his aggressive stance, tapping one toe on the floor, ready to joust with Dr. Lenz.

A couple of minutes later, Dr. Lenz, my father, and I gather around my mother's bed. Lenz clutches her clipboard, which she holds at an angle like a shield against my mother's misery. My father comes up behind me and touches my elbow. When I turn my head, he's two feet away from me, fingering his tie clip, as if straightening it will bring order to the chaos inside and around him.

My mother's propped up on three pillows. Her pale hands, folded in front, are a collection of bones held together by thin white skin. She points at her travel bag. "Lipstick."

I hand it to her and, with a trembling hand, she tries to apply it to her lips, but it smears, like a child coloring outside the lines with a red crayon. "Utte, would you?"

Dr. Lenz reaches down, takes the lipstick from my mother's hand, and rubs away the smudged color. My mother takes hold of Lenz's wrist and guides her hand around lips so skillfully I wonder if she's done this before.

My father sees this too, clenching and unclenching the muscles at the corners of his jaw.

I am now struck by something I've never thought before— even in my role as absent-minded math and meteorology whiz. What a big difference a small gesture makes when it tells us,

138

without words, what we didn't know. In this case, my mother asserts her right to ask Dr. Lenz to put lipstick on, showing my father that she can do what he's been doing for years.

"Thank you, Utte," whispers my mother. "I'm tired," she says, closing her eyes and easing back onto her pillow.

Lenz tries to calm us. "She may have a persistent spinal fluid leak, brain herniation. Perhaps a rise in intracranial pressure, with displacement of intracranial structures." She makes a note. "It should resolve itself in a day or two."

My mother's eyes spring open. "Isn't this the perfect room to die in?" she says in a tiny voice.

"Florence, please," says my father, making white-knuckled fists.

"Arthur, it's *my* death."

"Florence, I've been thinking, as soon as you're better, we'll take a trip."

My mother gives him a weak smile.

"Where would you like to go?" he says.

"Berlin."

"The Berlin in New Hampshire?"

"Germany. November." She closes her eyes again and breathes deeply and slowly.

He walks around the end of the bed and stands next to Dr. Lenz, cradling his left arm at the elbow, like a broken wing. "Doctor, please tell her she's in no condition to travel."

"Florence," says Dr. Lenz, reaching down to stroke my mother's cheek. "Let's get you better first."

"No," says my mother, holding Dr. Lenz's wrist as she caresses my mother's cheek.

My mother lets go of Lenz's wrist, and Lenz steps back to her place next to my father. My mother takes a deep breath and lifts her head off the pillow. "Ben . . ."

I lean down, put my ear near her glossy lips. Her breath warms my cheek. "Ben, you book the tickets. Berlin, Thanksgiving."

"I'll look into it," I say in a half whisper. I don't have the strength to tell her she's not going. I understand her desire: she often describes her honeymoon to Berlin, Paris, and Vienna as the best time of her marriage. *I was in love with your father, and I was in love with the idea of being married.*

My father's face goes bright red. "I'm sorry, Florence, but it's out of the question." He has his hand on the metal bed frame, knuckles white as mothballs.

All of us are flummoxed by the stalling conversation.

Dr. Lenz holds up my mother's chart and flips through her death-tracker notes. Her eyes move slowly my way from behind smudged glasses. "I wanted to share the latest test results." She inches nearer my mother, a trace of rubbing alcohol stirring the air.

Outside, behind the dingy curtain, rain spatters the window, and I have to strain to hear Lenz's next words.

Lenz says, haltingly, as if she's translating, "A parasite's infected Mrs. Heald." She nods three times. "This confirms my hypothesis." Her breasts expand almost audibly against her starched lab coat. "*Trypanosomo brucei gambiense*," she says, aiming a mulling stare my father's way.

He flutters his eyes, letting it sink in.

I say, "African trypanosomiasis. Sleeping sickness?"

"*Richtig.*" Color has come into her face, and from where I'm standing, I get a whiff of her perfume, lilac notes. "Caused by extra-cellular protozoa." Dr. Lenz touches my mother's knee over the blanket.

My father opens his mouth to comment but stops before letting any words out.

Seeing this, Dr Lenz peers yet again at my mother's chart, a smile tugging at the corners of her mouth. It's not clear to me why she's smiling. Maybe because my father is silent, now touching the wisps of black-gray hair above his ears. She returns her gaze, first to my mother and then to us. "She probably caught it in Uganda, which has a very high incidence of insect-born parasites."

At this, my father shakes his head. "How could this happen, Doctor?"

"Perhaps she was bitten by a tsetse fly; sometimes people don't even notice the bite."

After a long silence, my mother says, "Congo Basin, something bit me." She studies the back of one bluish hand. "Pinprick."

My father studies the end of his tie, slow and distracted, an act with all the world of sadness in it.

"It's an ulceration," I explain. "The symptoms of East African trypanosomiasis occur within months to years after getting infected. The disease involves two stages."

This pleases Lenz. Over her glasses, she offers me a half-hearted smile.

"When my mother got sick a few weeks after you came back, I figured she must have caught something in East Africa. So, I went to the public library, and they gave me a paper by Castellani called 'On the Discovery of a Species of Trypanosoma in the Cerebro-Spinal Fluid of Cases of Sleeping Sickness.'"

Lenz pats me on the shoulder, then turns to my father. "Your son is very bright, Mr. Heald."

"Sometimes," he says, with a huge grin, "too bright for his own good."

Dr. Lenz lets her clipboard, which is attached to a fine chain around her neck, fall to her side. "In the early phase," I continue, "the parasites dwell in the lymphatic system and bloodstream. The trypanosomes multiply in subcutaneous tissues: blood and lymph. This is also called the hemolymphatic stage, which entails bouts of fever, severe headaches, swollen lymph nodes, joint pains, extreme fatigue, and an itchy rash."

"Maybe one day you should study medicine." The compliment reddens my face. She adds, "Visit my lab tomorrow, I'll show you around and tell you about my work on sleeping sickness, especially the efficacy of arsenic as a palliative." She chews on the end of her pencil for a few moments. "As I was saying, in the second stage the parasites cross the blood-brain barrier to invade the central nervous system. This is the neurological or meningo encephalic stage. Brain damage, with symptoms like weight loss, personality changes, slurred speech, confusion, irritability, loss of coordination, seizures, difficulty walking, and of course, disturbance of the sleep cycle—sleeping all day, insomnia all night."

My father lights a cigarette, gripping the butt between his thumb and forefinger.

Lenz wags an index finger at him. "Please, Mr. Heald, we have a smoking area next to the waiting room."

He shakes his head, goes to the sink, turns on the tap, and puts out the cigarette with a hiss. He plants himself across the bed from Lenz and rests his straight arms on the mattress as if he's the boss. "If I'm following you," he says, "My wife was bitten by a real-life insect vampire."

"*Ja*, it's"—Lenz speaks with a forced cheer that wouldn't fool a dog—"not a friendly disease."

My father chuckles bitterly. "What would you call a friendly disease?"

"Influenza. Shingles." A flash of lightning strobes outside the window, lighting Lenz's face with a glaring blast of light. "So," she says, "no immediate travel now."

We fall silent.

Lenz jerks her head once. "Without treatment, sleeping sickness is fatal. Florence may live another ten years. Or she may cease to breathe five minutes from now."

A clap of thunder rattles my mother's IV Pentothal bottle. The din of the rain now makes a sound like sand falling through trees.

Tears flood my father's eyes. I've never seen him so emotional. "What's the treatment, Doctor?"

"That depends whether she's in the early phase of the disease, or whether she's in the third phase of the disease, the neurological phase. I believe she's in phase three. I'm making tests these days to see the number of vectors that are still in her brain after the first round of treatments. That's why the lumbar puncture before."

"And your arsenical drugs will cure her?"

"There is no guarantee, Mr. Heald, but with luck, the arsenic will completely eliminate the vectors that have crossed the blood-brain barrier, and she should be out of the woods by Labor Day."

"What about convalescence?"

"I recommend Quogue to recover her strength; the sea air will do her good."

"Arsenic is poison, right?"

"*Jawohl*, it can cause certain complications such as fatal allergic reaction, kidney or liver damage, or inflammation of the brain. Close monitoring is required now. But afterwards, she should go back to light daily activities, which is why Quogue will be a good course of action."

"So, she's going to need live-in care?"

"Probably."

"For how long?"

"Maybe a year.

"Then she's going to be OK?"

"Depends what you mean by *OK*. She's unlikely ever to return to full strength; in New York or Quogue, she's going to need household help."

My father goes back to the sink and splashes cold water on his face, spattering his damp shirt. He rolls up his sleeves and runs his arms under the cold stream. He's talking to himself, but I can't make out the words, though his voice has angry bass notes.

Dr. Lenz consults her watch. "Here is the conclusion."

My father swings around and, facing us again, lets the water drip off his fingers. "What?"

I lean against the railing of my mother's bed.

"You were right to bring her here, Mr. Heald. And none too soon."

"We should have brought her sooner, only she didn't seem so sick."

"You couldn't have known, and if you had, the treatment would have been the same."

"That's what I tell myself," he says, now drumming his hands on the edge of the sink and staring into Dr. Lenz's eyes. "But she could die in the next few hours."

"Yes, that is possible. But now that we know, we have no time to waste." She shrugs. "The next hours will be critical."

"We should have known," says my father, "Somehow one of us should have known. Don't you think?"

Dr. Lenz pricks her eyebrows. "*Selbsrekrimination*—"

"Self-discrimination?" I say.

"*Ja, ja,*" she says. "It brings nothing. The main thing now, we need to intensify our arsenic therapy."

"Ach," says my father. "This African trypano-thing isn't a thing, it's an endless series of setbacks ending in who knows what. And it's losing its charm."

18

After the visit to my mother's room, my father leaves in a huff and stays back, sitting in the waiting room. The door is once again pulled open, this time by Gloria. A dozen people in rumpled clothes rush in, some holding a rolled copy of the morning *Post*, one of them the same elderly Ukrainian woman from a few days ago, wearing a black leather jacket and a headscarf decorated with white edelweiss. She opens her metal lunch box; takes out another hard-boiled egg, this one colored green; and a thermos; and pours herself a tea. She catches my eye but doesn't offer me any tea this time, no doubt remembering that I declined her offer the last time.

Gloria's wearing a crisp, white cotton uniform with a wide belt, and her hair is in a messy bob. We know each other from my previous visits, though this is the first time I've had a chance to talk to her alone.

"Hi," I say, in my friendliest I'm-normal voice.

"You're probably waiting for your mother," she says. "She'll be done in a half hour."

I point at the old woman. "I've seen her here often. She here every day?"

"She's here for her husband, but she's become a fixture of the place for us all. She comes in every day with the same metal lunch box and offers tea to everyone."

"My father would never do that."

"Neither would my mother," she says, staring at me intently, as if she's suddenly more present, seeing me for the first time.

"What's going on with my mother?"

"She's having another lumbar puncture this morning."

"Good lord. Why?"

"Dr. Lenz wants to see if the arsenic treatment and rehydration therapy are working, if your mother's spinal fluid is free of vectors and she's better. Only another LP will show that."

"How's she doing?" She has no reason to give me any details, since those are reserved for Dr. Lenz, but that's the most natural-sounding thing I can think to say. Next to Gloria's starched white uniform, I'm feeling underdressed in my cords, double-knit polo, and V-neck sweater.

"It's touch and go with your mother," Gloria says, her voice oddly cheerful, "but Dr. Lenz says the treatment is going well, and your mother has a good chance of recovering."

"Great," I say, crossing my legs and patting my hair. The room is stifling hot. Two seats down from the Ukrainian grandmother, a woman is crying. Most of the men in the row of seats are staring at Gloria. The one with the *Post* holds the paper up high, pretending not to steal peeks over the top, but he's obviously fascinated. I can't stop staring at her—one look and I can't think straight. My stomach is squeezing itself and I'm getting excited, wanting to do things that would get me thrown out of the hospital.

Gloria has a shiny, scrubbed pretty face and lustrous skin that anybody in the waiting room would wish were theirs. She is, all of us can see, well-to-do. She probably went to a boarding school like Brearley, one of the top private schools, on East Eighty-Third Street.

I feel like an awkward schoolboy who meets his beautiful teacher in Saks Fifth and shakes hands with her, for the first time, outside of school where she has a life of her own.

"It's not easy, having your mother in the hospital," Gloria says.

"It's fine," I say. "At least she has a chance to get better." For some reason, I'm short of breath. "I was just on my way to swim practice."

"I used to swim, but I gave it up when I finished high school. I bet you're good, so tall and all."

The heat in the room is getting to me, and tiny beads of perspiration are showing above Gloria's lip. My fixation on lips is taking on a life of its own. Has anyone noticed me staring? The Ukrainian woman catches my eye and gives me a big, fat wink, and says something in a Slavic language.

"Your father's taking it pretty hard," Gloria says.

"When he's at the store, he's great, but he hates hospitals and doctors. He says people who go into the hospital come out feet first."

"If they're sitting in a wheelchair." She laughs. "That's our mission—to wheel healthy patients out the door feet first."

"He'll be OK, so long as my mother gets better."

She plays with the stethoscope around her neck. Her forearms are smooth and covered with fine hair, like golden fur. She's the most imposing young woman I've ever seen. Suddenly, unexpectedly, she smiles a different smile, not the smile she reserves for all her patients, but a smile full of interest in me, as if she wants to hear more about me. She swivels her head around and regards the large window in the far wall. "Let's go over to the window," she says. "It's my favorite place. You can see the tall oak trees from there. Imagine how many generations of people have lived during the life of that one tree."

"I read that the famous Angel Oak near Johns Island, South Carolina, is estimated to be nearly fifteen hundred years old. That means the trees started to grow when Attila was made king of the Huns."

"Jeez," she says. "The things you know."

I join her at the window and get lost in her peppermint-gum smell.

"Your mother talks about you nonstop." She lifts a hand to her lustrous neck, which disappears into her wide collar, where a gold chain glints in the light from the window. "Just yesterday she called you 'our little genius.' I wish my mother were that proud of me."

"Believe me," I say, my face red, "it has it's downsides."

"Like what?"

"She used to parade me in front of her famous artist and writer friends, and sometimes she made me do math tricks."

"Like what?"

"Really?"

"Show me. Pretty please."

"OK. Name a date, any date in the past."

"November 17, 1849."

"It was a Saturday."

"You're making that up," she says, laughing.

"You can go to the library and look it up."

"Any other hidden talents?"

"I'm the All-City swimming champion in the two-hundred-yard freestyle."

She reaches out and squeezes my biceps. "Most impressive," she says, with a clucking sound.

My face heats up again, and I'm lost for words, so I point at a pile of glossy magazines on a nearby table. "I read an article in

Life that claims Amelia Earhart's flight was an elaborate scheme to spy on the Japanese, and that after she crashed, they captured her and held her prisoner on Saipan until she died. I have my own theory: she missed her refueling stop at Howland Island, ran out of fuel, and crashed into an uninhabited coral atoll." I want to impress her, but judging by the way her eyes are darting around, I've had the opposite effect. I expect she's going to leave.

But she surprises me. She checks her watch, a small gold Timex. Then she says, "I've got another fifteen minutes—let's go." She leads me out the door and into another room two doors down—freshly painted, with bookcases filled with medical texts, a coffee pot by the metal sink, and a table for two by a sunny window. Everything about it is cheerful, including a poster of a Swiss mountain scene— "Visit Wengen and Mürren: Ski Paradise of the Bernese Oberland"—and a painting of a sleek ketch. All clean and bright. No bad news of the sick and dying here.

"If anyone asks, you're my cousin from Providence," she says, sitting at the table by the window.

"May I?" I say, pointing at the table.

"OK. Sure. You bet you can, Mr. Swim Champion." I sit down and wait for some agreeable words to come to me.

Her breath creates another peppermint cloud where I'm sitting. Gloria's blue eyes and expansive forehead lean forward at me now to signal something important coming. "Your mother is very ill. She almost went into a coma four nights ago." She lifts her chin, her lips in a tight line. "She went into hyperpyrexia."

"That's a fever spike of 106 degrees, right?"

"She was confused, breathing rapidly, and her heart was irregular."

"You said she's better."

"We got the fever down with a cold bath and ice packs. Dr.

Lenz thinks the fever came from the arsenic treatment. The next morning her temperature was normal, and she seemed much better. Since then, she's getting stronger every day." Her face is a mixture of solemnity, respect, sorrow, empathy, consideration, and a hundred other expressions I can't name, now that she's delivered this news.

"Thank you for telling me," I say meekly. "You didn't have to tell me."

"It seemed like the right thing."

"Does my father know?"

"Dr. Lenz think it's best not to upset him, now that she's much better."

"Before she got really sick, my mother used to tell me, when my father wasn't around, 'If I have no hope of recovery, let me go.'"

Gloria's chest expands almost audibly against her nurse's smock, advancing her stethoscope out toward me then back again. "Your mother is a trouper; she never complains."

"It's kind of you to say that."

"What do you mean?"

"When I was a kid, she used to complain when I didn't do what she asked. 'You're not leaving the house in that sweater. Speak up, Ben. You also have to get A's in English.'"

"Maybe she wanted the best for you."

"Possibly," I say, avoiding her eyes for fear of losing myself in desire.

She touches the back of my hand. She's wearing a thin ring with a blue stone on her right hand, no doubt from an admirer, probably a tall, agreeable football player she goes on dates with and thinks about marrying.

She notices that I'm staring at the ring. "My father gave it to me. He's—" She gathers herself. "He's got late-stage pancreatic cancer."

"OK." This sounds so uncaring I wish I could take it back.

"Pancreatic—it's spreading to his liver, lungs, and brain." She takes a pair of reading glasses from her waist pocket, then slides them up her nose to where furrows mark her brow.

"That's terrible."

"Well, he's going where we all go." She sounds calm, but she has a terrified expression. "It's ironic. My father is a patient in my hospital."

"That must be hard, seeing him every day."

"No. It's against hospital policy for relatives to care for im-mediate family," she says. "I visit him every day at seven thirty," she says. "I don't know how much longer . . ." Her voice is a low whimper. She waves her hand in front of her face, as if she's dry-ing tears. Then she touches my hand again, and a warm and tin-gling sensation starts at my scalp and moves down my neck and spine. She takes her hand in mine, turns it palm up, so my wrist is exposed. Then she puts in the earpieces of her stethoscope and sets the chest piece against my wrist.

"My resting pulse is fifty, from swimming," I say almost more to myself than to her.

"My goodness, it's eighty now." She smiles.

"OK." I say.

"Do you want to ask me something, Ben?"

"When's your next day off?"

"Saturday," she says. "Why?"

"I can get the afternoon off from the store."

"Are you asking me on a date, Mr. Heald?"

"Um. Yes," I say, almost inaudibly.

"You took your sweet time."

"Let's meet at our apartment on Fifth. The address must be on my mother's admission form."

"I'd like that." She tears a page from a reporter's notebook and writes her telephone number in small precise letters. While she does this, she bites her lower lip. Then she folds the paper into a small pointy figure, like origami, and hands it to me. She stands up, smooths her uniform over her hips, walks to the door, stops, turns around, and smiles. "Nice to meet you, Ben Heald."

$p^3; \dfrac{\sin\varphi}{n}=1 \quad \dfrac{7}{8\sqrt{2}} \quad \ln\dfrac{x^2-x\sqrt{2}+1}{x^2-x\sqrt{2}+1}; \sin\beta=c_0 \quad g'=-2\pi Dg \quad \dfrac{1}{2}(1$

$g(x\sqrt{2}-1)\Big|_0^\infty =x \qquad \dfrac{\pi}{2\sqrt{3}} \quad \dfrac{5v_i\cdot 5v}{\sin\beta}=n=\eta(\mu, \qquad m=\lim\sum_{i=1}^{m}$

$s, n_1, i_1)$

$x^2\pi.$

$a^3z; \quad n=$

19

Since I first told my father I want to go to MIT, he has become adept at all things blame and disaster. In particular, he's been painting the horrors of my not coming in. My mother will die because he can't pay her enough attention, young men won't come to the store because they want a salesman my age, the business—again the old specious argument—will go bankrupt. Here, I fit nicely into his latest theory: Heald Shoes is going to go bust because I want to be a professor. He hasn't said this, but I know he thinks it, and I expect it each time I talk with him.

He does, however, list all the ways it's going to be wonderful when I come in.

You're going to love it. I can't wait to put your name on the awning. Father and son, my dream. The customers can't wait to meet you. I'll teach you how to play good-cop bad-cop, take you to the suppliers in upper New York State and Chicopee, Massachusetts. He thinks he's in control, but I've got a new strategy: give him the silent treatment until I get into MIT. I got the idea from my Loomsfield history class, where we learned that the ancient Greeks expelled for ten years citizens who were thought to be a threat to democracy, and early American settlers banished people accused of practicing witchcraft. I'm banishing my father for practicing undue psychological pressure. I lock myself in my room when he's home and pretend to be asleep when he knocks. The last few days I don't answer him when he talks to me, and

I leave him alone when he's in the living room with his scotch. I'm hoping my silent treatment causes him so much stress that he relents. Last Saturday, September third, I shadowed him in the store from 9:00 a.m. to 4:00 p.m. and never said a word. He grew increasingly nonplussed and, finally, sent me home.

Locked in my room yesterday evening, while I was learning Fourier Analysis, which is fascinating because of its practical application in fluid dynamics, the truth about my uncle's situation was flashing in my brain. No matter how he, or his new director, manages Whispering Palms in the near future, he'll never be able to pay Abner Zwillman fifty thousand dollars, plus twenty-five points. By my calculation—and with the luck of a good season —no hurricanes, no snow, and no Red Tide—he'll be able to pay Zwillman back in two years, and still build the reserves he needs to run the place. But that's not fast enough for Jesse.

He wants me to steal fifty thousand dollars from the cash my father keeps in the safe. "Artie never counts it. He'll never know it's gone." I know this to be wrong; my father knows exactly how much he has in the yellow envelope with the metal clasp. This feels too reckless to me, and stealing is as foreign to me as selling shoes. I can get my aunt involved, skimming small amounts, say, fifteen hundred dollars each month from the current account, and convince Zwillman to accept a three-year repayment scheme. My uncle can rob a bank, escape to Havana, or divorce my aunt and marry a wealthy widow in Palm Beach. He can even tell my father the truth and hope that my father bails him out. Or I can tell my father. Although these options give me a sense of agency, none holds much hope of success. What I'm feeling is the cold recklessness of any involvement with Zwillman. But I really like Jesse, despite what my father says, or maybe because of it, and I figure I'll get farther with Zwillman than Jesse can.

Zwillman won't hurt a sixteen-year-old; maybe he'll show me some leniency.

I find out from my uncle that he often meets Zwillman at the *Nuova Villa Tammaro* restaurant. So, at 10:00 a.m. on Wednesday, September 7, I take a bus out to Coney Island, ride for an hour, and wait for Zwillman to show up for a late lunch.

I'm fascinated by the restaurant. It's spooky, knowing that this is where Joe "The Boss" Masseria was gunned down on April 15, 1931. It's unlike any restaurant I've ever seen: nondescript, with brick and flaking stucco, and curtains over the windows. Every few minutes, a huge late-model car pulls up and lets out Italian-speaking men in black suits who enter the building through a black door to the side. It's so plain, so broken down, if I hadn't seen the men go inside, I would have thought it was an abandoned one-family tenement.

Zwillman never comes. I tell the large bald man at the door that I need to speak with Zwillman. Winking as if my request is a joke, he tells me to come back tomorrow at one o'clock. As I walk away, he mumbles something in Italian.

The next day, I ride the Coney Island bus again. I wonder what my father would think of me meeting a New Jersey mob boss who controls the numbers racket and smuggles whiskey to New Jersey from Canada.

The same bulky man with a shiny head is standing at the door, just under a hanging lantern with a single burning light bulb, even at midday. He smiles, but I can't tell why. He tells me to go around the side of the building and wait in the alley.

I wait, locating myself so I can see the parking area. Business seems poor, and the few cars that arrive are ostentatious: a Packard 12 Custom Convertible Victoria, Chrysler CL Imperial Dual-Windshield Phaeton, and others I don't recognize, but all are long and black. Heat lightning flashes overhead, and the air over Brooklyn has the sweet, pungent smell of ozone, like a burning wire.

A silver Bentley pulls up on the dirt parking area, long and wide as a cruise ship. The driver leaves the engine growling. The bulky man who told me to wait walks over, the back-seat window of the Bentley comes down, and the man confers with somebody inside. Then he straightens up and goes back to his post by the front door.

Zwillman gets out, moving slowly in an Italian double-breasted suit and handmade, alligator-skin Testonis with gold side buckles. He's over six feet, wide, and meaty. His black hair, shiny with gel, is parted on the left and swept back over his head in two waves over a droopy left eye. The driver has a pointy chin and a peaked head, and while I watch he drapes a blanket over his lap.

Is that a gun?

Zwillman walks over to me.

I step back, but bump into the wall. My hands are shaking.

"You wanted to speak with me." It isn't a question.

I'm taller, but he's bigger, and I'm terrified. "Yes, sir."

He tilts his head to one side, giving me a quizzical expression. "Do I know you?"

"No, sir. I mean, yes, I'm Jesse Heald's nephew."

"You have a name, Jesse Heald's nephew?"

"Ben, it's Ben."

"So, where's your uncle?"

"Don't know, sir."

"He give you a message?" he says, smoothing his hair.

"No, sir." My knees start to buckle.

"Easy, kid. I'm not gonna hurt you." His voice is polite and warm, like a headmaster.

"Yes, sir."

"The money?"

I nod briefly.

He smiles. Though the flattened curve of his mouth could be a threat.

"That's the thing," I say, making my voice small.

"What's the thing?" He grabs my wrist with a hand adorned with a diamond on its forefinger and a wedding band. His grip is not tight, but I can feel the threat of violence in it.

"I don't have it."

"You asked to meet me, instead of your uncle, and you show up without the money." Again, not a question. He nods with painful slowness, still holding my wrist, as if he's taking the measure of me.

I pull my hand away and the man in the Bentley jumps out, holding a shotgun. Zwillman waves him back. "So why are you here, Ben Heald?"

"I wanna help my uncle."

"I see." He unbuttons his coat. "How do you plan to help? You don't have the money, and you know that accidents happen to people who don't bring me the money." His voice is patient and easy to listen to; he could be a Latin teacher, or on the radio, only he's larger, bulkier, and more handsome. He reminds me of my uncle, so sure of himself, which intimidates me, though I try not to show it.

"You work for your uncle?"

"Um, not exactly."

"Well, Mr. Not-Exactly," he says, lowering his voice. "You come all the way out here and ask for my time . . . how old are you?"

"Sixteen."

"Well, you've got some guts, kid," he says, bursting out laughing.

I step back, scared.

"So, tell me, Ben Heald, what are you going to do for me, if you don't have the money?"

"Mr. Zwillman," I say, "my uncle bought a hotel in Florida and I'm helping with the books. I calculated that he won't be turning a profit for two years, and right now, he's short of cash."

"Do you hear the violins, kid?"

"I don't understand."

"I'm not interested in sob stories." He grins. "You tell your uncle, he stiffs me again, I'll see to it that he stays away for good."

"Mr. Zwillman, I think if you give him a year, he could make twelve smaller installments, and then a balloon payment in September 1939 at forty points. You won't get that at a bank, and you can't rely on the stock market, not after the crash. If my uncle, um, stays away for good, you won't get your money."

He whistles. "Smart kid." He takes my wrist and squeezes it again. This time, his grip is like a pair of pliers. I'm in considerable pain.

"Listen, Ben Heald, I'm going to take the deal—not because I like your uncle; he's in way over his head, with the shoes, the old speakeasies and now the cellar bars—but because you impressed me. It took cojones to come out here." He pats me on the cheek, hard enough to start an electric hum like tinnitus. "I can find you any place, any time, for any reason. Next time we won't be drinking Earl Grey." He gives me a cold, unblinking stare. "Where do you go to school?"

"Loomsfield Prep. I'll be a senior."

"Good school. Your uncle tells me you're a math genius."

"I don't know about that, sir." My voice is thin and reedy.

"It would be a pity if you never graduated from Loomsfield Prep." He starts lumbering away.

"Mr. Zwillman?"

He turns to reveal his profile, which is hard, like a boxer's, with a flat, narrow nose.

"My uncle would like an IOU."

He smiles, the droopy eye closed, which makes him seem thoughtful. "Your uncle Jesse, the one with the death wish?"

"He asked, is all."

He takes a pen from his shirt pocket, inspects the nib. He says, "Give me your shoe."

I don't move, not sure I heard him right.

"Your shoe." He holds out his butcher's hand.

I kneel, slide off my Weejun and, stand slightly off kilter, and hand it to him.

He says, "You know the expression, clothes make the man,?"

"Yes, sir."

"Some advice?"

"Sir?"

"New shoes."

He turns the shoe over in his hand and writes on the sole: "Owed by J. Heald to Zwillman." He stops. "How much is forty points on fifty k?"

"Twenty thousand."

He carries on writing. "*70K due Sept. 4, 1939.*" Pleased with himself, he winks. In a well-modulated voice, lower register, he says, "I wouldn't wear that if I were you."

"No, sir."

He turns slightly, takes out a miniature mister, and sprays his hands; he rubs them for what seems like minutes and, to complete his ritual, dries them with his handkerchief.

My nose is flooded with the stench of isopropyl alcohol. I wonder if Zwillman has nerve damage from it.

"Germs," he says with a tone of distaste.

I give him a lowly smile, remembering that my father does the same things every time we leave the hospital.

"You ever want a job, I can use a math genius like you, kid."

"Thanks, Mr. Zwillman. I'm planning on going to MIT."

"Great school," he says, impressed. He lumbers back to his Bentley, his broad shoulders rolling; languidly opens the door; arranges his hefty mass in the back seat; and closes the door as the car rolls away. I get it: the draw of secrecy, power, crime, guns, bags of money, threats, and the violence. I have a queer feeling, as if I've stepped out of my life completely, into a stranger's—a confused boy standing on the sidewalk with one shoe in his hand.

$$\frac{\sin\varphi}{n}=1 \quad \frac{1}{8\sqrt{2}} \quad \ln\frac{x^2+x\sqrt{2}+1}{x^2-x\sqrt{2}+1} \; ; \; \overline{\sin\beta}=c_v \quad g'=-2\pi Dg \quad \frac{1}{2}($$

$$g\left(x\sqrt{2}-1\right)\Big|_0^\infty = x \quad \frac{\pi}{2\sqrt{\cdot}} \quad \frac{5v_i\cdot5v}{\sin\beta}= n = \eta(\mu, \qquad m=\lim\sum_{i=1}^{m}$$

$$s, n_1, i_1) \qquad\qquad\qquad\qquad\qquad\qquad\qquad a^3z; \; n=$$

$$x^2\pi\cdot.$$

20

This morning, I wander across the park and up Madison to Jesse's store. There is a ground fog and a cold sun behind cirrus clouds, making the park seem quiet, even for a Wednesday. I can't wait to tell him about the deal I made with Zwillman. In the store, which is buzzing with customers, I approach one of the sales guys, a short young man shaped like an eggplant. His head is shaved above his ears, and on top, he has a thick nest of hair.

"Hi, Ben," he says. "Walter. We met at the Christmas party, two years ago."

The last thing I want to do is make small talk with Walter. "Have you seen my uncle?" I demand, extracting myself from the chitchat. "I need to talk to him."

Walter shrugs. "Haven't seen him all morning," he says. He catches the attention of Miler, who worked for my father until two years ago, when he got fired ago for flirting with my aunt. Ironically, Uncle Jesse had no problem hiring him for his store. I saw him get fired. My father wanted me to "see how it's done." And what I saw soured me on the people part of the business. I don't know how anybody can fire a man with a mortgage and two kids, but it didn't seem to bother my father, who told me, "Miler crossed the line. He needed to be sanctioned, otherwise word gets around that he made a move on your aunt, and I didn't do anything. I would have lost their respect." I still wonder what the line was that he crossed, since I know my aunt often makes things up.

Miler nods, comes over, and stands in front of me, but he doesn't meet my eye.

"You know where my uncle is?" I say.

"Not here."

"Or when's he coming back?"

"He's gone." His face is so red it's almost glowing, and even from five feet away I can smell the cheap alcohol on his breath.

Tension fills the space between us, and I try to ignore the fact that Miler's being uncooperative and that I am on the verge of saying something I'll regret. An apology for my father's firing him might help, but I can't say the words that might have helped Miler feel better. It's not my responsibility to apologize for my father. But I have the feeling that Miler thinks differently, which makes no sense. But people make no sense, most of the time.

I thrust my right hand into my pocket and press the nail of my right index finger into the tip of my thumb until it hurts, and then take a deep breath. "Do you know where he's gone?"

"Florida."

"What?"

"Florida Keys, to Whispering Pines, his hotel."

"Whispering *Palms.*"

"Whatever," he says, kicking at an invisible spot on the floor.

"When?"

"Yesterday," says Miler.

"Did he leave something for me?"

"Like?"

"A yellow envelope, maybe?"

"I'm not his secretary," says Miler, holding a stare. He's preparing to say something about the firing, I can feel it. I put a stick of Wrigley's in my mouth and, to calm my nerves, I dig my nail deeper into the tip of my thumb, my latest tick. "I'll never forgive you for what you did," he says, the muscles of his jaw working.

"Me? What did *I* do?"

"When your father accused me of making a pass at Myrtle, you watched. You knew your aunt was lying, and you didn't say anything. Flex believed her and called *me* a liar. Then he threw my money on the floor, so I'd have to stoop to pick it up. When I told my wife, she cried for two days. You made me feel so small."

"I was scared," I say.

"That's your excuse?"

"I can't control my father."

"But you can have an opinion," he says, with a crooked smile tugging at his lips. "You're a coward, Ben."

"I'm just a kid."

"Cowardice has no age," he says, and walks away shaking his head, with Walter close behind, leaving me alone to wonder why my uncle didn't tell me he was leaving.

On Thursday morning, my father arranges a ride for me back to Loomsfield, with two steamer trunks, my swim gear, two calculus texts, and weather notebooks, for a day of orientation, a day of class introductions and getting to know the other seniors, and then a "Welcome Back Weekend," with many parents in attendance (not mine, of course).

After a two-hour drive through Danbury, Waterbury, New Britain, and Hartford, we drive through the school gate in Windermere, and I stare out the window at the Loomsfield main office building, with its four Doric columns. Though it's a familiar sight, my eyes linger as the morning light glows against the eighteenth-century classroom buildings, the senior dorm, and the boathouse hugging the Fairfield River. The first time I saw the quad, it was a peaceful thing where I felt safe: isolated and sheltered from negative influences. But seen up close, lived day to day, Loomsfield isn't safe. Its thick, knotted ivy and the conservative lines and angles of its brown-brick buildings seem perverse, since what goes on among the students within those walls can be so cruel. Off to the right, a lone mower is clipping the football field for a preseason game against Choate, and beyond that, a track, tennis courts, and baseball diamond look manicured as an abbey. It is as if the grounds were designed by a British aristocrat who wanted to create order among a group of privileged boys, an impossible task. I think, climbing out of the car, that living here another year will either crush me or make me stronger. Beyond the clipped fields and rows of poplars, the late-morning sun falls on low hills where the freak Cape May hurricane of August 1924 washed away small trees and flooded the meadows along the river. The leaves are starting to turn orange, yellow, and red.

After a fitful night, the first day of orientation passes without a hitch, which is regrettable since it lulls me into thinking my life at Loomsfield as a senior will be different. On Friday, the first official day of classes, more an introduction to the subject than an actual class, I eat breakfast alone at the only empty table. The bell for first class rings and I cross the quad to Thornton Hall, unofficially the science building, for my first session of senior calculus, the class I've been preparing for since Hedjhal came to visit us in Quogue. I'm a little worried that the hazing from last year will start again.

Senior calculus is held in the biology lab, which is like having class in an underground garage. I sit in the back, at the end of the last row. Next to me is the specimen shelf—shark liver, calf's brain, and fetal raccoon. The other eight students straggle in, all football players and rowers, needling each other about their summer conquests of girls. Judging by their confidence, they've all had their first kiss.

Hedjhal arrives five minutes late wearing a green bow tie like the host of the children's hour. His improbable talents are cause for talk. He multiplies, adds, divides, and subtracts twenty-digit numbers in his head. He can tell you what day of the week September 20, 2030, will be, and he can name every species of butterfly known to man. He does complex calculus without paper or pencil and teaches whole semesters of math with no notes. He has—another rumor—memorized our math textbooks verbatim. Anywhere else, his eccentricity might have landed him in a psychiatrist's care, but he's Loomsfield's endearing genius—the teacher who forgets where he parked his car.

"Today, we're going to review all mathematical knowledge up to calculus." He strolls over to the end of my row, tapping the slate tip of his pointer on a jar of sheep's eyes. Click. Click. Click.

I suffer a sensation like my heart squeezing air. Everyone's watching me. The new kid, the brainiac, the loser.

"Heald," says Hedjhal. A long, bluish hand reaches down and clamps my notebook shut. "Get in the cage."

The cage is a square of tape on the floor in front of the chalk board, like the spike tape on a stage for actors.

"Heald," he says, drumming the fingers of his free hand on my desk.

I notice the sheep's eyes, which are spookily staring every which way.

"Something wrong?" Hedjhal stops his finger-drumming.

"Thinking."

"Think up front."

A titter goes through the room.

I trudge to the front. Inside my head is a threshing sound, like hail.

Hedjhal comes back to the board, fingers a nugget of yellow chalk, and writes: "Circle Formulas. Ben Heald." He holds the nub of chalk out to me.

I take it. In my head, I picture a diagram. I trace a circle at the top of the board by slowly arcing my arm around. But at three o'clock, the chalk breaks. A surge of laughter. To students in the front row, I'm quite possibly an alien from a cigar-shaped ship. Someone yells, "Loser."

I finish the circle in three arcs that don't match up. I step back and inspect the damage: a lopsided pumpkin.

Another yells, "What's the matter, brainiac, cat got your hand?" More laughter from the first-kiss crowd.

"Heald, no one's expecting Tintoretto. Get on with it." He turns to the class. "You'll have your turn . . . he who laughs last."

The class goes silent, except for the light scratching of pens on notebooks.

Working slowly, I list every circle formula and element I remember. Circumference, area, arcs, chords, secants, tangents.

"Excellent," says Hedjhal. "Now the trig functions."

Trig functions? This I know. Within seconds, the lab disappears—Hedjhal evaporates, the students cease to exist—and my hand fills the right side of the board with sine, cosine, tangent, cosecant . . . a kaleidoscope of formulas. I feel like I do in the swimming pool: no self-consciousness, just intense serenity with no sense of time. My mind is reeling in a good way. I can do anything I like. I'm done before I realize that I'm done, and when I realize it, I can't believe I filled the board with formulas.

Hedjhal climbs down from his perch and goes to the board. "Well, that's superb." He turns to the class, a smile opening on his preoccupied, boyish face. "This is what I expect from all of you."

Eight sets of eyes aim their dark augers of anger at me.

Chills strafe my back. We're all doomed to isolation, since it's what holds us together in the forced camaraderie of boys brought together at random. But now I see that my performance is my doom, since it sets me apart and breaks the Loomsfield Code: never make your classmates look bad.

Ten seconds pass. I'm still standing in the cage, waiting to be dismissed.

The edges of my field of vision blur. My pants feel too tight. Hedjhal is talking about vectors and matrices, but I don't comprehend the words. Just a voice. The overwhelming stench of formaldehyde. What's next is that my vision goes wonky. White sharp-edged objects, like snowflakes, float across my eyes. The faucet, a piece of chalk, the faces in the front row, and the stuffed head of a skunk mounted above the board—all dissolve into flickering, mercurial spots of light. Swaying, I lean over the sink. And then, below me in a dissecting tray: a frog splayed on its back, with a pin through the web of each foot. A surgical slice has opened the white, glistening belly from the jaw to the V of its legs. Two flaps of white skin are pulled back and pinned to the tray. The stomach, heart, lungs, and intestines shine like jellied consommé. And next to the corpse, in the corner of the dissecting tray, lie the heart, discarded and skewered—a miniature Aztec sacrifice. I'm ready to hurl.

"Heald, take your seat."

Someone shouts, "Hey Heald, time for lunch." I see them peripherally. They're all laughing so loud, their heads craned in my direction.

I yawn uncontrollably, gasp for air, and vomit. My stomach is leaving my body through my throat. In inexorable waves, a yellow brown liquid splashes my shoes. Three dry heaves leave me gasping.

I bolt from the room, leave Thornton Hall, traverse the quad, and don't stop running until I get to the end of the boathouse dock. I sit where a wooden ladder leads into the lazy current. I'm feeling more alone here than almost any time before, except standing in the crowded Heald Store. I'm oddly distant. Bits of duckweed gather at my feet in the flat, brown river.

"Hi, Ben."

"Dr. Hedjhal?"

He reaches me, takes off his shoes, and sits with his stockinged feet stretched out in front of him, one blue sock with yellow canaries and one red argyle. "You did an excellent job with the trig functions . . . and your vomit had an interesting trajectory."

"They think I'm weird," I say. "I feel so alone."

"You are alone. They can't appreciate what it's like being you. To them, your talent is creepy and unsettling." He smiles as if he's summarized my whole life in one sentence. "It's not their fault." He wraps his arms around himself. "You and I, we see things others don't see, our minds do things their minds can't do. I see numbers as colors and remember the comma in a footnote on page 290. We see connections no one else sees."

"It's horrible."

"It's a gift, a terrible, wonderful, lonely gift." He peers at me through lenses that make his eyes as large and moist, it seems, as sea anemones. "These next weeks are going to be tough. Sleep is a luxury." He laughs agreeably. "You want to go to MIT?"

"Yes."

"On the matter of your future, the only important thing, Ben, is what you want." He scans my face. His looks sad, which doesn't match his words: his lips are saying one thing, but his eyes are saying something else. "The world is rife with things we're afraid to do, afraid to say, afraid to see. We avoid one thing we're afraid of after another, and pretty soon, if we're really good at being careful and avoiding all risk, fear chooses for us." He wraps his arms around me and squeezes, and for once, I feel warm and protected. At that, I relax, and let my head fall onto his shoulders. I hear loud sobs escape from me. And still, he holds on, not saying anything, holding me tight, while I cry into his shirt. I know that I will return to this moment from now on, whenever I'm alone. I'll close my eyes and remember Hedjhal's kind words. What is it about them? He takes me seriously. He says *we*.

After my disaster in first-period calculus, I have Latin III, French II, organic chemistry, and senior English, which is both a success and a disaster.

Ten minutes before the bell, the other eighteen students in senior English file in, their arms loaded with books, their ties loose or even undone, and pens in their shirt pockets. A late student rushes in, yelling, "He's coming, he's coming." Every student in the room ties his tie into a neat knot and flattens his shirt with his palm like an iron. They place their books in a neat pile and line up their pens and pencils. Dr. Shore is a stickler for propriety and brooks no laziness. Rumor has it that neatness and exactitude are 50 percent of our grade. And if he can't read one of our weekly essays, we have to write it again in all capitals.

Dr. Shore is a small, short, thin man with narrow shoulders and a mop of thick, unruly red hair that breaks every one of his tidiness rules. He walks on the balls of his feet, like a dancer, and seems to glide across the space between the door and his desk, mimicking the astounding adroitness of his mind, which makes me think of lightning in a bottle. One story making the rounds is that when Dr. Shore was at Harvard, he took a Shakespeare course that required him to read all the plays—comedies and tragedies—in a book as thick and heavy as a cinder block. On the final exam, students were asked to identify one hundred quotes, what play they were from, and which character said them. Shore not only got 100 percent correct, but just to show off, he listed what page in the book the quote came from. His essay answer, written in two hours, won him an undergraduate essay award.

Shore puts our textbook on the desk and, without delay, launches his attack on our preparedness, starting with me. It's not out of a sadistic streak, so far as I can tell, but because he wants to gauge how well the "new" students have done their homework (the new students being anyone he didn't intimidate and thrill through junior English).

"Heald!"

I hold his gaze. "Dr. Shore."

"I hear you're quite the math student."

I shrug while a titter travels through the class.

"Let's see if you're quite the English student."

I open my copy of *Macbeth*, the play we're reading and discussing this week, to keep Shore in the dark about my eidetic memory, and not to look like I'm bluffing in front of the other seniors, most of whom don't yet know about my eidetic memory since the school year started only a week ago.

"I'm going to give you part of a quote. You finish it, and you give us the explanation. Got it?"

"Explanation, sir?"

"What it means, why it's important, maybe a little context, how it fits in the themes of the play."

"OK, sir."

"Ready?"

I nod, close my eyes, and prepare to see the pages of the book in my mind's eye.

'Be bloody, bold, and resolute . . .'" says Shore, then raps a knuckle on the desk.

"'. . . Laugh to scorn the power of man, for none of woman born shall harm Macbeth."

Shore smiles, smugly, as if he's to thank for my answer.

I go on. "The second of the three apparitions says this to Macbeth. This convinces Macbeth that he is invincible, since he will never be killed by another man. He chooses to neglect the first apparition which warned him of Macduff and doesn't realize that the 'bloody child' is in fact the infant Macduff covered with the blood of the untimely ripped womb of his mother."

"Excellent, Heald. Excellent," says Shore, pacing back and forth to burn off his excess energy. "Fair is foul . . .'"

"'. . . and foul is fair," I whisper. "This quote is said by the witches. I think it means things are opposite to what they appear. Maybe it also means that Macbeth's world will turn upside down and he will do things he considers foul or unfair, disregarding what appears fair to him. I think it describes the theme of the play."

"Two for two, Heald. One more: 'Here's the smell of the blood still . . .'

'. . . All the perfumes of Arabia will not sweeten this little hand," I take a deep breath to gather my thoughts.

"Stumped," says Shore.

"No, sir. This line is from the famous sleepwalking scene after which Lady Macbeth commits suicide off stage. Lady Macbeth is traumatized and guilt ridden. She says she cannot get rid of the smell of blood from her hands, not even with all the perfumes of Arabia. This is in sharp contrast to her statement to Macbeth, when he murdered Duncan, that 'a little water clears us of this deed.' Knowing that she was the prime force that led Macbeth down his murderous path, her guilt dominates her thoughts, and she is unable to turn away from what she now considers sins."

Dr. Shore stops pacing, and looks at me, one eyebrow lifted. "Outstanding, Heald. You have lived up to your reputation," he says. He pokes an alarmingly large index finger at the others. "Let that be our standard, men."

I sink into my seat, assuming Dr. Shore has just relegated me to social infamy. No one likes a smartass. And sure enough, twenty minutes later, as everybody's milling around by the classroom door, a senior I don't know, except that he plays football, grabs my shoulder. "Bad enough that you have special dispensation to go home on Fridays—"

"How do you . . . ?"

"Everybody knows, mama's boy," he says, tousling my hair like I'm a three-year-old. "Not only are you a mama's boy brainiac, but you've also made us all look like fools. You're so dead. You might as well order your gravestone."

I walk out of the building with my head down and rush to the indoor pool. Minutes later, whoosh, splash. I'm back in my element again, face down in the flowing wet, forgetting my first day of classes and feeling the water flow over my face and back. At one point, I take off my goggles and swim with my eyes closed, feeling the pressure of the cool water against my face. No worries about ordering my gravestone or soon being dead.

At eight o'clock, after my five-thousand-yard workout (the high point of my first-day ordeal) and eating dinner alone at one of the long tables the headmaster says are designed to turn the dining hall into Loomsfield's meeting place (I didn't meet anybody), I stand at the hallway phone in my dorm and dial my uncle's number at Whispering Palms.

"Whispering Palms Hotel and Restaurant," a cheerful young woman's voice says.

"Hi," I say. "It's Ben Heald calling. I'm trying to reach my uncle Jesse Heald. I left him two messages. I'm just trying again." My heart's kicking inside my rib cage. I know already, because he hasn't called me back, this is probably a mistake. Maybe a bad one. On the other end of the line, I hear a rustling, then nothing. I begin returning the handset to its wall cradle.

"Ben, is that you?" A deep baritone hums through the extended handset, trapping me with my name. Why do I want to talk with him so badly? "Ben?" My uncle has me now, so I'm going to have to talk to him. A big cough boils up through the line. I should probably hang up so I don't have to talk with him, but he'll be happy that I tried. "Are you . . . Ben?" He's shouting over music with conga drums and women's voices. "Damn it, Martha," he says. "Not now."

"I'm here," I say tentatively.

"You're there, good."

A warm female voice says, "OK, good," from the background.

"Everything OK, Ben?" In the pause, ice cubes clink against glass. "I don't have much time."

"Well . . . look, Uncle Jesse . . ."

"Why the hell didn't you call me back?" Kissing sounds. A laugh. "Jesus, Martha."

"I am calling you back," I say irritably. "Actually, I called you three times since yesterday."

"Oh, right. Right."

"I've got some good news," I say. "I talked with Zwillman."

"Thanks, but that was a stupid thing to do."

"I knew he wouldn't hurt a sixteen-year-old kid," I say. "He offered me a job."

"You shouldn't have gotten into my business."

"I . . ."

"It's my goddamned business, got it?"

"Sure, I get it."

"You could have gotten me killed, since Zwillman thinks I sent you."

"I told him I came on my own."

"That's damned naive." The mellow voice is gone. "Do you have any idea what you did?"

"I negotiated a new payment schedule."

"Yeah, I talked with Zwillman." Something is ruffling his handset like a piece of clothing. "Listen, Ben, I'm in kind of a hurry."

"I was just trying . . ."

"Why don't you come down to Florida, you can help the new manager straighten things out." Kissing noises. A woman's moan.

"I have school," I say quickly, disappointed and miserable. "I'm sixteen."

"Right."

A whisper in the background: "I'm waiting."

"I'll send you my best occupancy rate calculations."

"Good, Ben, I just . . ." Then the line is empty between us. I'm alone and discouraged. Outside the window next to me, from the chapel, the bell rings for curfew. My heart's beating funny; my hand is still clutching the handset from which my uncle was speaking but is now gone, without a thank you. There was no acknowledgment of my help. This wasn't my plan. I need to start making more realistic plans, since my last ones have gone awry. And I need to get it into my head that my uncle doesn't care about me any more than my father does. I need to avoid such moments as this, since I can handle the stress of senior year, but I can't handle the rest.

In my dorm an hour later, I sit at my desk, reflecting on calculus class and my call with my uncle. I'm embarrassed and disappointed. A prism of light from a lamp in the quad passes through the window, brightening a spot on my advanced calculus book like a reminder of my top priorities: MIT and my first kiss. I'm not sure what did it, but I suspect the gradual dawn of contempt I experienced—a contempt for my father and my uncle, for different reasons; my inability to believe either one has my best interests at heart—had to do with my being angry at my father and overly impressed by my uncle. The gap between what they want and what I want is widening and unbridgeable.

My uncle, who, until recently, seemed fascinating to me, has begun to seem selfish, elevating his needs above my own, but camouflaging them behind flattery. I analyzed his business plan, gave him a checklist for his new director, explained to him about the ideal occupancy rate, and gave him ten hours that I could have spent on calculus, something I love way more than helping Jesse. And then I suffer through a call in which he barely thanks me, says I did a stupid thing, and invites me to Islamorada to help in his hotel. My motivation with both my father and Jesse is clear to me now—to earn their love and respect by keeping quiet and shadowing him (my father) or doing him favors (my uncle). I've done all sorts of things I don't want to, and for what? From my father, I get no appreciation for trying to like the business, and from my uncle there's only the most cursory thank-you for making a deal with Zwillman and saving him thousands, and maybe even his life.

My father tells me I'm being an egomaniac, disrespectful, and way too introverted. I don't respond, not only because it's my new strategy, but also because no counterargument exists. He's right. He dislikes in me what I dislike in him: impatience about things that don't go his way. The question isn't whether I'm becoming those things—I am—but what that means for my future. One thing is clearer than ever before: I'm going to go to MIT, and it's time to dig in.

$\frac{\sin\varphi}{n}=1$ $\frac{1}{8\sqrt{2}}$ $\ln\frac{x^2+x\sqrt{2}+1}{x^2-x\sqrt{2}+1}$; $\sin\beta=c_5$ $g'=-2\pi\nu g$ $\frac{1}{2}$

$g(x\sqrt{2}-1)\Big|_0^\infty=x$ $\frac{\pi}{2\Gamma^9}$ $\frac{5v_i\cdot5v}{\sin\beta}=n=\eta(\mu,$ $m=\lim\sum_{i=1}^{m}$

$,n_1,i_1)$ a^3z ; $n=$

$x^2\pi$.

21

The Loomsfield indoor pool house is a one-story wood-arched building with a curved roof, like a mysterious outpost on the moon. Inside, I feel like I'm standing in a church; there's cathedral-like silence except for the faint hum of the pumps. It's the nearest place I know to a haven, where I'm safe, comfortable, and confident. I've come for my afternoon workout on the third day of the new semester. I'm feeling like the odd man out, a young senior in advanced classes with people two years older than I am, the subject of whispers and rumors.

We have a new coach this year, Frank Masters. He's a tall whip of a man who looks to be around forty and dresses in Loomsfield tracksuits. He's pale, like he lives in chlorinated water and never goes outside into the sun. His reading glasses hang around his neck on a silver chain. He's standing next to a group of breaststroke swimmers. He sees me, and says, "Afternoon, Heald. Workout's on the chalkboard; warmup is five hundred yards easy, then five thousand yards broken freestyle in sets of three hundreds, two hundreds, hundreds, and fifties. Varying effort, with five hundred yards' cooldown."

I dive in, feeling the shock of the first cold, a million bubbles rising around me in a shimmering cloud—it's the best moment of my day. When I'm swimming laps, it's just me and the water. Today, the breaststrokers aren't encroaching on my lane. For twenty minutes, I tune out the world and focus on my swim stats: three breaths per lap, twelve strokes per twenty-five yards, twenty-six strokes per fifty yards, maximizing my distance per stroke.

Halfway into my warmup, staring down at the endless lane line, I've been playing around with my father's expectations on the edges of my mind, counting laps. I used to think coming into Heald Shoes would be the result of one colossal moment, either when he announces that I'm coming in, since the lawyers have already drawn up the papers, or he dies, and I suddenly inherit the company. But now it occurs to me that it's happening so gradually, I don't feel a sudden rush of panic or end up at a table at the lawyers' office with a pen in my hand. Right now, these two inflection points don't seem likely. At three hundred yards, I have a thought I've never had before: people say your life can change in a second. But, it's three events that are altering the course of my life: my mother's sickness, the calculus challenge, and my father pushing me into a partnership. Alone, I can handle the stress of my mother's mystery disease. Calculus is just a matter of working harder than I've ever worked before on something I love almost as much as swimming. But my father's unrelenting pressure to bring me in is a strategy of attrition. My father's going to keep wearing me down until I cave. Maybe my Aunt Myrtle and Dr. Hedjhal are right: I don't have the luxury of saying no after a single event. I'll have to find the moxie to choose my own moment to say no.

After five hundred yards, my hand touches the wall, my heart beating at ease, and my lungs opening and closing like billows.

"Heald! A minute," Coach Masters yells.

I'm bobbing in a draft from the open door by the diving tower and quickly my teeth are chattering.

"I see you with a grim face." He watches the breaststrokers

gunning it to the wall, their heads plowing small waves. He blows his whistle for the sprint group to start, then lets the whistle fall from his mouth and focuses on me over the rims of his reading glasses. "What's wrong?"

"Nothing."

"I've been doing this too long for you to con me."

"I'm cold."

"I mean, what's going on with *you*?"

"Nothing."

He turns, watches the others in lane two, yells, "Early catch, and let's see some serious kicking!" Then he turns again to me. "What's the problem, Heald?"

"I'm not holding the water."

"You're a smart kid, you've been swimming ten years, you know that elite swimmers have good days and bad days. On the bad days we can't feel the water." He scans the notes on his clipboard. "What's really eating at you?"

I'm getting defensive. "I'm uncertain about what time I can swim at the New England Championships in Winchendon."

"Doc Woodworth at the NYAC tells me you swam some good times at the Club this summer."

"You talked with him?"

"I know Doc from my days as a Bruin." He sighs. "He said you've got the best feeling for the water of any age-grouper he's ever seen, but you think too much."

"What does that mean?"

"You're too much in your head, trying too hard to stick to a plan, counting with that huge brain of yours."

"I memorize every workout, times, distances, breaths, strokes, and kicks per length and per event."

"Impressive, but not fast," he says, standing a yard away

from me, shaking his head. "I want to see you swimming more intuitively."

"I don't know what that means."

"You've got to pay better attention to your body, your position in the water . . . feel the drag forces, adjust your hand position, reduce the amplitude in your kick by using your ankles more, making sure you're relaxed." He opens his mouth, blows his whistle, and gives the sprint group their next set. "Twenty times twenty-fives, alternating fly and free. Medium effort. Twenty seconds rest." He angles back toward me. "You're swimming doggedly, Heald. I see you not having fun."

"I'm pushing myself above my limits, that's all."

"But if you're always pushing your limits," he says warmly, "over time, you'll swim more slowly, you'll lose your spark. It happened to me my freshman year at UCLA. Three weeks before the NCAAs, I worked out harder than ever, and when I got to the meet, my times were two seconds off my best." He winks at me. "We taper before big meets for a reason."

"Rest and recovery."

"Every workout has a mini-taper or two," he says, with genuine sympathy for my obtuseness. "Get it?"

"How do I know when to taper?"

"Do you trust me, Heald?"

"I don't know."

"You may be the next John Stuart Mill, but I know more about swimming than you do," he says, reaching down and rubbing my head briefly. "Just follow my workouts—the taper is built in."

"Yes, Coach."

He looks his stopwatch, then at the breaststrokers. "Five fifties at ninety percent, then four twenty-fives underwater, and four hundred cooldown, forty percent effort." Then he swings his attention back to me. "Where was I?" he says.

I swim to within two feet of him. "Relaxation."

"Ah, yes, relaxation," he says. "Are you sleeping enough?"

"Yes."

"The point is lost if you're not having fun."

"I've got a lot on my plate, skipping junior year."

"Everything OK with your family?"

"I guess so."

"You guess? Either it's OK, or it's not."

"My mother's got African trypanosomiasis."

A moment of vague confusion passes over his face.

"My mother may be dying."

"Tough break, Heald." He turns back to the pool. "Dinkel, head down, the water should flow over the top of your head." He angles his head toward me. "You need some time off?"

"No, sir."

"Struggling in your courses?"

"No."

"You enjoying Loomsfield?"

"Sure," I say. "Why are you asking?"

Winters stares at Dinkel, Loomsfield's fastest fifty-yard man, then shakes his head, clicks his tongue in disapproval. "Jesus H., Dinkel, don't stare at us—get your damned head down, eyes on the bottom of the pool, when you see the T, go in for your turn." Winters aims his gaze back at me. "I'm no shrink, Heald, but you'll never swim fast if you're miserable."

Instead of saying anything, I climb out, take my towel from the bench behind him, and drape it over my shoulders. "I'm fine, really, Coach."

"Not my impression," he says. He yells again at the sprint

group: "Arms straight in the last fifteen, no glide to the wall." Putting his hand on my hip, he says, "You can pull a mean puss anywhere else, if you need to, but not here." He screws his features into lines of frustration, mirroring me. "My job is to worry about team morale, and your face is hurting the team."

"What does my face have to do with team morale?"

"We work out as a team, we compete as a team, we lose as a team, we win as a team."

"That's obvious," I say.

He gazes at me disapprovingly over his glasses. He reaches out and puts his other hand on my hip, and comes so close to my face, he could be inspecting my teeth. "This is not just about swimming; this is also about character and teamwork."

"But swimming is an individual sport. It's each of us against the clock."

"You're the fastest mid- and long-distance guy we've got. Your name is on the school record board. You're practically the captain. I hear you're the smartest guy in the school; the guys look up to you."

"They make fun of me, mostly."

"That's all bravado. They're impressed; they're going to follow you."

"I can see how we're a team by definition, since we're all Loomsfield competing against Choate, Milton, and Andover. But we're not swimming together as a team. Otherwise, we'd only swim relay."

"That's not the point, Heald," he leans back a little. "If you can't see how your behavior affects the others, you and this team have no future."

"Are you kicking me out?" A shock flashes through me.

"Not yet, Heald, but consider this a warning," he says.

"Teamwork is about making a personal sacrifice for the group, supporting the other players, even the slower ones. When you swim for Loomsfield, you represent the school and stand with your teammates. It's about achieving a common goal, not just winning the thousand-yard freestyle, but about winning as a team."

Getting kicked off the team would be a disaster, since I depend on my hours in the pool to feel good about myself. "Sorry, Coach."

"If we weren't a team, you could train alone and compete alone, and you'd probably win, but you'd miss out on the camaraderie and the chance to make a personal sacrifice—watching the others compete, swimming an event that's not your best, like the two hundred fly, and motivating the others to do better than they think they can."

"OK." I have no clue what else to say.

"You have to stop making this all about yourself, and more about the others." He takes a deep breath. "Why do you think we get in a circle, hold hands, and do our chant?"

"*On three. After me. We will not yield, Loomsfield,*" I say. "It seems kind of silly."

"The chant may be silly to you, but it's not silly to the others. It's about the common bond among all of us. It's *motivating*." He swallows hard, like he has a lump in his throat. "Spell it for me."

"What, now?"

He nods.

"M-o-t-i-v-a-t-i-o-n."

"Right. 'Desire or willingness to do something, enthusiasm.'" He glares at me, no longer agreeable. "From the word *motive*." He's too loud now. "You got a motive?"

"I want to win the New England Championships."

"Winning's only a part of it, Heald." He makes a harrumph. "You're a great swimmer. You've got talent—a great build and flippers on the ends of your legs—and you've got grit, but you've got to be a team player."

"I see what you're saying, in theory."

"This isn't theory, like some axiom in geometry; this is practice." He turns quickly to the sprinters. "Dinkel, damn it, let's see you step on the gas, set the pace now, no dawdling." Now he addresses me again. "Are you hearing me, Heald?"

"I get it, Coach."

"Good. Good. I respect you, Heald," he says, tapping me on the shoulder with his overly large hand, like a cold warning. "But if you pull that narcissistic crap again, I'll cut you from the squad."

At dinner, Bobby Hinckley, another senior on the swim team who's also in senior English, sits kitty-corner to me at an otherwise-empty table, as if he and I have leprosy and the other students are afraid to get the bacteria.

"Tough workout today," he says.

"I swam well." I give him my classmate smile number two (I have three)—big, but not too big.

"Good. Keep it up, we need you in the relays."

"I think I could hold the water better."

"If you hold the water any better, you'll lap us in the fifteen hundred," he says, grinning. "Can I ask you a question, Heald?"

I know he can, but that's not what he's asking; he's asking if he's allowed to. I learned that from my uncle. "OK."

"How did you remember all those lines from *Macbeth*?"

"I read them."

"I mean what's your trick?"

"Sometimes I read them slowly."

He rubs his eyes with alarmingly long, thin fingers, perfect for a sprinter, with his wide wingspan. "Dr. Shore gave you a hard time," he says, trading his wide grin for a sharp little arc, like something drawn with a protractor. "He's a damned nasty bastard. I had him for freshman composition. Every time he came through the door—"

"—How did he come through the door when it was closed?"

He nods, with a baffled expression, and saws at his chicken cacciatore so hard it's an act of revenge. "I mean every time he came to class, he drove us all nuts."

"I think he's really smart, and Shakespeare is cool."

Hinckley spots somebody and waves him over. It's Winston Bell III, a short red-haired kid from Paramus, New Jersey, who rolls his shoulder muscles when he walks. He sits down next to Hinckley, ignores me, and laughs. "Bobby, my man, sitting with the Loomsfield brainiac is going ruin your reputation."

"What?"

"Not a day passes without Heald showing us all how smart he is." Winston Bell III attacks his chicken too, hacking at it like it's a weed. "Right, Hinckley? What do you think?"

"I think Heald's too smart for his own good," he says. "And for our good too."

"It's not my fault," I say. "I remember things." This is a simple fact that no one can argue with.

"It's your fault that you're always showing off," says Bell.

"I'm interested in *Macbeth*. Lady Macbeth and Macbeth remind me of my parents."

"Well, Macbeth Junior, be interested somewhere else," Bell

says with a sneer before he forks off a slab of chocolate cake, and adds, with his mouth full, "Keep your mouth shut in class."

"You blame me because I know the answers?"

"No, we're blaming you because you say the answers," says Hinckley, taking a sip of the nameless Loomsfield red drink. "You're a fucking brownnose. Just like you're always swimming too fast in warmup, passing us so we look slow."

"My swim speed actually has no effect on how fast you look."

Bell's eyes widen, and his mouth hangs open. He smashes his peas into a paste with his fork. "You ever think about doing something with us? Last year you never came."

"Who's us?"

"Swim team."

"You're not on the swim team."

"Big diff."

"Yes, sure."

"So, you'll join us?"

"No, I often think about it. What's the something you want to do?"

"Dunno," says Hinckley, spreading his hands flat on the table, like he's steadying himself. "Maybe join our chemistry study group, share a smoke behind the boat house."

"I learn better alone, and I don't smoke."

"You know what happens if you don't join in." Bell's voice is half an octave higher, like he's suddenly talking to a five-year-old. He spreads his pea paste on a slice of industrial white bread and takes a huge bite, bulging his cheeks. After a mighty swallow, he says, "You become an outcast. A flake."

"What kind of flake?"

"You know, a flake."

"Do you mean a crazy flake or an eccentric flake?"

"Fuck I know," says Hinckley. "Somebody who doesn't fit in."

"I already don't fit in." I say this without any feeling whatsoever, like I'm talking about someone else.

Hinckley smiles at Bell. "Hey, give him the frog problem." Then he clinks his fork against his plate, like someone making a toast at a wedding.

"You're such a fucking brainiac, right?" says Bell.

I don't answer the question I'm busy smearing mustard on my hamburger.

"You ready?"

"OK."

"A frog is ten yards away from a pond. On the first day, it jumps halfway, five yards towards the pond. On the second day, the frog jumps halfway again, two and one-half yards towards the pond. On the third day, it jumps halfway again, one and one-quarter yards, towards the pond. Every day it jumps exactly halfway towards the pond."

"What time of day does the frog jump?"

"No idea."

"Does it have access to water?"

"How do I know? It's hypothetical."

"How much does the frog weigh?"

"Jesus, Heald, it doesn't fucking matter."

"It may matter," I say, again stating the obvious.

"So," says Bell, "here's the question: will the frog ever reach the pond?

"No, of course not."

"What's the reason?"

"The frog is an amphibian, and if it goes three days without water, its skin will dry up and it will die."

"What's the matter with you, Heald?"

"Nothing."

"What's the mathematical reason?"

"It's intuitively obvious . . . mathematically, if the frog gets enough water to stay alive, and if it always goes half the remaining distance, it will never go the whole way."

Hinckley is starting to look the way I imagine Macbeth looks: eyebrows turned inward, raised upper lip, winkled nose, and a rise in cheek muscles. He touches Bell's tray. "Let's get outta here."

Then Bell pours his milk over my chocolate cake. "Jesus, Heald, you're not a flake, you're a fucking freak. Enjoy your chocolate soup."

After my dinner with Hinckley and Bell, ending with my cake floating in a saucer of milk, I call Gloria at the hospital. It's a bold move for me and may be reckless; it's something I've never done—call a girl.

"Gloria?"

"Ben? Hi. Are you at school?"

"Since yesterday. It's great to talk with you."

"You too." She giggles, but in a low voice, self-confident, in a way I recognize but don't recognize. Is this really Gloria? Eventually she says, "I'm sorry I can't talk long, I'm starting my night shift. We have a meeting first with Dr. Lenz to discuss the patients. We've got lots of work, blood pressure, medications, shots, dressings." Her warm voice reaches me from New York. "Sometimes we just listen. They're lonely."

"Don't let me hold you up, then."

"No, it's OK. I really want to talk. I was thinking about calling you today, but I was afraid I'd bother you, starting your senior year."

"Yeah, well, a lot's going on, but everything's great. Calculus is going great and I'm swimming—"

"I'm glad."

"Well, we haven't had any swim meets yet, and Coach Winters wants me to be more of a team player."

"Oh, no, you'll be fine."

I hear her talking to another nurse. I imagine her at the nurse's station, and immediately I'm excited. One of the seniors from my calculus class—it may be Thayer—appears at the end of the hall. He comes up to me. "Weirdo," he says and walks away, with a laugh like a cackle. I watch his narrow frame disappear into his room and lean back into my conversation with Gloria.

Then I remember what Jesse told me: girls like to be called beautiful. And so, with a deep breath, I say words that characters in books and movies say all the time, but I've never said before. "You're beautiful, Gloria."

Gloria giggles.

"So are you, Ben Heald."

"You like it?"

"What?"

"Working in the hospital."

"Mostly, but not always. Your mother's my favorite patient."

"Oh, god." I knew it, my mother's already working her public charm on Gloria.

"She likes to talk, that's for sure," Gloria says, louder. "She's always telling everybody what for, even Dr. Lenz." Papers rustle from the background, and Gloria laughs with another nurse, who has a heavy New York accent. "Ben?"

"I'm here."

"I can't believe they went to Africa together."

"Yeah . . ." I can't think of another question, or what to say.

"Wow," Gloria says. "Your mother's really doing better now."

"Good."

"Yeah . . . it's good."

"So, anything new?" Another question my uncle taught me.

"My father had his appendix out."

"How is he?"

"Complaining about the food. But good. Really good."

"That's good."

"Yeah," Gloria says as our conversation gets stuck. "Um, my father told me when you find someone you like, make sure they know it."

"Makes sense."

"He knows things I don't."

"What?"

"How to appreciate the small things, like this call." She giggles. "I always giggle, it's a terrible habit."

"I like it. It reminds me of you."

"I've really gotta go. Dr. Lenz is coming. She's always in a hurry."

"When I see her, she's running down the hall."

"Oh . . . yeah, she uses this weird expression, 'Hurry up and wait.'"

"Yeah, well, thanks for talking with me."

"Yeah, let's do it again."

"Maybe I'll see you at the hospital this weekend."

"Or call me," she says quickly. "I'd like to see you, or talk to you, Ben. I mean it. Will you?"

"Sure, I will."

"I wish I could talk longer."

"Me too."

"Bye."

"Bye."

And then she's no longer on the line, I've got the handset in my hands, and for some reason I don't understand, I feel empty and a little disappointed.

22

I've got a dispensation from Friday afternoon classes and swim practices—the subject of much innuendo and gossip, most of which suggests I'm a mama's boy. Why that's an insult is a mystery to me, since we're all mama's boys—so I'm back in the city again to visit my mother. At the Flower Hospital, my mother is now in another new room, one floor up, two doors from Dr. Lenz's lab, room 4-D. Gloria will have already announced me, since I called ahead, so I'm expecting to find my mother's door open and a welcoming smile. A nurse I've never seen before asks me my name, then waves me past the nurse's station.

I'm ready to knock on the door when there's a big crash inside. The door opens before I can rap my knuckles on the wood, and Gloria rushes out, nearly running into me. "Hi, Ben, we can talk later, I need to get some bandages." Then she's gone, moving away quickly, her blond ponytail swinging back and forth, shoulders squared, earrings glittering, her heart-shaped calves poking out from under the hem of her white uniform. I turn and look inside, and see my mother sitting on the floor, supporting herself on straight arms, her legs splayed out before her. Her varicose veins look like bright blue webs. Dr. Lenz is bent over her, whispering in her ear. On the bed is a camera.

I go right to her. I bend over, next to Dr. Lenz, and get my mother's attention. I'm shaken by the smell of urine, and my mother's murmuring, which I strain to understand but can't. I ask her if she's OK, and she whispers she's fine and asks me how I'm doing. I whisper the same. She seems far away, and I can't pull her back from whatever planet she's on, and while Dr. Lenz is brushing the hair from my mother's eyes, I take her hand in mine—this is what I've seen people in movies do with accident victims. I squeeze but she doesn't squeeze back, so I take my hand away and get to my feet.

My mother tells Dr. Lenz and Gloria, who just came back, that they should see to other patients, but they don't. Dr. Lenz helps my mother back into bed while Gloria is fussing with the sheets, tucking in perfect hospital corners. The overhead fan isn't turning; the room is stifling, at least seventy-five degrees and humid, with that alcohol smell in the air. Dr. Lenz asks me to step outside.

For twenty minutes I don't hear any talk from inside the room, which worries me: perhaps she's suffered a concussion or a stroke. Fear squeezes my stomach, and my heart is beating like it does after a fifty-yard sprint.

Twenty minutes later, they call me back into my mother's room. Dr. Lenz and Gloria are hovering on either side of the bed, smiling, with my mother looking surprisingly fresh, as if she never fell out of bed and nearly broke her hip or wrist or something else. They've gotten my mother cleaned up, put her in a fresh hospital gown, brushed her hair into place, reinserted her hydrotherapy drip, and resettled her into bed, where she sits, propped on two pillows. The whole scene is composed, like a Christmas photograph of the perfect family: my mother and her two women.

I'm not panicked any more, I'm awed. When I rejoin them at the foot of the bed, I apologize for coming in before, and Gloria laughs. "It's OK, Ben. It's good you're here."

I'm embarrassed by her remark, so I say, "Thank you. You too," and immediately feel awkward.

"Isn't this crazy?" proclaims my mother. "I fell out of bed. I've never fallen out of bed."

"What happened?" I ask.

"We were taking pictures," Dr. Lenz points to a small black camera on the nightstand.

"That doesn't make any sense," I say. "Why were you taking pictures?"

"Your mother's much better," Dr. Lenz says. "She will probably not stay here much longer, so we wanted to create memories before she goes to the summer cottage."

"To Quogue?"

"*Ja, ja.* Next week, probably."

"Who's going to take care of her?"

"Myrtle," my mother says dismissively, as if this is obvious. "But that's neither here nor there. I sat up and swung my feet over the edge of the bed because I wanted a picture of me standing, instead of prone in that infernal bed, but then I got really dizzy and next thing I know, I'm on the floor in a puddle of sweat. Somehow, when I toppled over, I must have missed the bed."

"Poor Florence. First trypanosomiasis, and now she falls from the bed." Dr. Lenz laughs, not taking my mother's accident as seriously as I do, though my mother seems to be OK, just a little shaken. "You are lucky and unlucky," says Dr. Lenz. It could be that she's just being friendly, but it seems like more—the way she sneaks glances at my mother, and the way my mother laughs at her attempts at humor. This makes me uncomfortable, since I don't want to imagine them doing things in bed, so I distract myself from the picture in my head by imagining that I'm kissing Dr. Lenz.

Gloria's holding the camera now. "I guess we'll be wanting pictures of you two," she says in a perky voice, pointing at my mother and Dr. Lenz. "And you'll want one of your Ben, right, Florence?" She says this as though there are hundreds of Bens, and she just happens to have one. It makes Gloria seem much older, like a mother with children.

My mother smiles. "Of course I want one of our boy genius."

Following first Gloria's, and then Dr. Lenz's directorial instructions, photographs are taken of my mother and Dr. Lenz, cheek to cheek—what's going on?—Gloria and my mother with their arms around each other's waists, Gloria and me, and then, finally, my mother and me. But when I sit next to her on the bed and I rest my hand on hers, she bats it away. I get up and go to the window. Gloria comes over. "Don't be too hard on your mother," she whispers in my ear, "She's had a hard go of it."

"What does that have to do with her slapping my hand?"

"Nothing," she says, "It's just that long-term patients do odd things; the treatment may be affecting her mind."

Dr. Lenz joins us. "It was nice to see you again, Ben, I'm off for my rounds." Gloria turns sideways and asks my mother if she needs anything; when she declines, Gloria winks at me and leaves, camera in hand, carrying the proof of a bond between Dr. Lenz and my mother that I don't quite understand.

I return to my mother's bedside.

"Your father hasn't come for a visit in three days. Have you . . ." My mother starts to say. The smile leaves her face as she puts both hands behind her head and angles it toward me. Not finishing sentences is something new for her. Before, she delivered declarative statements whole born, like a professional stickler for grammar.

"I see him before work sometimes."

196

"How's he doing?"

"I'm not sure."

"You're what?" My mother doesn't hear as well as she used to. Maybe it's a symptom of sleeping sickness.

"I couldn't say."

"He never talks about me, then?" Displeased, she draws her mouth into a tight radius of effort.

"Not really. Mostly he talks about the company and how much he's looking forward to when we're partners." Over the years, she's regularly asked me about my father, and I used to feel flattered because it made me feel special. During a recent visit, she told me he might not have been the greatest husband, but he was a good father, better than most. I can't judge, because I've had only one father, but I've seen other fathers who seem to be home more than my father, and who are more interested in their families. So, I'd give him a C+.

"Promise me something, Ben," she says, lowering her hands to her sides and pressing them against the sheets, as if she has a pain deep inside. "Think about his offer. He's got his heart set on bringing you in. In his own way, he loves you."

Sometimes I think I'm talking when I'm thinking. This is apparently one of those times.

"Ben?"

"OK. I'll think about his offer."

"You look a little pale. Do you want Dr. Lenz to look at you?"

This is one of her standard observations when she doesn't know what else to say. Sometimes she says I look fragile. Or peaked. Sometimes she says I can calculate ten-digit numbers, but can't manage to match my socks, or that being a genius is a social burden which has destroyed many famous men. And sometimes, she says I'm acting just like my father: not listening, storming around . . . I hate hearing this, but it's mostly true. I'm often surprised to learn that other people know either things about me I'm trying to keep secret, or things about me I don't know myself. Like I sometimes act just like my father.

"Can I ask you a question, Mother?"

"Why don't you sit down, Ben."

I sit on the edge of the bed, take a paper from my back pocket, and unfold it.

"What's that?" she says.

"It's my birth certificate."

"May I see it?"

I ignore her question. I read it out loud:

"'This is to certify that the Certificate of Birth has been filed in this office for Ben Heald who was born on May 18, 1922, and whose parents are Jesse Heald (Father) and Florence Heald (Mother).'"

My mother coughs. "Oh, that," she says. "That was a party gag your father pulled."

"It says that Jesse is my biological father. Right here," I say, pointing at the words, "Jesse Heald and Florence Heald."

She touches a tissue to her lips. "Your father—Arthur, I mean, is your father."

"I have a right to the truth."

My mother moans. "Of course, dear," she says dryly. "Have you asked your father?"

"Last night."

"What did he say?"

"Nothing to tell."

"So, it's what I said."

"He told me this birth certificate is a party gag he had made five years ago as a joke for my uncle." I rest the paper on my lap.

"I don't get what's so funny."

"Well, if you must, dear. Jesse was always chiding Arthur, saying he couldn't be your father because his sperm were weak swimmers."

"That's not funny."

"You don't understand the humor of two Jewish brothers. To embarrass Jesse, who's childless, Arthur had the counterfeit birth certificate made up."

"I don't believe you," I say, impatient now. "You've been lying to me for sixteen years."

She laughs so hard she chokes. "Lying? Don't be ridiculous."

"It's real, it has the date of my birthday."

"Of course, it had to look real. He paid some guy in the Bronx, a well-known counterfeiter." My mother's explanation is weak as tissue paper.

"Birth certificates aren't made, they're vital official state documents that record the birth of a child."

"Where did you find this so-called birth certificate?"

"In his office at home, in the drawer he keeps locked."

"Which you opened."

I ignore this red herring. "I went into his office for a pencil and the drawer was open."

"You went through your father's things?"

"Sorry, I didn't mean to." Immediately I regret saying I'm sorry, since I have nothing to be sorry for.

"Think about this logically, Ben. Why would your father keep a birth certificate in a place where he knows you'd find it?"

"I don't know, that's why I'm asking you."

"What would he gain from that?"

"I'm not sure."

"Put yourself in his shoes. Imagine for a moment: What might motivate you to leave it where your son can find it?"

This thought has never occurred to me, which isn't surprising because I'm clueless when it comes to my father's unspoken intentions. "I don't know. I always wondered why I'm so tall, when the only tall person in the family is Uncle Jesse. And that would explain my gift for swimming. You and Father aren't athletic."

"You sound piqued, dear."

"I'm pretty angry." I fold the paper and put it back in my pocket, then rest my hands flat on my thighs. "You could at least give me an explanation that *sounds* true."

She loses her smile. "Ben, think about it this way: the whole story is so obviously ridiculous it can only be true." She sits up and props her back against her two pillows. "Are you still mad at your old mother?"

"More . . . confused." I smile a smile that I hope will elicit mutual understanding.

"I know you want everything to work by some neat logic, but human behavior isn't always logical." She mutters a low sound, like aha. She turns sideways and looks out at the rain smudging the view. "You'd think with all this humidity and rain, the hospital would bring me the fan I asked for, but no; my pleas do nothing." My mother turns back and tugs at my ear. "I know this is bothering you, dear, but you can let it go. Your father, Arthur, really is your father." She curls her hair behind her ears. "I'm very tired," she says, staring at the door, which I take to be a hint for me to leave. "Come back tomorrow?"

I get up and walk to the door. "Sure," I say, and leave, gently closing the door behind me.

Walking down the hall to the elevators, the smell of floor wax in the air, it occurs to me that they're all lying to me. My father is five feet, six inches, I'm six feet, two inches. So is my uncle. My father hates sports, especially baseball. My uncle played for the Yankees, and I have the same build: wide shoulders, narrow waist, and long arms. My parents have black hair. Mine is brown, like my uncle's. I want the truth, and I'm going to find out one way or another.

23

Inside the New York City Athletic Club, early morning, Saturday, September 10, it's hard to believe that in four weeks I'll be standing on the blocks in the pool at the New England Swimming Championships in Winchendon, Massachusetts. The Athletic Club pool is narrow, only four lanes, but the building housing it is two stories high and has wrap-around galleries for water polo spectators. It's like standing in a warm, humid chapel in deep silence. It's the nearest place I know of in New York City where I feel safe and comfortable, the same as in the Loomsfield Prep pool house. Only here, nobody knows me except Doc Woodworth, my childhood coach.

Two other swimmers are in the pool, chest deep in the blue-green water, laughing loudly, other things besides swimming on their minds. I wonder if I could swim faster if I cared less; nevertheless, I'm feeling surprisingly good about this workout, the whole six thousand yards—240 laps—yet to come. The taste of chlorine in my mouth is getting stronger, even though I'm not in the water yet.

"All right, now, all right, Heald." A voice I know—Doc Woodworth—comes out of the men's locker room, ready to hand me my day's sets on yellow legal paper that gets soggy as I swim, and finally disintegrates, as if to remind me to look forward and not overanalyze the past. "Saturday gift," he yells out and smiles at me as if my last workouts went well (they didn't) and this one's going to be the best one yet (very likely, since the last three I missed my times and collapsed after three thousand yards of broken three hundreds).

"Saturday gift," I say back, waving in the most enthusiastic way I know. I've been working with Doc Woodworth again since my mother and I got back from Quogue, and he'll be coaching me every weekend I'm in the city. I like to think I know him, just as I like to think I know my parents, my aunt, and my uncle, but I don't. Doc Woodworth is large, maybe six feet, but heavy in the shoulders and arms and, in the last few years, thickening around the midriff. He smiles a lot and sometimes glares, depending on how well I swim. He's a dynamo in a UCLA tracksuit.

He knows more about the physics and fluid dynamics of swimming than anybody I've ever met, and his scientific analysis of my stroke mechanics is easy for me to understand. He doesn't just say, "Do it because I told you so," but rather, "Do it because it increases propulsion and reduces drag," and drag is the bogeyman of fast, efficient swimming. I've spent more time with him these last three weeks than with anybody in my family, or with Gloria, without having to know him well or be friends. Doc Woodworth is the best coach I've ever had. He's around forty, and coaches age groupers plus the NYAC elite team, including Olympic medal winner, George Kovak, and spends a few hours a week helping at a soup kitchen in the Bowery. Compared to my father, he's solid and dependable. The father I always wished for.

From back in the bowels of the locker room, I hear again the radio playing Tommy Dorsey's "Marie," which has me thinking of Gloria.

Doc Woodworth walks over to me. "You ready, Heald? This one's a doozy," he says, smiling as if he has a secret.

But it's no secret. It's all on the paper he hands me. Free-style and butterfly sets, totaling six thousand yards. At least three thousand have to be all out freestyle (three one-thousand-yard sets with ten minutes rest). "Saturday doozy," I say. He is as supportive of me as anyone I know, but I'm going to need help getting through this monster workout. "Are you trying to kill me, Coach?" I say, dipping one toe into the water.

"Oh yeah," he says, chuckling. Although he's huge, the human version of a silverback, he's precise in his movements, and it's easy to imagine him powering to wins in national-level college swimming. He studies his stopwatch again, the way he always does while he calculates the split-times he expects from me. "This one's going to remind you about endurance, breathing, and maintaining speed, which you didn't manage last time."

My first thought is *I'll never make it. Either too slow or too fast.*

Doc Woodworth goes to the row of blocks, squats by the edge of the pool, swizzles his hands in the water, and nods. "Water's good today, not too warm." Then he's headed back toward me in the wet heat.

"No excuse, right?" I say. No need to think about an answer; I already know it. Swimming is an individual sport with no one to blame but yourself.

He drapes a meaty arm around my shoulders. "When I was trying to qualify for the US Olympic team, I learned to pace myself in practices. After two months, I didn't even need the clock to know if I was hitting my times." A trace of hair tonic accompanies him around the deck, like his sweet-spicy personal fog. "Now you're gonna learn it, so when you get to Winchendon, you'll know intuitively whether you're on pace." He's nodding, his cheeks partly inflated by thought. Swimming is serious to him. An opportunity to develop yourself. "You ready, kid?"

Before I can answer, he gives me a hefty shove, and into the drink I go. I'm unexpectedly, then, trapped in the instant—too much cold, too much water. I sink to the bottom, get used to the cold, then bob up again, bubbles swarming all around me. He smiles at me—or at his playful push—and I smile back. It becomes a moment of bonding I otherwise never experience.

I do the five-hundred-yard warmup, mixed strokes and drills, then the first thousand in the red zone, about 90 percent effort.

My hand touches the wall.

Doc Woodworth shrills his whistle.

I lie on my back, kicking lightly, negotiating a ceasefire with my lungs.

"Ben?"

"Yes sir." I'm bobbing in a draft from the locker room door. My arms are shivering and my teeth chatter.

Doc Woodworth lets the whistle fall from his mouth, like a disappointed teacher. "What's going on with your pull?"

"Feels OK to me."

He turns, watches the others in lane two, yells, "Early catch, and let's see some serious kicking!" then turns again to me. "Why are you swimming so fast?"

"You told me faster."

"For god's sake, Heald, blood is spurting from your ears." At this, he shakes his head. "You'll never make another five thousand yards."

"Forty-five hundred yards, actually."

"Forgive me, Einstein," he says. "Now swim the rest in red, not purple."

"I'm trying to get ready for the championships."

"Tell me, Heald, why do you have your afterburners on?"

"I'm not holding the water, so I'm speeding up my cadence."

"Give it time, Heald."

"What if it never comes back?"

"Your answer is to go all out in the first thousand?" He obviously believes that the effort question doesn't require an answer, because he goes on. "A brilliant kid like you should know better."

I touch my fingers to my goggle strap, adjusting the cupped lenses better to my eye sockets. "I'm unsure about the two hundred free, I'm not used to swimming such a short event."

"You won't get used to it exhausting yourself in the first thousand."

"I don't feel exhausted."

"That's the problem, Heald." He sighs. "I told you this last week," he says, his voice pinched with frustration now. "You've got to be more aware of your body." He opens his mouth to say more but stops himself. "So, this time keep it red, one minute, ten second hundred splits."

"I was."

"No, you weren't. I clocked you at fifty-eight-second splits."

"It felt slower."

He threads his hands through his hair. He gets down on his knees and touches my shoulder. "You need to follow my instructions. This is not just about swimming, this is also about knowing yourself, testing your limits, feeling what you can and can't do."

"I'll try."

He swallows hard, his Adam's apple bobbing like a fishing lure. "You're a good swimmer, Heald, maybe one day a great one. You've got talent—but you've got to pay attention to what's going on below your prefrontal cortex."

I realize, for the first time, that he's not criticizing me. He's talking to me elite swimmer to elite swimmer. Unlike my father, he wants me to make the most of my swimming talent.

"All right, then," he says, moving to the row of benches along the deck. With the stopwatch in one hand, he smiles at me again. "Stick to the pace this time?" he says in a surprisingly soft voice.

"I'll try," I say.

He shakes my hand in his amazingly large one. "I'm watching you," he says.

All has been said that needs to be said. The rest is up to me. I sink into the water, position myself, and push off, the water streaming around my arms, head, and shoulders; and the day is saved.

$\frac{\sin \varphi}{\pi}=1 \quad 8\sqrt{2} \quad \ln \frac{x^2+x\sqrt{2}+1}{x^2-x\sqrt{2}+1} \; ; \; \sin \beta \quad y=-2\pi\nu g$

$g(x\sqrt{2}-1)\big|_0^\infty = x \quad \frac{\pi}{2\sqrt{9}} \quad \frac{5\nu_i - 5\nu_i}{\sin \beta} = n = \eta(\mu, \quad m = \lim \sum_{i=1}^m$

$s, n_i, i_i) \quad a^3 z; \; n=$

$x^2 \pi \cdot$

24

On Monday morning, thirty-six hours after my mother fell out of bed, a note comes sliding under my dorm room door at 6:00 a.m. I recognize the handwriting: Hedjhal asking me to take over his freshman geometry class at ten that morning. He has an emergency appointment at the dentist. At 9:45 a.m., after breakfast and senior English—we're still discussing the role of Lady Macbeth in Macbeth's downfall—I'm standing in Hedjhal's third-floor classroom watching the ninth-graders come in the way freshmen always do—nervous, their eyes darting everywhere, not knowing that I'm more nervous than they are.

At first, I feel out of control, uncertain of what's going to happen next. But then something unexpected happens. I think about geometry, especially transformations, circles, trigonometry, conic sections, and the laws of sines and cosines. I love all of it. And I'm fascinated. It's unlike any feeling I've ever had in school. I'm buoyant, teeming with laughter, shouting, a feeling of great music coming, an expectation in the air. The snatches of talk I overhear are of football tryouts; Mr. Johnson, their Latin I teacher, who speaks Latin in class; the breakfast eggs; gossip. I'm startled to hear the suggestion that this year Loomsfield Football, the Nittany Lions, will win the New England Prep School league, which seems like a statistical improbability.

The classroom smells like a place I could call home: the detergent used to clean the desks, freshly laundered Oxford-cloth button-down shirts, and the distant sound of rain on the roof catch my attention. It's warm in here, the first warmth I've felt in days. I want to stay here, even if my heart is beating itself into a fury. A smile tugs at my mouth. I bring my index finger to my lips.

The class quiets.

I thread my fingers through my hair, faking confidence. "Dr. Hedjhal is unable to be here. He should be back tomorrow. I'm Ben Heald. I'm a senior here. This is freshman geometry, and today is your introduction to the year's work. Your textbooks are in the back. You won't be needing them today, but you should pick them up on your way out. Questions?"

I check attendance. Then I do what Hedjhal does; I stand by the student sitting front and center, nearest to me. "You are Mister . . ."

"Dunbar."

"Mr. Dunbar."

"Yes . . . sir."

"Heald is fine," I say. "What is geometry?"

Giggles in the class.

"Lines, circles, triangles, all that Euclid stuff."

"Thank you, Dunbar. Geometry is the branch of mathematics concerned with the properties and relations of points, lines, surfaces, solids, and, for those of you who are interested in math, higher-dimensional analogues. We live in a world of shapes and sizes. They are part of our daily lives. We are surrounded by space and different shapes and sizes." They already look like they could fall asleep, so I pull another Hedjhal trick. "Get into pairs and make a list of all the reasons we need geometry in our lives. You've got ten minutes." Immediately the room buzzes with talk, not all of it about geometry. A hand goes up. I check my roll. "Sunderland?"

"Can you give us an example?" More giggles.

"Many different scientific and technological fields require knowledge of geometry. Especially in more advanced and specialized fields, the use and knowledge of geometry is essential."

Ten minutes later, the class comes up with a long list of reasons, some good, some worthless, but I haven't felt so animated since I started my calculus work for Dr. Hedjhal. I lose track of time, and we're still discussing their ideas when the bell rings. The class leaves, most of them grinning. I think, *I'll be happy doing this the rest of my life.*

At lunch, I get a message that my father wants to meet me at 4:00 p.m. After swim practice, I cross the Loomsfield quad and, for a time, I hear the rumbling of my father's yellow Stutz in the school parking area. The engine settles into idle.

I reach the car and climb in, hoping no one sees me getting into the bright-yellow wannabe power car.

"Gotten your first A yet?" he asks.

I'm liking his train of thought. "It's my first week, so no A's yet." I shake my wet hair. "But I taught freshman geometry."

"They let you do that?"

"No, I broke about ten school rules, and I will be expelled."

Turning to me, he laughs. "How'd it go?"

"Well."

"I see," he says. He puts the car in gear and, as we're pulling out of the lot, rolls down the window and holds his hand out, like a baffle. "I've been waiting for this moment since the day you were born," he says, turning his head to wink at me. But his voice is lonely.

Above us, a hawk begins a savage, plaintive call.

He's waiting for me to pick up the conversation. "What moment?"

"Going to the lawyers to sign the papers that make my son a partner in the business." He gives me a grin, his face streaming with light.

This whole business of bringing me in is getting on my nerves. He's been harping on it since my mother first got sick in June. I've told him I'm not interested, but with each rebuff, he gets more stubborn about it, trying to argue me into it. But no argument's going to persuade me. The lawyers' offices are in Norwalk. I've got about an hour to figure out how to say *no* to being his partner. But instead of *no*, I say, "Great." I don't know why, but I regret it immediately.

To keep out of the conversation, I close my eyes and lie back against the plush seat. For the next half hour, I keep quiet, listening to the swing tunes on the car radio, all the way from Loomsfield, through Hartford, New Haven, and New Britain.

Midway between Bridgeport and Norwalk, on Route 1, a rushing sound wakes me up. My father steers us into a fog of spray from a milk truck in front of us, and for a few seconds, we can't see anything but white spray, like a wave is breaking over the car. Whoa." My father stretches out the word. "Pure terror, like flying through cloud. Never know what's ahead, or if you'll see in time." He eases off the gas and frowns, squinting and chattering to himself. We clear the spray. "I've got an idea," he says, in a high pinched voice, glancing at me and then back at the road. "You can tell me how excited you are about coming in."

"I've told you a thousand times, but you don't listen."

He takes a long, pained breath and drops one hand from the wheel and rests it on my thigh. It's a warm gesture, like maybe he's suddenly changed his mind. But then, just when I feel some hope, he dashes it again.

"I hear every word you say, even if I don't acknowledge it," he says. "I just don't agree."

I lean back hard against the seat, my face flushed. "Do I have a say in the matter?

"No, not really," he says, with cold finality. "Life is about letting things go."

Not wanting to argue anymore, I turn on the radio, close my eyes again, and listen to Benny Goodman.

"Everything could be worse," my father says over Benny's clarinet.

He's right, of course. Everything could be worse, much worse—and it's about to be.

In Norwalk, I follow my father two blocks to the Law and Tax offices of Edelmann and Petschevsky. Beside the converted bungalow is a sign that declares "Welcome to Norwalk," with a rusty bullet hole in the final *o*. Inside, a receptionist with a nest of dark hair greets us and presses the button on an intercom contraption. A tall, black-haired man comes in cradling a *Laque de Chine* pen and points it at me. "Ben?"

I nod.

"Abdown Edelmann."

"Nice to meet you, Mr. Edelmann."

"Ab to you."

We shake, and I feel the soft hands of a man used to working with a pencil and telephone.

My father and I trail him into the small, boxy conference

room. It's got one window, like a minimum-security jail cell. We take our seats across from Ab. Then Edelmann's partner, Petschevsky, comes in and hands each of us a sheaf of heavy-bond paper bound with a gold wire clip durable enough to attach an airplane wing.

We sit in silence for half a minute, edged by the ringing of a phone in the next room. I thumb through my allotment: business plan 1938, 1937 balance sheet, income statement, detailed breakdown of the company's assets, first and second quarter financials from all fourteen stores, sales predictions for the next five years, report on the company's general position in the shoe industry, bank statements, personnel files, and plans for expansion into men's and women's casual wear. Nothing of interest. Already, I'm feeling pinched.

"These documents," says Edelmann, tapping his copy with a manicured forefinger, "lay out the agreement to give Ben part ownership of Heald Shoes."

"What part?" I ask.

The corners of my father's mouth turn down, as if he doesn't want me asking questions.

"Fifty percent," says Petschevsky.

No one speaks for a moment. My mind is churning. Unsure, I stare at the orchids sprouting from a Chinese vase on the shelf by the window. A clock somewhere in the suite begins to strike 5:00 p.m.

Petschevsky rolls up his sleeves to reveal powerful forearms. "Ben, if you have any questions, I'm happy to answer them. Anything you don't understand?"

"I'm fine," I say. "I need a few minutes."

"Could I get a cup of coffee?" my father asks. "Black, no sugar." He taps a cigarette from a gold case with his initials on the front, doesn't light it, then grinds the end against the bottom of a glass ashtray. "You don't need to read everything, Ben. You can trust these guys, if that's the problem."

It occurs to me that it's not Edelmann and Petschevsky I don't trust; it's my father. I don't believe we could be fifty-fifty partners. He would never accept that; I'll still be his kid.

"I need some time, that's all."

Edelmann gets to his feet, looks at his watch, a *Jaeger-Le-Coultre Reverso*, and says, "Well, seems we're at an impasse." His eyes are suddenly alert, and I detect a light slouch in the small of his back. "Ten-minute break." He angles himself toward me. "It's a big step, Ben, so take your time. You can sign the agreement when we come back." He uncaps his pen and recaps it with thoughtful slowness. In a warm, sonorous voice that's easy to hear—and no doubt the reason for his success—he says, "OK with you, Arthur?"

My father gives Edelmann an apologetic smile. "Fine."

Edelmann and Petschevsky leave the room.

My father now regards me with curiosity, like he's seeing me for the first time, though my resistance can't be a surprise to him.

I get up, go to the window, and watch a New York 40 in full sail on the horizon, wishing I was on it, headed to Florida where I'd stay in my uncle's hotel. I know what my father wants from me, but I don't know how to do it. I don't know how to pick up the pen and sign my name and give up my MIT future. It seems so permanent and irreversible. When I imagine signing the agreement, my breath comes in short gasps and I see myself at fifty, running around the Heald Store, avoiding customers, feeling full of regret for not becoming a professor.

The two lawyers return and angle themselves into their seats.

I sit down again and fold my hands in my lap under the table to hide my shaking.

Edelmann shrugs his sharp shoulders. "Ben?"

I'm feeling out maneuvered, like I'm an unwitting actor in a play in which all the other actors know their lines and choreography, but I've never read the script. "You can't just make me decide my future like this," I say.

"Ben," says my father. "We've talked about this."

"*You* talked about this." I pull some slack from my tie, and it bites into my neck. "I told you what I want."

"I remember how hard it was for me to sign my name on the new ownership papers after my father died," he says. "My hand was shaking so hard, I could hardly form the letters. Since then, my signature is just AH." Now he gets up, goes to the window, and opens it. Fresh air trails in. He groans. When he wheels around . . . eyes are blue ice. "You've had enough time," he says with the seriousness of a judge passing sentence. "No putting off the inevitable."

Petschevsky pulls a sheaf of papers from his briefcase, a hand-worked leather job; stands; and, counting the clipped bundles under his breath, comes around the table and spreads them out in front of me, one at a time with great formality, like's he's laying out the Magna Carta of Connecticut. "These first ones change the documents of incorporation, making you a co-owner."

A secretary comes in and gives us each an ornate blue pen with Edelmann & Petschevsky embossed in gold on the barrel.

Edelmann holds his up to the light. "Mozart's *Requiem*."

I pick mine up, feel the weight of my father's expectations. My heart is thumping so hard it shakes my body. I skim a few sentences, stare at the words.

"Jesus, Ben," barks my father, squinting like he's experiencing bladder pain, "just sign."

What registers, and registers quickly, in rapid increments, is that he wants me to sign because he wants me to be like him, a man who lives in memories of potential. It's not a simple moment, thinking that your father wants you to give up on a dream, just like he did.

"Ben, why don't you sign and read them later? We can amend them," says Edelmann, easing some slack into the tight wires of his face.

I uncap the pen and line up the papers for signature.

A smile brightens my father's face like a small city of bright lights. He reaches across the table and rests his fingers on my wrist. The tremors in his hand feel like faint shocks.

Petschevsky stands up and nears me, bends close enough for me to hear his breathing, and points at the first line where I'm to sign. "John Hancock goes here and here, and everywhere with a penciled X. Don't forget the date, and the location: Norwalk." He places his hand on my shoulder, where it rests like a mitten of warm sand.

"I'm done," I say.

"What?" says Edelmann.

"I'm leaving."

"You haven't signed," says Petschevsky.

"I'm not signing."

"But—" says Petschevsky.

"Let him go," says Edelmann. "He can sign later."

My father's lips move, but no words come out. Tears well up in his eyes.

I put down the pen, loosen my Loomsfield tie, stand up, and walk to the door, my back to them. It's not a simple moment, to be leaving the offices of your father's lawyers to step out into an uncertain future, determined, yet feeling guilty for letting your father down. He's now slumped over the table with his face in his hands. Disappointing my father is a way worse feeling than him being mad at me, since he's giving me unearned guilt, the worst kind.

$$\frac{\sin\varphi}{n}=1 \quad \frac{1}{8\sqrt{2}} \quad \ln\frac{x+x\sqrt{2}+1}{x^2-x\sqrt{2}+1} \quad ; \sin\beta=c_2 \quad g'=-2\pi\nu g \quad \frac{1}{2}($$

$$g\left(x\sqrt{2}-1\right)\Big|_0^\infty=x \quad \frac{\pi}{2\sqrt{9}} \quad \frac{\partial v_i-5v_\cdot}{\sin\beta}=n=\eta\left(\mu, \quad m=\lim\sum_{i=1}^m$$

$$s,n,i_\downarrow) \quad a^3z; \quad n=$$

$$x^2\pi.$$

25

By the time we get back to the Stutz, the truth of what I've done is sinking in, and I don't know what to do with it. The recklessness I feel about my refusal to sign is as foreign to me as the one-story bungalows and rows of mailboxes along Route 1. I can find no answer in any of it, not in my father's sagging features, not in my calculus book, nor in the billboards outside Hartford: Wrigley's, Pep, Martinelli's Cider. What I'm feeling is the cold repudiation of letting my father down.

I wait in silence, chewing on a Tootsie Roll and watching cars, until my father gives me a nod. "How could you do this to me?"

"I'm afraid I'll lose myself." I sound sheepish, which isn't my intention, but I can't help it.

"Fuck does that mean?" he says, hunched forward a little, stroking his chin with his thumb and forefinger. "You're like an alien, you know that?" he says with an amused smile. In one quick motion, he gives me an affectionate punch on the shoulder. "You're like from Mars or something," he says, with the shadow he has under his cheekbones when he's worn out. "What set you off?"

"I don't know."

"I think you do," he says, waving a hand dismissively.

I'm not sure what to say.

He doesn't look mean; he just looks like my father: dark half moons under his eyes, unshaven, a messy crown of hair. He leans back into the bucket seat and pulls up behind a cement truck, braking late, recklessly close. Is he hoping for an accident? "I had the feeling that when you said *no* you meant *yes*, or *maybe*," he says, glancing at me. "I figured you were testing how far I'd go."

"Sometimes at night, in my dorm room at school, I squeeze my eyes shut and imagine how it might be to be a professor. It doesn't seem so far-fetched to me that I might go to MIT or another university where this might be possible. I like to think about having an office in the MIT Earth, Atmospheric, and Planetary Sciences Building. I imagine my office—a desk with a lamp, a shelf of textbooks I've written, papers to grade and theses to read—or I see myself standing in a classroom with that smell of paper, pencil shavings, floor wax, and old chairs. The scratching of chalk on the board, which is covered with equations. I love those equations: integrals, derivatives, series, Greek letters, trigonometric functions. I believe that I'm meant to be a professor. I knew this the first time I met my Loomsfield math teacher, Dr. Hedjhal. I'm just like him, I've got no other way to be."

Instead of arguing with me, his usual gambit, something shifts inside my father; he falls into silence, like he's heard what I was saying and is running it through his mind.

Twenty minutes later, an hour south of Loomsfield, my father makes a left turn toward the ocean. "Let's go out to Shippan Point. We can talk in the little pavilion."

Ten minutes later, he's sitting on a wooden bench, tilted slightly to one side, pulling at his ear. I'm sitting beside him, an arm's length away. He crosses one leg over the other, wincing as he adjusts himself. Then he gets a twinkle in his eyes, like he's about to try one of his sales techniques on me. I'm expecting him to try to disarm me with a message hidden in a joke. *A father says to his son, "So, my college boy, exactly what did Einstein do that was so smart?" The son says, "He revolutionized physics! He proved matter is energy! That when light goes past the sun, it bends. That—" "Awright, awright!" says the old man. "But from this he made a living?"*

My father leans toward me, his arm along the back of the bench. "You don't know this, Ben, but I was never supposed to be in shoes." He takes in a long breath. "When we were in high school, my father chose Jesse to run the company, not me. I thought it was the most natural thing in the world. I was so proud—and a little jealous—Jesse was so smart and handsome and charming." He shakes his head. "So gifted at baseball and in school—he never talks about that, but he was an A student. I understood that even though I was the oldest, that was the way it was supposed to be—Jesse was obviously better suited to marketing and sales—I mean, every woman in Manhattan would buy shoes from your uncle just to be near him." He stares right past me in the direction of the ocean. For a moment, he seems lost. "Everybody thought that way then, back when he was fifteen. Jesse was the perfect choice." He leans away from me again and folds both hands in his lap. His shoulders are hunched. "Then I went off to flight school, which didn't work out, and New York University." He's breathing hard. "I was, well, if not happy, at least contented in my life the way it was." He takes two labored breaths. "But then when Jesse went into the Yankees farm system, it broke my father's heart." He lowers his voice to a whisper. "The succession plan fell apart," he says, turning his head to stare down at the water. "And then my father died. I found him under the piano, his eyes bulging, and it was just . . . I was nineteen years old, and I had never had a job. I'd worked a little in the store, but my father had trained Jesse to take over, and now, my mother asked me to take over." He sighs again. "I didn't love shoes, but I learned to love the idea of running the company, expanding it, getting to know our customers, making the sale. Now I love the company. I love the elevators. And I don't want to be the one to let down the memory of my father, or let down your mother, or the sales guys. Sometimes, I lie awake at night and I'm afraid that if you won't come in, I'm going to let everybody down." He stands, pacing back and forth. "I've let people down, and people have let me down, but I'm not going to let myself down, not this time."

"I can't sign," I say, avoiding his eyes.

"But you will." He stops and turns to face me straight on. "Because you'll learn to love it like I did, and you'll become Young Man Heald, and together we'll open stores all the way to Miami." He takes a step toward me, then another. "Let your professor dream go. You won't be the first to let a dream go, and you won't be the last. It's the nature of things; life is about letting things go." He's standing still with his hands folded before him like a mourning cherub. "I'll get the papers. You can sign them now." He comes back and sets the sheaf of papers beside me and holds out a pen.

I take the pen, and turn it in my hands, inspecting it for his fingerprints.

He smiles, and a new energy lights his face, arms, and legs, making him seem years younger. "You're wrong," I say.

"About what?"

"Everything."

I stand up and walk to the edge of the retaining wall above the rocky beach. Then I swing my arm back, pen in hand, gather my strength, and launch the pen into the air, where it spins and wobbles like a bad rocket. It plops into the water, making the waves of my quiet rebellion: the dark rings of my confusion in a confusing family in a confusing world, lost in the midst of finding me.

26

The next Saturday, one week after our trip to the lawyer's (and an uneventful week at Loomsfield), the roof of our apartment building looks like a glistening jungle from the intermittent drizzle. It's the two of us—Gloria and me—outside on this wet afternoon. It's the rainiest September I've ever recorded in my weather notebook. The forecast is more rain on the way.

Gloria's got on a sunflower-print dress, the irony of which, on another rainy day, isn't lost on me, and her hair is tied back with a blue ribbon. When we get to the door of the greenhouse, Gloria suddenly hugs me, which takes me by surprise, so I hug her back stiffly. A current of damp, cloudy air shifts around us. We walk into the glass house where my mother used to tend to her flowers. Inside is a spider plant, two Chinese money plants, an inch plant, a deep-purple moth orchid, ten sansevierias, a weeping fig, and a pothos.

"Are these all yours?" she says.

"After she got sick, my mother took up gardening, but she's not much of a green thumb, so I try to take care of them," I say. I water the Chinese money plant with the watering can my mother brought home from Paris. "But now that I have to go back to school, unless my mother comes home soon, they'll die. Except the five Christmas cactuses, which do well indoors and can adapt to low-light environments."

"I'll take them."

"I'll have to ask my mother."

"I'll ask her—I see her every day."

I don't want my mother knowing I'm spending time with Gloria because she'll ask a thousand questions, pry the details from Gloria, and tell me what to do. "I'll ask her tomorrow when I visit."

"That would be great. My mother would love them; she needs something to do," she says, touching a leaf on the Chinese money plant.

Light rain hisses on the glass walls.

Gloria goes to stand in front of one of the orange trees. She stares up into the sky in the direction of the thunder. Her face looks fragile, questioning.

"The rapid expansion and heating of air caused by lightning produces the accompanying loud clap of thunder," I say. I come to within a few feet of her, and I'm talking down. "A lightning strike hits somewhere on the earth's surface approximately forty-four times every second, a total of nearly 1.4 billion lightning strikes every year."

She turns to me and smiles patiently. Close up, I can see the smoothness of her skin, which so enthralls me, I have to make a conscious effort not to touch her cheek.

"Why don't we go out on the roof," I say. "You can see the Empire State Building. Well, most of it."

We exit the mini-greenhouse and traverse the flagstone path with my mother's row of large ceramic planters filled with Vernonia, blanket flowers, aster, and cornflowers.

The raw sun is trying to shine, but far off, over Long Island Sound, louder thunder rattles the horizon.

Gloria climbs up on the guard wall, which is no more than a foot wide, sits, and dangles her legs over the void.

Trouble could be brewing. "If I were you," I say, "I'd get down. You might fall."

Gloria takes no notice. "Don't be such a worrywart," she says in a determined tone.

I'm suddenly slightly panicked, since she really could fall. Or she might turn on me, angry about my warning and seeing what kind of a worrier I am. She must sense my panic.

"For heaven's sake, Ben, I'm not going to fall, no need to look so scared," she says, giggling. "You boys are all the same, all talk, but at heart stretched toddlers."

I turn back, gazing into her eyes again, and my worry subsides.

She points at a bird, her finger tracing its zigzagging flight. "Do birds get sad when it rains?" she hollers.

"Bird don't have feelings," I say.

"And how, exactly, do you know that, Ben Heald?"

"It's logical; their brains aren't as developed as ours."

"They have other ways of knowing, besides logic. People die suddenly, with no logical explanation, or the doctors tell the family that the patient won't survive, but they survive anyway."

"Maybe you're right," I say, not arguing with her, for fear of hurting my chances of a kiss.

She stands up and walks along the edge of the roof, balancing herself by fanning her arms, like a tightrope walker. Then she lowers herself onto the flagstones, which are spotted with rain, and my sense of relief is palpable. My pulse settles into its resting rate.

Lightning flashes to the south, thunder follows, and the breeze pushes a few dry leaves across the path.

She stands in the corner of the terrace, near my weather station. She crinkles her nose. "What's that smell?"

"You mean that mixture of sweet and pungent?"

"Yes, exactly," she says.

I come to stand within four feet of her, not letting my eyes roam anywhere but into contact with hers. Gloria magically becomes the recipient of a lecture on ozone. "That's ozone. It's a form of oxygen. O^3. Lightning splits nitrogen and oxygen molecules in the atmosphere into separate atoms. Some of them recombine into nitric oxide, which reacts with other chemicals and sometimes produces a molecule made up of three oxygen atoms—ozone, or O^3. Downdrafts from that thunderstorm carry the O^3 from higher altitudes to nose level." I feel like an idiot again, lecturing her like a meteorology class at MIT.

Another silence builds between us. With no coat, I'm cold. I want to go back inside the building and stand by a heating vent, but I don't want to leave. No matter how she scared me, or how cold I am, Gloria is the girl I want to kiss.

The sun has gone into hiding behind a massive raft of cumulonimbus. A denser drizzle begins.

I reach around her and open the door to my weather station, revealing a collection of gauges, the names of which I now list, as if that interests her: "Thermometer, barometer, hygrometer, anemometer, wind vane, rain gauge—"

"What's the one that's like a sextant?"

"Ceiling projector. It measures the height of the base of a cloud above the ground."

"You're an odd bird, Ben Heald," she says, and I fear she's given up on me, the weirdo on the Quogue beach, but she laughs.

"I take measurements every day and record them in my notebook," I say, inspired by her laugh. "Weather's one of my hobbies. I'm a weather observation volunteer for the National Weather Service." I feel a spasm of panic as I stare into her narrow, bored eyes. "With observation data, we can track big storms and hurricanes and get out of their way."

"I like to read," she says.

"What's your favorite book?"

"I'm reading *Of Time and the River*."

"Thomas Wolfe. He wrote *Look Homeward, Angel*, right?"

She nods, impressed.

"My mother said it was an 'affecting work of fiction,' though it could have benefitted from editing."

"It's very long, but you can get lost in it, the way you do in your weather observations."

"What's it about?"

"It takes place in 1920, and the main character, Eugene Gant, leaves the South for Harvard, New York, and Europe. He's really determined to become a writer. On the boat home, he meets Esther Jack and falls in love." She takes in the city below, then stares at me. "Thomas Wolfe is so passionate."

Incredibly, for a few seconds, the sun breaks through the thunderheads, red orange and half squashed. Bright panels of light illuminate the buildings along Fifth Avenue, and those four blocks west on Ninetieth Street. Central Park floats below like a rich, green pond of good fortune.

Suddenly, Gloria puts a hand on my waist and pulls me close, the heat of her hip coming through my trousers. She holds out her hand and lets a few raindrops fall into her palm. "I bet you can't measure how the raindrops feel."

She tilts her head to one side and plays with a lock of her hair. She goes up on her toes and whispers in my ear. "You've never kissed a girl, have you?"

"A few times," I lie. I've always been a bad liar, but I've been telling myself this lie so often that I almost sound convincing now.

She smiles as if she knows I've only imagined kissing girls.

The sun fades again, and the drizzle is now a steady rain. Fog has spread through the greenery, as if one of the clouds has lowered itself onto the roof. A wet, earthy smell is all around. In the blue-white mist, a flock of birds—pigeons, maybe—is spiriting around.

"We need to act quickly," Gloria says. Droplets stream down her face. She's soaked to the skin, her hair clinging heavily to her neck. "Let's go back in the greenhouse." She takes my hand and pulls me into the small glass house.

The fog thickens.

"How come clouds don't fall?" she says.

"Clouds are full of water. A cloud one mile by one mile weighs a ton. But they're actually made of tiny particles and ice crystals called hydrometeors that have a very big surface area compared to their size. And because the sun constantly heats up the surface of the earth, the surface warms the air and the warm air rises. The rising warm air pushes upwards and stops the tiny particles in the cloud from falling."

Huge white droplets hit the glass walls, and the wind whistles through the uncaulked cracks. Lighting strobes above us. Thunder blows the sky apart, and rain rips the leaves off the climbing hydrangea by the door.

Gloria nears me like she's floating. Her bangs are wet, and her mascara is running. Her smile reveals her white teeth which glisten like wet porcelain. She tilts herself toward me on her toes. She puts her hand on the back of my neck. Her cold hand sends a shiver down my back. My heart flutters. Her eyes are dreamy. She's so near I feel her breath on my lips and see the laugh lines around her eyes. She studies me, from my eyes to my lips, and I'm doing the same, and we come closer and closer. Right before our lips touch, I stop.

"Are you going to kiss me, or what, Ben Heald?"

I lower my lips to hers and we kiss.

She laces her hands with mine by our cheeks, and I notice how small they are, now that her palms are pressed into mine. I can wrap my fingers around her entire hand. No more awkward pauses, no second thoughts, no worries about what I'm doing wrong—only me and Gloria and our hands fitting together like puzzle pieces.

She smiles at me with a hundred words behind her sapphire eyes.

I kiss her again. She responds with such enthusiasm that I'm taken aback at first, but I quickly regain my composure and re-mind myself of what is happening. I am really kissing Gloria, she is really kissing me, and the rainstorm around us is meaningless.

Nothing can possibly mean more than us right now; nothing can have more beauty than this moment: her small hands pressed into mine, the way her round eyes flutter to a close. Gloria lean-ing into me, her kiss like the beating of a butterfly's wings, soft as the cool breeze of a summer evening in Quogue. It is gentle as trickling rain by the Fairfield River at school and the hooting of doves outside my dorm.

It should never end, the feel of Gloria so close to me. I'm unsure of where I end and she begins. Her entrancing eyes, her smile against my lips, her laugh when I give another stupid lec-ture on the weather, her hair that smells like coconut and how it falls over her shoulder, her raspy voice when she's talking to my mother, and her hands, those strong, tiny hands, squeezing and loosening in my bony fingers in perfect rhythm with my lips touching hers.

But my stupid, *stupid* lungs have to find air, like swimming the two-hundred-yard butterfly, and I'm forced to separate from her with the feeling of an earthquake splitting me in two. Somehow, she manages to inch backwards and disconnect her hands from mine (with another pitiful drop in my stomach) so she can run them through my disheveled hair, and I close my eyes at her touch.

When I open them again, she's radiating such an inviting warmth that I want to kiss her again, but I'm not sure she likes it. When I don't kiss her again, she pulls away. I take a step back, heat rising to my face. "Sorry—shouldn't have done that."

"What are you talking about?" she says softly, watching me bemusedly. "That was . . . it was fine."

"F—fine?" My voice is hoarse. I clear my throat, laughing a little before she makes a move to kiss me again.

I finally notice how close she truly is when my lips close on hers; soft yet immersive, gentle yet powerful all at once, just the two of us, or one of us, rather, and all I feel is Gloria: vanilla, cinnamon, fresh laundry, and lavender in my nose, blond hair and blue eyes on my mind. I want more, so much more, and she knows it, but this time her kiss is short and wet and strawberry sweet. "That was fine. Just fine, Ben Heald."

$\frac{\sin\varphi}{\pi} = 1$ $8\sqrt{2}$ $\ln\frac{x + x\sqrt{2} + 1}{x^2 - x\sqrt{2} + 1}$; $\sin\beta = c_2$ $g^{-} : -2\pi Dg$ $\frac{1}{2}(\frac{1}{\varphi}$

$(x\sqrt{2}-1)\Big/\begin{smallmatrix}\infty\\0\end{smallmatrix} = x$ $\frac{\pi}{2\sqrt{\cdot}}$ $\frac{\partial v_t \cdot 5v}{\sin\beta} = n = \eta(u,$ $m = \lim\sum_{i=1}^{m}$

$n, i_t)$ $a^3 z; \quad n = n$
$^2\pi$.

27

The big Loomsfield pool, which I haven't been in since I kissed Gloria, is in full training stress when I walk in. The sound of voices, splashing, and the coach's shrill whistle are amplified by the arching wooden roof. In every lane, one of the groups—sprint, long distance, and individual medley, all of whom were doing butterfly and breaststroke repeats—are just at that moment winding down. Winded swimmers push off in exhaustion and hang on the end of the pool, winded, sucking air, and waiting for their hearts to slow.

"Go!"

The entire row of butterfliers—and a few freestyle sprinters—angle themselves into the water, then resurface after a few yards, breaking out at full force.

"Go!"

Again, the row of swimmers launches themselves toward the far end, struggling to keep going, praying their hearts won't give out, their legs and arms in severe lactic acid stress. Some of them suddenly, in the middle of the pool, lose all their coordination, and their strike turns into a sloppy thrashing as if their nerve cells have stopped communicating. Eventually, all of them get to the end of the pool, their lungs heaving, their faces barely above the water.

"Awright, good job!"

I dive in without checking in with Coach Winters, so excited by the chance to get back in the water. My dive goes deep, and I swim a lap underwater, turn hard, and sprint all the way back, feeling strong and at peace with a great crazed smile on my face, screaming underwater, "Yes!" I keep thinking, *It doesn't get any better than this, oh my god, Jesus H, I kissed Gloria and said* no *to my father.* The next four laps, I push my muscle cells to their adenosine triphosphate limits, swinging my arms like rotating vectors: straight, with a deep pull. I maximize my hip rotation and keep my head down, my chin pressed against my chest. With a hard six-beat kick, just like the sprinters, I feel for the first time like I could be a real, deadly threat at the New England Championships.

Swimming hard is the only weapon I have against my frustration. I'll do twenty-five-yard sprints until my arms fail, aiming for thirteen seconds per lap. It's exactly the opposite of what I said I'll do, which would be active recovery, "taper" in Coach Winters's words. The first twenty-five, I'm feeling pretty glorious. I'm averaging thirteen-second laps without opening the carburetors. In my head, my father's voice is loud. *You're a self-involved sixteen-year-old. You're not listening to me.* After one lap, at the end of the pool, a JV breaststroker says, "Christ, Heald, I'm swallowing water from your waves." On the twentieth twenty-five-yard sprint, my breakout's still tight and relatively drag free. The breaststroker who swallowed my wave gets out, stares at me, and stomps off to the locker room. Sweat is trailing down my forehead. I'm winded, manage three thirteen-second reps on the next laps, but slow to a series of fourteen-second laps after that. *You don't care about what I want. You're an ungrateful son,* I hear my father saying. I'm slowing down, too tired to take my goggles off my eyes. I'm not a sprinter. I tell myself to stop gliding so much, relax my cramping shoulders, and feet, and stop stroking like a spastic. Every two strokes,

I breathe to my offside to give my dominant shoulder a break. At the wall, a sprinter yells, "You on benzos, Heald?" The next lap's a thrashing fifteen seconds. I hang onto the side of the pool for five minutes. The last fifteen laps are seventeen seconds, giving me time for two haggard breaths before setting off again. This is getting ugly. The last five laps are agony. I beach myself onto the pool deck and lie on my side like a dying whale. How long have I been here? No clue. Delicious fatigue blackout.

"Heald!"

The pool area reverberates with Coach Winters's basso voice.

I open my eyes to see Coach Winters's deck shoes and the wet cuffs of his chinos. Three varsity swimmers are standing next to him, snapping towels at each other, yelping. "What in the name of God are you doing?"

"Resting." I stay on the deck, flat-out busted like the wind's been knocked out of me.

"Explain what you're doing with your hands on each stroke."

"I've been thinking a lot about freestyle technique," I say. "When your hand enters the water, you want to minimize the frontal drag from the hand and the arm. So, first you keep your arm straight with the wrist and the hand in alignment with the forearm. Before your hand enters the water, squeeze your fingers and thumb together, and keep them squeezed when they enter the water."

"Your point?"

"I'm trying to reduce frontal drag maximally after my hand enters the water, so I rotate my little finger on my breathing side."

"You turn your pinky finger down?"

"Of course, it's logical. Turning the pinky down reduces lift, and it reduces frontal drag too. The pinky-down technique in freestyle works great for longer events, since the power comes more from the hips than from the shoulders."

"Heald, when your hand enters the water, I want you to angle your fingers downward and bend the wrist, with the palm down."

"Coach, that's not a good idea."

"That's how the fastest distance swimmers do it."

"Doing that adds significant frontal drag."

"OK, Professor-of-Fluid-Mechanics Heald. What do you suggest?"

"I position my hand in the water with fingers and thumb squeezed together pointing forward, either palm down or, preferably, if time allows, pinky down."

"And then what?"

"Once my hand starts pulling with downward force, I switch to fingers pointing down as quickly as I can, with my hand just inside my elbow."

"And that squeezing you mentioned?"

"I separate my fingers and thumb slightly in order to maximize the pulling force, since once my hand begins moving quickly downward or backward, the flow of water through the small spaces between my fingers becomes turbulent, which effectively increases the surface area of my hand. My thinking is that the larger the effective surface of my hands, the more potential I've got to increase propulsion."

Coach Winters shakes his head. "I heard you want to go to MIT."

"Yes, sir."

"Well, you'll fit right in. They have a lousy swimming program—they all think too much—but everyone's smarter than Einstein."

"OK, Coach."

"What is it you want, swimming like a banshee?"

"I—I'm not sure."

"You gotta be kidding me, Heald. You don't know why you were murdering the water when I asked you explicitly to take it easy. What part of *taper* don't you understand?" Frustration contorts his face.

"Sorry, Coach."

"Why did I ban you in the first place?"

"I didn't follow your plan," I say, noticing that the other swimmers have gone quiet, listening intently to my dressing down, a few of them sniggering, their belief that I'm a flake confirmed yet again. "Sorry, Coach."

"Sorry? Sorry?" says Coach Winters. He taps one foot on the deck, making little explosions in the gutter wash. "I don't know any way to get through to you."

"My father and I had a huge fight. I was kind of upset."

Now his face warms. "Anything I can do?"

"It's OK."

"I'll call your father, if you want."

"I'm not asking you to do anything."

He wags his head, with a squiggly mouth. "I don't get it. I ask you to go easy and you do God-knows-how-many twenty-fives full out and drive one of my breast strokers out of the pool, and the rest see you ignoring my instructions. I tailor your workouts to your needs, every day a new distance set. What the hell am I supposed to do about you?"

"Nothing, Coach."

"A brilliant kid like you, with everything going for him. But you just don't listen. I don't get it. Why do you keep messing up your swim training?"

"I don't think I'm messing it up. I've done pretty well so far on my own."

Coach Winters is silent, staring at me. Then finally, "OK, I've had it. You're a big kid now, and actions have consequences. I'm not letting you in the pool for two weeks. You remember that."

"You're suspending me?"

"You need to taper, and I need you out of here, so yeah, the pool is off limits for two weeks."

"Two weeks? That's not fair."

"T-w-o."

"Please Coach, just one week, you don't understand."

"Oh, I understand better than you know," he says, grinning at some memory he's not going to share with me.

"I need to swim."

"Good, you can come back a week before the championships, but only if you convince me you're serious about listening to me."

"How?"

"That's for you to figure out, Heald."

"But—"

"Get the hell out of my pool." He walks away, his feet sopped from the wavelets the butterfliers are stirring up, still wagging his head.

I want to tell him it's not his pool; it's the school's pool, so it's theoretically the students' pool, but I think the better of it, choosing instead to act like I'm listening. Coach Winters is wrong. I am listening to him. I hear every word. I remember almost every word he's ever said to me. Problem is, for some reason, I just don't do what he says, and I don't even know why. I get to my feet, sit on the bench next to my towel, and watch the other swimmers doing exactly what Coach Winters tells them to do. Suddenly, things are much worse than they were.

28

The day after Coach Winters bans me from the Loomsfield pool, I come out of Thornton Hall after an hour of calculus catch-up with Dr. Hedjhal and stand under the oaks that are positioned around the quad in two rows of perfect symmetry. It's a blue-and-gold Indian-summer day, and I stand on the shadowy side to avoid a group of senior football players who like to make fun of me, who knock my books to the ground, or give me messages from the office that often turn out to be phony. So, the one today—*Heald, you have a message from the office, your uncle is waiting to meet you by the main gate*—may or not be true. I act all nonchalant, but they can smell my doubt, laugh, and walk on. If I walk to the main gate down a long, curved drive and my uncle's nowhere to be seen, the students will have one more reason to call me a flake.

Carrying my calculus book under my arm, I hurry down the drive. And it occurs to me that one of the main qualities of Loomsfield Prep isn't that the education is better than at another prep school or even the best public high schools; it's that, at first glance, Loomsfield gives you a feeling of everything being better here. And not just that it's better than other nearby schools, but that it's better than anywhere you've ever been, so that the nasty details of prep school social life are like the inconveniences of a luxury cruise ship—nothing to complain about.

After ten minutes of waiting for Jesse, I'm ready to turn around, but then he stands suddenly before me on the other side of the iron gate. He must have been behind the brick column that holds up the gate. Below his Florida-sun-bleached hair, his muscled arms are zipping up his trousers and tucking in his short-sleeved fruit-salad shirt—he's been letting water, my father's euphemism—out of sight of curious Loomsfield eyes. He waves, like a New York Yankee greeting his fans, and I feel small and unsure.

I wave, wondering what he's doing here.

Somehow, I know, by the confident way he swings his arm, the other dangling easily at his side, that I'm going to be surprised by what he's about to tell me, and I will then have it in my mind forever. Some days I'm tired of remembering everything, too much junk in my head. Whenever he's about to deliver bad news or tell me something that will change my life, he fidgets like a reluctant witness to some minor Heald scandal or another. I immediately assume he wants more help with Whispering Palms, where he spent the last two weeks. And I feel my anger boil up, since whenever I agree to help him, he forgets to thank me.

He runs his hands through his hair. "Come on out, Ben."

"Why are you here?"

"Need to show you something."

I swing open the heavy gate, like the portcullis of a medieval castle, and walk over to him gingerly, trying to control my anger.

"Well?" he says.

"I thought you were in Florida." I'm surprised by my steely tone. I step back, my face flaming.

He gives me a contemplative stare. "Long story," he says. "Short story, I'm here now."

"You never thanked me for the Zwillman deal."

"Sure, I did." He takes a cigarette from a gold case he keeps in his back pocket and lights it.

"You said you had more important things on your mind." I put my hands in my pockets and make fists. "It sounded like you were having intercourse."

After a long drag, he waves it. "Trying," he says, winking again. "Kissing, that's what you heard."

"You called me stupid, because it could have gotten *you* killed."

"It *was* stupid," he says, twisting his mouth.

"I took a risk for you and helped with your business plan."

"Don't get all whiny, Ben. Women don't like it." He shakes his head and takes another drag. "Ben, it's not like I'm ungrateful."

"Yes, it is."

"Don't do that. Not now. We've got more important things on our dance cards," he says, walking toward his car, which is parked fifty yards away. I follow, still drawn to my uncle like a magnet, although I'm still angry at him. We climb into a car I've never seen before, a Bahamas-blue 1935 Lincoln K convertible roadster.

After a twenty-minute drive past houses that were built during the American Revolution, my uncle turns onto a dirt track. He steers the car into a pull-off, hits the brake hard, eases up under a tree, cuts the engine, and says, "Short walk from here."

We tromp through some piney woods and come to a large clearing where the sun is lighting the tops of the trees gold green. Before us stands a relic from the National Weather Service's past: a wooden observation tower, an airstrip the weeds have commandeered, two Quonset-huts, and a low building with a tin roof.

My uncle leads me to the low building, fishes a key from his pocket, and opens the padlock. We go into a windowless room that smells like wet newsprint, which he sweeps with a flashlight. He flips a switch, and five wall lights flicker on. The room is surprisingly well furnished in dark teak, like the galley of a schooner.

He walks over to the miniature bar, which is draped with an American flag and hosts a row of bottles with no labels, and gives me a wry smile. "Want a drink?"

"I don't drink."

"Not even a beer?" he says, with an impish smile.

"I'm in training, New England Championships in three weeks."

He nods. "The reason I brought you here—"

"It smells like alcohol."

"This is the little room in the woods where I print money."

"Counterfeit?"

He chuckles, but his eyes are hard as flagstones. "Listen now, very carefully. Before you come into our shoe business, you need to know certain things."

"OK," I say extra obligingly. But a worry flashes behind my eyes. Here's the part where he tells me things I don't want to know and will never be able to forget, just like my father, mother, and aunt. I never know what to say, so again, I nod like I'm listening, but I'm thinking about how to improve my freestyle stroke. *How much do I bend my knees when I'm kicking?*

My uncle sits at a small round table that would be perfect for a four-hand game of poker. Fanning the room with his arm, he says, "You need to know how all this fits into the Heald scheme of things."

"I'm not coming to work for you."

"Before you go work for Arthur," he says, scanning my face. "You need to know how Heald Shoes *really* works."

I pluck at my lip. *What's the most efficient way to pull my arm backward in freestyle?* I wonder.

"Arthur isn't who he pretends to be."

"He isn't my biological father, right?" I don't know it for a fact, but I'm convinced of it.

"No, that's not it," he says, with a weak avuncular smile. "It's the business that isn't what it seems to be." He purses his lips and exhales a loud breath. "It hasn't turned a profit since 1929."

"I'd know that; I've helped with the books."

"You helped with the *official* books." Tension, like acrid woodsmoke, spans the space between us. "Not the *actual* books."

I stand motionless, stunned. Either he's lying to me, or I'm completely wrong about Heald Shoes. I can tell you his pitching statistics from his days in the Yankees farm system—I memorized them every week—but I'm still struggling to read him.

He takes a second loud breath. "When Arthur was out selling Thousand Milers to the Irish Policemen's Union, ingratiating himself with the suits, and schtuping salesgirls from Bergdorf-Goodman, who ran the company?"

I mull it over. "Myrtle?"

"She kept the books," he says, his arm bent over a chair back.

I nod and pluck my lip again.

"I ran it," he says, a scrim of pride in his voice. "And how do you think I kept the store afloat after '29, when nobody was buying shoes?" He rubs his thumbs and forefingers together.

"Lease holds."

"That was Artie's story," he says, gulping. "Make sense to you?"

"I always wondered." Again, I can't believe I missed something so obvious.

"Lease holds don't bring in enough," he says. "So, I opened

a bunch of speakeasies. Underneath most of our stores, some in separate locations with heavy foot traffic and ample parking." He flashes his huge beaming smile. "You never figured it out? Amazing."

I shake my head. Words are failing me more than usual. I search my mind for clues I must have overseen. Finding nothing, I sit at the table across from him and wait for more. Better to let him explain.

He gets up, comes toward me, glancing left, then right, seemingly assessing whether I'm buying his story, which is, in my mind, unbelievable. It's downright bad.

"It's all pretty simple," he says, opening a Genesee 12 Horse Ale. "Old Man Heald and Heald Elevators are good brands, but shoe retail doesn't bring in the shekels. Henry Morgan's made Heald Shoes a household name." He goes over to the rows of bottles, picks one up, and points it at me like a weapon. "In 1923, I opened a drinking and gambling club under my store on Madison and started making buckets of money. Things were fine until '31 when Prohibition ended in the city. Then I had to convert them into bars, but I offered more than drinks. I've still got most of my patrons, though I'm paying heavy protection. I've got them in Manhattan, the Bronx, Brooklyn, Queens, Staten Island, and two in Jersey." He spreads his arms to show me that he's talking about the big wide world. "Just like this one, only bigger and more profitable. Plus, three out on Long Island—one in Quogue, by the way, which makes it nineteen. And a new one in Islamorada, called the Tiki Bar, opening next week, the twentieth." He puts the bottle back on the shelf. "Whispering Palms is a cover for washing the cash from my illicit trade."

"Illicit?"

"Gambling, prostitution, narcotics." He tilts his head, as if he's waiting for the right words to form in his brain. "I needed your help with the business plan because Whispering Palms needs to look legit." He makes an exhaling noise. "In 1935, I cleared half a million a month, and I pumped ninety percent of it back into Heald Shoes." He beams with obvious pride.

"*Cleared* a half million a month?"

"The cops on Long Island and New Jersey stopped playing ball, so I shut ten of the locales. Now we're down to two hundred thousand a month."

I swat away a fly buzzing around my head. "But why here, in an old airfield?"

He squints at me. "Your father wanted to keep it open while you're at Loomsfield, but closed it last spring because the police were on to us."

"The whole time, my father knew?"

"He was helping me put the stacks of cash in bags three nights a week."

I get up and move to a couch across from him and close my eyes for a few moments to ponder these revelations. I've got a thousand questions, but I settle on what seems like the most important one. "How come you're telling me this now?"

"In case you come into the business."

My uncle could be making this all up for some reason I don't understand. My father's words echo in my mind: *Jesse never tells the truth, or he only tells the truth that suits him.* But then again, what he's saying makes sense. I've never seen my father do anything that resembled *running* a business. Once, for the fun of it, I calculated that, to make a profit, the business would have to sell ten times the number of shoes at higher margins. What worries me is how I could have missed the now-obvious signs. I saw what I wanted to see. My father is good with people and a gifted salesman, but that doesn't mean he's good at the other aspects of the business, or that the business is sustainable.

The conversation stalls out.

My uncle makes a tight smile and turns in his chair. "What are you going to do?"

"First, let me get this straight: my father is pushing me into a shoe business that's only making money because of your mob connections."

"If you put it that way."

"He's been trying to bring me on board a sinking ship at the *fucking* expense of my academic dreams." I've never said the word *fuck* before to anyone in my family. I turn and go out the door into a cloudburst. The rain pelts the trees with the sound of a threshing machine, and I aim my face upward.

The door behind me opens, and my uncle comes out. "Ben . . ."

"He's conning me," I yell, water streaming down my cheeks. "Just like you're conning me."

"We were *protecting* you."

"No," I scream, adrenaline raging inside me. "You were protecting yourselves. And I get to go back to school where the old-money kids will find out I'm actually a nouveau-rich kid whose family made it big off its mob connections."

"I know how you feel."

"You have no idea how I feel, and neither does my father."

The rain is falling harder than in a shower.

He grabs my wrists quickly, so hard it aches. "I care about you. More than you know."

I don't know what to do with this revelation; the rain is obscuring my vision and running down my back under my shirt.

"You're not made for the shoe business, Ben," he says, straightening to his full height.

"I know. That's why I told my father I'm not coming in."

"That's good. You're proficient at exactly nothing the business requires, except accounting and taxes." He glances at me, then releases my wrist, which throbs.

I move under a tree where the rain eases off, and he follows me. "My father's really disappointed. I'm afraid he'll never speak to me again or disown me."

Then Jesse says something that surprises me. "When I left home at eighteen to play ball"—his throat is choked up—"my father didn't speak to me for two years."

I feel a smile start. It is a little thing, this admission, but it helps. I can see he is trying to help me. If Jesse could survive his father's silent treatment, maybe I can, too.

"You have a passion for math, and if I've learned anything, it's that life is happier if we follow our passions."

"I know, I know. You make it sound easy. I feel confident now, but I'm afraid I'm not strong enough for this."

He pats my shoulder soothingly. "When you were a kid, you were skinny as a popsicle stick, you stuttered when you got nervous, and you were afraid to say what you wanted. I know. I was there a lot. But that's all over now. You'll be strong. You know why?"

"Why?"

"Because you're like me. You're not going to give up on your dream, because you know that if you do, you'll regret it for the rest of your life, and that scares you more than saying no to the business."

"Will you help me, Jesse?"

"Of course, Ben. I love you like a son."

This admission feels like something I've always wanted.
My uncle gives me a bright wink. "And Ben . . ."
"Yeah?"
"I was never here."

$\frac{\sin\varphi}{\pi}=1$ $\overline{8\sqrt{2}}$ $\ln\frac{x-x\sqrt{2}+1}{x^2-x\sqrt{2}-1}$; $\sin\beta=c_2$ $g'=-2\pi\nu g$ $\frac{1}{2}(3\varphi$

$(x\sqrt{2}-1)\big|_0^\infty=x$ $\frac{\pi}{2\sqrt{9}}$ $\frac{\partial v_i \cdot 5v}{\sin A}=n=\eta(\mu,$ $m=\lim\sum_{i=1}^{m}c$

$n_i(i_i)$ a^3z ; $n=r$

$^2\pi$.

29

Today, Friday, September 23, two weeks into my senior year at Loomsfield Prep, I take the early afternoon bus from Windermere back to the city to visit my mother. For a few weeks, I've been observing my family's nonstop talk about my mother's condition. Much of what's said is highly speculative; some is downright conspiratorial and even ridiculous.

My father believes Dr. Lenz is trying to keep my mother in the hospital so they can see more of each other. Aunt Myrtle builds on my father's theory, believing that Dr. Lenz infected my mother intentionally so she could discover a new arsenic treatment for African Sleeping Sickness ("I don't trust those Austrians.") My uncle drops hints that Dr. Lenz is "lavender" and "in the life," and she has brainwashed my mother into some kind of perverse dependency. From what I can tell, evidence for any of these bizarre beliefs doesn't exist, since my mother most likely caught the disease from an infected mosquito and is slowly recovering thanks to Dr. Lenz' research and treatment, which has nothing to do with Dr. Lenz and a queen-size bed.

So, late this afternoon, two hours after I hop off the Greyhound at Penn Station, I'm at the hospital waiting for my mother to wake up. I'm washing my hands in her room and listening for the first footfalls of Gloria's crepe soles (she's the real reason I'm here, after a week of late-night phone calls), when I hear Henry Morgan's voice over the radio: "Old Man Heald is the man to see when you want to be taller than she. Old Man Heald does a lot for you. Confidentially with his elevator, elevator, elevator el-e-va-tor shoes. There is one Heald shoe store at 128 West Forty-Second Street."

My mother has changed dramatically from the last time I saw her. A week ago, she was still an advertisement for death warmed over. Now, what's happened to my mother's appearance is nothing short of amazing; I didn't know it was possible to recover so fast. Her yellow-brown curls are back, her hair shiny. Her small face, previously pale as onion skin, with deep dark grooves under her eyes, is smoothed out. The deep grooves are mere shadows. My mother was never a beauty queen, and the sleeping sickness had made her small mouth and pointy chin fade into a face dominated by a wide nose and rough skin. But now she's taken years off her appearance. Her eyes are bright and her skin shines like it's been resurfaced. You could call her handsome again. She's no longer wearing the green smock of a week ago, but rather a white dress with a low collar and long, wide sleeves. To make her happy, I'm wearing my Brooks Brothers blazer, slacks, and a pair of Heald loafers with a penny in the leather strip across the uppers.

A knock rattles the door, and Gloria walks in. She winks at me, then bends toward my mother, "Time for your IV therapy, Florence." I do a double take, surprised by the familiarity. She takes out a thick syringe with tubes that lead into a bag full of clear liquid.

"It beats dying," my mother says, her eyes half closed.

"What's that?" I say, finding Gloria's eyes.

"Saline solution, for fluid therapy." She's at my mother's side, rubbing alcohol into her forearm with a cotton swab. "Dr. Lenz got the idea from cholera treatment, where they cure the patient by rehydration."

I brace myself for what's coming next: the needle.

Gloria pushes the sharp silver tip into the fine skin in the crook of my mother's elbow.

My mother gasps, twists her face in pain, clenches her hands into white fists, and lets out a ragged sigh.

Gloria tapes the needle flat against the skin and squeezes the rubber bottle. My mother says, "I feel flush," and rests her head back on the pillow.

Gloria checks the drip bottle, flicking it with her middle finger, and puts more needles in a line on the instrument tray.

I notice Gloria staring at me, like she did when we were on the roof and I was explaining why clouds don't fall. It's almost as if she wants to ask me, "Who are you?" Or more to the point, "What are you thinking?"

"How do we know she's dehydrated?" I ask.

"Dr. Lenz says so."

"How does she know?"

"Florence hasn't been eating or drinking enough." Again, the use of my mother's first name strikes me.

"So, she doesn't actually *know*."

"It's more of a hunch, I guess." She smiles, patient as ever, her eyes as blue as a spring sky. "Any more questions, Dr. Heald?"

"I read about the risks: kidney failure, soggy lung, air in the line, phlebitis, disrupted organ function, intravascular injection, hematoma. Isn't this risky?" I say. "What about an allergic reaction to the electrolytes?"

Gloria makes a tsk-tsk. "At worst, swelling in the surrounding tissue."

"Please, Ben," my mother croaks toward me. "Enough of the third degree." And then to Gloria, "That needle is fatter than a metal straw. Any more instruments of torture today?"

"Mother, a carelessly placed drip can kill you." I bite at my lower lip.

Gloria turns to me, glaring. "I've seen a hundred people die. I know the signs, and your mother doesn't exhibit any of them." Gloria wrinkles her nose as if she smells something bad. "Still worried?" she says.

"Not so much."

She gives me a forgiving smile. "I'm on break now. Join me in the cafeteria?"

"Sure."

She holds out her hand to shake and, when I take it, she tickles my palm with her middle finger. Immediately I'm aroused.

I find Gloria in the cafeteria, talking with Dr. Lenz. I walk over to them. "Your mother is a medical wonder," says Dr. Lenz. "She seems to be recovering. Recovery is rare, but cases have been documented in England and Paris. She's doing so well, I'm going to release her after this round of rehydration therapy. She'll go out to Quogue to recover, and your aunt—"

"Myrtle," I say.

"*Ja. Ja.* Myrtle will live with her until she recovers . . . well, gets her strength back. She's never going to recover fully from the collateral nerve damage. There will likely be some lasting neurological phenomena."

"When?"

"Now that the disease vectors are in minimal numbers and no longer attacking her brain, and she's tolerated the arsenic well, she should recover in two months."

"I meant, when is she going to Quogue?"

"Tomorrow morning."

"Already?"

"There's no point in your mother staying here longer, and the sea air and quiet in Quogue will be better for her."

"OK, Doctor," I say. I doubt this seriously, and I worry about a relapse, especially since Myrtle is anything but stable, but it's clear I have no say in the matter.

Dr. Lenz inspects her watch, a new Swiss military model. "I'll let you two talk." She says this as if she knows that Gloria has something important to tell me. Have they been talking about me? "I'll be back in a few minutes," she whispers, again with a hint of secrecy, and marches decisively out the door and down the hall.

Gloria gives me what my mother would call a look: hip thrown, mouth mumped, brows worried, arms crossed, like she's been standing in line too long. "Will you tell me something, Ben?" She brings the tips of her fingers together.

"I'll try," I say, a shiver shooting down my back.

"You're a senior at Loomsfield, right?"

"You know I am."

"How old are you?"

"Sixteen."

"Oh," she says. "You never told me. I thought . . ." she whispers.

"I thought you knew," I say.

"How could I know? You told me you're a senior."

"I am, I'm just younger than most seniors."

She starts to say something more, "Oh never mind," she says with a shake of her head. Then she turns away.

I touch her shoulder and she turns back to face me, tears in her eyes.

"How old are you?" I say.

"Nineteen. Twenty in November." Tears leave glistening trails on her cheeks. She tamps them dry with a hankie.

I have no idea why she's crying. Her pretty face and mouth are so near. Possibly she's sad about her father being so near to death. "Is your father all right?" I ask.

"We're careful not to be too optimistic." She fingers the nurse's pin on her chest.

Stuck, I pause.

She sniffles.

"May I ask you something, Gloria?"

She nods, wipes her cheeks with the flowered hankie.

"You know how I feel about you," I say.

"That's not a question." Her voice is clipped, dismissive.

For some reason, I'm feeling dread and defeat, but some hope too. "I don't have a question, I—" I pull her into a hug, tentatively at first, and then more determined, getting lost for a moment in the raspberry notes of her perfume. This feels like home. I could stay here forever.

She pries my arms free and steps back. "—Please, Ben," she says, shaking her head fervently. "Don't do that and not here."

Suddenly I know what's going on, and I feel the floor drop out from under my feet. "Gloria, please."

She rests her hand on my wrist. "Don't say it, Ben."

"I thought, I mean, I felt that . . . there's something . . ."

Gloria takes a long, pained breath and drops her hand. "I felt it too."

But then, just as my heart speeds with hope, she dashes it with almost clinical precision. "Ben, be realistic. There are so many obstacles, I can't even begin to list them." But then she begins listing them anyway. "Our ages, our plans, our interests, our wishes, our backgrounds, our families."

"There must be a way."

"Why try? I'm moving with my family to California in December, so when my father recovers, we'll be nearer to my mother's family in San Diego. If my father has a relapse, my grandparents and uncles can help take care of my father. And I've got a job at Mercy Hospital."

"That's great." Doom is constricting my stomach.

"I've got a life you know nothing about. Plans. Plans that don't include you."

"I see." What else can I say? I step back, my face scorched, and stick my hands in pockets, faking nonchalance.

She rests her hand on my shoulder. "It's not that I don't care." She sniffs.

I give her my handkerchief.

She wipes her eyes and nose with it.

I try to keep my chin from quivering. "I–I–"

"Please, Ben, don't. I have to work."

Dr. Lenz returns, taps the toe of one utilitarian shoe on the linoleum. Sighs.

"Ben," says Gloria, "I have to go."

"But–"

"—Let's just leave things as they are."

"How *are* things?"

"Two young people who met at a special time, shared a couple of moments—lovely moments—nothing more. Who agree to let it go."

"I don't know how."

"We're good friends. Friends is all."

"Friends."

"Good friends."

"But why?"

"I don't want to talk about it," she says with half a laugh. It's so cold in here, the coldest I've felt in days. And then Gloria walks away, leaving me in the hallway, more alone than I've ever felt.

$\frac{\sin\varphi}{\pi}=1$ $8\sqrt{2}$ $\ln\dfrac{x^{-2}\sqrt{\alpha}+1}{x^2-x\sqrt{2}-1}$; $\sin\beta = c_3$ $g'=-2\pi vg$ $\frac{1}{2}\sqrt{3}\varphi$

$\left(x\sqrt{2}-1\right)\Big|_0^\infty = x$ $\dfrac{\pi}{2\sqrt{9}}$ $\dfrac{9v_i\cdot 5v}{\sin\beta}= n=\eta\left(\mu,\right.$ $m=\lim\sum_{i=1}^{m}c$

$n_i i_i)$

$^2\pi$.

30

The next morning, my father, my aunt, and I are at Flower Hospital for my mother's release from what she now calls her "infernal captivity." Dr. Lenz, but not Gloria, joins us at the entrance to celebrate my mother's wholly unexpected recovery—Dr. Lenz has published a paper about it in the *New England Journal of Medicine*—and to wave my mother off. I'm hurt and still confused about Gloria's remoteness; I feel like a schoolboy who waits for the girl who never shows up. Into my aunt's car, a black 1930 Plymouth 30-U with a wide band radiator, a surprisingly middle-class and staid choice for a woman who wears purple dresses and tennis sneakers. We load two steamer trunks and three suitcases into my aunt's car, the collection of clothes my mother gathered during her month at Flower. My mother is a little unsteady in the drizzle, and we watch as my aunt takes my mother's elbow and slowly helps her into the front seat. My aunt starts the engine, puts it into gear, waves, and weaves out into the traffic for the two-hour drive to Quogue. My uncle will be coming later from a meeting in New Jersey, I'm guessing with Zwillman, and my father and I will head out later this afternoon, after he oversees the Saturday morning rush, the busiest of the week.

I spend the day studying first- and second-order linear equations, and by the time my father and I head out to Quogue, I'm so exhausted even my father can't bother me.

When we get out of the city, the rain becomes hard, popping pellets. Drops bounce off the hood of the Stutz. It's coming down so thickly, it would be easy to plow into another car. Out in Queens, through layers of pummeling rain, oncoming traffic is terrifyingly invisible, each car a cloud of spray above slick pavement. This fall has, by now, become famous for its rainfall and torrential downpours. "The devil's doing his laundry," my father says, squinting toward the windshield, seeing not more than fifty feet ahead on Route 27, even though it's still light and he's got the high beams on. The happy reunion with the family still lies ahead—if we don't go off the road into a ditch.

"You excited about the reunion?" my father asks.

"Sure."

"I've got some big news."

"What?"

"You'll find out soon enough."

He's not going to say more no matter what I ask, so I close my eyes and drowse for an hour until we're outside Quogue. When I wake up, the windshield wipers still can't keep up and the sidewalk gutters are small rivers. Squinting to see better, my father shifts down and steers onto Dune Road. "Will you look at that," he says. "The summer places are boarded up. I could never live out here." He's supremely self-satisfied at his choice not to live out here. "It's as if Quogue is holding its breath waiting for the first winter storm."

For a moment, I wish it were summer again, when everything was simpler and more ordered: before my mother got really sick, when my father was in New York City with two hours between me and his expectations, and when I could take readings from the weather station, swim in the surf, and watch the Girardin brothers, Margaret, and Peggy at the beach.

A mile up Dune Road, with high surf to our right sending salt spray into the passenger-side window, my father navigates the Stutz into a gap in the beach-plum hedge, the tires crunching on the crushed shell surface as we pass the sign he had made—Temporary Sanity—and pull up next to my aunt's Plymouth and my uncle's new convertible.

Though I can't imagine anything more excruciating than a family get-together, on the good side, I'm relieved to finally be here. We avoided a head-on crash and stayed out of a ditch. The tension in my neck has given up, and my head doesn't hurt.

"Your uncle changes cars more often than women." There's a note of jealousy in my father's voice, which I understand, because I often wonder how it must be to not have to work for a kiss, to have women throw themselves at you, the only work being to decide which ones to kiss and which ones to decline. "He's just not reliable, your uncle," he says, as if this makes Jesse's animal magnetism somehow less painful to behold. "Hey! Your Aunt." He points over excitedly at her, as though he's just seen Myrna Loy, who's sitting on the porch swing behind sheets of rain, watching us pull into the driveway.

My father gets out of the car in the squall, opens his umbrella, and heads for the front door, leaving me alone in the passenger seat. It's as if he's forgotten that I'm sitting in the car, and I'm feeling the unsettling sensation of being unseen. Raindrops as big as white grapes are making little explosions on the hood. Inside the car is a rushing sound; the windows are quickly steaming up. Sitting in the downpour, it strikes me that the front of the house, even though it's protected by a cement retaining wall, is only two feet above sea level, dangerously low for a full-moon high tide, which starts tonight.

My father tromps halfway to the house before he stops and bangs his palm on his forehead. He comes back, his ring of hair plastered to his skull, water streaming down his face, and opens the door for me. "Hi, are you Ben? I'm Artie, you can call me Flex. What kind of shoes can I do you for?" He's making light of his distractedness, and once again, I understand why customers love him: he can make you feel that life can be light, that you are the most important person in the world, because he can be suddenly, unexpectedly present.

When we get to the porch, my aunt hugs me and I'm lost in her perfume, something with lilac and cinnamon notes. She leans back, still holding my waist. "Well, Mr. Tall and Handsome."

At the small distance of a foot, not looking at her, I let my eyes roam anywhere but into contact with hers. My aunt has become, not her old self, but the person who wouldn't tell me the truth about my paternity.

"Taller than your uncle," she says, letting her hands fall from my sides. "And much more cleverer."

"That's not a word," I say, cold and wet, though not wanting to leave. "And the grammar's wrong."

She winks, as if she's pulled one over on me, which I suppose she has. "Maybe it's not," she says, "but it's all the truer." She takes my hand and leads me inside.

I notice, as I cross the living room into the large kitchen—passing the picture window with the wide view of a gray dome of cloud—that a pungent gravlax and garlic-bread smell is floating about, as if the celebratory catered food my mother ordered stands in contrast to the tense atmosphere of my family getting together.

Ten minutes later, everybody's in the kitchen, which is as large as the living room. There's a table for eight in the center, a restaurant stove, a wide counter, and cabinets with square holes in the doors so you can see the flatware. My mother is arranging canapés, corn on the cob, and salads—potato, iceberg, tomato and red onion, coleslaw—on silver trays. She's put out rows of gravlax and bagels, my father's favorite lunch. Jesse is standing at the window, leaning against the frame, smoking a cigarette like an actor waiting for his next scene. When he spots me, he gives me his own big smile that says a whole world of things have happened between us, and more will likely happen today. My aunt is sitting at the table, her hands folded in front of her like she's praying. My father's sitting at the opposite end of the table from my aunt, swirling the ice cubes in his scotch on the rocks, waiting for the right time to share the big news he's been wanting to spring on us.

"Where did you get all this," I say to my mother.

"Fratelli's, next to the public library," she says. "Incidentally, I saw that Apthorp girl . . ."

"Peggy," I say, smiling.

"Why yes, she mentioned that she saw you on the beach. Are you two a thing?" She sniffs a lax canapé and looks down at her new pumps.

"Haven't heard from her." My parents don't know about Gloria, which is how I want things to remain.

"You know who's a thing?" my father asks.

"Who, dear?"

"You and I, my gorgeous Florence." He gets up and hugs my mother from behind. She drops a fork, seemingly surprised by the embrace.

He picks it up, bowing like a court jester as he holds it out to her with a big comical clown smile.

"Put it in the sink, dear, it's been on the floor." Her expression, a weak version of her old smile, has disapproval for my father's antics written all over it.

He takes a step back, pouting like a wounded child.

Although she's much improved, she's still tired and brittle: hollow crags mark her cheeks, like rough dents. But her hair is a perfectly coiffed helmet. "I invited Dr. Lenz for some medical advice," she says.

"I thought we agreed," my father hisses. "Only *family*."

"After her ordeal," my uncle says, "Lenz practically is family. She spent more time with Flo than you ever did. And besides, if she has any brains, she won't try to drive out in this rain. She could be flooded right off the road," he says, with a wide, laughing mouth.

"So now you're the family shrink?" my father barks.

My uncle straightens up unexpectedly, his bearing erect, points an index finger at my father like a pistol, and makes a shooting sound.

"You missed," my father says.

The tension is making me uncomfortable. So much is going on between the words, I want to run away. I only want them to get along—which, I see, they sort of do.

My mother drops her keys at her feet. "How clumsy," she says. "My arm still hurts from all those transfusions."

Relieved by the distraction, I pick them up and hold them out to her.

"Sweet boy," she says.

My uncle comes over to us. "Anything else we can do for you, Flo?" He plants his hand on my mother's rump. I've never heard my uncle call my mother Flo to her face, in front of my father, and the familiarity of it takes me aback.

"No, not really," says my mother in a weak voice. She's usually a confident hostess, but now, with her frail appearance, even though she's supposedly in recovery, I feel like my mother is slowly disappearing, and it scares me.

I go to the side window. A few nautical miles offshore, dense clouds are amassing, and the sun is shining weakly as if through rice paper. My father joins me. "Those clouds are weird, kinda low, and ragged."

"Scud clouds. They form when warm air from outside a thunderstorm is lifted by the updraft. Those big, thick ones are cumulonimbus and nimbostratus."

"Smarty pants," he says and gives my thigh a friendly slap. Then he goes back to his place at the table and clinks a spoon against his glass.

A silence descends on the room, like a fog of tension.

I raise my hand like a third-grader and feel stupid again. "I've got a question," I say.

"OK, partner," my father responds.

My mother gives me a worried stare, as if she's anticipated that I'm about to shatter her catered idyll.

"I want to know who my father is."

"Ben, please, not now," my mother says. "I thought we agreed to let this go." This time, her smile is strained and her large eyes, suspicious.

"You agreed with yourself to let it go," I say, not smiling. "I never agreed." But it's obvious I'm not getting any further without one of them stepping in. So, I offer an I'm-sorry smile to my father, hoping to play off his expansive mood. I hold his gaze, and watch his cheeks turn red. "The answer to your question is simple," he says, "but like most things, it's complicated."

"Wha-at?" I say. *Calm down*, I tell myself. But I can't calm down. I feel like picking my father up and throwing him through the living room window. *I hate you*, I want to shout, but I don't. I can't. Again, I'm on the verge of saying what I feel, but I don't want to make a scene or say something I might regret.

My uncle gives me a fierce gaze. "You want the truth?"

"Yes."

"Really?"

"I wouldn't have asked."

"You can't handle it."

"Try me."

"You're expecting more from the truth than the truth can deliver—you think knowing one way or another is going to make a difference, but I can tell you, it's not, you're still who you are."

"Jesse, don't," my mother pleads.

Precisely what's happening here, between them, I don't really know. Dark intimations are in the air, but I can't give voice to them.

Ignoring my mother, my uncle grins and kneads his fingers, like he's warming up to throw a fastball.

And then, without him saying anything, I catch on—I'm always the last to catch the most obvious signals. I know exactly what he's going to say.

"Artie isn't your biological father," he says. "I am, and Florence is your biological mother."

Although I've known this intellectually for weeks, my uncle's pronouncement makes me feel lonelier than I've ever felt, so lonely my feet are cold and my neck is stiffening up. I'm trembling. I look at my father again. I look around at the others, waiting for comfort, though I don't know what comfort would look like. What helps when you learn that you've been living a lie and been lied to for sixteen years? What helps when you found your birth certificate that proves the lie, and they've made you feel like an idiot? I feel like I'm going to be sick. I look at each of them, one after the other, and not one of them catches my eye. I go to the sink, splash water on my face, walk to the table, and sit. My hands and face are still wet. There's tremors in my legs. I've left the water running.

My mother goes to the sink and turns off the faucet with a shaking hand, the back of which has kept its blue tint. Then she looks over at me. "I dreaded this day for sixteen years."

"You should have told me."

"Why?"

"Because I had a right to know."

"But you turned out fine, dear."

"That's not . . . you're confusing the morality of not telling me with the good result of my upbringing." I don't want to listen to her—or rather, their duplicity.

"I've been wrong about many things," she says, "but I wasn't wrong about this—*we* weren't wrong about this."

"So, you all agreed to lie to me?"

"It wasn't a lie, it was . . . an alternative fact."

"What? That's not logical. A fact is a fact, and here's another fact: you kept the truth from me. That's a conspiracy."

"Ben," my mother reasons. "You are who are. It's hard not to be. The question of who conceived you makes no difference. I'm your mother, your father is your father, and Jesse loves you like a father."

"He *is* my father."

"We all love you," she says in a syrupy whisper. "You've got it better than millions of other young men."

Still trembling, I turn to my aunt. "You told me you have no right to share certain things. I knew you weren't telling me the truth. You were too afraid to tell me to answer my question." Then I turn my gaze back to my father. "I asked you if Jesse's my father. I asked you umpteen times, and you said Jesse was just pretending to be my father because he's a loser." I stop to catch my breath. "That's what you said, *Jesse claims to be your father,* but that he and Mother *never had intercourse.* You said the very idea of it was preposterous."

"I never said that," my father says.

"That's exactly what you said."

"Ben, calm down." My mother is speaking in some kind of soft, psychiatrist tone.

I'm gasping for air. "Just last week, you told me my birth certificate was a party gag." I pick up a fork and squeeze the prongs into my palms.

"Ben, you need to hear this, really listen. Can you do that?"

I squeeze harder. "Yes."

"When your mother and I got married, we couldn't have children. We were having a bad time. I did some things I'm not proud of—"

"Things?"

"With other . . ." He casts his eyes down and lowers his head. "And. And your mother and Jesse . . ." He nods sadly, then sits on his hands and rocks back and forth.

"They had intercourse."

"Your mother got pregnant with you." He turns his head toward my uncle and meets his sad stare. "We agreed that your mother and I would raise you." He drops his head further until his chin rests on his chest. "And you were—are—the best thing that ever happened to me." Suddenly, he's a small man who couldn't conceive a child and whose wife had intercourse with his taller, movie-handsome brother. And now he has to admit it to his adopted son, in front of his brother. He's shrinking with shame.

My mother leans forward and rests her desiccated hand on my father's wrist. "At the risk of redundancy . . . Arthur is your father, dear," she says, now calm, like a person used to arguing. "He read you King Arthur stories in bed, he paid for everything, he took you skating in the park and rowing in the swan boats— he was a good father."

My father touches her hip.

I catch my mother's odd expression of anger and shame and regret. "Why didn't you tell me sooner?" I say to her.

My father comes to her rescue. "I—we planned to tell you, every birthday since you were ten. I had a speech ready, but then I couldn't do it," he rasps. "If we'd told you sooner, you'd have been traumatized for life."

"So why now?"

My mother whispers in my father's ear. He smiles and leans back in his chair, as if to clear the way for her to speak. "We're all getting older, my health is fragile, you were asking questions, Dr. Lenz recommended it."

"You mean, Utte, your girlfriend?"

"Dr. Lenz."

"Did Dr. Lenz tell you how I'm supposed to deal with this?"

"Time."

"An hour, a week, seventeen days, three months, how much time?"

"Dr. Lenz says trauma manifests itself in different ways in different people."

My father, who's been resting his head on folded hands at the table, sits up. "I'm sorry we didn't admit the truth a long time ago."

Although I expected this news, hearing it, the actual words, goes through me like an electric shock. Before I can even catch my breath, I understand that everything has changed—that my heritage, family history, relationships, and even my original birth certificate were bogus. My identity has collapsed like a building imploded, all because my father isn't my real father.

I'd always felt like an outsider in my family, but never believed I was one. I explained away my closeness to my uncle and my height as a lucky draw from the gene pool. I like my uncle more than my father. He's funny, confident, and handsome, the kind of man a kid my age wants to have as a dad. His pride in me sometimes seems like the scaffolding of my life.

It's been easy enough to explain feeling like a misfit. If I had little in common with my father, I convinced myself it was because I got more of my mother's genes, though she seemed unlike me in many ways. And when gut feelings of being a stranger among strangers gnawed at me, I only had to look in the mirror at my brown hair, long arms, and six-foot frame that I shared with my uncle to be convinced that my father wasn't my biological father.

But I didn't really believe it was possible that Arthur wasn't my father, because that required me to imagine my mother doing things with another man that I didn't want to imagine. So now, I'm really upset. I don't have words for the combination of horror at the monstrous lie, disappointment for being so gullible, sadness at the loss of my sense of self, and the thrill—yes, the thrill—of feeling free to say what I've been trying to say for so long. But the words won't come from my lips.

My father's still resting his praying hands on the table, with my mother's hand on his shoulder blade. Jesse's still standing by the window, expressionless, like a man accused of murder listening to the judge pronounce his life sentence, trying to keep expression off his face. My aunt is weeping quietly at the far end of the table. She knew all along but refused to tell me the truth.

"I've had it with all of you," I say, feeling the power of being free to say what I mean. "So, here's my news." I pause. "I'm not coming into the business."

"You can wait until you graduate," my father accedes.

"I'm not coming in now, next week, next month, next spring, not ever."

"Ben, take a few days to think it over. We'll sign the papers later." He stands up and reaches a hand toward me. "Let's just shake on it for now."

I hesitate, step back toward the kitchen door, and close my eyes, searching my head for the right words. But the nerves in my brain are on fire, filling my head with smoke. I can't think clearly, so I'm going to open my mouth and see what happens. I'm terrified and thrilled. I pick up the empty champagne bottle and bang it on the table. "I'm going to MIT. I don't care if none of you ever speaks to me again; you can disown me. You're a pack of liars and conmen—or is it con people? I'll be happy to get away from you," I say, and then, in a huge nebula of adrenaline and rage, I smash the bottle into the door frame, and it shatters into a thousand pieces spread around my feet.

My father comes around the table, his hand still extended. "Ben, wait."

"Don't come near me," I yell. I run from the kitchen up the two flights of stairs to the attic, lock the door, and go out to the roof, where I stare at the gathering storm clouds—mostly cumulus—and feel my heart finally slowing.

$$\frac{\sin\varphi}{\pi}=1 \quad \frac{1}{8\sqrt{2}} \quad \ln\frac{x+x\sqrt{2}+1}{x^2-x\sqrt{2}+1} \; ; \; \sin\beta = c_0 \quad g'=-2\pi\nu g \quad \frac{1}{2}(1$$

$$g\left(x\sqrt{2}-1\right)\Big|_0^\infty = x \qquad \frac{\pi}{2\sqrt{9}} \qquad \frac{5v_i \cdot 5v_a}{\sin\beta} = n = \eta\left(\mu, \quad m = \lim\sum_{i=1}^{m} J\right)$$

$$S, n_1, i_a) \qquad\qquad a^3z; \; n=$$

$$x^2\pi .$$

31

Two hours later, I come down from the attic, descending the stairs sheepishly, afraid my father will start harping again on my coming in, but everyone, including my father, is acting like nothing's happened, chitchatting about the shoe business, my mother's recovery, and her plans to move out here with Myrtle, who will quit her job doing the Heald books.

"We've been waiting for you," my father says. "Get a drink and join us."

I pour myself a tonic, my favorite, with a quarter-inch slice of lime and watch the effervescence dance around the ice cubes like mini fireworks. Then I sit on the couch to watch my family lie to one another, and to me.

My father stands in front of us, like a general before his troops. "The other day I was talking to Bud Hirschmann—you know Bud, partner at Hirschmann and Haddon—who was buying his third pair of elevators, and he said something pretty deep. It got me thinking. He said, 'We like to believe that everything's under control, but the truth is that nothing is.'" He sits down at the head of the dining room table. "I've got some big news, but first I'd like to propose a toast to Florence, my long-suffering wife, who's put up with me all these years—my best friend." He clutches his side for a moment, then sets his shoulders firmly. "We thought we'd lost you, dear Florence, but you're the first member of this family not to leave Flower Hospital feet first."

He raises his tumbler of scotch. "Here's to the prettiest, here's to the wittiest, here's to the truest of all who are true, here's to the sweetest one, here's to them all in one—here's to you, Florence."

My mother unbuttons the top button on her Peter Pan collar, stylish and pricey as always, then fans herself with a napkin and rolls up her sleeves, revealing the purple-black bruises from the rehydration therapy that, with the arsenic treatment, saved her life. "Go ahead and stare," she says. "I have these wounds to remind myself that I survived sleeping sickness."

My father inhales a considerable breath, then lets it out slowly.

All at once I sense I'm about to hear something that's going to change my life—again.

"What I've been waiting to tell you is, I have prostate cancer."

"What?" my uncle says.

"I've got prostate cancer, but don't worry, I'm not infectious," he says with a laugh, but his beleaguered eyes reveal his worry.

"That's terrible, Arthur." My aunt walks over and gives him a big hug. They stay in a tight embrace for a few moments, and, when she lets go, my uncle joins them and cups the back of my father's head, resting his own head on my father's shoulder for a long moment.

The sun goes behind a thick cloud and gray light seeps in around the edges of the curtains. The wind has turned, and sunlight bursts in through the side window, the first and last rays we'll see today, judging by the clouds piling up to the south over Long Island.

"Jesus, Artie." My uncle raises his head and clasps my father's face in his hands. "What can we do?"

"Find me a new prostate," he says, with a clipped voice. "One that's free of tumors and functions the way mine did when I was thirty."

"When did you find out?" My aunt wipes a tear from her eye with her sleeve.

"It started when I was having pain in my hips. I figured it was arthritis, so I ignored it. But then I had problems letting water go, which I had to do more often at night, and the stream was weak. About a month ago, my urine was suddenly blood red. And then I began to lose control of my bladder. So, I went to a guy at Flower and he confirmed it: prostate cancer, with cancerous growths pressing on the spinal cord."

"I had no idea," my uncle says.

"I told Florence as soon as I found out."

"What's the treatment?" my uncle asks.

"None. Surgical removal of the testes or parts of the gland, but the operation has had limited success and terrible side effects. Incontinence, impotence, frequent infections, loss of control," he says, shaking his head. He pulls at his chin. "I've decided to forego treatment."

"But that means . . ." My aunt can't say it.

"I have six months, maybe eight," he croaks. "I'll say one thing: whoever invented cancer did a great job. It's probably German, it's so efficient. Two months ago I had pains in my pelvis, and now I'm dying."

My uncle pours himself and my aunt another scotch, while my mother takes a seat beside my father. And then my aunt and uncle sit at the table too.

"So, you're dying," I say.

"For heaven's sake, Ben," my mother says. "Have a little decorum."

"He just said he has six to eight months to live."

"It's OK, Florence," my father says. "He's right. We start dying the day we're born, but I'm not leaving you all quite yet." He smiles at me. "We've still got time for me to show you the ropes in the store. We'll leave the awning and stationery as it is: no need for Heald & Son."

"Didn't you hear me before? I'm not coming in." My voice is the loudest it's ever been with my parents. It will take a disaster of major proportions to change my perspective.

"Oh, Ben." My father's voice is unnervingly warm. "I understand your resistance."

"You don't have cancer. It's just another way to get me to come into the business, and then you'll announce that it wasn't true, or you'll tell us you had a miraculous remission."

"How can you be so mean and unfeeling? I don't recognize you anymore." My mother is shocked at my outburst.

My father brings his drink to his lips and coughs again, and this time, he groans. My mother, my uncle, and my aunt surround my father like a heartfelt scrum and console him with offers of support. Meanwhile, I'm sitting on the couch in a daze. I'm shocked by my self-righteous attack. These feelings! They're not easy to explain. I failed to keep a lid on them, though considering how angry I am at my father, my outburst could have been worse. I wanted to punch him, or twist his arm. Still, I just belittled a man who's dying of prostate cancer, a man who's not my biological father but who nonetheless raised me. If you can die of guilt, I'm terminal.

I get up from the couch, walk quietly across the room, hoping they won't bother with me, go out the side door to the lawn, walk down to the dock that juts out into the duck pond, strip down to my underwear, and dive in, my head breaking through a layer of green algae and silty, brackish water.

Ten minutes later, I'm sitting on the raft in the middle of the duck pond. Kelly-green water-lily pads crowd the surface. In the lee of the onshore wind, there's a putrid smell of rotting seaweed: dimethyl sulfide, with notes of creamed corn and rotting boiled cabbage. Dark clouds are piling up on the horizon. Above me seagulls swoop and dive over the four dormers and twin chimneys.

Since my parents told me that Jesse's my father and Arthur announced that he has cancer, no way forward comes to my mind. I can run away. I can leave for school, try to get a scholarship for my last year, get into MIT, and never come back. I can pretend, the way they did until today, that my family arrangement falls within the norm. My sense of shock is still nagging at me when I see my father come out of the house wearing his trunks.

He stands on the flagstone walk, talking to himself in a pair of blue Jantzens and a black tank top. He checks out the darkening sky, walks out to the end of the dock, and dives in. A couple of minutes later, he swims up to the raft and holds his hand out to me. I'm pleased to have already gotten over my outburst, my telling him he doesn't really have cancer. I'm still breathing hard from my swim out to the raft.

I hoist him up onto the raft planks.

Water is running down his face. Then he coughs, a scraping retch that sounds as though it's stripping soft fibrous tissue from deep inside his lungs.

The sun ducks behind a cloud.

"I hope it doesn't rain again," I say.

"I don't mind a little rain."

"Those clouds are the typical vortex for a hurricane, which is weird, since the only big storm is forecast to veer out toward Bermuda after it leaves the Carolinas. And since we got here, we've been having gusts and showers, interspersed with calm periods. Typical for an approaching hurricane."

"OK, doc," he says. "So do we have to board up the house?"

"It's too late now anyway. Nice to get a break in the rain. See how the chop is getting bigger, and with the tide coming in, the waves might wash up over the seawall."

He makes a sweeping gesture. "Well, if it isn't washed away, this will all be yours by the end of the year." He stirs the air with his arm sadly. He's expecting us to hug and make up, but I'm not ready—I may never be ready. "Listen, Ben, about before, I'm so sorry."

"What, before?"

"The whole father thing."

"I thought you meant the cancer."

"That too, I guess."

I have no urge to touch or hug him. I keep three feet between us. I say, "So why did you tell us now?"

"It was time."

"No, really, why *today?*"

"Good question." He laughs with abandon, but quickly his laugh turns into hacking from deep in his lungs. "The day you were born, I had a vision: *Heald & Son.* I wanted a legacy. It's a cliché, but it's a true cliché."

"There's no logical correlation. I want to go to MIT. You could let me go and still have your legacy: the elevator shoe."

A smile tugs at the corners of his mouth. "Bringing you in makes me feel safe and secure and cared for." He's clenching his molars. "When you're in the showroom with me, or doing the books, I feel young, like I can do anything. I'm so proud of you—we'll corner the North American shoe market, beat Florsheim at its own game."

I hold back a smile, since the correlation he makes between his pride in me and conquering the retail shoe market is absurd. I look down at him to let him understand I know this is important to him, and that the next thing he says will also be important to me.

"I know I'm hard on you and expect a lot," he says. "Your mother thinks I'm unfair. So many things are harder for me than for you. I wanted to wrestle, but I was too slow for the take-down; I wanted to be a pilot, but my eyes kept me out; I wanted to go to City College to study business, but I was afraid; I want-ed to marry Laurel Lindblatt, but her parents said I wasn't good enough, and I was afraid to fight for her; but having you in the business, that erases all those failures."

He catches my hand and brings it to his mouth. Kisses it, King Arthur to Ben, his knight. He sighs, holds his breath, kicks his feet in the brown water, leans back to rest on his outstretched arms, and says, "You want to know why I'm bringing you in now? Well, here's the truth: I'm scared, that's why. I'm afraid I'll go out of this world with no pride left to my name. After I go, I want people to say, 'That brilliant, accomplished businessman is Ben Heald, Artie's kid.' I'm scared that when I go, people will forget I was ever here—that when I'm gone, nobody will re-member me." He stares down at his bony knees, thin, atrophied legs. "You're my hope. I thought that bringing you in could save me, especially since I got the diagnosis."

To this admission, my mother or Jesse would have hugged him, or said, "I'm sorry, I'm with you, I'm here for you." He must be expecting me to say something like that: *You've been a decent father, and you've helped me through some rough times, like when I was being bullied at PS18. I'm going to be here for you the way you were always here for me.* But we both know that would be a lie. And then it dawns on me that my shock isn't my father's revelation; the shock is that, at least right now, I feel nothing. It's more of an intellectual thing for me.

My father sits, shivering, on the edge of the raft, his feet swinging forward and back in the brown water. His skin is white as calcite, and he's so skinny his Jantzens are three sizes too big. Plus, the weak sun has given him a reddish allergy-pallor.

I don't know how to comfort him, the sixteen-year-old son ministering to the father. So, I do the only thing I know how to do: I pump him with questions. "How long have you known?"

"Three weeks." He pulls at an earlobe. "I'm getting up five, six times a night, figure I'll die from lack of sleep. For months, I explain the frequent urge and the weak stream as symptoms of coffee. A few weeks ago, it's burning like hell when I pee, like a red-hot catheter. Ten days ago, I get up at night, and stand by the toilet waiting and waiting. Nothing happens. I turn on the tap. That makes me want to go even more badly, but nothing comes. I panic. I'm going to explode. I can't tell you the pain. I go to the hospital. They catheterize me to empty my bladder. That hurt, I tell you. Turns out I have a urinary infection. The course of penicillin helped. The burning stops, but I still can't pee, it comes out like yellow raindrops. My urologist does the bend-over-and-cough exam, with his finger—well, you know where—and he's poking and prodding. He hits a spot that hurts so sharp it brings tears to my eyes. He does a biopsy, and the results confirm: "' bulky, poorly differentiated lesions. '"

"What's that?"

"Tumor on the prostate, with likely involvement of the lymph nodes, hip bones, and bladder."

"So, how are you doing, I mean day to day?" I've heard people in the hospital asking this question. I hope it sounds like I care. I'm not much of a thespian.

"I have moments where I don't think about it, and other moments when I break out in a cold sweat." He chews on nothing, grinding his teeth. "We both know it's a death sentence, but then again, so is birth . . . I said that before, didn't I?" He appraises me. "Too late for surgery, but a doctor at Columbia has tried an experimental estrogen treatment." His eyes scan the moving water of Long Island Sound. "With luck, I might have a year and half, but it won't be pretty, and I'm considering my end-of-life options."

"What does that mean?"

"It means I know a doctor, and if I pay him enough, he'll help me out . . . out, if you know what I mean." He goes wistful. "To answer your question—why today—when I die, it's better to have the company in your name." He slides to the front edge of the raft, preparing a quick exit if the conversation gets too uncomfortable.

I don't want to think or talk about his dying.

My father goes on. "I don't want to peer down from heaven—or stare up with a periscope—and watch you and Jesse scrap over succession. The main thing now is to make you a partner. So, we're going to settle this at the lawyer's next week."

He rubs his sad blue thighs, lost momentarily in thought. He clambers to his feet, winces with what I imagine must be pelvic pain, comes around, lowers himself onto his haunches, and rests his elbows on his own knees. He pants a few shallow breaths. "Please hear me out," he says. "I tell you this knowing I'm going to die. One of our customers, Daniel Wilinsky, spent a summer at Bell Labs. At the end of the summer, his boss told him that he'd love to hire him, but he couldn't, because the men on the work crews would never accept him because of his religious persuasion."

"I've never even been in a synagogue."

"I've asked around; academia won't accept you either."

"You don't get it."

"Of course I do, that's what I'm telling you."

"For me, this isn't a choice. I'm going to MIT."

And with those words, he gets up, walks around me, and kisses me once on the forehead, still frustrated with me; then he says, "Race you back to shore," and launches himself out over the water. For a moment, he's suspended in midair. Then he slides into the brown-green pond, does three frog kicks under water, and surfaces, shaking the water from his head.

Watching his surprisingly elegant stroke, I sense I'm at a threshold. I sense a change in things, but I can't describe it. I'm starting a new and clearly defined relationship to my father. I'm about to feel more empathy for him (actually, to feel *any* empathy for him). I blast into the pond, kick underwater through the brown-green murk, and break through the lily pads, and in twenty strokes, I catch him at the dock. He's winded, and so am I. Between gasps, he says, "Thank you, son. It's been so long since I've felt pleased with the world."

$$; \frac{\sin\varphi}{\pi} = 1 \quad \frac{1}{8\sqrt{2}} \quad \ln\frac{x^2 + x\sqrt{2} + 1}{x^2 - x\sqrt{2} + 1} \;;\; \sin\beta \quad g' = 2\pi\nu g \quad$$

$$g\left(x\sqrt{2} - 1\right)\Big|_0^\infty = x \qquad \frac{\pi}{2\sqrt{9}} \qquad \frac{\partial v_i - 5v}{\sin\beta} = n = \eta\left(\mu, \qquad m = \lim\sum_{i=1}^m$$

$$s, n_i, i_i) \qquad \qquad a^3 z; \; n =$$

$$x^2\pi.$$

32

After our swim, my father and I walk back to the house, shivering in onshore gusts that are whipping up white caps and blowing dry seaweed along the beach. To the southwest, there's a rim of black cloud like the wall of a massive cliff moving toward us slowly.

"Jesus, that's as frightful as the sandstorm I once saw in Egypt, outside Cairo," my father says. "It swallowed up everything in its path. People died; buildings collapsed."

"Shelf cloud, typical for a hurricane," I explain.

"This far north?" My father peers at me over his reading glasses like a stern teacher. "Not much chance."

"Actually," I say, watching him blanch.

"Don't tell me—"

"—Yup. On August 25, 1635, the Great Colonial Hurricane struck Rhode Island, killing at least forty-six people. It was the most intense hurricane to hit New England since its European colonization."

"Ben, that was three hundred and three years ago."

"A twenty-foot storm surge wiped out hundreds of houses in Narragansett Bay, and extensive damage was recorded in Rhode Island, Connecticut, and Massachusetts."

"The forecast is for sunny spells, with a chance of showers this afternoon." My father's eyes are cold, the flecks of light like mica. "That sound like a hurricane?"

278

"It's possible, theoretically, under certain meteorological conditions."

He smiles at me appraisingly, but I can see that his patience is, once again, wearing thin. He stops, turns, and stares back at the raft, which is bobbing so hard in the waves that I fear it's going to break its mooring.

The wind is picking up fast. The gusts feel twice as strong as when we were sitting on the raft. While I watch, the raft rides up high on a wave, and the wind gets under it, flipping it and breaking the chains.

"Shit, now I'll have to call Lombardo, the guys who installed it. God, this house is a hole in the sand into which I'm throwing hundred-dollar bills. I keep telling your mother to sell it; we can use the money in the business; but she won't have it, something about sentimental value."

Inside the house, there's the smell of fresh-brewed coffee and apple pie. My mother is waiting at the dining room table, her eyebrows raised expectantly. "Well, at least you didn't drown your father," she says to me.

"Changed my mind."

She takes a sip of ginger tea, her favorite. "Could you help your aunt finish setting the table? Use the long, white candles. They're in the kitchen. Otherwise the table looks sad." She has traded her wide grin for a pensive smile.

My father wanders over to the Philco, tuning it to WROR. Tommy Dorsey's "I'm Getting Sentimental Over You" plays. "Dear," he says, sashaying over to my mother. "Care to dance?"

"Please, Arthur."

"I've got some fine moves," he says, doing a sort of shuffle two-step.

"I'm not one your secretaries."

My father paces a little back and forth in front of my mother. He's hunched forward. I expect him to be angry, but he surprises me. "That's true," he says. "You're a class act." That she talks openly about his schtups gives me pause. *What kind of deal do they have? I've misunderstood so many things about my parents—this is just another one.*

My father glides over to the drink cart and pours himself two fingers of Glenfiddich with ice he crushed with a hammer. Then, in one swift motion, he crumples up a copy of the *New York Times* front page and lobs it toward my uncle, who catches it before it bounces off his head.

"Jesus, Artie, you're acting like a teenager."

"I keep trying to do better."

"You've got a lot of work to do," says my uncle. "Sometimes you're kind of an asshole, but that's kind of rare lately." He smooths the paper and scans the headlines with his finger. "The girl with the topaz eyes died."

"Who?" I ask.

"Pauline Frederick. She played Madame Chung in *Thank You, Mr. Moto*. Jesus, she was only fifty-five, but her eyes were to die for."

"What about mine?" my aunt asks.

"Yours too," Jesse says, as sentimental as a mollusk.

To my mother, he says, "Anything I can do in the kitchen, Florence?"

"You can turn off the oven and take the pie out." She stands up, teetering. "I'm going into the cellar to get the blackberry cordial for the ice cream and pie."

My uncle walks into the kitchen, whistling "I'm a Yankee Doodle Dandy."

By an excellent stroke of luck, the three of them are so busy with each other, they've forgotten to notice me. So, I go to the living room window and look out at the dunes. The wind leaking through the window frames sounds like a small woman wailing. The grass leading out to the dunes is bent flat, and three- to five-foot waves are pounding the beach. Spray rises over the retaining wall and lands as foam on the front lawn. With no trees or shrubs, as the tide comes in, the house will flood.

The wall of cloud, now dark and menacing as before a tornado, is nearing Quogue at an alarming rate. It's the fastest storm front I've ever seen, at least fifty miles an hour.

My aunt comes over and stands next to me at the living room window, whispering to herself. "That cloud is going to swallow us up."

I check my watch. "It's three o'clock," I say. "The leading wall of the low-pressure system is going to hit us in an hour, maybe less."

"The wind on the water is whipping up great shapes, like moving sculptures." My aunt's voice is lonely, and I wonder if it's because of what Jesse told me, leaving her like the odd person out, where the other three have a bond she can't share. I feel something for her that I think may be pity.

"This morning, the wind was blowing into Long Island Sound," I say, "but now it's shifted south, causing the water to blow in from the Sound."

"Is that bad?"

"Every gram of water, a volume about the size of a man's thumb, releases 540 calories of heat as it condenses into water vapor. As the warm tropical air continually rises and condenses, this huge energy flow powers a deadly and driving machine that can't be stopped." As I watch, fascinated by the immense power of the cloud, the outer bands of the storm bear down on us with strong gusts of at least sixty-five miles an hour. It hurls sand and pebbles against the picture window like millions of tiny ball bearings. If the velocity of the wind increases, the flying debris will shatter the window and the rising water will flood the living room.

My aunt, faced by the approaching calamity, is the only adult taking it seriously, for now. "We have to do something," she says. "I have the same feeling I had before my insulin therapy. Something's not right. I don't want to die."

Although I don't agree we're going to die, I do agree that we have to do something.

I go up to the attic and turn my radio to WEAF, the station I use to get my time signals and weather reports. A deadpan voice comes over the speaker: "The West Indies hurricane that has been off of Cape Hatteras seems to be changing course and may hit Long Island." I race back downstairs and gather everybody in the living room in front of the picture window, which is now a picture of wind-and-water destruction. "It's a hurricane, and it's going to hit us within the hour. Air pressure's 945 millibar; the rain gauge measured half an inch in two hours, and the wind is gusting to seventy miles an hour."

"I'm going to go check on the car and see if we can get out of here." My father goes out the side door, drink still in hand.

My uncle tries to call for help, but the phone's not working. "Power's out," he says. "Jesus, was this in the forecast?"

"No," I say, going back to the living room window. Wind sweeps across the dunes and the lily pond, driving beach debris—a Traveler's Motor Oil cannister, an orange buoy, and a segment of rope—into the living room window. Lightning streaks across the horizon to the south.

My father comes in the front door, his shirt clinging to his bony frame and the glass of scotch nowhere to be seen. "Jesus, it's an apocalypse. I tried to get into the car to move it into the lee of the wind, but the wind held it closed. With all my might, I couldn't pull it open. I had to hang on to the door handle for support."

My mother's been gone ten minutes, so my father goes to check on her. They come back moments later, both breathing hard, my mother clutching a magnum of Bordeaux. "My shoes are floating," she says. "Even my favorites from Barcelona."

"Ben," my uncle says. "Let's go."

A smell of foul seawater meets us halfway down the narrow steps. I dangle my hand in the water, and watch the brown muck rise up my wrist.

"Jesus," says my uncle, "I could see it rising up your arm. Where's it coming from?"

"The pond, from underneath, maybe the sewer system."

Back upstairs, my uncle and I join my father and my aunt, who, to a T, are staring out the front window, paralyzed by inaction, which is no surprise, since a tragedy is unfolding before our eyes. A quarter mile offshore, a white and red lobster boat battles into Little Narragansett Bay. The bow pitches and dives under waves that sweep over the deck and flow out the transom. It lunges forward when the stern rises, throwing its spinning propeller free of water. Struck from all directions, it rolls forty degrees, the port rail disappearing in a torrent of water. Slowly, it rights itself and plunges on. A man on deck in a yellow slicker and Sou'wester hat frantically waves for help. A monster wave—more than fifty feet—carries it up and sends it careening into a trough before the wave breaks over the wheelhouse, blowing out the windows. The boat turns turtle, and another wave swallows it up. The hull rights itself again, bobs up. The man is gone.

"Jesus," my uncle says. "If the water keeps rising, that's what's going to happen to us?" His eyes are glistening with concern.

My father puts his open hand on the glass, like a spectator at a zoo watching the shark in a tank tearing small fish to shreds. "I can feel the vibrations of the waves hitting the beach. We should have left two hours ago."

"We've gotta get to the attic," yells my uncle.

I go into the kitchen to stop my mother from packing like she's going on a three-week Caribbean cruise. Oblivious to the danger, or ignoring it, my mother is packing a picnic basket with bread, crackers, cheese, canned soup, bananas, and apples. She covers it with a red-and-white checkered cloth. She hastily throws in a can opener, knives, and soup spoons. Then she picks up a large metal soup ladle.

A humming fills the kitchen.

"Put the spoon down."

"Don't be silly, dear," she says, walking across the kitchen to the metal bread box.

Static electricity crawls over my skin. My hair stands on end, and so does my mother's. She has quickly become a witch with wild hair. Still holding the metal serving spoon, she picks up the breadbox. She draws her brows together, making two creases between them. "It's buzzing," she says.

The spoon is radiating a bluish-violet light. "Drop it," I yell, "and get away from the table."

"What's happening?" she says, in a small, high-pitched voice.

"St. Elmo's Fire. The metal's attracting static electricity. Thousands of volts. The electric field around the spoon is causing ionization of the air molecules. Lightning's going to strike."

A blinding light blows the world apart. The linden tree next to the dock teeters, leans, and, with agonizing slowness, topples like the mast of a great ship, coming to rest on the front lawn, the branches spread across the drive and yard. *Boom!* The thunder is like a plane crashing into the house. The front door blows in. Muddy water surges in, a foot of rushing water flooding the living room and kitchen.

The water catches my aunt, sweeping her feet out from under her.

My uncle lifts her out of the water and carries her up the stairs, and the rest of us follow.

My uncle kicks a hole in the roof, for our escape. I poke my head out to see a huge wave, higher than the roof, swell up out of the black-brown water. The house lifts with creaks and groans, and the wave careens over us, tons of water rushing into the hole in the roof and the broken dormer window.

I'm blinded. I turn my head away from the oncoming surge, grabbing my mother's arm. Now she's swinging free; I think she's let go and slipped free and I call frantically, still grabbing for her hand or arm. I can see nothing—only a rushing confusion of water and debris swirling around my head. The attic floor breaks away from the rest of the house, bobbing and twisting, a makeshift raft. My father, my uncle, and I grab a pipe protruding from the middle of the raft. My uncle frantically yells at my aunt to stop screaming. Half kneeling, my father grabs my legs and tells me to catch my mother. Now, lying prone, I grasp my mother's wrist and begin dragging her, inch by inch, toward the middle of the raft, with my father holding my ankle, myself on the verge of falling into the current.

Waves pound our makeshift raft, we break free, and now we're drifting out to sea, with the wind whipping us at eighty miles an hour. We breech upward and go almost vertical. At the top of the crest, the platform catches the wind and lifts and lifts, careening over the top and falling into the next trough, dunking us in the freezing water. Visibility is less than a half mile, though I can make out the submerged houses in ruins along the shore of Little Narragansett Bay.

I'm clutching the pipe with one arm and my mother's wrist with the other arm. Her lips are blue, and she's muttering "Utte, Utte" over and over. My uncle has one arm around the pipe and, with his free hand, clutches my aunt's blouse.

Spray hits me in the face, and I blink. My vision begins to clear.

"Watch out," my father yells.

We hit something, bumping and scraping, like a boat going aground. But we're too far offshore to hit bottom. It's a tree poking out of the water; brown, leafy branches sway in the current. We bump into more submerged trees, their crowns poking out of the water like pointed hats.

"We've drifted south," I scream. "We're over land."

"How's that help us?" asks my uncle. "The water's still fifty feet deep, and the current's going to pull us out into deeper water. We're going to drown."

"We just have to hang on," my father says. "We'll be rescued."

For a few moments, our raft levels out, and the wind dies. "We're in the eye," I say. "The worst is over."

First the grace notes of hope, then the unthinkable. A monster rogue wave bellies up from the roiling depths. Ten feet. Twenty feet. Thirty feet. Forty. Fifty. We rise with it, our stomachs twisting, but the crest is too steep. The raft nears the top; the wave breaks over us, submerging us in black water. We plummet down the backside and come to rest in the trough. But the wave rips me, my aunt, and my father off the raft.

I hear a cry. My aunt, or maybe my mother.

The rain comes harder, pocking the water. An oil can flies by three feet in the air and spinning.

"Myrtle? Myrtle?"

My father is bobbing nearby. He takes a breath, dunks under, and comes up gasping, shaking his head. "Help me, Ben, I'm not going to make it."

The wind is now massive, unstoppable blocks of pure momentum. Millions of volts crackle over us as the storm comes back full force.

I hear a voice or a moan. My aunt is nowhere to be seen. I yell. No luck.

My father bobs up again, barely getting his chin above the water.

"Myrtle," my uncle yells. "Myrtle's gone. She's gone, Ben."

I'm galvanized into action. "No." I swim downwind. My aunt's back, white as porcelain, is floating just below the surface.

"Myrtle. No. Not now. No." I swim over to her, turn her over, and get her into a dead man's float, holding her face above the water. As I do this, my father, twenty feet upwind, bobs up again. "Help me, somebody help me." He sinks again.

My aunt moans. She has an empty non-expression, and her lips shine blue. I squeeze her wrist. A pulse. I wrap my arm around her waist and pull. Her body rolls partway, but it's caught. I tug on her ankle, feel resistance, pull until the flesh gives way. Her body floats into my arms. A tree branch has impaled her thigh. The wound where the wood protrudes is proud, but not lethal. I tow my aunt back toward the raft. "I don't think it hit an artery," I yell to my uncle. "She may be OK."

My mother moans.

My uncle crawls over to her. He comes back to the edge near me. "She's exhausted and scared. She keeps calling for her doctor."

I can't pull my aunt through waves with the stick in her leg. I try to break off the protruding ends.

No chance. I jerk it back and forth gingerly, and blood seeps into the water.

"Leave it, Ben," my uncle says. "Just get her over here and I'll pull her up onto the raft. Then we'll deal with the stick."

Before I start swimming again, I check my aunt's pulse. It's weaker, and her breaths are shallow and sporadic. She's been semi conscious for more than ten minutes. If I don't get her onto the raft immediately so my uncle can do mouth-to-mouth resuscitation, she'll have permanent brain damage or die.

I take two strokes, kicking frantically, and before I get a yard nearer the raft, my father's face emerges from the murky water, like a ghost in a dream.

"Help," he croaks, his voice no more than low, squeezed notes. "Somebody, help me." His face disappears into the murk.

If I save him, dive down after him, by the time I get him to the surface, my aunt will be dead, or brain dead. If I save her, my father will drown.

For a fraction of a second, I waver, my only wavering.

I wrap one hand around my aunt's torso, and with the other hand feel the rough, wet bark. I work my jaw muscles to keep my gorge down, clutch my aunt's waist harder, kick for my life, and pull her toward the raft. Another fury of kicking brings her to the raft.

My uncle grabs my aunt's arm and lifts her onto the raft, careful not to snag the stick protruding from her leg. A trickle of blood runs down my aunt's leg. My uncle starts giving her mouth-to-mouth, alternating with chest massage. He counts as he does this, his strong arms pressing down on her heart. After a while, she sputters, gasps, and takes a massive breath. My uncle turns her on her side, and the water flows from her mouth between breaths. My uncle removes his shirt, twists it into a tourniquet, and wraps it around her thigh, stress making his mouth into a ragged line.

"I'm going back for my father."

My uncle draws back in shock. "No, he's gone."

p^3; $\dfrac{\sin \varphi}{\pi} = 1$ $\dfrac{1}{8\sqrt{2}}$ $\ln \dfrac{x + x\sqrt{2} + 1}{x^2 - x\sqrt{2} + 1}$; $\sin \beta = c_0$ $g' = -2\pi \nu g$ $\dfrac{1}{2}(1$

$g(x\sqrt{2} - 1)\Big|_0^\infty = x$ $\dfrac{\pi}{2\Gamma^0}$ $\dfrac{5\nu_i \cdot 5\nu_i}{\sin \beta} = n = \eta(\mu,$ $m = \lim \sum\limits_{i=1}^{m}$

$'s, n, i_x)$ $a^3 z$; $n =$

$x^2 \pi$.

33

At 6:30 p.m.—my watch is still working—the calm waters of
Little Narragansett Bay give no hint of the fury that only hours
before, nearly obliterated us. It's as if we imagined the ordeal.
The sky is vibrating blue; sunlight is slipping through the clouds,
glinting off the waves like burning acetylene. It quickly becomes
clear that the storm surge carried us about three miles west over
Dune Road to Reedy Island in Moneyboque Bay.

We've come to ground on a strip of beach on the south side
of Reedy Island. The ruined beach alarms me. The wrongness of
it, like the scene of a bombing, is alarmingly quiet, reminding
us of what we've been through the last hours. I may well be in
shock; at least I've got the symptoms of being amazed at being
alive: the objects on the beach seem larger, in sharper focus: the
stranded red-beard sponges and horseshoe crabs, shattered and
tangled lobster traps, transoms of boats, a plank from a ruined
jetty, and a yellow rubber boot.

And then I remember: *My father sinks down under the surface,
his face disappearing as he goes down into the murk, just out of
reach, like the face in a nightmare.*

With my cut index finger—when did I get this deep gash?—I
rake out my wet hair. My mother is sitting on a downed phone
pole next to my uncle, who's kicking an oil drum. By the water
line, my aunt lies on the stony sand, kelp in her hair, Jesse's
tourniquet still cinching her thigh and waves lapping at her feet.

I pull my aunt onto drier sand.

My uncle comes over, rubbing a deep gash from his cheekbone to his jaw, which makes him ever more handsome, the wounded sheriff. "This is a really bad thing," he says. "I think she's dead."

"Her pulse is weak, but she's still breathing, and I think the bleeding has stopped."

"I just woke up," my uncle says, making circles with his head. "I must have hit my head. It feels like it's filled with sponges." His confused eyes grab mine.

My aunt gives a pinched cry of distress, like a feral animal with its leg in a trap. She raises her head. "Help me."

My uncle is shaking his head. He's struggling to focus, and keeps gazing out over the sparkling Sound, like he's trying to figure out how we ended up here. Then he strides over to my aunt and strokes her cheek with the back of his hand. Between moans are faint rasps, she opens her eyes, smiles, and lets her head fall back. Finally, her breathing evens out, and for a short while, she seems to be free of pain.

"There's nothing we can do now except wait for rescue. I'm going to go check on your mother, Ben." He walks over a heap of seaweed to where my mother hasn't moved. She looks old and exhausted; hopelessness is leaking from her eyes. They hold hands and exchange words. I still can't imagine the two of them having intercourse, and the thought turns my face red. That my mind would conjure this image with my father dead and my aunt dying shocks me. My uncle wraps his arm around her shoulder, connected again to his confident, energetic self.

"How's she doing?" I ask when he returns.

"Your mother's going to be all right."

And then miraculously, as if she got a memo from the high-society police telling her to buck up, she is all right; she's on her feet, tiptoeing around the washed-up detritus. I can imagine her tidying up, her motto being, "Keep moving, keep busy, everything will fall into place, it always has." Except my father is dead, and I have no idea what she's feeling or thinking.

In the piercing sunlight, during the seconds it takes me to cup my aunt's hand in mine, I feel for the first time the impact of my father's death—the plain fact of his absence. The recognition is brought on by familiar sounds and smells that I'd never paid much attention to: his cologne, his Lucky Strikes, the shoe polish he kept in his office, swing bands, Henry Morgan's grating voice. I had talked about him to my mother, my aunt, and my uncle, and I had thought of him too, in snatches during my calculus review, or recording my weather data, or drifting into sleep, and until right now I had never really missed him in my heart, or felt the stinging insult, the shock of knowing I will never see him or hear him again. He was my father, the father who had raised me, and he's gone.

For a moment, I feel doubt, but when I glance at my mother, I can see her tense jaw and the flinty hardness of her eyes, and the determination of her expression gives me the resolve I need. A blue chest of drawers sits among the rocks. Inside the drawers, a child's clothes, wet through, are still folded in tight squares. I see my reflection in the mirror attached to the top. *My eyes are too big, my nose too wide. My cheeks are puffy, and my lips are bluish. The person in the mirror is ten years older than I was yesterday.* I slide the mirror out of its frame and walk to the edge of the water, going through the motions, but not participating in the movements of my arms and legs. My feet rest in the shallow water. *Why aren't they cold? I feel nothing.* I aim the mirror so that anybody offshore can see the glints of light.

My mother comes over, leans forward, and squints. "A boat,"

she says, looking toward the horizon. "A boat." She raises her hand, waves, puts on her best smile.

And then I see it too.

A tiny speck bobs and jinks toward us from the Westhampton harbor.

It approaches slowly, its engines turning over with a low rumble, louder when the props break the water. Three men are waving from the afterdeck. Twice, it stops, and one of the men grapples an object out of the way with a boathook. The boat, a forty-foot trawler with four deep-sea rods protruding from the back and a pile of nets aft, comes to within twenty feet of us and throws out an anchor in waist-deep water. It swings around to aim the bow into the waves, and the name comes into view: *Seas the Day.*

"Need a hand?" says a bearded man in rubber overalls and a wool cap. "Captain Hoar," he announces in a deep baritone. "Headed back to Westhampton boatyard." He scratches his beard, then clasps his hands behind his body. "If it hasn't been washed away." With firm, precise movements, he gathers a rope-and-wood ladder from a storage box in the stern. "We got the worst of the blow. Dune Road area of Westhampton Beach is obliterated."

"Our cottage is on Dune Road."

"'Fraid that's gone. There's nothing left of the whole shoreline all the ways out to Montauk Light." He makes a sucking noise. "Thirty dead in Westhampton. Twenty-one more out east. Storm surge flooded the south fork at Napeague, washed out the tracks of the Long Island Railroad, and cut off Montauk." He lowers the ladder. "Storm tide was fifteen feet—never seen waves that big, least thirty feet, some fifty." His tired eyes shift over to me. "Take you people in?"

I point to my aunt. "She's hurt pretty badly."

"We'll use the lift." He sounds like a captain now, standing straight and pushing his chest out. "Come aboard," he says. "Injured first."

The radio in the wheelhouse crackles a marine forecast. Captain Hoar radios in his location and returns to our rescue. "You'll have to wade out a few feet. Careful, you never know what washed up."

I fetch my mother and my uncle. One by one, I lead them through the swirling water behind the transom, my mother rasping and my uncle teetering a little, his face flushed. Then I volunteer to carry my aunt's body toward the boat. Two crew members in yellow waders attach painters to her hands and legs and lift her on board with a small swordfish derrick. My uncle helps my mother navigate the saggy ladder. He follows her, then pulls me up and pulls the ladder in.

The deck is a gray-and-black space stained with fish blood. It smells of rotting fish. We sit on the deck in a row, our backs against the gunwales, shivering in the sun and warming ourselves on the heat from the engine. My aunt is lying on the deck at our feet. Captain Hoar gives us each a blanket and covers my aunt up to her neck.

One of the crew, a young man with a thick scar on his cheek, asks Hoar for the course. "Westhampton boatyard."

My uncle takes a cigarette from one of the crew and sets fire to it. My mother sits next to him, her head resting on his shoulder.

An hour goes by.

Captain Hoar calls it in, announcing to some unseen radio operator that he's got a woman with a serious injury on board, seeking assistance.

At ten minutes to seven, the engines slow to a purr. Five minutes later, the bow bumps against the remains of a jetty that survived the blow in the lee of a large boat storage warehouse. Captain Hoar jumps up on to the dock and extends his hand to us. My mother climbs out first, the others follow, and we stand on the edge of a congregation of onlookers curious to see my aunt's body.

They stand around watching us, three men from the boatyard in working clothes, two policemen in wet uniforms, a boat supply man, a handful of lobstermen, and a reporter from the *Long Island Daily Press*. They ask a few questions about our escape from Quogue to Reedy Island, a photo is taken, and I stand next to a tall man in oil-stained clothes.

"How bad's the damage?" I ask him.

He considers carefully before he replies, as if he wants to be sure that his terrible news is accurate. His eyes grow from soft to hard. "Misquamicut's wiped out. Napatree Point's gone. Fifty dead. Scores of bodies washed ashore. New England has been devastated," he says, lowering his head. In a wrenching whisper, he says, "God forgot us."

Everything around me—fuel pumps, fishing boats, fish guts on the dock, nets, lines, and a large anchor—seems unreal, like in those moments between waking and sleeping. As the world recedes, I wonder if there's a pattern or order to the things in your life, not one like the Pythagorean theorem, or Newtonian physics, but one that works on you just the same, one as inevitable as gravity, that explains events and makes them easier to accept, even if they seem wrong. Or does everything just happen? For the first time I think, *I will be alone in the world. And that seems all right.*

An hour later, I'm in the Quogue police station, sitting in a grey room with a metal chair and table that reminds me of my mother's rooms in the Flower Hospital. A fleshy-faced man in a blue uniform approaches me from down the hall. As he swaggers toward me, his nightstick slaps his leg. "I'm Chief Comeau," he says. "Ben Heald?"

I nod.

He takes off his cap and clamps it between his arm and his side. "I'm sorry for your loss, son, but we're going to need a statement," he says, his voice warm with empathy. "Just to make everything official."

I wait for him to go on, watching him write my name slowly on his steno pad. He stops chewing his gum. "So, Ben, tell me what happened out there, in your own words."

"It's a blur."

He blinks twice, thinking for a moment. "What *can* you recall?"

I tell him word for word what I've been telling myself for hours. "Our house on Dune Road was caught in the storm surge and washed out into the Atlantic. We saved ourselves on part of the roof, like a raft. There were thirty-foot waves and hundred-mile-an-hour gusts. My father and my aunt fell into the water. I dived in and saved my aunt, but when I swam to where I'd last seen my father, he was gone. I kept diving to find him, but the waves pushed me back, over and over, and then he was gone, and I couldn't see him in the black waves." This is, of course, the truth as my memory has recreated it. Every time I remember an event, I recreate it as suits me, adding details and omitting others.

"Thank you, Ben." He forces a smile, and I can tell that what I said is bothering him.

In my mind, the ghostly images of my aunt and my father last only a moment before fading away, as all traumatic events are wont to do.

He puts all his weight on one leg and crosses his arms. "Anything to add?" he whispers.

I'm feeling overwhelmed. His question strikes me as absurd. I could add that I don't deserve his sympathy. I could add that I don't understand why I had to choose between my father and my aunt. I could add that I can't explain why I saved my aunt. I could add that I don't know what happened, not really *know* the way I know calculus. I could add that I'm appalled by how little I'm feeling right now. I'm waiting for the tears of grief, but my eyes are dry. I have a lot to add, but I'm not adding it now.

An awkward stillness enwraps us.

Chief Comeau pats me on the hip. "I'm so sorry," he says, opening his mouth to show a row of yellowed, misaligned teeth. He's not a handsome man; his beefy face and thick nose look confident, though. "I don't mean to upset you."

I stare, amazed that he's made it to chief with yellow teeth. Must be the confidence. Or luck.

He leans forward, squinting at me.

I smile a little and look down. Is he going to ask me if I chose between my father and my aunt? Is he going to ask me if I'm happy with my choice?

If he senses that there's more to my story than I've said, he's not letting on. "Do you need a doctor, Ben?"

I wag my head.

"Are you sure?"

"I'm fine," I say, although I'm not sure this is true. What does he want from me? I'm definitely feeling out of my depth.

The Chief bulges his cheek with his tongue, wets his finger, and uses it to flip back a few pages in his notebook. He nods again slowly, reviews his notes, then says, "What a tragedy." He takes my hand and squeezes.

I pull my hand away, and then, standing back, I can't believe how good it feels that our conversation is almost over. Suddenly, I'm feeling detached, like we're talking about a drowned man who wasn't my father, and an accident that didn't happen to me. I wait for the emotional blow of what I've done, but it doesn't come. Behind me, rain drums on the window. "It's raining," I mumble.

Chief Comeau frowns. "I didn't mean to upset you, Ben."

"It just started raining again."

"Ben? Everything okay?" He closes his eyes a moment, then opens them, clicks his pen twice.

"It was an accident," I say. "An accident can be defined as an unfortunate incident that happens unexpectedly and unintentionally, typically resulting in damage or injury. My father's drowning was, by definition, an accident." I stop to give him time to add this to his notes.

He puts his cap on, cocks his head to one side, clamps the pen between his teeth, and slaps his detective pad closed. "Well," he says, louder but still gently, "I believe we're done here." And with that, he backpedals two steps, turns, and lumbers languidly down the hall, pushing the elevator button to go up, while I feel like I'm going down.

34

A week after the storm, I'm still remembering the hours on the raft as vividly as in a nightmare, but I go back to school anyway. The soccer and football fields are still flooded, and two guards have been hired to keep students off them. Personally, I don't see the attraction of wading through soppy ankle-deep grass, but other students found ways to sneak onto the fields. This is as near as many Loomsfield students will ever get to the damage caused by GH38. So, they question me, an endless drill of detail-seeking. Whenever one of them wants to know what it must be like to be swept away in a hurricane, he comes to me. At first, I'm proud. But then I'm confused by the attention. After all, I've been treated as an outsider for a year and mocked for being a brainiac, a weirdo, and a flake. But trauma has made me attractive.

My family's experience on the raft separates me even further from my classmates. They just aren't interested in my personal catastrophe, and if they are interested, they aren't interested in me per se, but are rather interested in what it was like to watch my father drown: his struggle, first the panic, and the resignation on his face when he sank for the last time, what it must be like to take what fishermen call "the big gulp." I have no idea. I'm still here, after all. What for them was nothing more than an exciting northeaster, was for me a nightmare that I relive every day and that I'm sure will flicker in my daydreams and nightmares for the rest of my life. It now seems to me that trauma has both the power to destroy and the power to transform and resurrect; that's the paradox.

My Loomsfield classmates treat me like a rare animal, alternately afraid and mocking. I find myself more alone than ever, with only Dr. Hedjhal and Coach Winters on my side, and occasionally Dr. Shore, when he gives me an "Excellent, Heald," for remembering, verbatim, some lines or other from the tragedies.

Out of habit, I call my mother every evening, an hour after dinner. Sometimes, my Aunt Myrtle answers, and twice, Dr. Lenz picked up. I have a feeling that they're moving on without me, now that I'm probably going to MIT, which makes me feel like I'm drifting in space, cut loose from the mother ship, spinning into deep black, alone, but oddly, not lonely.

During last night's call, I asked my mother where Jesse is; I need to talk to him about the business. She says that's good, since my father left half of it to me. My father got his wish: I'm a partner in Heald Shoes.

"He went back to Florida for a few days," my mother says.

"Say when he'd be back?"

"No."

"Any idea how I can reach him?"

She gives me a number. "He's usually not in."

I want to tell him that I'm selling the business. I've already asked the lawyers to find a buyer, probably Florsheim, with its five Chicago factories and 2,500 employees, seventy-one stores partly or entirely company-owned, and nine thousand stores around the US selling Florsheim. He'll get half the proceeds, easily a few million, which would ease the financial strain of Whispering Palms. So, he won't be needing me, which is fine, since I want nothing more to do with him.

I try calling the number I got from my mother, but a receptionist at the hotel answers and tells me my uncle is out fishing. "Will you call again?"

"It's very important."

"I'm afraid he's not here, and I have no way of reaching him."

As I know my uncle, he's got his arms around the receptionist right now, kissing the back of her neck. So I hang up on my uncle, and move him into the drawer of experience I call: *Done*.

I stand in the dorm hallway for a few moments, watching students meandering from the study hall, which is in the Finnegan Library from 6:30 to 8:30 p.m. They're jostling each other in a way that they never jostle me, friendly; not mocking nor taunting. Dr. Hedjhal's advice echoes in my brain: "Listen, Heald, let them go. They're jealous of you—you're a sixteen-year-old senior. You're smarter. You hold school swimming records. You're taller, and you're a good-looking kid. Focus on what you do well, and remember, it's OK to be different."

One of the juniors starts to ask me questions about advanced algebra, but I break away and go hastily back to my room to review my calculus notes. My MIT admission test is on Friday, October 21, from 8:00 a.m. to noon, the day before the New England Swimming Championships.

Since my visit to the police station a week ago, it's been pretty much nonstop hurricane talk at Loomsfield. In the hallways, in the dorms, on the quad, and before classes, the particular focus has been on whether I'm a hero for saving my aunt, or a gangly sixteen-year-old weirdo whose famous father drowned in the storm.

But I'm preoccupied with the widely shared meteorological statistics: the Great Hurricane of 1938—the Long Island Express, or GH38—was the strongest, most devastating storm ever to hit New England. As morbid as it is, I'm fascinated by the destructive power of the storm. Some families and some communities will never recover physically, economically, or spiritually. Much of the talk among my Loomsfield classmates turns out to be highly speculative. The National Weather Service is taking a lot of criticism for not predicting the oncoming storm.

A surprisingly large number of New Englanders believe cows were blown into trees, a house from Napatree Point floated north west to Hartford, or an ocean liner capsized off Fire Island and sank within three minutes with its full crew on board. Another rumor is that all the patients of the Pilgrim Hospital in Brentwood, Long Island, escaped and went on a murder spree.

Callers to radio shows pointed out the strange green fog that preceded the storm. They claimed it was a gas planted on the sea floor by German submarines, and that these cannisters of gas caused the hurricane to build strength and wipe out the New England coastline.

The reality is more disturbing, because it is real. The Great Hurricane of 1938, or GH38, as it is now called, humbled New England. 708 people were injured, 4,500 homes and buildings were destroyed, more than 1,500 homes, cottages, and farm buildings were damaged, nineteen thousand families applied for assistance, 2,605 boats were lost, and 3,369 were damaged. Twenty-six thousand automobiles were smashed; 275 million trees were snapped off or uprooted; nearly twenty thousand miles of electric power and telephone lines were blown or knocked down. 1,675 head of livestock and an estimated 750,000 chickens were killed. Like many disasters, what distinguished GH38 from other storms at other times and places was the surprise that accompanied it. The storm struck a vulnerable part of the country when it was in a weakened economic state, and it came without warning, like the sudden violent death of a member of your family.

On the evening of September 30, a week after GH38, as I stand washing my face in the sink in my dorm room, I hear a voice on my shortwave radio. I've heard the voice before, the last time I was in the car with my father. It's hard to believe this is a coincidence, but I've trained my mind to see coincidence.

It begins, ". . . Morgan here, with some sad news. Yeah. OK. So, I'm still grieving the loss of my dearest friend, Artie Heald. Yes, we've lost New York's Great Shoe Man, OK, Old Man Heald, to the Great Storm. I've been listening to all our radio spots, feeling sorry for myself just for being alive, which Artie would hate. I always imagined Artie would outlive us all I've been living with this thought for a long time, and now that he's gone, I'm ready to cash it all in. No replays. No do-overs. No returns for a new pair. Since Old Man Heald came into my life ten years ago, I always had something new to say, but now I'm out of quips, and I've got no one to make fun of, no one to needle on air, no one who gets as angry as Artie Heald and then forgives me. Listen, folks, I don't know why I'm telling you. It's worrisome; maybe Morgan's going crazy. I'm going to clear my desk, the one I don't have, and get out of the studio and go down to the Heald Store and appreciate what Old Man Heald meant to all of us. The world is so unpredictable. That's what this hurricane was telling us. We have to pay attention. Things happen suddenly, unexpectedly. We want to feel we're in control of our own existence. In some ways we are—we can decide to buy Heald Elevator Shoes, which, incidentally, I've been wearing for years—but in some ways, we're not. We are ruled by the forces of chance and coincidence."

"OK," Morgan says, "Here's another one about the Old Man. . . . Old Man Heald is sitting on a park bench crying his eyes out.

A young man comes by and asks him what's the matter. Old Man Heald says 'I'm a multimillionaire, my elevator shoe business is booming, I know Gene Kelley, I have a mansion in the sky, a 1928 Bugatti Type 37-A, and I just married a beautiful bombshell who satisfies me every night in bed whether I like it or not.' The young man says, 'Man, you've got everything I've ever dreamed for in my life. What could be so wrong that you're sitting here in the park crying?' Old Man Heald says, 'I can't remember where I live.' So that's it for tonight, folks. If there's one thing Artie Heald taught me, it's this: remember, we must remember."

The next Monday morning, October 3, as I'm eating my break-fast toast and eggs in the dining hall with a bunch of guys from the Loomsfield swim team, listening to them joking about the New England Championships coming up this weekend, Dr. Hedjhal comes over and taps me on the shoulder.

I'm surprised. "Thanks for the problem set," I say.

Hedjhal doesn't reply.

"And for writing my recommendation for MIT," I add. He had written a recommendation and called his Harvard college roommate, now director of the MIT Co-op Program, and put in a good word for me. He'd told me I was "practically a shoe-in, what with my sponsorship, Loomsfield swim record, and likely score on the admissions test."

"I was really sorry to hear about your father, Heald," he says. He is suddenly, unexpectedly, shy. "I meant to tell you sooner, but I was in the city taking care of my mother. She had a stroke three weeks ago and has limited motor movement on her left side."

"What about your father?"

"He died four years ago, congestive heart failure."

I don't know what to say to people who express their empathy. Some of them tell me it will take time to adjust to his loss, but I believe his death has now become part of my life. "My mother's recovering."

"That's a surprise, isn't it?"

"Yeah, a new arsenic and rehydration therapy worked. No one expected her to recover."

A moment of silence. Then Hedjhal turns and heads toward the door, stops, and motions for me to join him. We cross the quad and enter the arched entrance to the Saltonstall Building, a stone corridor like St. Patrick's Cathedral, and park ourselves in the sunshine.

"You must be having a hard time," he says, for the first time trading his shy smile for an empathetic stare, like the school counselor, only with the Loomsfield blazer and blue tie with the gold lion.

"It's OK," I say, not wanting to talk about my feelings.

"Everybody's talking about how you saved your aunt," he says. His empathy is strained. As a school counselor, he'd be a flop.

"What are they saying?"

"They're saying you swam through thirty-foot waves to save your aunt. You risked your life."

"I tried to save my father, but . . ." The last image of my father flashes across my eyes.

Silence.

Now he changes in some small but significant way. I get the sense he's not trying to be my teacher or my mentor, just Dennis Hedjhal. Dennis to Ben. Friend to friend.

Hedjhal stoops a little and sneaks a sideward glance at me. He takes a slide rule from his back pocket and moves the cursor back and forth. "One thing I learned when I left home at sixteen after a huge fight with my father: it's almost impossible not to be who you are."

"I kept trying to do better," I say. "I wanted to be what my father wanted me to be, but I couldn't . . ."

"That's the way things are."

"What does that mean?"

"It means accept who you are, and what happened. Learn from it. Grow from it. It doesn't matter what you've done, or not done: what matters is what you do from here."

"Like going to swim practice."

"Don't be obtuse, Heald." He stabs the slide rule back into his pocket. "When I was in high school in Chicago, I was in a gang. I never went to school, and I was failing all my subjects. I got into fights all the time, once with a knife. My father had his own agency: Hedjhal Insurance. I didn't know what I wanted to do until my senior year when I took high school exams, like Regents, and scored the highest in the city. I won a scholarship to Harvard. Harvard opened my eyes to a world I'd never known, where I could become my own man, and I never left." His soft lips are bent into a look of familiar concern. "Academia gave me something I know you crave."

"Sounds good," I say, though I sound indecisive.

"Independence from the messiness of your family, a place where you can become your own man, like being here at Loomsfield."

"The weirdo sixteen-year-old?"

"No. Ben Heald, gifted mathematician and pretty decent swimmer."

The first-period bell rings.

Hedjhal waits a moment, studying my face; then he loops his arm over my shoulder, pulls me close, and kisses my ear—something he's never done before—and I don't know what to make of it. I lean into his shoulder, smell the pipe smoke on his blazer, and close my eyes. We stay like that for ten seconds; then I open my eyes and fix my gaze on the arched roof of the swimming pool building at the end of the long row of oaks, now starting to turn colors.

Hedjhal takes his arm away, comes around in front of me, and stares, smiling like a concerned uncle. "Want to tell me what's wrong, Heald?"

All at once, feeling Hedjhal's warmth, I realize I'm not numb. My father's accident isn't in that drawer called Done. It's real, it hurts, and I'm devastated. I've never felt like this before. Tears stream down my cheeks. "It keeps coming, this weight. How do I stop it? I feel like I'm suffocating." I see that my hands are shaking.

Hedjhal takes my hands in his, and squeezes lightly, and I'm lost in his warmth.

"I need—I need to breathe again, it's like holding my breath underwater too long."

"You can't control everything." He scratches his neck under his ear. "Terrible, wonderful, devastating things happen all the time. When you're least ready for it, nature has cruel, yet cunning ways of finding our weakest spots."

"I just want to understand."

"Who the hell are you to know why?"

"I'm me. I just want to understand."

"Life isn't calculus, Ben." He's coming toward me now, a smile opening on his long, narrow face, as if he knows I'll remember these words the rest of my life, and he means to get them just right. "You may feel like you deserve to understand, you can make up reasons, but they're made up. Who the hell are you to know, to understand, why your aunt lived and your father drowned, why your mother was bitten by a tsetse fly? People die all the time—a child gets hit by a bus, a mother has a stroke, a Bell worker gets electrocuted in a transformer accident, a boy in my class at Andover drops dead during football practice from an aneurysm. My wife hears voices calling her and walks out a forty-story window. You don't get to know why, any more than I do. I don't know why your father died. You don't either. And neither one of us gets to. You either believe in life's value, or you believe it's all cruel and random and pointless. You have a huge talent, and I envy you. If you don't use it . . . what a waste! The world is full of brokenness, and it's our work to feel, not just to think. You may not want to feel right now. But I'll tell you one thing: I'll never have your talent. What you do with it is your business, but don't choose something that demands nothing of your talent and wears your heart out. You and I have talents, but we're just like other people—we're all in need and in pain. I'm here for you. I'll be here for you at MIT when I start my associate professorship next fall. That may not feel like much consolation *now*, but it will. Just remember: right now, you've got sorrow and pain, but don't block it out, don't try to understand it, let it be, go with it, and one day, maybe only for a minute, you will experience something that most people call joy."

35

That afternoon, Coach Winters gives me what he likes to call a "fun" workout. "You're going to have fun today, Heald, understood?"

"Yes, sir."

"You're not going to beat yourself up until the blood spurts from your ears, understood?"

"Yes, sir."

"You're going to swim easy and relaxed, with long rests. I challenge you to swim a few sets as slowly as you can."

The recovery set is a little longer than three thousand yards, with a warmup. A pre-set, a main set, and a cool-down. It's a mix of all four strokes, with lots of drills, including my favorite three-three-three: three left arm, three right arm, three normal crawl strokes.

As soon as my fingertips slice into the water, I taste the delicious blue liquid sweeping over my face, arms, and back. My balance is perfect and my position in the water is good. Stroke after stroke, with flip turns in between, three breaths a length, I spool off the yards, floating above the black line below me.

The Junior Varsity swimmers pass me. The breast strokers pass me. I fall into a steady rhythm, and Coach Winters gives me the thumbs-up every time I breathe to his side of the pool.

For the first time since GH38, my mind is quiet, and I feel my arms and legs gaining power. My default self-consciousness is gone. After the main set, I tread water at the end of the pool and feel a wonderful sense of well-being, my contentment stronger than ever before. By the time I get to the five-hundred-yard cooldown, I can't remember why I was so upset. I'm untroubled by what happened in Quogue before and during the storm. I hear the whisper of the water, feel my toes interacting with the water, my face relaxed, my head down, chin almost against my chest, my arms swinging wide and easy, my upper arms vertical in recovery, then extended out front, with a long glide and an easy breath. The light in the pool is amazing, bluish rings. And I feel totally connected to the water.

When I finish, I hang on the end of pool, resting my chin on the gutter, smelling the chlorine, and blinking as the water runs down the front of my cap. I put my goggles up and watch the sprint group. I see myself in them, pounding the water, faces tense and red with effort, kicking hard, stroking at a very high cadence. I can do that too, but not today.

Coach Winters comes over, bends down, and taps the top of my head. "Heald."

"Coach."

"That was your best workout yet." He's beaming. "A great, easy practice. I knew you had it in you, I could feel it, but you wouldn't let yourself enjoy it."

"It was great, Coach."

"Can you feel the difference?"

"That was fun; the other way of swimming is work. It's kind of grueling."

"There's a time to push ourselves, but sometimes we need to let ourselves remember why we swim."

"Coach?"

"Joy, Heald. Joy," he says.

"Dr. Hedjhal just told me the same thing."

"He's a swimmer?"

"He swims with his mind."

On the afternoon of October 12, I spot Aunt Myrtle standing outside the senior dorm after a swim practice that was really tough, but went well. I swam my best time in the hundred free-style. She's pacing back and forth in her absent, preoccupied way, her hands out in front of her as if she's talking to someone, her head bobbing back and forth, adapting itself to whatever strange thoughts are ricocheting in her mind. Just as I near her, she stops to inspect a yellow leaf. Suddenly she hears me, and walks toward me, her arms spread wide for a hug.

"What's the matter, Ben? You don't want to welcome your old Aunt Myrtle?"

"Not after what you did to me."

"Don't be an offended liver sausage," she says quickly. "What's the matter with you? I drove all the way out here through the wrecked roads to see you. Still angry?"

"Aunt Myrtle," I say, "why did you lie to me all these years?"

She stares at me without a word, and I know she has no excuse, and feels guilty. I start to turn away to go back to my room, but she steps after me and grabs my arm.

"I didn't lie to you," she says. "I just didn't tell you the truth. When I told you there are some things I have no right to share, I still believe that; it wasn't any of my business."

"You didn't think I had a right to know?"

"Of course, I did, but not from me."

"I thought we were friends," I say derisively. "All those years you helped with the books, you never told me Arthur and Jesse had close connections to the Families, made corrupt deals with the Irish police, kept two sets of books to hide their illicit income, and ran speakeasies in the basements of the stores."

"What if I'd told you? What were you going to do? Call the cops, report them to the Internal Revenue Service, volunteer to keep the second books? No, you were a child. Naïve and even younger than your years. It would have ruined your childhood."

I have nothing to say, except the one fact that remains: I trusted her, and she betrayed that trust.

"And if you think it was easy for me not to tell you, think again. When I went out to the Pilgrim, and the doctor asked me about you, I broke down and cried like a baby. That's how much I suffered not telling you. But I'd promised Florence, Arthur, and Jesse that I wouldn't tell anyone, especially not you. Either about the business or Jesse being your father. By God, it was awful."

My eyes follow three students crossing the quad from the study hall that I don't have to attend because of my perfect grades. I want to forgive my aunt, because in a way, I love her, or care more for her than for the other three, but I can't feel sorry for her or forgive her, and I'm not sure how I feel about her. But I also understand what they did to her. Demanding that she not tell me anything must have hurt, so I can see that she must have suffered. But not as much as I did. The other three are careless people, and she got trapped. It's all very selfish and greedy. They do whatever they please, and retreat back into their mansions in the sky, cottage in Quogue, or hotel in Islamorada, leaving the rest of us to deal with the wreckage. I feel suddenly like her being here is also selfish. "Do you need something, Aunt Myrtle?"

"I wanted to talk about what happened."

"I don't."

"It would be nice to see you again in the city."

"You were part of the conspiracy, and I don't want any more to do with it." I'm feeling uncomfortable, but confident. The risk of my refusal is that she will stop talking to me. This used to terrify me, but not anymore. "I know you mean well, Aunt Myrtle, but . . ." I hold my hand out. We shake.

"Maybe we'll see you at Thanksgiving." Something sad has crept into her voice. "With your father gone, your mother misses you."

"I'm pretty busy with calculus and swimming."

"Oh," she says, smiling weakly. She kisses me on the cheek and walks toward the parking lot. She stops once, looks back, and waves.

But this time I don't care. I wave back, but I've got calculus on my mind, and I feel relieved: now I can find my way to mastery of differential equations.

⧗

Two days later, a busy Saturday, October 15 in Central Park, my wristwatch now says 4:15 p.m. It's an hour after I get off the bus from Norwalk. I stayed an extra night at Loomsfield to get in another taper practice for the New England Championships. Now, I follow East Drive toward the lake, pass the Bethesda Fountain, and head for the Bow Bridge, which is lit with gold beams of late sunlight. The swans are cruising the lake like miniature warships.

Two tiny, distant figures on Bow Bridge come clearly into view. They turn out to be my mother and Dr. Lenz, making the same tour, I assume, as when I saw them the last time, two Fridays ago. They must see me, since they don't move from the bridge. They're huddled close, which makes sense because the cold wind has an edge, though I'm still wondering about their relationship, and can only get from my mother a curt "Some things aren't any of your business," which I take to mean they're having intercourse, or whatever women have when the bedroom curtains are closed.

I approach, and suddenly we're very close to each other, Dr. Lenz craning to see over the edge of the bridge railing and my mother holding a white box. "Ben, we weren't expecting you until tomorrow."

"Coach Winters gave me the day off, so I took the earlier bus," I say, my hands stinging with cold. "What's in the box?"

My mother comes so close she can whisper. "I don't quite have the words for this . . . it's your father."

"But . . . they never found his body."

Dr. Lenz straightens up and rests her hand on my mother's arm. "It's ashes, from the morgue—unclaimed deceased person—symbolic, for closure."

This revelation distresses me, and I want to leave, but don't, for my mother's sake.

"Your father didn't leave any instructions," my mother says, succumbing to tears. "He thought he had more time." She gets herself back under control. She sniffles and wipes her nose and eyes with a paisley handkerchief, one of my father's, I notice. "I can't make sense of it, your father reduced to a shoebox," she says bitterly. "What an irony."

I take the box. *Arthur Heald* in gold letters. It's like something you'd carry expensive stationery in. "It must be five pounds," I say.

My mother says, "It's heavier than one would expect." She's confused, it seems, by her own grief, which has come unexpectedly after all those nights alone while the man whose ashes she holds in her hands was out with his schtups. "I thought when you burn something the ashes are lighter."

"Like when you burn a log in the fireplace?"

"Exactly. What's left is a handful of feathery ash."

I shake the box and something hard inside rattles against the inside walls. *Are those the teeth? Probably not, as they would be reduced to calcium oxide, like the bones, which leave plenty of ash, and shard too.* I put the box down and, just because it seems like the right thing to do, I step into my mother's arms and she pulls me toward her, her shoulder bones hard stones in my hands, and her lilac-scented hair at my cheek. It's like holding my father's brittle body on the raft, all fleshy vitality gone.

"When I die, Ben, my wish is that you scatter my ashes here too." She wraps her hands around my waist. "I need a favor from you, Ben."

"What?"

"Would you scatter his ashes for me? I can't bring myself to do it."

"It's illegal."

"Just be careful."

"Right now, in broad daylight?"

"I'll tell you if somebody's coming. If the police come, you're clever, you'll think up a good story."

"You want me to take the blame?" My gorge rises.

"We don't want your mother having trouble with the *polizei . . .* police," quips Dr. Lenz.

My mother releases me, turns her face away, rests her hands on the edge of the railing, and rocks forward and back, sobbing quietly.

"It's OK," I say loudly over a gust, which is about the stupidest thing I could say, since there's nothing OK about watching your father's ashes sink into the Central Park Lake.

"Everyone expects me to be OK," my mother says. Close up, I can see the lines of grief etched around her eyes. "So I'm OK." She balls her fist and thumps it on the railing. "My husband is extinguished in a freak hurricane, I've been incapacitated for months by some protozoan infestation, and my son is going to sell the family business his father gave his life to build. What's not to be OK with?" She dries her tears with her sleeve, and just stares at me.

I give her thirty seconds. She rubs her knees as if to press out the arthritis. "You'll take care of the scattering?"

"Now?"

"Please, Ben. I shouldn't have to repeat myself, but the thought of your father sifting through my fingers is more than I can bear."

I step back, crack open the box slowly, and lift the lid, dreading what I'm about to see. Inside the box is a uniform pale-to-dark-gray powder that looks like the coarse sand on the Quogue beach. Clearly, they're not his ashes, but they could be his ashes, full of pulverized bone fragments. It's already getting hard to remember my father as flesh and blood. I set the box on the railing, remove the lid, and finger the dust, letting the gray powder flow over my hand. A handful of my father. How light. How inconsequential. Chips of bone catch, fall into the water, and float there. A shard of hip. Femur. Skull. The fine dust makes a gray fan in the light breeze. It swirls and drifts down onto the surface of the lake, where it forms a gray stain that moves slowly under the bridge with the quacking ducks.

I repeat this act many times, letting my father slip through my fingers, and finally throwing the chips of bone. When the box is almost empty, I tip the rest into the air and watch the fine powder of my father drift along the shiny black surface of the water. Below me, his ghostly gray remains spread into nothing, like smoke, as if he had never been.

The swirls of ash remind me that I'm going to have to forgive him and myself and let my pain go, or I will never be happy. I discover that I'm weeping, but not for my father—no, for me—for the conversations that will never take place, for the chances I will never have with him to make things right. I don't miss him; I miss the chance to get to know him well enough to miss him.

The three of us stand on the bridge for ten minutes, my mother still weeping and Dr. Lenz stroking her cheek, watching the ducks glide in and out of the shadows thrown by the massive trees, as if the pond has tidal currents tugging them along. I check to see if anybody's seen us, and keep my eyes out for mounted police, but as far as I can tell, our little code violation hasn't been spotted.

All of a sudden, I don't want to be here—at all. Whatever good intentions I came here with have withered away and rendered me superfluous. My mother and Utte Lenz are happy together. They don't need me any more than I need them. I thought my mother needed me to be her good son, Ben, which is why I ventured down here every two weeks, but I now see I didn't need to today, or anymore. For this first time, I have a sensation that I need to be my own man, just like Hedjhal said, and academia in Cambridge will give me that chance. Not New York, but a future lit by the bright lights of MIT labs, like sunshine spreading across the bridge as the sun comes out from behind a cloud.

As I'm about to say goodbye, Dr. Lenz breaks the silence. "Ben, call me Utte."

"OK."

"Did you know that your mother and I come here every day since Arthur died?"

"Um, no. She never mentioned it."

"Every day at 3:00 p.m."

My mother sniffles again, her face drooping with sadness, or maybe shock.

I keep my head down, waiting to leave without being impolite.

Two ducks bob by, quacking like mad, working out some duck dispute or another.

Utte watches them disappear under the bridge. "Ducks are surprisingly intelligent: they put themselves to bed at night, quack when they need something, find food and water, separate friend from foe, and take shelter when needed."

"Smarter than some people," I say.

Utte laughs, pushes her fingers back through both sides of her black bangs, clears her throat, and leans forward to drop a stray bone fragment that fell onto the bridge. "Ducks are calm on the surface of the water," she says, "but underneath they paddle. Like crazy."

She takes a bag of peanuts from her coat pocket and empties it onto the sidewalk, and my mother uses her toe to scatter the peanuts evenly. *In life, order is more than half the game.*

"Ducks know what they like," she says. "They're stubborn, and they'll fight like hell to get their way." She sniffs and looks hard at me. With growing discomfort, I turn my eyes away, letting them roam to the line of moored swan boats.

"It's a myth that ugly ducklings become swans," she explains, with a kindly smile. "They become tough confident duck brawlers that take charge of the pond and quack their problems away." And with that deep bit of ornithological psychoanalysis, she says,

"Ben, you look *farmisht*."

"You speak Yiddish?"

"Utte comes from a well-known Viennese Jewish family." My mother sounds more than a little prideful.

"A little," says Utte. "My surname, Lenz, comes from the Ashkenazi." She brushes her hands together to scatter the dust from the peanut shells. "What life expects from us, sometimes I think, is not worth the trouble." She crosses her arms. "Have you ever read Franz Kafka?"

"*Metamorphosis*. Last year in sophomore English."

"Ah, *Die Verwandlung*," she says, tugging at the silver hoop in her left ear. "Kafka says the meaning of life is that it stops."

"I don't understand."

"From now on," Utte says, consulting her watch, "remember the most important lesson I learned being a doctor: all the world will not save you from death." She thinks for a moment. "If Moses died, who then will not," she says, pulling at her smooth chin and making a pout with her lips, which I suddenly want to kiss, feeling ashamed of my urge. And at that, I start thinking hard, for the first time, about what choosing life actually means. Something about fear, not letting fear stop me. I will leave my fear on the Bow Bridge, on the exact spot where I scattered pieces of my father into black water.

$; \dfrac{\sin\varphi}{\pi}=1 \quad 8\sqrt{2} \quad \ln \dfrac{x^2+x\sqrt{2}+1}{x^2-x\sqrt{2}+1} ; \sin\beta = c \quad g'=2\pi\nu g \quad 2$

$g(x\sqrt{2}-1)\Big|_0^\infty = x \qquad \dfrac{\pi}{2\sqrt{9}} \qquad \dfrac{\partial v_i \cdot 5 v_i}{\sin\beta} = n = \eta(\mu, \qquad m = \lim \sum_{i=1}^m$

$s, n_1, i_1)$

$x^2\pi.$ $\qquad a^3 z; \quad n=$

36

Coming to the Winchendon YMCA pool two years after the last New England Age-Group Swimming Championships makes me feel stronger, a little more reckless, and as I walk through the locker room—pausing one moment to listen to a coach in a green tracksuit pepping up his swimmers—I realize the pool is also making me feel more confident. I'm ready to execute the split-times strategy Doc Woodworth and I worked out. I pass, then, into the pool—timers huddling in a corner, one-meter diving board, scoreboard large as the screen at a drive-in movie, swimmers swinging their arms, coaches lugging duffel bags of gear, friends and parents murmuring in the bleachers.

I'm feeling free of my usual anxiety. The last time I was here, I was fourteen. Other swimmers cowed me. I believed I couldn't win, and I came in second to last. The pool, the bleachers, the large timing clock—all of them made me feel unsure. Now, after the events of the last two months, the pool area appears smaller, the other swimmers less daunting, my nerves calmer. Two years ago, the stern-faced judges with stopwatches looked like they were waiting to record my slow times. Now I take them to be friendly, waiting for me to set a meet record.

My mother likes to say, "Fold your clothes and you've already accomplished one good thing in a day." I walk over to the edge of the pool, bend down, and slowly drag my hand over the surface, letting the water slide through my fingers.

"New England Swimming Championships," I whisper. I take a folded piece of paper from my pocket and open it. A message from Coach Winters:

Who's the only one who can beat you?

I study it for a long time, and it gets me thinking about all that has happened since I came home from Quogue in August. I wish I had seen what was coming. I wish I had been able to take the hints about my father's illness and put them into a clear picture of what he was doing and why. It makes me think about what I was doing then and where I was going. It makes me think of Jesse, my mother, Gloria, and choosing to save my aunt. And it makes me know the answer to the question on the piece of paper.

"Just me," I say out loud.

And that's when I look up to find my uncle waving to me from a seat in the front row of the bleachers. He's wearing a white shirt with a leather jacket. He's had his hair lightened, like a man who has spent hours in the Hollywood sun. It has attracted two women three rows up. He beckons me over.

"How did you know I was here?" I ask. Concentrating on my race strategy, I'm put off by his presence.

"Your mother," he says laconically, with his arms draped over the railing, like a ball player waiting to bat. "I have to tell you something," he says quickly, his chest expanding under his white shirt.

"Not a good time," I say. I'm still unsure how to talk to him—as a father, an uncle, or some mixture of biological father and uncle-mentor. But I'm curious what's so important, that he chose this inopportune moment.

"I have to get this out of my head," he says, pointing to his temple. "You're old enough to hear it now. It was love, what your mother and I had." He's staring fiercely and confidently, his warm eyes blinking.

At least I believe that's what Jesse just said. His apologetic face indicates he thinks he said something important, and potentially hurtful.

"What?" I could've heard him wrong, with all the noise. Neither one of us is talking very loudly. In case I'm right, I say "Why are you telling me this?" "It's obvious, you had intercourse."

"No, it wasn't just a fling." He grabs my wrist. "I loved your mother, in a way that I still love your mother."

"What?" I say again, not much louder but pushing in a little closer.

For a moment, my uncle seems incapable of speaking. He coughs. He clears his throat and then says very quickly, "Your father was in Europe for months, and Myrtle was in the hospital recovering from a total abdominal hysterectomy, so your mother was alone, and I was alone, and we spent a lot of time together, talking and going to the theater and, believe it or not, baseball games. I wanted a divorce, but your mother was against it."

"What?" I say a third time. "When my father was on a buying trip for the company and Myrtle was in the hospital?" A pause. "Divorce?" Another pause. "My mother and father?"

It isn't so much that I'm saying these words as much as they're coming through me. I hear them when Jesse does.

"I could have told you earlier," he says, gulping, then averts his gaze as if he wants to recede into the seat behind him. In the pool, the last swimmers are warming up. Two are throwing down long and graceful butterfly strokes. "I fell in love with your mother, Ben," Jesse's low baritone manages, his impossibly handsome face still staring away. "I wanted her to come live with me in a new place I bought on Central Park West. Your mother said no. She loved your father, and she wanted the two of them to raise you. I don't want to go back to Florida without telling you. I'm so sorry." He sighs. What's the difference?

"Why . . ." I'm about to say something I'm not really sure about. *Why* are you telling me this? *Why* should I believe you? *Why* are you bringing this up now? *Why* would I want to hear this? I'm staring down at Jesse, unblinking. I have no clue what my face is telling him. It occurs to me that I have no words or feelings for what Jesse's just told me.

"You were conceived out of love, and I wanted to raise you," he says speedily, as if I've got my hands around his neck.

"Well," I say, and think a moment. "What's the difference?" I'm surprised by how calm I am. I just don't care. "You're not my father. Arthur was. He's gone, and whatever you wanted sixteen years ago, doesn't matter now." I watch the last swimmers clear the pool. "You can't make the clock go backwards. Not so far as I know."

"I know," Jesse whispers. "I'd like to get to know you better. What do you think?" A note of regret has seeped into his voice.

"Yes," I say. "Yes, I like you, as an uncle, I don't love you like a father. Whatever father love feels like, I don't really know. How could I? Now's the time for me to go to the marshalling area."

"Tell me what I can do, Ben." My attention isn't on him anymore. It's claimed by the chief judge posting the list of starters for the men's thousand-yard freestyle, with my name next to Lane Four, reserved for the second-fastest qualifier.

"I don't know, Uncle Jesse." I figure he wants me to tell him that he can be like a father to me. But it's too late. And I've got my race on my mind. "It doesn't change anything, Jesse," I say, not knowing what else to say, and anyway, it seems like the truest thing I can say. Maybe my uncle wants me to punch him, or yell at him, but I'm not mad. I've moved on. I have a race to win, and my uncle can't help me.

"This is really bothering me, Ben," Jesse says, "It's been haunting me since we met in the Big Hat and I asked you to review my business plan." He squeezes his eyes shut in the effort to be honest with me. "Things get stuck in my head, and they won't go away."

"Same here," I say taking a step back. I'm headed for Lane Four.

Over the loudspeaker, a deep voice announces the thousand-yard freestyle.

"You'll think about it?" he says, his catcher's mitt hand smoothing his leading-man hair.

"Sure," I say, raising my hand like a traffic cop. Enough.

"Ben?"

Now over the loudspeaker, the basso voice asks us to assemble at the blocks.

I'm gone.

⧗

I go to Lane Four. I remember hearing that the blocks in Winchendon are really slippery.

"You should dry them with your towel," one of the coaches said in the locker room. I run my hand over the damp surface, but it seems grippy enough, and I don't want to get my towel wet, since I'm always cold after my races. I'm using a both-feet-forward start to get a stronger jump, so I don't need to worry.

A wavelet splashes over my feet, and I take a hasty step back from the surprisingly cold water. For the first time, I feel tall and invincible next to the other six swimmers, most of whom

I've known for years. I look the kid in Lane Two in the eye. He smiles and waves, and I remember something else Doc Woodworth told me: *look the competition right in the eye, never back down, never give up, never give in.* At one time, Woodworth's fighting words seemed laughable, but now I see that he's right: the other swimmers don't back down or give in either.

A whistle shrills.

Then a deep voice, with descending pitch: "Men's thousand-yard freestyle. Step up."

The seven of us ascend the blocks, shake out our shoulders, kick our legs like marionettes, and settle. All noise—the voices in the stands, the announcements, the water in the gutters—goes silent. I lower my goggles and check the strap. Tensed, I wait for the signal. And then suddenly, wondrously, instead of being nervous, I am fully immersed in the instant. My face is reflected back up to me from the green-blue chlorinated water.

"Take your mark."

I'm careful not to jump too early, to give into reflexes and be disqualified. I've gotten my start down over the years. Crouch. Hands on the front edge of the blocks. Big leap just as the starter's gun goes off. Aerodynamic streamline, arms forward, followed by the underwater kick. Usually, I come up ahead of the pack.

The starter flexes his arm, and the starting gun resounds with a shattering crack.

I swing my arms back and then forward. My feet slide along the block's surface as though it's been greased with lard. I push as hard as I can with my legs; my toes burn from sliding across the rough blue surface, unable to get any purchase. I launch myself into the air. But my body overbalances, arms and legs akimbo and flailing, midsection parallel to the water. I hit the water flat, and not more than two yards from the wall. A cloud of effervescent bubbles, silvery blue reflections play underneath the surface. My goggles have come off, so I can't see. I'll have to count my strokes.

I'm a yard behind. I swing my arms in high, wide arcs, pulling long and easy. At the first turn, the swimmers to my right and left are a body-length ahead of me. I up my cadence, speed up my kick. At each turn, I'm closing the gap. At each hundred yards, I kick harder and swing my arms faster. After nine hundred yards, I'm in second, an arm-length behind. One hundred to go. I straighten my arms for the last fifty yards, dig deep in the water, thrash my legs, up my cadence again, windmill my straight arms, and then—head down, no breathing—the wall.

The time flashes on the board. New meet record. Tied for first with the kid who waved at me. He drifts over to my lane, reaches over the lane line. "Nice race, I didn't think you'd catch me."

"Neither did I," I say.

I sink into the depth. My feet touch the bottom of the pool, bubbles rising to the mercury surface. Five feet under, I say all the words I never dare say. They aren't coherent words. They're just angry, lost words, words of hope and despair. Then, I push off the bottom and float upwards, rising with my bubbles. I break the surface and fill my lungs. All content leaves my head to be replaced—briefly, oh too briefly—by a wonderful happy vacancy. Here I am.

Gordon Adler is a writer, communication expert, and swim fanatic. Originally from Concord, Massachusetts, Gordon now lives in Switzerland, where he owns and operates Adler Way, his professional consultancy that helps business people improve their communication skills.

Gordon is a Harvard University alumnus with an MFA and a doctorate degree. He is the author of several business and communication books such as *Management Communication: Financial Times Briefing, Case Writing For Executive Education: A Survival Guide,* and *Winning at Service: Lessons from Service Leaders.*

In his free time, Gordon is an avid reader with an affinity for autobiographies. He loves international cuisine, smartphone photography, and, every once in a while, the binging of a Netflix show. On early mornings, he can be found in his local pool, perfecting his butterfly technique.

Here. I. Am. is Gordon's homage to true events that shaped his own family, such as the New England hurricane of 1938, boarding school life, and his father's tumultuous experiences as a young man in New York City.

Printed in Poland
by Amazon Fulfillment
Poland Sp. z o.o., Wrocław

22970510R00188